Resounding praise for
GREGORY BENFORD
and
EATER

"Benford is a rarity: a scientist who writes with verve and insight not only about black holes and cosmic strings, but about human desires and fears."
New York Times Book Review

"One of the leading exponents of hard SF . . . takes one of the oldest SF plots—first contact—and spruces it up with great success . . . His astronomer-protagonists . . . are nicely drawn and highly believable. His alien is, well, incredibly alien and endlessly fascinating . . . Full of astronomical pyrotechnics and the kind of intellectual verbal fencing that seems to go along with creative scientific thinking, Benford's latest should delight any serious reader of SF."
Publishers Weekly (*Starred Review*)

"The scientific equivalent of a taut police procedural . . . Benford's deft, suspenseful weaving of the struggle between Eater and humanity blends two threads with maximal impact."
Newark Star Ledger

"One of the top writers in the genre."
Chicago Tribune

GREGORY BENFORD

EATER

An Imprint of HarperCollinsPublishers

EOS
An Imprint of HarperCollins *Publishers*
10 East 53rd Street
New York, New York 10022-5299

First Eos paperback printing: May 2001
First Eos hardcover printing: May 2000

Eos Trademark Reg. U.S. Pat. Off. and in Other Countries,
Marca Registrada, Hecho en U.S.A.
HarperCollins ® is a trademark of HarperCollins Publishers Inc.

Printed in the U.S.A.

10 9 8 7 6 5 4 3

To
Mark Martin,
Jennifer Brehl,
Ralph Vicinanza
and
Vince Gerardis
. . . who all did their part.

Man is a small thing,
and the night is very large
and full of wonders

—LORD DUNSANY,
The Laughter of the Gods

PART ONE
BURSTER

1

It began quietly.

Amy Major came into Benjamin's office and with studied care placed a sheet in front of his tired eyes. "Got a funny one for you."

Benjamin stared at the graph. In the middle of the page, a sharp peak poked up to a high level, then fell slowly to his right. He glanced at the bottom axis, showing time, and said, "So it died away in a few seconds. What's so odd?"

Amy gave him an angular grin that he knew she thought made her look tough-minded and skeptical. He had always read that expression as stubborn, but then, she so often disagreed with him. "Here's the second."

"Second?" Maybe her grin was deserved.

With a suppressed smile, she handed him another sheet. Same sort of peak, subsiding into the background noise in four seconds. "Ho hum." He raised his eyebrows in question, a look he had trained the staff to interpret as *Why are you wasting my time?*

"Could be any ordinary burster, right?"

"Yes." Amy liked to play the elephantine game out in full.

"Only it's a repeater."

"Ah. How close?"

"In space, dead on. The prelim position is right on top of the first one's." Dramatic pause. "In time, 13.45 hours."

"What?" Was this a joke? "Thirteen hours?"

3

"Yup."

Gamma-ray bursters were cosmological explosions, the biggest Creation had ever devised. They showed up in the highest energy spectrum of all, the fat, powerful light that emerged when atomic nuclei fell apart. The preferred model describing bursters invoked a big black hole swallowing something else quite substantial, like a massive star. Bursters were the dyspeptic belch of a spectacularly large astrophysical meal. Each one devastated a seared region of the host galaxy.

Eaten once, a star could not be ingested again, thirteen hours later.

On the off chance that this was still a joke, he said with measured deliberation, "Now, that *is* interesting." Always be positive at the beginning, or else staff would not come to you at all. He smiled wanly. "But the preliminary position is in a big box."

This was more than a judicious reservation. It was almost certainly the true explanation. The two would prove to come from different points in the sky.

They got from the discovering instrument a rough location of the burster—a box drawn on the sky map, with the source within it somewhere. Sharpening that took other instruments specially designed for the job. Same for the second burster. Once they knew accurately where this second burst was, he was sure it would turn out to be far from the earlier burst, and the excitement would be over. Best to let her down slowly, though. "Still, let's hope it's something new."

"Uh, I thought it was worth mentioning, Dr. Knowlton." Her rawboned face retreated into defensive mode, mouth pursing up as if she had drawn a string through both lips. She had been the origin of the staff's private name for him, Dr. Know-It-All-ton. That had hurt more than he had ever let on.

"And it is, it is. You asked Space Array for a quick location?"

"Sure, and sent out an alert to everybody on Gamma Net."

"Great."

She let her skeptic-hardnose mask slip a little. "It's a real repeater. I just know it."

"I hope you're right." He had been through dozens of cases of mistaken identity and Amy had not. She was a fine operations astronomer, skilled at sampling the steady stream of data that flowed through the High Energy Astrophysics Center, though a bit too earnest for his taste.

"I know, nobody's ever seen a repeater this delayed," she said.

"Minutes, yes. Hours, no."

"But the prelim spectra look similar."

"How many data points in the spectrum?"

"Uh, four."

"Not nearly enough to tell anything for sure."

"I've got a hunch."

"And I have a crowded schedule."

"I really think—"

"Hard for me to see what the rush is."

"We might want to alert some other 'scopes right away, if this is important."

Patience, patience. "I see."

"I'm getting the first one's full spectrum any minute," she went on, beginning to pace. He realized that she had been holding herself in check until now. He reminded himself that enthusiasm was always good, though it needed guidance.

"I'll give Attilio a ring, see if I can hurry things along," he said, touching his desk and punching in a code.

"Oh, *great*, Dr. Knowlton." A sudden smile.

He saw that this was the real point of her telling him so soon, before confirming evidence was in. He could help. Despite himself, he felt pleased. Not at this implied acknowledgment of his power, but at being included.

Every once in a while he got to analyze raw data. Perhaps even to invent an explanation, try it out, see his work as a whole thing. Every once in a while.

As he punched his finder-phone keypad, Amy started to leave. He waved her back. "No, stay."

He got straight through and jollied Attilio with a moment of banter, speaking into the four-mike set in his desk. Attilio's replies came through, clear and rich, though his lanky, always elegantly attired body was sitting in the shadow of the Alps. "You knew I would be in here this very morning," Attilio said. "We are both working too hard."

"We're addicts."

"Science addicts, yes, an obscure vice."

Benjamin asked for a "little bit of a speedup" in processing and checking the two events. This took about fifteen minutes, most of it devoted to chat, but getting the job done all the same. An e-mail might have gotten the same results, but in his experience, not. All the talk of being systematic and highly organized left out the human need to gossip, even with people you seldom saw.

He finished the call with a promise from Attilio to get together next time Benjamin was in Europe and also, just incidentally, could he look into this second source right away?

"I was hoping you'd do that," Amy said. She had been sitting on the edge of her seat the whole conversation, when she wasn't up and pacing quickly, her long hair trailing in the air.

"I wanted you to hear the conversation, get a little experience with greasing the international gears." Studying gamma-ray bursters was now not merely international but interplanetary, if one counted the many robot observers orbiting in the solar system. At least the spacecraft did not take so much massaging. Or grand meals at Center expense.

"Oh, I've learned pretty well how to work the system."

"Sure, but you don't know Attilio yet. He's a great guy. I'll take you to dinner with him, next AAS meeting. He's giving an invited talk, I hear."

"Meaning, you're on the program committee."

Benjamin grinned. "Caught me out." As in every field, having friends on the right committees and boards and con-

ferences was important, a game Benjamin had played quite
often. "And I appreciate your bringing this to me so soon. I
do like to look up from the paperwork every year or three
and act like a real astronomer again."

"Glad to."

"You've been doing a good job here. Don't think I don't
notice."

She was nominally a postdoctoral researcher under his direction, but her appointment was about to convert over to
full-time staff. Might as well build her up a bit for the dis-
appointment to come, when Attilio called back.

Astronomy treated its students kindly, providing many
tasks that were true, solid science and even might lead to an
important result. The universe was still so poorly known
that surprises lurked everywhere, especially when one had
a new instrument with greater seeing power, or the ability
to peer into a fresh region of the spectrum. The newer
'scopes were mostly distant hardware operated by a corps
of technicians. Astronomers themselves ruled these by long
distance, asking for spots in the night sky to be scrutinized,
all over a Net connection. Nobody squinted through eye-
pieces anymore.

So it was with gamma-ray bursters. Long known, and still
imperfectly understood, they now rewarded only the diligent
with new phenomena. Amy was careful and energetic, perfect for mining the profusion of data. Bursters were still interesting but not really a hot topic any more. Benjamin ran
the group that did most of the burster data organizing,
plunked down here in Hawaii more for political reasons than
scientific ones.

Since they dwelled at the very edge of the perceptible
universe, bursters yielded their secrets only to careful study.
As there was no telling where and when a burster would
burst, one had to survey the entire sky. When a burster spat
out its virulent, high-energy emissions, a network of telescopes went into operation, recording its brief life.

If a burster was truly different, a crowd of experienced observers would rush in, analyzing data and offering interpretations at the speed of e-mail.

But Amy—and he—would have the honor of discovery.

"Hope it pans out," he said kindly.

"Got to play your hunches, right? I'll zap the VLA results to you at home if you want."

"Yes, do."

Had he been harder on her than he should have? He felt grumpy, a sure signal to withhold judgment. The situation with Channing had been getting so bleak lately, he had to defend against the black moods that could creep up on him whenever he got tired. He would have to watch that. It kept getting worse.

Amy went back to work and he noticed that it was well past 6 P.M. He had been due home half an hour ago. He felt a pang of guilt as he left, lugging his briefcase full of unread bureaucratic paper.

As he was getting into his convertible, a loud bang echoed from the rocky slope above. His head jerked up toward the radio array antennas perched along the upper plateau. Birds flapped away on the thin air. The array's "shotgun" fired several times at sunset to scare away birds, who showed a fascination with building nests in the dishes of the radio telescopes. It was incredibly loud, not a gun at all, but fuel ignited in a tube. It also served to keep the birds from getting into the great domes of the optical telescopes farther up the mountain. Still, the blasts always unnerved him. The "shotgun" was just another aspect of working at the true focus of astronomy, the observing sites. It had been a pure stroke of luck, being offered his position here at the High Energy Astrophysics Center. A university appointment would have been more comfortable, but less exciting. Even if he did mostly push paper around these days.

Here was where astronomy still had some vestige of hands-on immediacy. All the high, dry sites around the globe were now thronged with telescopes that spied upward in every band of the electromagnetic spectrum: radio to gamma ray, with many stops in between. Though data flew between observatories at the speed of light, there was still nothing quite like being able to walk over and talk to the people who had gathered it, see the new images as they formed on TV screens. Of course, the sharpest observations came from space, sent down by robot 'scopes. And he was quite sure that within a day those instruments would tell Amy that her second burster was no kin to the first.

He drove down the mountain, from the cool, thin air of the great slopes and into the moist clasp of Hawaii's sprawling big island. Mauna Kea was a massive stack of restless stone, giving great spreading views of misty green, but he noticed none of it as he sped a little too much on the way down. He felt guilty about being late. Channing would be home from her doctor's appointment and would probably have started making supper and he didn't want her doing that. Either he would make it, or else take her out. Visits to Dr. Mendenham usually made her withdrawn and wore down her precarious confidence.

That was it—a good meal at the Reefman, maybe even some dancing if she was up to it. He had forgotten about Amy's objects by the time he hit the easier part of the road, the lush tropical plain that ran down to the sea.

2 When the radiologist abruptly stopped his mechanically friendly chatter, she knew something was wrong. Again.

Immediately, Channing remembered when all this had started, back in the rosy dawn of time when she had been brimming with energy and going to live forever. Then she had felt the same reaction in a doctor and, in classic fashion, went through the Virtuous Girl list: *Nope, never drank, smoked, didn't use coffee or even tea, at least not much. Plenty of exercise, low-fat addict, even held her breath while walking by a coughing bus exhaust. Can't be me, Doc!*

Then why? *It's so unfair!* she had thought, then sourly saw that she was buying the Great Statistical Lie, which made you think there were no fluctuations, no mean deviations, no chance happenings in a world which her rational, fine-honed astronaut mind knew was jammed full of haphazard turns.

So she had heard the leaden words fall from the doctor's mouth: *lumpy tumor plus invaded lymph nodes, bad blood chem,* the full-course dinner.

So okay, I'll lose my hair. But I like hats, fine. And I can explore my inner drag queen by wearing wigs.

The chemo doctor had said with complete confidence, "You and I are going to be good friends," which had immediately put her guard up.

She had gone through the predictable symptoms, items on her checklist, just like pre-mission planning. Hair loss came right to the day, two weeks after chemo. She had a little party and turned it into a piece of performance art. *Atta girl!* Fatigue: she was ready, with new pillows and satiny sheets; sensual sleep, the manuals whispered. Nausea was tougher: she had never grown fond of vomiting. Possible infertility?: well past that anyway. Loss of libido: definitely a problem; maybe stock up on porn movies? Weight gain: bad news. She would waddle down the street, bald and unsteady, and instead of onlookers thinking, *Must be going through chemo,* they'd say, "Wow, she's really let herself go."

Plenty of phone calls: astronaut buddies, friends, college roommate, the support circuit—much-needed strokes. Bought a Vegas showgirl wig, stockpiled it for a late-night turn-on. Cut the hair back to a short, sassy 'do, so there wouldn't be a total clutter when it fell out. Bought a Bible: she was shocked to find they didn't have one in the house. Benjamin had never pretended to believe, and she supposed she didn't either, but what if God favored those who kept up appearances? It had always been one of those things she was going to read when there was time, like Tolstoy. When she had been in orbit for three months, doing tedious experiments, she actually had started in on *War and Peace* because it was in the tiny station library and she had forgotten to bring anything. She had finished it because it was good, to her surprise. *Okay, time for Dostoyevsky.*

Only she hadn't, of course; too depressing. More gloomy obsessions when she had quite enough already, thank you.

From the look on this tech's face, maybe she wasn't going to get another chance.

Then, without her noticing the transition, she was with good ole Dr. Mendenham, the tech was gone, and she knew she had passed through another little time jump. She had first noted this quaint little property of her mind when she was in astronaut training. Anxiety erased short-term memory. So to get through the protracted training, she had learned to skate over her anxieties, focus-focus-focus. Only now it didn't seem to work.

"Lie down. I need to put my hands on you," said one of the specialists with Mendenham.

"You have no idea how often I hear that from men," she said bravely, but the sally from her tight throat came off as forced. She had gotten used to having these men fondle her breasts but not used to the indifference they conspicuously displayed. A little nervous energy from them would have been appreciated, evidence that she hadn't entirely lost her attractions.

Then they were through and she was taking notes, pre-mission checklist style, preparing for a flight plan to a destination she didn't want to reach. The cancer had advanced in a way they had not expected. Despite the last therapy, which they reminded her was experimental, there were only slight signs of retarded growth.

Another jump. She was out of the clinic, in the car, rolling around the curves of the road home. *Focus-focus-focus, no point in becoming a traffic statistic when you have a classier demise on the way.* Hawaii's damp smells worked into her concentration, pleasant sweet air curling into her lungs and reminding her that the world did have its innocent delights. Even though plants, too, were trying to fend off animals with poisons and carcinogens, one of which had wormed into her.

Channing swerved a bit too fast into their driveway, spitting gravel, crunching to a stop just short of Copernicus, who was sunning himself. She got out and was suddenly immensely glad that he was there. She hugged him and babbled some as he tried to wag his tail off. With Copernicus she could make a fool of herself playing and he would respond by making an even bigger fool of himself. Still, his admiration was not conclusive evidence of one's wonderfulness. For that, she needed Benjamin, and where was he?

On cue, he rolled into the driveway, barely squeezing his sports car into the space. She had kidded him about mid-for-ties testosterone when he bought it, but he did indeed look great in the eggshell-blue convertible, top down, his concerned frown as he got out breaking over her like butterscotch sunlight, and then she was in his arms and the waterworks came on and she was past being embarrassed about it. She clung to him. He clung back. Chimpanzee nuzzling, maybe, but it worked.

She was unsteady going into the house with him and let its comfy feel envelop her. He asked about her medical and she told him and it all came in a rush then, all the sloppy emotions spilling out over the astronaut's shiny exterior. She finished up with some quiet sobs in his arms, feeling much better and also now slightly embarrassed, her usual combo.

"Sounds like you need some mahi-mahi therapy," Benjamin murmured into her left ear.

"I'd prefer some bed right away, thanks sir, but yep, my stomach's rumbling."

"Oh, I thought that was a plane going over."

"Maybe my knees knocking."

"You're braver than anyone I have ever known," in the soft tone he always used to creep up on the worst of it.

"What happens if you get scared half to death twice?"

"The blood analysis—"

"Yeah, worse." Cryptic, astronaut-casual. "Some physio, too."

"You have the printout? I'd—"

Breaking away, she made the timeout signal. "Lemme slap a flapjack of makeup on my face."

She got through the repair work without looking in the mirror much, a trick she had developed since the hair loss. The medical printouts went into her valise, along with the harvest of the fax machine. Brisk and efficient she was, carefully not thinking while she did all these neat little compartmented jobs. *She's steppin' out,* she sang to herself from an old Electric Light Orchestra number, letting the bouncy sound do its work. *Steppin' out.* Fake gaiety was better than none.

He drove them to the Reefman in rather gingerly fashion, not his born-to-the-road style. Hot white clouds hung stranded in a windless sky of shredded silver. The swanky driveway led them to a rambling building that appeared to be made of cinder from the island's volcano, an effect slightly too studied. Music boomed out from a spacious deck bar, heat shimmered over car hoods, the perpetual hovering presence of eternal summer thickening the air.

They ambled around the side garden approach to the beach tables. Her floppy hat would look appropriate there. She had two inches of fur now, creeping up on a presentable cut, but not quite there. The grounds were trying to cheer her up with their ambitious topiaries, laughing fountains, a beach below so white it ached to be trampled. They got a table and she remembered that this was one of those new-fangled home-style restaurants, with a few of the Unnotice-ables passing appetizers among the tables. She and Benjamin had lived here long enough to see the old Hawaiian informality give way to Advanced Tourism, so that one looked through the help and visitors never thought about who changed the sheets of the Rulers.

"Glass of wine?" Benjamin nudged her.

"Really shouldn't."

"I know, which is another reason to do it."

"Hey, that's my kind of line."

"I always steal from the best."

"I look like I need it pretty bad?"

"Let's say *I* need for you to."

She laughed and ordered a glass of fumé blanc, a thumb to the nose for Death, and even in her rickety state not enough to risk a hangover, the Wrath of Grapes.

"Okay, fill me in on the medical." Benjamin said this in his clear, official voice, a mannerism from work he used sometimes when the uncomfortable side of life came up. He was completely unaware of this habit, she knew. Rather than feeling affronted, she found it endearing, though she could not say why. When she was through, he said, "Damn," his voice tightening further. "Going to operate?"

"No, they want to let this new regime of drugs work on it awhile."

"How long?"

"Didn't say. I got the impression that they wouldn't give a solid answer."

"Well, it is experimental." He tried to put a little lilt in his tone to freight some optimism into the conversation, but it did not work because they both knew it.

"And I'm not up to more cutting anyway."

"True," he said miserably. "Damn, I feel so *powerless*."

An absolutely typical and endearing male trait. They wanted to *do*, and women supposedly more wanted to *be*. Well, her astronaut-self wanted to do something, too, but they were both far out of their depth here. Both technically and emotionally.

She watched him clench his fists for a long moment. They exchanged thin smiles, a long look. *Time to move on,* her intuition told her.

She opened her valise. They had always done paperwork at dinner, one of those odd habits couples acquire that seem, in retrospect, defining: workaholics in love. She shuffled the medical printouts to the side; best to get his mind off the subject. "Here, this looks like work."

He reached for it almost eagerly. "From Amy, relayed from the VLA."

She recognized the Very Large Array standard display, a gridded map made in the microwave spectrum. After tiring of the astronaut horse race, she had thrown herself into becoming a respectable astrophysicist. Mostly a data magician and skeptic, which fit her character fine. She had gotten her job here on her merits, not on glory inherited from being a space jockey; she had made sure of that.

Benjamin traced a finger along a ridge of dark lines. "Ummm, a linear feature. Must be a mistake."

"Why?" He told her quickly about Amy's supposedly repeating burster. He slid out a cover sheet and scrawled across the top was: I CHECKED—COORDINATES ARE RIGHT. THIS IS REAL. AMY

"She's found something?" Channing sipped her wine, liking its bite.

"Ummm. She wrote that note because she knew I'd doubt this like hell. This long filament is far larger than any burster could be. Must be a chance overlap with something ordinary. Looks like a galactic jet to me."

She nodded. In their early eras, galaxies often ejected jets of radiating electrons from their core regions. Channing had never studied galaxies very much—astronauts specialized in solar system objects, or studying the Earth from space—but she recalled that such jets were fairly common, and so one could easily turn up in the box that bounded the burster's location. Still . . . "What if it's not?"

"Then this is a burster that makes no sense."

"But that's what you'd like—something new."

He gazed skeptically at the long filament. "New yes, wrong no."

"You don't know it's wrong yet." He had been like this lately, doubting everything. Perhaps it came from her illness; medicine always rewarded a skeptical, informed use of the squeaky-wheel principle. He had loyally squeaked a lot in her defense.

"I'll bet it goes away tomorrow."

"And I bet not," she said impetuously.

"How much?" He gave her his satyr grin.

"Something kinky, say."

"Sounds like we can't lose."

"You bet." This evening was getting off to a good start, despite earlier signs. Now to glide by the hard part. "I want to go in with you tomorrow, have a look at this burster."

Concern flickered in his face, then he suppressed it. He was always urging her to stay home, rest up, but bless him, he didn't know how maddening that could be. She did still have a job and desk at the Center, even if both were getting covered in cobwebs.

"I don't think—"

"If this is important—and of course, you're probably right, it's not—I'd like to be in on it."

"As experiences go, it'll be pretty dull."

Lately, experience was something she never seemed to get until just after she needed it. "Better than daytime TV."

She let a little too much desperation creep into her voice, which was not fair, but at the moment maybe it was just being honest. She watched him struggle with that for a long moment. Visibly reluctant, he finally said, "Uh, okay."

"You always say you want your staff to be ambitious, look for the new."

"Well, sure . . ."

He was getting a bit too sober, she saw, the weight of her news pressing him down. How to rescue the evening?

"Standard executive cheerleading. Follow your dream, you say." She smiled and lowered her eyelids while giving him an up-from-under gaze—a dead-sure attention-getter, she knew, and just the sort of attention she wanted right now. "Unless, of course, it's that one about giving a speech to the International Astronomical Union dressed in sexy underwear."

3 Astronomy, Benjamin mused, was a lot like a detective story with the clues revealed first, and the actual body only later—if ever. Pulsars and quasars, both brilliant beacons glimpsed across the cosmos, had proved to be powered by small specks of compressed mass, resolved only decades after their emissions made them obvious. The clues were gaudy, the causes obscure. So it went with this latest mystery.

The next morning Channing was too worn out to come in with him after all. He lingered over breakfast, they talked about the news in ritual fashion, and finally she shooed him out of the house. "My bed beckons," she said. He was somewhat relieved, then, to get immediately to work with Amy when they got the "cleaned" radio map, chugged out by the ever-laboring computers. It showed the intensity of radio emissions, plotted like a topographical map. A long, spindly feature like a ridge line.

"A definite tail," Amy said. "Some kind of guided flow."

"A galactic jet?"

To his surprise, she shook her head. "That's what I figured. But I checked the old radio maps of this region. This thing wasn't there five years ago."

"What?" He flatly did not believe her, but kept that out of his voice. A mistake, surely. He did a quick calculation and realized that if this thing were a jet in a distant galaxy, it

18

could not possibly have grown so large in a few years. *Must be a mistake.* "It's too big—"

"Yeah, and too luminous. Couldn't have missed it before. This thing is new."

"But . . . but—" He traced out the size of the straight feature and checked his calculation again. "It would have to be the size of a galaxy, maybe bigger, to look this big."

Amy grinned. "Now you know why I only got three hours' sleep last night."

To appear suddenly and be galactic in scale meant that the entire structure had to light up at once, faster than allowed by the speed of light. "Got to be wrong," he said as amiably as he could.

So they spent an hour going over every number and map. And Amy was right. "So we're making a wrong assumption somewhere," she said cheerily. "And I bet I know where. Looks like a jet, so it must be extra-galactic, right? Wrong. It's in our galaxy."

He nodded. There were jets of radiant matter streaming out of star systems, all right. This must have just been born. "But why is it a gamma-ray source?"

"Must be it's got a black hole down at the base of it, gobbling up mass from a companion star." She scribbled some numbers. "And a hell of a bright one, too."

Benjamin checked her calculation. The radio luminosity was very high, and so was the gamma-ray intensity, if this were a source in the Milky Way galaxy. "Too high," he said. "This would be the brightest we've ever seen."

"Well, somebody's got to be the brightest," she said so flatly that he knew she implied the double meaning. She was quite bright herself; her intuition about this source had been right all along; it was damned interesting.

Time to throw a curveball, see how she swung. "I just got this by e-mail." He showed her a report from the Space Array. They had looked at the source and failed to resolve any feature.

"This just means it's tiny," Amy said. "Fits with the idea that the source is a star—"

"And here's the spectrum of the flare." He plunked it down. A mass of lines, many of them obviously from hydrogen. A joker in the deck for sure; gamma-ray bursters did not look like this at all.

That much Amy took in at a glance. "Um. I recognize some of these lines, but they're off . . ." Quick jottings. "They're split!"

"Right." Each of the major spectral lines had two peaks. "Never saw anything like this from a galactic jet or anything else."

"Maybe this will go away." This was code for a wrong measurement, to be caught when it was checked.

"Nope," he said merrily, "I saw this right away, of course, and got back to them. They looked it over, say it's all right."

"Must be Doppler shifts."

"Plausible." An emitter moving toward them would seem to give off hydrogen light slightly shifted up in frequency, toward the blue. One traveling away would seem red. "This guy gives us both at once? Makes no sense."

"Ummm. The blue shift is strongest."

They looked at each other and grinned. "This is the strangest damn thing I've ever seen," Benjamin said happily.

"Me, too. And it's real."

Nobody had to say anything more. Not a gamma-ray burster, not a galactic jet—something strange and bright and mysterious. Astronomers lived to find a wholly new class of object, and this looked a lot like one. And it had just fallen into their laps. It helped being bright, Benjamin thought, but being lucky would do just fine, thank you.

"Glad to hear it" came a voice from over his shoulder. Brisk, British, and even after many years, instantly recognizable. He turned and looked into the face of Kingsley Dart. "Caught a whisper of this while I was over on Honolulu," Dart went on in his quick, clipped accent. "Sounded intriguing. Thought I'd nip over and have a look."

Benjamin felt his face tighten. He could not make himself say a word. Amy jumped in with a startled salutation and

Benjamin found himself shaking Dart's hand under shelter of her gusher of greetings, but he could not force his grinding mind to think of anything at the moment beyond an incident decades before.

The question had come out of the colloquium audience like a lance, clear and sharp and cutting. Benjamin had just finished speaking, his last overhead image still splashed up on the screen. As well, both blackboards were covered with equations and quick sketches he had made when he found the confines of language too much.

A moment before he had stepped back and acknowledged the loud round of applause. It was not the mere pro forma pattering of palms, carrying the quality of gratitude that the speaker was finished and soon would come the after-colloquium tea or wine and cheese. They liked the ideas, and some genuine smiles reassured that they liked *him*. The colloquium chairman had then asked, as customary, "Any questions?" Swiftly the Oxbridge-accented sentences spiked out and Benjamin knew that he was in trouble.

His heart was already tripping fast. This was his first colloquium presentation, an unusual honor. At twenty-six, he was the bright boy of the astrophysics group at U.C. Berkeley, but even the best graduate students seldom got an invitation to speak in the Astronomy Department's most elevated venue. There were fifty, maybe sixty people in the audience, mostly graduate students, but with all the senior faculty in the first few rows. He had counted the crowd as it grew, been gratified; the heavy hitters had all turned out, not cutting it because Benjamin was in their minds still just a graduate student, or nearly so. It was an honor to be here and he had prepared for weeks, rehearsing with Channing, tailoring his viewgraphs, making up four-color computer graphics to show sinuous flows and ruby-red plasma currents.

His talk had been about the energetic jets that shoot out from the disks around black holes, a recurring hot topic in the field. As new windows opened for telescopes across the electromagnetic spectrum, the jets showed more detail, fresh mysteries.

In his talk he had used the entire modern arsenal of theoretical attack: calculations, computer simulations, and finally, to truly convince, some easily digested cartoons. Nobody really felt that they understood something unless they carried away a picture of how it worked. "Get it right in the 'cartoon approximation' and all else follows," his thesis adviser had sagely said.

Benjamin had shown that the jets were very probably confined by their own magnetic fields. This could only be so if they carried a net current out from their source, presumably a large black hole and its churning neighborhood. He had ended up with a simple declaration: "That is, in a sense the flows are self-organized." In other words, they neatly knit themselves up.

Then the knife question came from a figure Benjamin did not know, an angular face halfway back in the rows of chairs. Benjamin felt that he should know the face, there was something familiar about it, but there was no time to wonder about identity now. A quick riposte to an attack was essential in the brisk world of international astrophysics. Ideas had their moment in the sun, and if the glare revealed a blemish, they were banished.

The question subtly undermined his idea. In a slightly nasal Brit accent, the voice recalled that jets were probably born near the disk of matter rotating about black holes, but after that were at the mercy of the elements as they propagated outward, into the surrounding galaxy.

Smoothly the questioner pointed out that other ways to confine and shape the jets were easily imagined—for example, the pressure of the galaxy's own gas and dust—and "seemed more plausible, I should imagine." This last stab was within the allowed range of rebukes.

Benjamin took a second to assume an almost exaggerated pose of being at ease, putting his hands in his pockets and rocking back on one foot, letting the other foot rise, balanced on its heel. "Lack of imagination is not really an argument, is it?" he said mildly.

A gratifying ripple of laughter washed through the room. Those already half out of their seats paused, sensing a fight. Benjamin quickly went on, catching the momentum of the moment. "To collar a jet and make it run straight demands something special about the medium around it, some design on its part. But if the jet is self-managed, right from the moment it was born, back on the accretion disk—that solves the confinement problem."

Nods, murmurs. His opponent cast a shrewd look and again Benjamin could almost place that face, the clipped, precise English accent. The man said casually, "But you have no way of knowing if a disk will emit that much current. And as well, I should think that no relativistically exact result could tell you that in general." A smirk danced at the edges of the man's mouth. "And you do realize that the black hole region must be treated in accordance with *general* relativity, not merely *special* relativity?"

The audience had turned to hear this, eyes casting back, and Benjamin knew that this was somebody important. The shot about relativity was a clear put-down, questioning his credentials. A nasty insinuation to make about a fresh Ph.D., the ink barely dry on his diploma. He drew in a long breath and time slowed, the way it does in a traffic accident, and suddenly he realized that he was frightened.

His was the second colloquium of the academic year, a prestigious spot in itself. The Astronomy Department liked to get the year off with a bang, featuring bold, invigorating topics. The air was crisp with autumn smells, the campus alive with edgy expectation, and Channing was in the tenth row in her blue good-luck sweater.

Act. Say something. But what?

He caught her eyes on him and stepped forward, putting his hands behind his back in a classic pontifical pose, the way he had seen others signal that they were being thoughtful. In fact, he did not need to think, for the answer came to him out of nowhere, slipping into words as he began a sentence, not quite knowing where it was going.

"The disk dynamo has to give off a critical level of current," he said easily, getting the tone of bemused thought. "Otherwise it would not be able to coherently rotate."

He let the sentence hang in air. The senior figures in the department were watching him, waiting for further explanation, and he opened his mouth to give it. His nostrils flared and he saw with crystalline clarity that he should say nothing, leave the tantalizing sentence to sink in. Bait. This guy in the back was a Brit, dish out some of his own style to him.

He had gotten everyone's attention and now the audience sensed something, heads swiveling to watch the Englishman. *Stand pat? No.*

Benjamin decided to raise the stakes. A cool thrill ran through him as he added, "I would think that was physically clear."

Half the audience had already turned toward the back rows and when he spoke they quickly glanced around like a crowd at a tennis match following a fast volley.

The face in the back clouded, scowling, and then seemed to decide to challenge. "I should think that unlikely" came the drawl, lifting at the last word into a derisive lilt, *un-like-ly*.

Benjamin felt a prickly rush sweep over him. *Gotcha.*

"It follows directly from a conservation theorem," Benjamin said smoothly, savoring the line, striding to the overhead projector and slapping down a fresh viewgraph. He had not shown it in the talk because it was an arcane bit of mathematics, not the sort of thing to snag the attention of this crowd. No eye-catching graphics or dazzling data-crunching, just some lines of equations with double-integral signs, ripe with vector arrows over the symbols. A yawner—until now.

"Starting with Maxwell's equations," he began, pointing, then glanced up. "Which we know to be relativistically correct, yes?"

This jibe made a few of the theorists chuckle; everybody had learned this as undergraduates, but most had forgotten it long ago.

"So performing the integrals over a cylindrical volume . . ." He went through the steps quickly, knowing that nobody this late in the hour wanted to sit through five minutes of tedious calculations. The cat was out of the bag, anyway. Springing a crisp new viewgraph—and then two more to finish the argument, all tightly reasoned mathematics—tipped his hand. He had anticipated this question and prepared, deliberately left a hole in his argument. Or so the guy in the back would think—*was* thinking, from the deepening frown Benjamin saw now on the distant, narrow face—and knew that he had stepped into a trap.

Only it wasn't so. Benjamin had not really intended it that way, had left the three viewgraphs out because they seemed a minor digression of little interest to the hard-nosed astrophysicists who made up most of the audience.

"So we can see that this minimum level is quite enough to later on confine the jets, keep them pointing straight, solve the problem." He added this last little boast and stepped back.

The Brit face at the back curled up a lip, squinted eyes, but said nothing. A long moment passed as the colloquium chairman peered toward the back, rocking forward a little, and then saw that there would be no reply. *Game, point, match,* Benjamin thought, breathing in deeply of air that seemed cool and sharp.

There were two more questions, minor stuff about possible implications, easy to get through. In fact, he let himself strut a little. He expanded on some work he contemplated doing in the near future, once he and Channing had the wedding business over with and he could think, plan the next step in his career. He felt that he could get away with a slight, permissible brag.

Then it was over, the ritual incantation from the chairman, "There is wine and cheese in the usual place, to which you are all invited. Let us thank our speaker again . . ."

This applause was scattered and listless, as usual as everybody got up, and the crowd left. His major professor appeared at his elbow and said, "You handled that very well."

"Uh, thanks. Who is that guy?" Benjamin glanced at the crowd, not letting any concern into his face.

"Dart. Kingsley Dart."

"The similarity solutions guy from Oxford?"

"Right. Just blew in yesterday afternoon, visiting for a few days. Thought you had met him."

"I was squirreled away making viewgraphs."

"You sure nailed Dart with those last three."

"I hadn't really planned it that way—"

An amused grin. "Oh, sure."

"I didn't!"

"Nobody gets timing like that without setting it up."

"Well, my Benjamin did," Channing said, slipping an arm around his. "I know, because he had them in the very first version of the talk."

Benjamin smiled. "And you told me to drop them."

"It worked perfectly, didn't it?" she said, all innocence.

He laughed, liking the feeling of release it brought, liking that she had made him seem a lot more the savvy Machiavellian than he was, liking the whole damned thing so much it clutched at his heart somehow in the frozen moment of triumph. Off to the side two of the big names of the department were talking about the implications of his work and he liked the sound of that, too, his name wafting pleasantly in the nearly empty room. He could smell the aging, polished wood, the astringent solvent reek of the dry markers from the blackboard, a moist gathering in the cloying air of late afternoon. Channing kept her arm in his and walked proudly beside him up the two flights to the wine and cheese.

"You were *great*." She looked up at him seriously and he saw that she had feared for him in this last hour. Berkeley was notorious for cutting criticisms, arch comments, savage seminars that dissected years of research in minutes of coldly delivered condemnation.

She had kept close to him through the aftermath, when white-haired savants of the field came up to him, holding plastic glasses of an indifferent red wine, and probed him on details, implications, even gossip. Treating him like a member of the club, a colleague at last. She had tugged at his arm and nodded when Dart came into view, earnestly talking to a grand old observing astronomer. Dart had a way of skating over a crowd, dipping in where he wanted, like a hummingbird seeking the sweet bulbs. Eventually he worked his way around to Benjamin, lifting eyebrows as he approached, his face in fact running through the entire suite of ironic messages, very Euro, before shooting out a hand and saying, "Kingsley Dart. Liked the talk."

Firm handshake. "You seemed to disagree with most of it."

A shrug. "Testing the ideas, just testing."

He said, a little testily, Benjamin thought. "I had dropped those viewgraphs, the proof, out of the talk. I didn't think most of the audience would care."

Abrupt nods, three very quick, then a long one, as though deliberating. "Probably right. Only people like me and thee care."

Ah, Benjamin thought, *instant inclusion in the fraternity of people-like-us.* "It's a major point, I should have brought it up."

"No, you were right, would've blunted your momentum."

Why is he being so chummy? Channing's glance asked, eyebrows pinched in. He had no idea. Not knowing where to go with this conversation, he said, "My fiancée, Channing Blythe," and they went through the usual presentations. But Kingsley kept eyeing him with a gaze that lapsed into frowning speculation, as though they were still feeling each other out. And maybe they were. Within minutes they were at it, throwing ideas and clipped phrases back and forth, talking the shorthand of those who spent a lot of time living in their heads and were glad to meet someone who shared the same interior territory. It was the start of a formal friendship and a real, never acknowledged rivalry, two poles that defined them in the decades that followed.

Twenty years. Could it have been that long?

And now here he was, the famous Royal Astronomer, first on the scene when something potentially big was breaking. Perfect timing was a gift, and Kingsley had it.

Forcing a smile onto his stiff face, Benjamin felt a sharp, hot spike of genuine hatred.

4 Channing planned her invasion of the High Energy Astrophysics Center carefully. First, what were the right clothes to stage a dramatic reappearance at work, after a month away, presumed by all to be no longer a real player?

When she had worked at NASA Headquarters the dress code had been easy: modified East Coast style, basically a matter of getting her blacks to match. Did a mascara-dark midlength skirt go with a charcoal turtleneck? Close enough and she was okay for either NASA's labyrinths, the opera, or a smoky dive.

But amid tropical glare and endless vibrant bougainvillea, her outfits had seemed like dressing as a vampire at an Easter egg hunt. Here, slouchy sweaters and scuffed tennis shoes appeared at "dressy casual" receptions, right next to Italian silk ties, subtle diamond bracelets, and high heels sinking into the sandy sod. She had seen jeans worn with a tiara, "leisure gowns" looking like pajamas, and a tux top with black shorts. Yet finding a studied casual look took her an hour of careful weighing, all to seem as though she had thrown them on fifteen minutes ago without a second thought. On top of that, you never knew how the day would proceed later, whether you were dressing for an evening on a humid, warm patio or inside, in air-conditioning set for the comfort zone of a snow leopard. *Maddening.*

She eyed herself carefully in the mirror. Now, thanks to

weight loss, she had a great, tight butt: *Gluteus to the Maximus!* But her breasts, once ample enough, thank you, were sagging, or as she preferred to think in TV terms, losing their vertical hold.

Getting over vanity had been the hardest part of adjusting to the cancer. A vain man would check himself out passing a mirror. An absolutely ordinary woman could pick out her reflections in store windows, spoons, bald men's heads. Channing, as a photogenic astronaut type, had been ever-aware of How She Looked. All women faced the Looks Issue, as she had thought of it as a teenager, whether as a positive element or a negative one. Not that it had not done her good now and then. At NASA it had helped her through earnest committee meetings in which she was the only woman in the room. Now, thank God, all that was behind her.

Still, she was not at all ready to enter the working bay, looking for Benjamin, and find Kingsley Dart in his uniform: slightly pouchy brown suit, white shirt, tie drawn tight in a knot of unknown style. Down-market Oxford, so utterly out of place that his attire advertised Dart's unconcern for such trivial matters. Since she had seen him in a tux when the situation demanded, and yet he had somehow achieved the same effect of unconscious indifference, she was sure it was all quite conscious.

She went through the clothes analysis automatically while trying to absorb the shock. She was suddenly self-conscious, and then angry about being so. He still had the power to throw her into momentary confusion. And the way he lifted his head to smile, with just a whiff of hauteur, still delighted her. *Damn him.*

"Channing, how wonderful to see you," Kingsley said smoothly.

He looked into her face with a worried frown, much as everyone did these days, as if they could read the state of her health there. Well, maybe they could; she was past the stage of trying to hide behind cosmetics. She knew that her skin was yellow and papery, her eyes rimmed with a dark under-layer, her once strong arms thin and showing swelling at the joints. It no longer even bothered her that people glanced at her out of the corner of their eyes, not wanting to stare but still drawn to hints of the eternal mystery—of what her mother called "passing," as if there were a clear destination firmly in mind.

"Thought I'd come in, see what all the excitement's about."

"Is there much?" Kingsley said to Benjamin with deceptive lightness. "Have you made any announcement?"

"Oh no, much too soon for that," Benjamin said quickly.

"Don't want to just announce a mystery," Amy put in.

"But it's all over the IAU Notices," Kingsley said.

This was the global notification system of the International Astronomical Union, used to focus workers on the newest comet or supernova or pulsar of interest. "Sure, but we've got to be cautious," Benjamin said. "If this is a new class of object—"

"Then you should enlist as many people and observing windows as possible," Kingsley finished for him.

Channing smiled, remembering. Kingsley had the annoying pattern of quickly disagreeing with you and often being right, plus the even worse property of agreeing with you and getting there first.

Benjamin pursed his lips and plowed on. "I think the big issue is how this thing can repeat."

Kingsley said carefully, "I must admit, when I saw your Notices piece, I thought it most likely an error."

Amy said flatly, "It's not an error, I can tell you that."

"I'm quite relieved to hear it." Channing noted that with this phrase Kingsley was not actually agreeing with Amy, only reacting, but his choice of words avoided rankling her.

"Look at it this way," Benjamin put in. "At the very least, this object throws into doubt the standard picture of gamma-ray bursters."

Kingsley's lips drew into a thin, skeptical line. "With many thousands observed, one exception does not disprove the model."

Since he had taken a major hand in building up the conventional view of gamma-ray bursters, this was predictable, Channing felt. She said amiably, "Similar appearance does not mean similar cause."

Kingsley nodded but Amy said, "Shouldn't we follow Occam's razor—prefer the simplest explanation? Then this is an odd kind of burster, but one in our galaxy."

Benjamin said, "Sure, but don't throw out data just because it makes your job harder. We don't understand the visible light data, either."

This led to a long discussion of the mysterious Doppler shifts. Channing had come up today mainly to see this data, and it was strange indeed. "It's as though some of the thing's coming toward us, some away. A rotating disk? We'd get the red shifts from the receding edge, blue shifts from the approaching one."

They all looked at her. "Good idea," Benjamin said happily, winking and grinning. She could see that they were surprised in two ways—by the proposal itself, and because she had made it. She had come into astronomy as an observing astronaut, doing yeoman labor in the last stages of the space shuttle era, then doing dutiful time on the space station. The more academically based astronomers regarded these as rather showy, unserious pursuits. She had never risen very far here at the Center and had always wondered if that bias held her back. In the slightly startled expressions of Dart and Amy—but not, bless him, Benjamin—she saw confirmation.

Kingsley said incisively, "I rather like that."

"But a disk?" Amy frowned doubtfully. "I'd say these are kinda large, but I'll have to check . . ."

"Good," Kingsley said quickly. "At the moment we *have* no other hypothesis to test. I wish we did."

Channing was not the only one to notice that his use of *we* included Kingsley in the team. Benjamin's eyes narrowed in a way she understood and he said, "Just wait. Theorists will jump on this like it was candy."

"They can theorize all they like," Amy said. "We have all the data."

"Which we should make quick use of," Kingsley said. "Let's do some preliminary calculations, shall we?"

Channing went with them to a seminar room and they reviewed the data. Some fresh observations came in over the satellite links as they worked, providing fresh fodder. She kept up with the discussions, but to her this branch of astrophysics was like a French Impressionist painting of a cow: suggestive, artful maybe, but some things never looked quite right and it was in the end not a reliable source of nourishing milk. Plus, she was woefully out of date on current theory. Still she found pleasure in watching Benjamin and Kingsley spar, using quickly jotted equations as weapons. Amy joined in, too, her tone a bit less canny and insidious, but holding her own.

Kingsley jabbed verbally, challenging others' ideas while seeming at first to be going along with them, inserting doubt slyly as he carried the discussion forward, ferret-eyed in his intensity. Just as decades before, he saw this as a delightful game played with chalk and sliding tones of voice.

Channing found her attention drifting. Looking back, she could remember liking contests like this from decades past. Benjamin would always see Kingsley as a rival; that was set in his mind like a fossil print of their first meeting. Benjamin was a perfectly respectable theorist, but not in Kingsley's class. That was simply a fact, but she knew quite well that Benjamin would never fully accept it. After all, who did not need a little illusion to get through life?

Having bested Kingsley in a colloquium encounter set their relationship, as far as Benjamin was concerned. Never mind that Kingsley had done better work on bigger problems, and on top of it displayed remarkable skills in the political circus that science had become. She could barely recall that incident, but knew that it burned in Benjamin's mind whenever he crossed Kingsley's path. Probably Kingsley had forgotten it entirely. This seemingly small difference was precisely why they seldom saw each other. Too bad, really, because she had always found Kingsley more amusing than the usual run of academic astronomers. In their bull moose rivalries, men missed a lot.

Would her own career at NASA have gone better, she mused, if she had been a man? Nobody in passing conversation would glance at your chest. You wouldn't have to pretend to be "freshening up" to go to the goddamn john. Nobody cared if you didn't remember their birthday. You could rationalize any behavior error with the all-purpose "Screw it." In late-night jokes in a bar, you could really see something hilarious in punting a small dog, preferably a poodle. You didn't give a rat's ass whether anybody heeded your new haircut. Thank God, they never noticed if you'd lost or gained weight. Men had some things so easy! With the Other Side, flowers fixed anything. And as the years closed in, gray hair and wrinkles would add character. Hell, you could dine out on that alone. Lean over the bar, belch originally, and declaim about the old days when rocket boosters kicked you in the ass so hard you thought you had a prostate problem. And what the hell, you could always look forward to being a dirty old man.

5 He had expected the next day to be hours of more muddling along, with data trickling in and more idea-bashing with Kingsley and Amy. Instead, it proved decisive.

The Very Large Baseline Interferometer reported in promptly, to everyone's surprise. This network had grown from a few stations strewn around the world into an intricate system that now included radio telescopes orbiting farther away than the moon. Its "baseline" then made it effectively an instrument of enormous equivalent resolution, like having a dim eye of astronomical size. Getting a measurement quickly was pure luck. The distant SpaceWeb satellites had been looking in roughly the right portion of the sky, and Benjamin's request came in at the very end of a rather tedious job. Instrument tenders were human, too, and the mystery had caught their attention.

The radio plume was thin, bright—and moving. Comparison with the earlier map showed definite changes in the filaments making up the thin image. Now they had two maps at different times show changing luminosity and position.

"But these were taken only a day or so apart!" Kingsley jabbed at the differences between the maps with a bony finger.

"So?" Benjamin gave him a slight smile.

"Must be wrong."

Benjamin said, "No, it means this object is local—very local."

"You took the rate of change of these features and worked it into a distance estimate?" Amy asked.

"Nothing moves faster than light—so I used that to set a bound. I came in early, had a chance to work through the numbers, and checked them by e-mail with the guys in Socorro." The site of the now-outdated Very Large Array, Socorro, New Mexico, still had a practiced set of house theorists and observers, and Benjamin knew several of them well. "Jean Ellik, an old hand there, agrees: this thing can't be much farther away than the Oort cloud."

"But it's a *radio* object."

The Oort cloud was a huge spherical swarm of icy fragments orbiting beyond the orbit of Pluto. Objects there were frigid and unenergetic, exceptionally difficult to detect.

"Something has found a way to light itself up, out there in the cold and dark," Benjamin said happily. The look of consternation on Kingsley's face was all he had been hoping for. He could not resist rubbing it in. "That added hypothesis you were asking for yesterday—here it is."

They quickly went to the head of the Center, Victoria Martinez, and got permission for added resources. "Get everybody on it," she said intently. Martinez was a good astronomer who had been deflected into administration. Benjamin worried that he would drift along the same path, getting more disconnected from the science all the while. He was happy that she saw the implications immediately.

They wrote a carefully phrased alert for the IAU Notices, asking for any and all observations of the object, in all frequency bands, because in Kingsley's phrase, "inasmuch as this is a wholly unanticipated finding, no data is irrelevant." "Let's keep the media out of it for the moment," Martinez said carefully, and they all agreed. Everyone remembered past embarrassments: mistaken reports of asteroids that might hit Earth, misidentified massive stars, spurious discovered planets around nearby stars.

Kingsley was atypically silent. Apparently he had decided to "hang about" for a few days out of curiosity.

Coaxed, Kingsley said, "Admittedly, all along I had thought that it would turn out to be a relativistic jet—yes, my favorite object. Indeed, one pointed very nearly straight at us. That would neatly explain its huge luminosity. Also, we would naturally see all the jet's variations as occurring quickly, as they would be time-squeezed by relativity. Alas"—a touch of the theatrical here, holding a pen aloft like a phony sword—"it was not to be."

The gamma-ray signature had surfaced as crucial, and within hours Kingsley had a new idea.

"Let us face facts, uncomfortable as they may be to conventional views," he began to a small band in the seminar room, including Amy and Benjamin at the front. "It makes no sense if you suppose this is an object passing through the interstellar medium, a very thin gas. It would emit radiation, then, because it was striking objects in its way. A quick calculation"—he proceeded to produce this in quick, jabbing strokes on a blackboard as he spoke—"shows that one needs to expend only a trivial amount of power to overcome the friction of the interstellar hydrogen." He dropped the chalk dramatically. "There is simply not enough matter nearby our solar system for it to run into."

He turned to the audience, which agreed. Or at least nodded; Kingsley's reputation for incisive analysis was enough to silence the timid. Several were checking his numbers and did not look up.

Channing had heard the news and was sitting in on the impromptu seminar that had developed spontaneously down the hall from Benjamin's office. She saw her chance and stepped into the silence. "Okay, then we have to look elsewhere. It's reasonably nearby, or else it couldn't possibly be so luminous. So as savvy Kingsley implies, why is it luminous? Because it's not gliding through, it's *accelerating*."

Benjamin had not even known that Channing was in the room. He turned to look at her, a spark of uneasy pride at her speaking up so readily. Uneasy because Kingsley had a reputation for leaving questions hanging, only to knock them down when anyone ventured to take the next step without thinking it through. But this time the narrow, hatchet face showed only real puzzlement as it nodded. Kingsley put his hands behind his back, as if to disarm himself, and said slowly, "Perhaps, but why? There are no unusual signatures near it, nothing to be propelling it forward."

Benjamin got her drift. "Exactly. But what if it's decelerating?"

Kingsley shot back, "I just showed that the interstellar medium slows things very slowly. Nothing would naturally—"

Channing broke in. "Suppose it's not natural? What if it's a starship?"

Benjamin's jaw dropped, but out of loyalty he tried to fill the skeptical silence that greeted her question. "P-passing near us?"

To his amazement, she rose from her seat and stepped with fragile grace to the front, taking the chalk from Kingsley's hand. Everyone in the room knew of her illness, but he sensed that her command of them came from the quality that had made her a successful astronaut, a presence he could never name but that he sensed every day. He felt a burst of pride for her and a smile split his face, telltale of a joy he had not felt quite this way for a very long time. Since the illness, in fact.

This was a mere instant, for Channing did not pause to absorb the regard of the room. Quickly she did her own swift calculation. It all depended upon the source's intrinsic luminosity. A bright source ten light-years away looked the same as one a light year away and a hundred times dimmer, so— she turned to the audience, neatly jotting $L = P/R^2$, and said, "With P the ship's power demand and R in light-years, we have—" More jotting. "How much does one need to ram a ship through the interstellar medium?"

The crowd now filled the room to overflowing, Benjamin

noticed, and from the packed faces came guesses: "The power level of a city?" and "No, nearer to all of North America."

She shook her head. "Try the whole planet."

A gasp of surprise. Not even acknowledging this, she went on to cite the Mouse, a runaway neutron star discovered decades before. It lay somewhere within a thousand light-years and looked vaguely like a fleeing rodent with a long tail, because it left behind a trail of excited electrons, which were discovered by a radio telescope. All the energy in that tail came from the shock waves the Mouse excited ahead of itself. The interstellar gas and dust was slowing it, braking an entire compacted star, and the energy expended by this splashed across the sky in an extravagant signature.

Of course, she allowed, the Mouse was just an analogy. There were details of how to estimate the braking, which demanded knowing the size of the "working surface" and interactions across it, shock waves—a zoo of astrophysical effects. Benjamin recognized areas she had worked on in her career, so her approach was not really surprising; to the man who owns a hammer, every problem looks like a nail. But this method came out of her life, giving her an assurance others lacked.

She turned from her calculations to confront them. "And this object is doing the same. But taking the luminosity, I can find the mass that's being slowed down by simple interstellar friction. Guess what it is."

She had them on puppet strings now and a pleased smile rippled. She waited.

"A neutron star . . . again?" a voice called, dribbling away in self doubt; she would not be *that* obvious.

"Jupiter-sized?"

"No, bigger!"

"An Earth mass, I would guess," Kingsley put in, not to be utterly upstaged, but smiling at her audacity. Benjamin suddenly saw in the wryly appreciative cast to his face that Kingsley had a deep affection for Channing. Somehow this had eluded him through all their clashes.

She drew it out to just the right point and then wrote a number on the board. Silence.

"That's about the mass of the moon," a voice called from the back.

"It's small."

"Nothing at all like a neutron star," a voice declared, sounding irked at being misled.

"True. With a moon's mass, but it makes gamma rays. Some kind of supermoon. Gentlemen, you have something really new on your hands."

She sat down in a free chair in the front row, next to Benjamin. As she settled in, he caught her letting go, giving way to the sudden body language of near-exhaustion. The room broke into applause. Not, Benjamin saw, at the particular brilliance of the analysis—anyone in the room could do the arithmetic and make estimates, and many no doubt would rush back to their offices and do just that, checking her—but because she had seen just the right calculation to do and had done it before anyone else. That was the trick in high-flying science: to pick the right problem just as it becomes worth doing. And she had brought it off. He had noticed that she had gotten up in the night, and in his fuzzy sleep had attributed it to her familiar medical woes. But no, she had been honing herself for this grand game, the clash of scientific ideas. *She still has it, my girl,* he thought with relish.

He leaned over to her and whispered, "I knew that I'd married Miss Right, okay—only I didn't know her first name was Always."

She gave him a proud, tired grin, followed by a kiss.

6 Most of the world's orbiting telescopes lost much time and flexibility from always having a huge bright object nearby—the Earth. Accidentally pointing the telescope that way for even a second would fry sensitive optical systems.

So astronomers avoided their home planet if they could. Placing large Big Eyes at Earth's Lagrangian points helped—orbiting sixty degrees fore and aft of the moon's position in its orbit, far from the blue-white glare of the planet's ocean and sky.

Without the sunlight reflected from the Earth's disk, telescopes could cool to a few degrees above absolute zero. This helped enormously when looking in the infrared, for then the telescope body itself did not emit much radiation at the crucial frequencies. With a hundred times the area of the much earlier Hubble Space Telescope, the Big Eyes could see dim objects a hundred times fainter.

But when pointed at the elusive quarry, the Big Eyes showed only a dim blur. They could not see in enough detail to tell what it was. As Kingsley remarked acerbically, two further days of effort on a global scale served merely to give it a name. One was suggested by Channing in an offhand moment: "X-1." She had explained, "X because we don't know what the hell it is, and one because there may be more."

41

But it sounded too much like a weapon or jet plane, so everyone just called it "the intruder."

Stymied, the worldwide network of observers went back to telescopes firmly fixed on Mother Earth.

Earth-based instruments used adaptive optics—mirrors that adjusted second to second, offsetting the dancing refractions of the air above them. Several of these sat atop Mauna Kea, the best all-around observing spot in the world. The aim of the newest sixteen-meter reflector 'scope, using adaptive mirrors, was to fetch forth images of Jupiter-sized planets orbiting nearby stars. Pricey Earth-based 'scopes were still far cheaper than space eyes, which had to carry a guidance system to keep them pointed accurately while orbiting at 27,000 kilometers per hour.

But the sixteen-meter 'scope could not resolve the blob of visible light that "X-1" gave off.

To reliably see another star's Jupiter-sized planets, humanity had to go to its own Jupiter—or rather, to send a robot. Able to see in the infrared with meticulous accuracy, the Deep Space Infrared Telescope hung as far from the sun as Jupiter itself, orbiting high above the ecliptic plane. This kept it cold and out of the plane of dust that clogged the inner solar system. The enemy of good, deep "seeing"—to use the astronomer's jargon—was the glow of sunlight scattered by that orbiting debris. Its dim radiance had been discovered in 1661 and it was still termed the "zodiacal light." In excellent seeing conditions, from Earth one could watch the plane of dim gray light stretch across a winter's night. This dust-reflected sunlight perpetually brightened the sky of the inner solar system. The dust declined in density far from the sun, and sunlight dimmed, so that now astronomers were driven to the outer reaches.

There a thin beam orbited, a hundred meters long and crafted to within a ten-thousandth of a millimeter: the Long Eye. To see a planet around another sun demanded that the Long Eye blot out the star's infrared emission, which was a million times brighter than the world being sought. Then the telescopes spaced at regular intervals along the length compared the phases of the light they received from near the star. Matching and subtracting, an onboard computer sifted through a torrent of noise for the faint, steady signal of a tiny planet, sending out the message of its own existence.

Standing beneath a clear sky, one's unaided eye could see details on the moon about a tenth of the moon's diameter. At the same distance, a Big Eye 'scope typical of those standing on Mauna Kea could make out an astronaut standing on the moon. With the Long Eye—and some luck—one could make out the astronaut holding up fingers—and count them.

The Long Eye was painstakingly studying the zone around likely candidate stars, seeking evidence of life. By looking carefully at each color of the light from the target world, it could in principle see the fine details of absorption by water, oxygen, or carbon dioxide—telltale gases of life.

This stretched array now searched for a dot at the very edge of the solar system, a target its designers had never conceived.

"Got it!" Amy cried, jabbing at a large computer screen. The data had just come over the astro-Net connection.

They crowded around. The de facto working group was only four: Amy, Kingsley, Benjamin, and Channing. Of course there were subgroups laboring over parts of the problem, but by unspoken agreement they had started meeting in each others' offices whenever a fresh piece of data seemed in the offing. Martinez had approved this catch-as-catch-can method, suggesting to Benjamin, "Whatever works, go for it."

They all took in the new result at a glance. There were small gasps. But they left it to Channing to note her own triumph. "Looks pretty small." A bright spot sat at one end of the radio finger: starship-like.

"It's fully resolved, though," Amy said. "Looks like a circle. A moon? At its distance, let's see . . . ten milliarc-seconds . . . Geez. No moon, not at all. It's only a few kilometers across."

"What? That can't be right." Kingsley peered at the screen's side panel of data and gazed off into space, making his own reckoning. He blinked. "Um. I'm afraid it is."

"Afraid?" Benjamin chided.

"Because it means something is wrong with Channing's rather nice piece of work from two days ago. This object cannot have the mass of a moon. It's far too small."

Benjamin wanted to defend her, but Channing spoke up quickly, despite a fog of fatigue that had descended upon her in the last hour. *Damned if I'll leave early today,* she thought adamantly, *and let Kingsley call the tune.*

If only her head would stop spinning . . . "Let's not rule out anything until we fit the pieces of this jigsaw puzzle together."

Kingsley said in a let's-be-reasonable tone, "Your estimate included a characteristic size, which we now see was far too large. So you derived a larger mass—"

"Not so fast," Channing said. "What's the rest of the Long Eye results?"

Benjamin punched some keys and peered at a sidebar that popped up. "They're logging in the spectrum . . . processing . . . Looks like an excess of blue shifts."

Channing beamed in a way that, from his expression, she could tell that Benjamin had not seen for a long time. "Which means it's decelerating."

"Just as you said," Kingsley allowed. "That I'll grant. But your calculation still makes no sense—quantitatively."

"Look," Channing pressed back, "I estimated in my first equation—"

"We're missing the big point, aren't we?" Plainly Benjamin decided to intervene before talk descended into another technical wrangle, as it had so much these last few days. Often the devil was indeed in the details, but he had a way of pulling specialists, including most definitely herself, away from their narrow issues to face the larger picture.

Kingsley smiled, seeing the point. "It is deliberately slowing to enter the solar system? The starship hypothesis."

"But to be so bright, it must have a huge mass," Channing said. "No starship would be so heavy."

Benjamin nodded. "A big contradiction."

Long silence. She had often heard historians of science go on about how a great scientist had the courage of his convictions, stuck it out through opposition, and so on. Until this moment she had not *felt* the implied sense—that sometimes you had to take the big leap: buy two apparently conflicting ideas and fuse them.

Should she? *What the hell, you only die once.*

"Maybe we're both right. It's a lot of mass packed into a tiny package." She had to put all her effort into getting the rest of the words out. Her mind was perking along just fine, but her body wanted to curl up and go to sleep. "After all, that few kilometers across is an upper scale. This thing must be lighting up a lot of gas around it. It could be smaller than we think. A lot smaller, even."

They all looked at each other. Another long silence.

She thought giddily, *He who laughs last just thinks slower,* but nobody laughed at her implication. To her vast and abstractly distant surprise, they all, one by one, nodded.

Within the hour, Channing was leaning back and breathing steadily, just holding on to watch the show. It took fewer muscles to smile than to frown, sure enough, and fewer still to ignore people completely. But she had shrugged off Benjamin's efforts to take her home.

She heard boss lady Martinez say tensely, "I've got to get up to NASA, NSF. Maybe even on to the White House." She smiled slightly, relishing the moment. Even if she was feeling light-headed and Martinez's words did come hollow-voiced, like a speech given down a long tin pipe.

Not a moon, no. Something much more interesting.

PART TWO
FAST LANE SCIENCE

1 The pinnacle of Mauna Kea stands a full mile above a deck of marshmallow clouds that at sunset turn salmon pink. In late afternoon the sun seems to lower into a softly burning plain that stretches to the horizons. When the volcanoes that built the island belch, the underbellies of the clouds take on a devilish cast where they hover over the seethe of lava. Beneath these, black chunks of razor-sharp, cooled lava render the landscape stark, brooding, and ominous. Nature here seems blunt, brutal, and remorseless.

Yet above all this churn, three hundred tons of gleaming steel and glass pirouette as gracefully as—and far more precisely than—any ballerina. No dancer has ever been required to set herself to within a tiny fraction of a millimeter.

Once in position, the biggest optical telescope in the world then commands the two jaws of the covering hatches to yawn, their slow grind echoing as the 'scope drinks the first light of evening. Here is where the best and brightest come to find the farthest and dimmest. That Hawaii is the most isolated landmass on Earth with the highest pinnacle gives it an advantage in the steadiness of its air. The flat ocean keeps the air stably warm over the islands. Air's usual small flutters cause stars to dance like shiny pennies seen at the bottom of a swimming pool. Over the peak of Mauna Kea air flows more smoothly than above any other high site in the world. The trade winds blow steady and level far beneath the realm of the telescopes.

These conditions drew astronomers, the only major lifeform at this height. Up a road left deliberately rough they brought their white observing pods, immaculate domes like enormous pale mushrooms. The venerable twin Keck telescopes had ruled over this realm since their construction in the 1990s, though they were no longer the largest of their breed. An even larger dome stood in the distance, but Benjamin thought the Kecks were the more beautiful. With two thirty-three-foot mirrors made from thirty-six segments, each such light-bucket was separately movable, swiveling in an echo to the dance of the heavens above. The two mirrors were in tubes eight stories tall, each floating so precisely on oil bearings that a single hand could move them.

Not that such maneuvers were left to mere human means. Elaborate systems guided these tubes, for the human mind operating at 13,800 feet quickly lost its edge. That was why Benjamin seldom came to this height, yet today, on a whim, he had driven up. To clear his head, he had explained to others, whereas the altitude had the opposite effect. He gasped for air after even a modest climb. Pointless, really, to think that he could mull over an idea up here, where his brain was losing cells every moment to oxygen starvation.

But today there was something about the perspective, in the slanted rays of late afternoon, that seemed to fit the scale of the idea he was carrying. Intelligence and technology ruled these barren heights. Against the cruel powers of vulcanism, which had shaped the islands, mere men had set up here a citadel of intricate artifice, dedicated to pure knowledge and the expansion of horizons. In the face of the world's raw rub, and especially whenever he allowed himself to truly think about what was coming for Channing, the view from this majestic height was ennobling.

Right now, he needed that. He drank it in.

If life could work its wonder upon so hostile a place, what other forbidding sites in the universe could play host to mentality? The 'scopes around him were preparing for the coming night, to chip away at answers to such questions. Eternal questions—until now.

Then his portable phone rang, dragging him back into the momentary world. It was a double ring, one of the codes they had introduced at the Center to get priority attention.

Well, it was about time, anyway. His walk up here had left him panting and somehow had clarified his resolve.

On his way down, he distracted himself by trying to find the FM station that played rock from the decade when you cared about it—the working definition of the Good Old Days.

Channing had insisted on being there when he presented his idea. Brimming now with resolve, he called her on the way down. She sounded quite cheery, her tone lifting at the end of sentences, a good sign. He had become fairly good at detecting when she was covering up. So when she came into the seminar room, he was startled at the drawn gray pallor of her face. Plainly it had cost her considerably to come up to the Center for this, a drive of several miles in the usual clogged traffic on narrow two-lane blacktop.

Above the gray cast her eyes sparkled with an energy that was intellectual, not physical—all that seemed capable of driving her now. He felt a pang of guilt; he should have driven home and picked her up. In fact, he had offered to, but she had shrugged it off, saying that she wanted to do some shopping later, anyway. This now looked completely implausible; he doubted that she would have the energy. But then, she had surprised him before with her desire to still visit dress shops, searching for just the right little item that would "cover the damage," as she put it. He embraced her gingerly, felt an answering throb in her body. Or at least he hoped it meant that, and was not one of the tremors he sometimes felt pass through her while she was asleep in bed, like an impersonal ocean wave bearing all before it.

He had decided to limit this to the usual four people, plus

Victoria Martinez. If he proved utterly wrong, which he had to admit was quite probable, at least the number of witnesses to his embarrassment would be manageable.

He got Channing a cup of tea and she took three of her pills along with it. By then the other three were gathered around the seminar table and he began, trying not to seem unsure, though he was.

"How many bursts from the intruder, this 'X-1' object, have we recorded so far, Amy?" He knew, of course, but like a lawyer in a courtroom, a seminar speaker should never ask a question whose answer was not readily at hand.

"Seven." She held out the trace printouts and he waved them aside.

"Far too many. That's my argument in a nutshell." Benjamin had wanted to create a dramatic effect, but saw instantly that this was too much of a jump. Victoria and Amy looked puzzled, Channing startled. He would have to be more orderly, he saw; one of his many speaking faults was a tendency to get ahead of himself. *A closed mouth gathers no feet.*

Kingsley frowned, his lips drawn into a thin skeptical line. "Since we don't know the mechanism . . ."

"But we all have one in mind, don't we?" Channing chimed in. "The energetic intruder smashing into iceteroids."

"Haven't heard that term before. Ice asteroids, is it?" Kingsley said amiably as he turned toward her, his face quickly changing to solicitous concern, voice filling with warmth. "True enough, I had been making a few calculations assuming that—"

"And they work out, don't they?" Benjamin said. "Order of magnitude, anyway."

Kingsley said, "I can get the gamma rays, all right. It's the radio tail I'm having trouble with. How does it form?"

Amy said, "Can't it be made pretty much the way galactic jets do?"

Benjamin was bemused by this, for he had not known

Amy to venture into that realm of astrophysics. Apparently, like the rest of them, she had been doing a lot of homework. He nodded. "It could. We can get to that. But let's stick to my main point. How often *should* we see a burst, if the iceteroid idea is right?"

"Depends on the thing's speed," Kingsley said.

"Which we know from the Doppler shifts to be about a hundredth of the speed of light," Amy said. "I just finished pulling that number out of the data. The spectral fields were sorta messed up, plenty of broad lines, a real jungle."

"Before we get to my reasoning, let's hear Amy's results." *She should have her chance to shine,* he thought, *and then I can get a fresh start myself.* She got up with a few viewgraphs, blushing becomingly.

If the entire solar system, including dim Pluto, were reduced to the size of a human fingertip, the bulk of the Oort cloud of iceballs would lie ten yards away from that finger. Space was indeed vast—and empty. But contrary to their first guesses, the intruder was not so far away. Amy had located it pretty decisively by timing the movements of bright parts of the radio tail and then making plausible arguments about how fast such radio-emitting plasma balls could move. She had showed that the intruder was only a bit beyond the distance of Pluto from the sun, or forty times the Earth–sun distance. A cometary nucleus would take years to fall inward 41 Astronomical Units, but this thing was moving much faster.

"Good work, yes," Kingsley said. He then offered his own reprise of her results—"to see if I've gotten it straight."

Benjamin noted how Kingsley often used the flattering conversational manner of beginning his next sentence by repeating another's words, peppering his talk with references to others' contributions and generally seeming modest. It paid off; scientists were stingy with praise and a few strokes worked wonders on their mood. After thrashing through the data a bit more, everyone present seemed settled.

The intruder was about 50 Astronomical Units out, somewhat beyond the range of Pluto's orbit. It was coming in at about a thirty-degree angle with respect to the plane the planets orbited in, the ecliptic. As Channing put it, "The thing's pretty close—and closing fast."

They all looked at each other. Unspoken was their growing sense of strangeness.

Now it was his turn. Benjamin began writing on the blackboard. Style mattered in bringing forth an argument, and he set the stage with numbers, bringing out the underlying contradiction.

The belt of iceteroids just beyond Pluto had been first imagined by Gerard Kuiper at the University of Chicago in the 1950s. The intruder could be hitting those. Little was known of them, despite their being much closer than the larger swarm in the Oort cloud farther out.

Benjamin drew out the point carefully. Models of the Kuiper Belt showed that the icy chunks were on average an Astronomical Unit apart—quite thinly spread. Typically they were a kilometer or two in size, about the same size as the apparent core dimension of the intruder, as seen in visible light.

"A coincidence, of course, their being about the same size," Benjamin said. "They can't be the same kind of thing. Point is, the odds of hitting an iceteroid in all that space are tiny." He followed with two viewgraphs giving the statistical argument, thick lines of calculations.

"If it's randomly hitting obstructions, then even at its colossal speed"—he paused to emphasize—"nearly a hundredth the speed of light!—then it would not strike one in a million years."

Gasps. They saw the point; a bullet fired into a light snowstorm had a far better chance of hitting a snowflake.

Kingsley looked up from scribbling in his leatherbound notebook, its ornate binding his only affectation. "In fact, it should take this intruder at least a day to fly from one iceteroid to the next—at the speed Amy worked out. Something is quite seriously wrong here."

"I believe there are two ways out"—Benjamin went on almost as if Kingsley had not spoken—"if we want to save our idea that the thing is striking iceteroids and processing their mass into highly energetic stuff. First, as Channing pointed out—"

"It's processing their mass in stages, holding some to chew later," she said for herself. "That would mean it can somehow save pieces of ice."

"Can't imagine how," Kingsley said laconically, looking down at his notes as if to avoid any conflict with her.

Amy said brusquely, "Me, either. But I think I see your second idea, Ben. It's not hitting these iceteroids at random. It's aiming for the next one, using the velocity change it got from consuming the last one."

Benjamin nodded. There it was, a clear leap into the unknown. Much better to have Amy make the jump. A genuinely crazy idea, however much he had tried to couch it in terms of times and distances and statistical probabilities.

"The 'starship hypothesis' again," Kingsley said incredulously. "Keeps popping up, despite its absurdity." This time he looked Benjamin full in the eye.

"How so?" Benjamin asked with a real effort at keeping his tone polite, though he knew what was coming.

"Calculate the flux of gamma radiation from the source. It's very bright. Any starship passengers near that flare would be crisped."

"I thought about that," Benjamin said, trying not to sound defensive, though of course that was just what he was. "As yet I have no answer—"

"Except that the ship need not be crewed at all," Channing put in smoothly, as though they had planned it this way. "Machines could tolerate gamma rays pretty well, if necessary."

Benjamin had not thought of this possibility. He smiled at her in silent thanks.

Kingsley waved this away with a quick flap of his wrist. "I'd hate to try to keep electronics alive in such an environment. *Nothing* could withstand it."

"I didn't use the term 'starship.' You did," Benjamin said hotly. "And—"

"I used it," Channing put in, grinning, "but only as a metaphor."

Kingsley looked irked but said levelly, "Metaphor for what?"

"Something unexpected, maybe obeying rules we haven't thought of yet," she said brightly. Benjamin could see the price she was paying for this in the darkening rims around her eyes.

"Or no rules at all," Kingsley said curtly.

"How else can you explain that it is hitting objects far more often than it should?" Benjamin pressed him.

"I look for another idea," Kingsley shot back, "one with some rules to bound it."

Benjamin saw suddenly a chink in the man's armor. *Just when you thought you were winning the rat race, along came faster rats.* Kingsley was unaccustomed to having his back to the wall in an argument. Perhaps his reputation kept him out of such scrapes now. Well, not here. "We don't need rules, we need ideas."

"Either we have a discussion hinged at one end by plausibility, or else—"

"Now, don't get—"

"Look," Amy said loudly. The two men stopped, both open-mouthed, and looked at her as if remembering where and who they were. Amy pretended not to notice and went on in the measured tones of one aware of being surrounded by her superiors, "The point is, this thing is decelerating at a rate we can't account for. Maybe it's ejecting its own mass to slow itself. Maybe it's a runaway neutron star—like that one Channing was talking about the other day, remember? The Mouse?" She looked around the seminar table; her long hair was pulled back and knotted, so she seemed more austere. "That could act pretty peculiarly. So let's not get pushed out of shape by this mystery, okay?"

Benjamin nodded, rueful that he had let the discussion

take so personal a turn. They were all under a lot of pressure, but that did not justify rubbing rhetorical salt into old wounds.

The talk swerved to other aspects of the problem. Data was pouring in from ground observers and space-based alike. The astronomical data streams on the Internet were thick with discussions and endless inquiries.

Already, theorists were demanding that they publish their findings on the Internet. Worse, some had written papers explaining various pieces of the puzzle, posting their hasty work to the high-display Net showcases. There were advantages to "publishing" electronically: considerable speed, nailing down credit for an idea, while not waiting for the reviewing process. Indeed, the more hot-topic areas of science now resembled a shouting mob more than a scholarly discourse, thanks to instant democratic communication.

They were all besieged by colleagues through e-mail. Others had simply buttonholed them in the Center corridors. Everyone local was working on sifting the data stream, but few knew what was up, overall, because there were so many pieces of the puzzle to assemble. And the Gang of Four arrangement had not facilitated communication, either, Benjamin had to admit, though it was efficient at giving ideas a thorough thrashing over before they escaped into the larger community. In a media-saturated culture, cloisters of reflection were invaluable.

"So what'll we do?" Amy asked the older and presumably wiser heads.

"Get out a paper?" Channing asked wanly. Plainly she had no desire to write it. The hunt was all for her, not talking about it afterward.

"I think not," Victoria Martinez said, jaw set firmly.

Benjamin had nearly forgotten that she was in the room. She sat at the far end of the table and had taken many notes, but she had added nothing until now. He was again embarrassed that she had seen the cut and thrust between him and Kingsley.

"Definitely not," she said, carefully looking at each of them in turn. "This is an enormously energetic object, behaving strangely, and if it continues at its present velocity, it will reach the inner solar system within a month. Am I correct?"

"Yes," Kingsley answered, "though remember, it is decelerating."

Benjamin became aware of a tension between Victoria and Kingsley, whose mouth had compressed into a thin line. The intruder's incredible velocity had moved it the distance between the Earth and the sun in about half a day. They all knew this, but the consensus among the Gang of Four had been that worrying about future effects was pointless until they got a good handle on what the thing was. Plainly Victoria did not feel the same.

"One point you've skipped over, I believe, is that it appears to be headed straight inward."

Amy said, "Well, yes, there's no sign of sideways movement yet. But at these velocities it would be hard to detect right away."

"But I take your drift," Kingsley said. "A possible danger."

Benjamin blinked. He had not thought along these lines in detail. "Of what? Chances of it coming near the Earth—"

"Are impossible to estimate, since it changes velocity with every encounter—correct?" Victoria Martinez said incisively.

Amy answered quietly, "Well, maybe. There's a little Doppler shift in the lines after every collision. If the gamma-ray bursts do represent collisions."

"Let's assume they do, until we have some better idea," Martinez said. "How else can it find its next iceteroid, unless it changes velocity?"

"Quite true," Kingsley said in his pontifical drawl, "but not yet cause for alarm."

"I agree, Dr. Dart, that it is hard to accept some of the ideas I've heard bandied about the room this last hour. But we have nothing more in the pot, and it's time to cook."

This metaphor went past Benjamin. " 'Cook'?"

"I have to get back to a lot of people about this. Word gets around. The NSF and NASA both fund this Center, and they do like to be kept in the loop. I've been shielding you folks while you worked, but I have to start speaking for you now. Unless you'd rather do it yourself?"

"Oh no," Benjamin said, knowing this was what she wanted. "You do it."

"Good. Then I'll be answering a lot of phone calls I've been stalling. And you four start writing up a statement."

"Statement?" Benjamin felt uncomfortably that he was asking stupid questions whose answers were obvious to the others.

"For the media," Kingsley said offhandedly. "Quite so."

Martinez said, "At its present speed, it could reach us within a month."

"I suggest we not emphasize that aspect," Benjamin said, choosing his diction so that it echoed Kingsley's precision. "Especially since it is not headed for us at all."

"Oh?" Martinez looked surprised.

He realized he had not shown his trajectory plots around yet. "It's curving in and downward, heading at an angle to the ecliptic plane. I can't pick out any destination. It will pass through the solar system and leave, as it is unbound. It is moving very fast."

2 She could remember drinking coffee to stay awake and keep working; now she needed it to wake up at all.

Running mostly on caffeine, Channing puttered around in her home office, immersed in cyberspatial bliss: sleek modern desk the size of a tennis court; ergonomic chair that was better than a shiatsu massage—and cheaper; picture window on the Pacific (today looking anything but); overstuffed leather chaise where she spent far too much time recouping; big tunnel skylight leading up to a turquoise tropical sky.

Self-respect demanded that she not work in pajamas. That left a lot of room in a vast sartorial wasteland, from T-shirts and khaki to turtlenecks down to jeans, running shorts, and tanks. All those were off the menu if she was going to do a visual conference with anybody, in which case she needed at least a decent frilly blouse, say, or even a full dress suit—top only needed, of course, since her camera had a carefully controlled field of view. She had heard of the new image managers that touched up your face as you spoke, smoothing out lines and wrinkles and even black eyes if you wanted. To order up one on the Net would be quick, easy to install . . . and the vanity of it would pester her inner schoolmarm for weeks. *Nope, let 'em see the truth. That's what science is about, right? Why not treat scientists the same way?*

Today something clingy, island-soft, and cool. In blue, it cheered her.

She had liked working at home the first month, despised it thereafter. After all, "I work at home" carried the delicate hint that you were in fact just about unemployed, or downsized out of the action, at the fringe of the Real World.

So she tried to be systematic. No distractions, that was the trouble. After years working at the Center, it was hard to get by with no coffee break, water cooler chat, endless meetings with clandestine notes passed ridiculing the speaker, business lunches, the sheer simple humanity of primates making a go of it together.

Work at home and you could never quite leave it. Slump onto the couch at nine at night when Benjamin was on a trip, all ready to kick back and veg out like any deserving, stressed adult . . . and down there at the end of the hall lurked the reproachful glimmer of the desk lamp. It was hard to walk down there and turn it off and walk back to a sitcom without checking the e-mail or looking at tomorrow's calendar, especially since its first screen was the latest selection from *Studmuffins of Science*.

She suspected her social skills, honed in the labyrinths of NASA and the NSF, were atrophying. So she did the next best thing, first off in the morning: answer vital e-mail, delete most without answering, and look over her notes. This kept her in a sort of abstract cyber-society.

The more traditional Net temptations no longer carried their zest. No point in doing an Ego Surf on her name; it showed up only on historical mesh sites now. Her Elvis Year, the time of popularity, was now long gone, back when shuttle missions made you a pseudo-celeb among some of the Internet tribes.

Since then she had been happier, more satisfied, steadily getting more obscure. Funny thing about contentment, some years just got lost. *Seen it, done it, can't recall most of it.*

Through those dimly recalled years, she had been happier with Benjamin than she probably had any right to be, and now that it was nearly over, to review it all seemed pointless. There were parts of the play she would have rewritten, especially the dialogue. Somehow, despite all her theories and ambitions, she still regretted not having children. The career had seemed more important, and maybe it still was to her, but regrets don't listen to theories. There were plenty of roads not taken and no maps.

She finished her e-mail and looked over the work she was doing on spectral analysis. The data pouring into the Center needed careful attention and she had been pitching in, giving the multitude of optical line profiles a thorough scrutiny. She popped the most puzzling ones up on her big screen and ran a whole suite of numerical codes, sniffing around. This took two hours and much intricate tedium. Still, the repetition was soothing, somehow: Zen Astrophysics. She was feeling the slow ebbing fatigue she knew so well when a clear result finally surfaced.

Three optical lines emitted from the intruder came out looking decidedly odd: each was split into two equal peaks. These were not the Doppler shifts they had spotted earlier. They were much smaller, imposed on the Doppler peaks themselves.

There are very few ways an atom can emit radiation at two very closely spaced intervals. The most common occurs if the atom is immersed in a magnetic field. Then its energy would depend upon whether its electrons aligned with the field or against it.

These three splittings she had pulled out of the noise, imposing several different observations from several different 'scopes. And they led to a surprising result: the magnetic field values needed to explain these up-and-down shifts were huge, several thousand times the Earth's field.

"Good grief," she muttered to herself, instantly suspicious.

Most amazing results were mistakes. She burned another hour making sure this one was not.

Then she sat and looked at the tiny twin peaks and liked

knowing that Benjamin would be thrilled by it. The give-and-take with the others at the Center, especially the Gang of Four, was great fun, but his reaction was still the crucial pleasure for her.

Abruptly she remembered her first experience of astronomy, as a little girl. Camping out, she had awakened after midnight, faceup. *There they were.* Even above the summer's heat, the stars were immensely cold. They glittered in the wheeling crystal dark, at the end of a span she could not imagine without dread. High, hard, hanging above her in a tunnel longer than humans could comprehend.

When she had first felt them that way, she had dug her fingers into the soft warm grass and *held on*—above a yawning abyss she felt in her body as both wonderful and terrible. Impossible to ignore.

She had not realized until years later how that moment had shaped her.

She took a break, stretched, felt the tiredness fall away a little, and glanced out a window. From the abstract astrophysical to the humid neighborhood, all in one lungful of moist air.

It was so easy to forget that she dwelled in what most people regarded as the nearest Earthly parallel to heaven. The volcanic soil was rich, lying beneath ample rains and sun. Irrigated paddies gave taro's starchy roots, which made *poi* when mashed. There were ginger and berries, mango, guava, Java plum, and of course bananas. The candlenut tree gave oily brown nuts, which, strung together, burned to give hours of flickering light. The sheer usefulness of candlenuts to humans seemed like an argument from design for a God-made world, customized to smart primates. But it was also a paradise with mosquitoes and lava flows—counterarguments. Well, she could settle the argument about God and paradise within a year. Probably less, the doctors said in their cagey way.

Her fatigue evaporated. The man she had been thinking of now for days was coming up the path.

There were Englishmen and then there were quintessential Englishmen, the types everyone expected to meet and never did. All had their points, in her experience, except maybe the ones whose accents were pasted on and covered over sentiments as soft as sidewalk. There was the jolly fellow who had many friends who would surely stand him a drink, all unfortunately out of the room just now. There was the erudite type who knew more about Shakespeare than anybody and so never went to see anything modern. He was better than the lit'ry one who kept rubbing his foot against your calf under the table while he wondered very earnestly what you did think of that recent novel, really? She liked the slim, athletic engineery types who were modest about their feats and never spoke of them but could fix a balky engine or conjugate a French verb, often simultaneously. They were even good in bed, though she got tired of the modesty because in the end it was fake, a social mannerism, a class signature.

The Englishman coming up the path from the driveway was none of these, but he did have that Brit habit of knowing an awful lot about the right subjects. He had known a lot about politics when people thought it mattered, was by his own description "infrared" until it became clear that the left was truly dead, and even recently could tell you the names of which ministers voted for what measure. He applied the same acuity to the currents of astronomy. Now he was just as sure of himself as ever, his instincts having carried him quite handily to the top. She felt that she should see him as something more than a somewhat scrawny man in a green suit badly wrinkled by the tropical damp.

She greeted him at the door with "Kingsley, what a surprise," though she had been half-expecting him and they both seemed to know that.

"Thought I'd drop by, was on my way to look at a flat."

They went into the spacious, sunlit living room and she sank a little too quickly onto a rattan couch. The trades stirred the wind chimes and she remembered to offer iced tea, which he gratefully accepted, drinking half of the glass straight off. She was infinitely glad that she had chosen the clingy blue dress, though did not let herself dwell on why. Best to keep things on a conversational level, certainly. He was being unusually quiet, getting by with a few compliments about the house, so—

"You're planning on staying for a while, then?" she prodded.

"I can put aside the Astronomer Royal business for a bit. If I am to be something of a scientific shepherd, I should be where things happen. I think it inevitable, given our experience of the last few days."

"Ummm. Lately, experience is something I never seem to get until just after I need it."

His face clouded and she could see he had been trying to keep this a strictly professional discussion. Well, too bad; she was feeling fragile and human now, and not very astrophysical after a morning of it.

After a pause, he said, "I'm so sorry about your condition."

"Oh Lord, Kingsley, I wasn't fishing for sympathy. I just meant that this intruder has taken me by surprise in a way I did not think possible anymore. I *like* it. Keeps me guessing."

She half-opened her mouth to bring up the magnetic field splittings, then decided to let Benjamin be the first. After all, she thought with a sudden wry turn of mind, Kingsley had been the first in an earlier, important way that Benjamin had probably always suspected.

"Sorry, um, again," he said lamely.

She felt a burst of warmth at this chink in the Astronomer Royal's armor. "You can just move here immediately?"

He smiled grimly. "My home situation is not the best. Angelica and I are separated, so I might just as well be here."

"Now it's my turn to be sorry."

"It's been coming for some time, years really."

"She's a brilliant woman," Channing said guardedly.

Friends with marital strife were tricky; some wanted you to slander their mates, like a weird sort of cheerleader.

A wobbly smile. "You've forgotten her mean side, I fear."

"Funny, I don't remember being absentminded," she said, hoping the weak joke would get him off the subject. He plainly did not want to go there, yet some portion of him did; a familiar pattern with divorces, she had found.

He laughed dutifully. "Tell me about your condition. I truly want to know."

"Bad, getting worse. A cancer they barely have the name for."

"I thought we had cracked the problem down at the cellular level by using an entire array of treatments."

"Oh, drugs help. I do well with what they call 'selective serotonin re-uptake inhibitors.' I take a whole alphabet's worth of them. Endless chemical adjustments known only by their acronyms, since no human could remember their true names—or want to."

He was regaining some of his composure, sitting on a stool and sipping. His voice recovered some of the High Oxbridge tones as he said, "Recalls, from my random reading, a line from Chekhov. 'If many remedies are prescribed for an illness, you may be certain that the illness has no cure.' As true in the twenty-first century as the nineteenth."

She shrugged. "I muddle through, to use a Brit expression."

"What was that old saying of yours? 'Life is complex; it has real and imaginary parts.' Quite so." He actually chuckled at this obscure mathematical pun, or else was a far better actor than he had been.

"Lately, the imaginary has been more fun."

"That reminds me of one of your sayings. 'I don't get even, I get odder.' Quite *Channing*, I used to think. Good to know you're still that way, that this damned thing hasn't . . ."

"Snuffed out one part of me at a time?" She might as well be up front about it. "That is the way it feels sometimes."

A sudden stark expression came onto his face and he said

nothing. She said soothingly, "I plan on living forever, Kingsley. So far, so good."

"I wish I had your, well, calm."

"It may be plain old exhaustion."

"No, you had it the other day, leading us all by our noses on that deceleration calculation. Energetic calm."

She could see that he meant it and thanked him warmly. "You've changed some, too."

He shrugged. "It is famously easier to get older than wiser."

"I have a lot of trust in your judgment."

He grinned. "You showed good judgment two decades ago, dumping me for Benjamin."

"I did *not* 'dump' you. I got the distinct impression that you were more interested in astronomy than in me.'

"Well, of course," he said quite innocently, then laughed at the baldness of the truth. "That is, I was a monomaniac then."

"Would Angelica say anything has changed?"

"Good point. Probably not."

"You weren't going to change, and Benjamin was what I wanted, anyway. Not that it wasn't fun . . ." She put a lot into the drawn-out last word.

He said seriously, "Yes, it certainly was."

They sat for a long, silent moment. The wind chimes sang merrily and the soft air caressed them both, a tangy sea scent filling the room as the trade winds built. She let the moment run, something she would not have done until recently. She relaxed into the sweet odors of plumeria and frangipani, both lush now in her garden. A few years before, she had not even known their names. The garden itself was a recent hobby, all due to the damned disease, which she fought by concentrating upon the present. Zen Dying.

Then Kingsley began taking his tie off, fingers prying the tight little knot loose. "I must remember where I am. Going to be here awhile, perhaps should buy one of those loud flowery shirts."

"And shorts."

"The world is not ready for the sight of my knees."

"Or mine anymore."

"Not so, they were and remain one of your best features."

"Say things like that a dozen more times and I'll get bored."

"I'd love the opportunity," he said brightly and then stopped, as if he saw which way this was headed. Visibly he sobered. A pause. Then he spoke carefully, so that she could hear all the commas in his sentences.

"I wanted to come here, in part, because I don't want to be overheard."

"That I can guarantee." She wondered at his sudden mood shift. "Prettier here than in that office the Center gave you, even if it is nice and big."

"I fear that the Center is not secure. Or at least, as I understand people like Victoria Martinez, I cannot be absolutely sure that my office is not eavesdropped upon." He looked at her edgily, as if this were being impolite. She liked his English delicate hesitation. "Already. But within a few days, almost certainly."

"That's also why you're looking for an apartment."

"Precisely. This is going to be ever so much larger and it is going to last quite a while."

"Once we've identified this new object—oh, I see." He made a tent of his hands and peered through them at the languid paradise out the window, like a prisoner contemplating an impossible escape. "I was shaken by Benjamin's calculation. His implication was clear."

"Martinez spoke of danger—"

"Only the obvious deduction."

Channing realized she had nowhere to go in this conversation without betraying Benjamin's own ideas. She stalled with "But no one in the room mentioned . . ."

"That obviously there are only two ways to reconcile his numbers."

He looked at her searchingly and she had to suppress a

smile at this coy game. Might as well play, though; he still had the old sly charm, damn him. "Either the thing's passing through a region of the outer solar system where the number of iceteroids is very high for some reason, or . . ." He let it hang there for a long moment and then gave up. "Or the thing is somehow seeking out lumps of ice and rock and processing them."

"Like a starship decelerating."

He slapped his knees, the sound scaring off a mynah bird from the windowsill, its quick white flash of wings a blur. "But my own point, that the gamma rays would kill anything—"

"A solid argument. So there's that pesky third choice."

"Third?"

She had to admit, he looked genuinely puzzled. "None of the above."

"But when you say 'starship,' you mean—"

"Something that flies between stars, period."

"Something crewed, even by silicon chip minds, would quite clearly still be vulnerable to—"

"Give it up, Kingsley. It's in a category we haven't thought of yet."

He fretted for a moment, his hatchet face with its large eyes drawing her gaze downward to a mouth that stirred restlessly, yet would not shape words. The default style in astronomy was to explain a new observation by assembling a brew of known ingredients—types of stars, orbiting or colliding in various ways, and emitting radiation in known channels, using familiar mechanisms. This worked nearly all the time. Kingsley had used it with speed and ingenuity decades before, explaining gamma-ray bursters quite handily with a little imagination and detailed calculations. Kingsley habitually worked in this mode, his papers couched in a style whose unstated message was to show, not just an interesting application of impressive techniques to a known problem, but also that he was a good deal better at doing this than his readers. Now his mouth worked and twisted with his dislike of working outside this lifelong mode.

"Then you two are thinking along the same lines as I."

"Sure—first, that this thing has to be enormously compressed, and the only object we know in its class of energy and power is . . . a black hole." She sipped her iced tea and watched his veiled surprise.

"One of . . ."

He was pulling it out of her, all right, but it was an amusing game. "About three times the mass of our moon."

"You derived that from the Doppler shifts from very close in to the core, I suppose?"

"Exactly. Didn't want to say so until I had more data."

"A black hole of that size is quite small, a meter or two across." He looked at her askance, skeptical.

She had looked up the theory. Primordial black holes could have been left over from the Big Bang, but there was no evidence for them. After birth, these tiny singularities in space-time could have survived their habit of radiating away sprays of particles—that is, black holes were not exactly black. This radiation had been worked out by Stephen Hawking, who showed that a small hole would have survived this evaporation, from the beginning of the universe until the present, if it had at least 10^{15} grams of mass. This was equivalent to an asteroid a hundred meters in radius.

The intruder, though, had a mass ten billion times greater. It had swallowed a lot, perhaps, in the last fifteen billion years as the universe ripened.

Where it came from was completely open. It could not have been born in a supernova collapse, which was the theorists' favorite recipe for making holes. Such a cataclysm would have produced a black hole of mass comparable to the sun. This intruder might have been built up by sucking in mass, all the way back to the Big Bang. *Might. Maybe. Perhaps* . . . the familiar wiggle room terms that accompanied most advanced astrophysical theory, which was starved for hard data. Until now.

Kingsley was enjoying this a bit too much, so she cut to

the chase. "So how's it guide itself, right? Like a fat man on skates, it should just shoot through in a straight line."

Kingsley allowed himself a smile. "I apologize for seeming to lead the conversation, but I have had the impression for several days that you know a great deal more than you are admitting."

"Being away from the scramble at the Center helps. The quiet gives me time to think."

"Particularly, to think of how this impossibility can exist."

"It's a black hole, almost certainly guiding itself with its magnetic fields. I've proved they're there, thousands of Gauss in strength, by looking in a small bit of the optical line data." There, the whole truth and nothing but. She was tired of all this precious waltzing around, as though they were all trying to get an ace journal paper out of this, or competing for a prize. She had operated under the assumption that Kingsley was, since he had quite a few prizes on his mantel already. But she now saw that he was beyond that, engaged at some different level.

"I see."

He had something to say now, she could tell, but wanted to be coaxed. "This object is not the only problem?"

"Sure, it's damned strange and people higher up—a hell of a lot higher up—are going to want to control the situation. But our position is equally odd."

"I try not to think beyond the astronomy."

"Alas, I must." He got up and paced, hesitating at the vision of leafy paradise beyond the window. "Quite predictably, we will be . . . enlisted."

"Benjamin feels the same way, but he didn't want to say it."

"Why didn't he mention it to me today at the Center?"

"You two have your own, uh, styles. They don't match up too well."

"A very polite way to say it. Bad blood between us, going back to . . ."

"Yes, you and me. He suspects, but I've never told him."

"Good." Quick nods of the head, a brisk manner. "No point."

"He got some hints from 'friends' around the time of our marriage. I could tell, from the way he edged around the subject, bringing you up at odd times. Then, years later, noticing very obviously your steady rise up the ladder. A professorship at Manchester—'Not bad for his age,' he said. Then a chair at Cambridge, how he envied that! Always in the back of his mind I could feel the question . . . but he never asked."

"It was over, done."

"Between men like you nothing is ever really over."

"Well, it is to me." He smiled very slightly. "With you, I mean."

"I know. Me, too. But you two are always going to be competitors."

"Inevitably." She could see him draw himself up, taking a cleansing breath, shoving the personal into a pocket of his mind. "And I fear my understanding of how power works in our tiny world implies that matters shall soon change radically."

"For the worse."

He looked soberly at her and she saw that he had enjoyed this bit of verbal jousting as much as she. But not as flirting, no—as nostalgia. He was shoring up memories of better times, against a grim future.

Not that she did not do the same, she reminded herself.

Kingsley gazed at the tropical wealth and sighed. "We're all going to be kept here, close to the incoming data, and 'encouraged' to work together. Of that I am sure. It's what you expect, isn't it?"

"I hadn't given it a thought."

He smiled. "Of course. You have far more important matters to attend. Quite right. I do hope I am wrong."

"Me, too . . ." She let the sentence trail off. His transition from the Kingsley of old to this astute observer of the corridors of power was unsettling.

"I can think of no better place to be incarcerated. Compared with my situation in Oxford, especially with the chilly winds blowing from Angelica, it is—"

"It's like paradise," she finished for him.

3 For centuries, physics and astronomy sought the big, glamorous governing equations for phenomena that were themselves ever-more grand: larger or smaller, hotter or colder, faster or slower than the narrow, comfortable human world. But shortly after the end of the TwenCen, science—particularly astronomy, with its pricey telescopes—approached the financial turnover, where ever-larger infusions of money yielded only incrementally more insight.

The universe kept upping the fare for further erudition. The particle physicists had hit that marginal realm with their massive accelerators. Now science increasingly shifted from the fundamental equations to discovering what emerged from those equations in the real, complex world.

One faction among scientists decried this turning to more applied problems. In their vision, physics resembled Latin— an important canon, essential for advanced work and kept alive by small bands of devoted advocates. This view failed to carry the day among those who gave funding. Applied problems had become the mainstream of physics and even astronomy, making the twenty-first century a more practical place, especially when compared with the great cathedrals of knowledge erected in the TwenCen, soaring to grand heights from the base of great theories.

Astronomers, with so many new observing windows

thrown open upon the universe, kept busy scrutinizing the zoo of objects available at ever-finer resolutions. Those who interpreted the observations evolved new approaches. Theorists now used pencil and paper in a blend with vast computer programs, asking questions with whatever tool seemed best.

Luckily, such intellectual armament proved to be the best for use against the problem of the intruder. Channing's discovery of high magnetic fields in the hottest, most luminous region of the object was the crucial fact that opened a rich realm of informed speculation.

Benjamin was particularly happy with the importance of magnetic fields. His doctoral thesis had focused on magnetic forces in galactic jets, and this thing definitely had a jet whose twists and filigrees the radio astronomers were enthusiastically mapping. They sent new charts daily.

Benjamin threw himself into the work, using a combination of imagination and rigorous computer programs. He was pleased to find that some of his hoary old methods were quite germane to this problem. It helped him keep up with Kingsley's darting skills at analysis. They had offices near each other and their meetings were contests between the speed of Kingsley's elegant fountain pen and Benjamin's custom keyboard.

Benjamin felt himself renewed. Like many scientists, he could trace his lifelong fascination with the natural world to a key, trigger moment. His father had showed him how a magnet always knew which way was north and explained it by saying the needle was forced to line up with the magnetic field. But he could not see or feel this field, so that meant there were invisible real things in the world, less substantial than air but able to act on iron across many miles.

This clue that something deeply mysterious lay behind the everyday world was a revelation and a source of quiet, persistent excitement, a note that had sounded happily throughout his life. Such excitements of the mind had come less often in the last decade as he felt his powers ebbing. In comparison with the bright postdocs who passed through the Center, he had felt slow to catch on to the latest currents. Now fashion, thanks to the intruder, had returned to his home turf.

"Magnetic fields act like rubber bands; it takes work to stretch or bend them," he said to several staff members who were assembled to talk, the usual crowd plus Kingsley and a few new ones. Even for informal talks, the crowd kept growing as data came in.

A newer staff woman who worked in another area was visibly struggling to keep up with the flood of ideas. "Those are the lines of force?" she asked, and he refrained from correcting. In his astrophysics textbook, he had once deliberately used that misleading phrase, then added a footnote that said: *The magnetic field lines are often called "lines of force." They are not. In fact, any forces exerted by the field are perpendicular to the fields themselves. The misnomer is perpetuated here to prepare the student for the treacheries of his profession.* A little prissy, maybe, and he could see this was not the time for such academic hair-splitting.

"That's exactly the point," Kingsley said. He had been sitting at the back of the seminar room, brooding, but now his voice was filled with vigor. "The intruder is exerting forces on itself by ejecting matter through its jet. Changing velocity, in a systematic way."

"How can you tell?" the woman asked. Benjamin smiled. She was unused to Kingsley's style of drawing the right questions from his audience, so that instead of lecturing people, he seemed to be merely answering them as they peppered him with their doubts. And doing it a bit serenely, too. The Cambridge touch.

Kingsley came forward and put a plastic sheet on the overhead projector. "I used these radio observations. By calculating the momentum delivered in each jet plume, I could find where the intruder was headed next, as a reaction to the matter it ejected. Here—"

The sly bastard's even got viewgraphs all ready, Benjamin thought admiringly, despite himself. *Playing us like a goddamn violin.*

The trajectory displayed was a jagged series of straight lines that nonetheless swooped inward along a persistent curve. No one had plotted these data in three dimensions yet and Benjamin saw that they had all been guilty of staying too close to the data. Kingsley stood silently, letting them digest the implication.

Benjamin jumped in. "The intruder is following a curve into the solar system. And it's finding iceteroids still, even though it's closer in than Pluto now."

"My esteemed colleague has stolen my points," Kingsley said with a stagy smile, though Benjamin knew this was exactly what he had wanted.

"It's guided," a postdoc said.

"It's *guiding*, I think, is the point," Kingsley said.

This provoked a rustle. If Dart had gone over to the "starship hypothesis," there were huge implications.

"Targets of opportunity," Benjamin said, not wanting to get into a broader discussion. "Every time it makes a course correction, it's headed for the nearest iceteroid that will help it follow this smooth path."

"But, my God," one of the staff said, "that would mean it can find chunks of ice and rock just a few hours' flying time away—"

"Some of them only a few tens of meters across, to judge by the variations in jet luminosity we detect—" another voice called out.

"And it can then fly unerringly to its next"—Kingsley paused just enough—"prey."

A long silence. "Where's that curve go?" a staffer whispered.

"Jupiter," Kingsley said simply.

Gasps.

"And quite quickly."

"That was an admirable result," Benjamin had to say to Kingsley. They were on their way a short while later, called to Victoria Martinez's office. "You must've spent a lot of time on it."

"I had help. Called in various orbital specialists, got some computer help—"

Victoria Martinez came into her office with a tall well-dressed man. "Sorry I was late, gentlemen. Mr. Arno has just arrived."

Handshakes all round, Benjamin wondering who this was. Not an astronomer, he was fairly sure; something about the eyes. He had little time to wonder. Arno sat on the edge of Martinez's desk, as if he owned the room. Martinez did not seem to mind, and instead settled into her own high-backed chair with an expression of hovering interest, an air of deference. Arno took the time to adjust the seams in his pressed light gray Mancetti suit, which went well with his blue and red tie based on a Japanese woodprint. An undefinable air of presence and power came across in the way he looked directly at Benjamin.

"I'm from the U Agency," he said, as if this banished all doubt. "We've been tracking your results here and think it's time to move."

"U Agency? Ubiquitous?"

Arno frowned at this joke, but then he managed a mirthless smile and said, "I'll have to remember that one."

Martinez's eyes widened slightly in alarm. This was a manager from the big time, her expression conveyed, not the sort given to minor banter. Arno waited just one beat for this to sink in and said, "No, we are an emergency arm of your government. I've been in touch with Dr. Dart here, and others, and we felt it was time to get some control of the situation. That means bringing you into the loop—in fact, everybody working here."

Benjamin had heard vague talk of a consolidated arm, usually called in to apply leverage in international crises. Arno must represent such shadowy forces. Benjamin paid little attention to the always-precarious balance of forces in the big power arena. The United States was wearying of being the perpetual fallback stabilizer, especially since the Mideast equilibrium had dissolved into ultranationalist and water rights issues. He knew the country was assuming more imperial modes, but cared little for the details. "What 'loop'—"

"Perhaps I can make this easier," Kingsley said smoothly. "I've been worried that this is moving too fast for us, and media attention is about to descend. Better to have it handled by people who can impose controls when needed."

Benjamin turned from Arno and shot back at Kingsley, "And what's that mean?"

"You see the implications of my trajectory analysis. It's *intelligent*—and hugely powerful. At the moment, it's headed toward Jupiter, but that, too, could change."

"Anything commanding those power levels is almost inconceivably dangerous," Martinez put in.

"Your authority to do this?" Benjamin asked.

"Direct from the White House," Arno said with casual assurance. He straightened the cuff on his long-sleeved shirt.

"The Science Adviser has been informed?" Benjamin persisted.

"Of course. Kingsley's reports came up through her."

Benjamin glanced at Kingsley and realized he had been played for a fool for the last few weeks. "I don't think I follow—"

"Look, this is presidential," Arno said, as if explaining to a child. "The U Agency has to run the show here. It's in your own interests. We'll handle the connections to the top and to outside—the media. You guys will be free to do your research. This Center will, from now on, be devoted entirely to coordinating international intelligence."

Benjamin tried not to let himself be put off by Arno's curt, aggressive style, which he recognized from his occasional dealings with other wings of government. Still, this guy was over the top. "U Agency people, then—"

"Will work closely with yours. We'll filter everything that goes in or out."

"How do you expect us to do research with you peering over our shoulders?"

"Just bring me the results. I'm a conduit, that's all. Believe me, we've got some able minds working for us. Our people will be, well, colleagues."

Benjamin was still trying to comprehend this sudden swerve. He had come into Martinez's office expecting a friendly discussion of how to deal with the growing circle of those who knew of the intruder. He should have realized that Kingsley was at his charismatic best when he sailed before prevailing political winds, well before others sensed them. Why hadn't he seen that Kingsley fit in with the U Agency style—and that something like this was inevitable? The astronomy of it had captivated him, blinded him.

Or so went his rationale later. Arno had ended with a warm handshake and an ingratiating, obviously phony smile, the sort of expression Benjamin always suspected people of rehearsing in front of mirrors at home. But that was merely cosmetic. Arno's staff began arriving within minutes, and he knew at a glance what was in store. The U personnel dressed alike, severe and stark in their dark slacks, jackets, and off-white shirts. At least they did not wear ties. The Center staff astronomers were Hawaiian hip, in shorts and gaudy flowered shirts and thongs.

Benjamin had to settle several immediate personnel problems, holding a quick general meeting to announce the "structural change," which included a layering of Deputy Administrators, Action Team Leaders, and Section Heads in a chart neatly printed for prominent display. With Kingsley and Arno beside him he answered a few questions, but thankfully most fell to Martinez.

Then he had to patrol the Center corridors as the U Agency types moved in, finding office space and mediating. It was like two different species having to suddenly share the same territory. "Colleagues," Arno had said, and this proved to mean that some of the U Agency people were faces he recognized. Apparently they had been hired as consultants, perhaps quite recently. Some of them seemed faintly embarrassed, but they moved with the same crisp efficiency as the others. Was there prior training to do this sort of thing?

It would have been easy to blame Kingsley for this, to see him as Benjamin's primary antagonist. But within three hours of this shock, the two men were bound down the mountain in Benjamin's car, headed for a dinner they had planned days before. They drove in silence, the aroma of burning sugarcane drifting up from the fields toward Hilo. They quite deliberately spoke only of Hawaii itself as Benjamin took the slope at high speed, tires howling on the curves, bamboo forests flickering past with their dry smells.

Kingsley seemed able to relax and truly enjoy the ride down to their beachfront home. After taking off their shoes in standard island good manners, Kingsley stopped to admire the photos in the entrance hall of Channing's career: aboard the space station, on an EVA, taking data in blazing sunlight. As he did, Benjamin sought out Channing and embraced her with a fervor that surprised him.

Channing sensed the soured mood of the men and quickly deflected it with drinks of mango and papaya and rum, amid soft Japanese music, all counterpointed by the wind chimes in their back garden. The air seemed layered with fragrances and talk ran to island gossip. But then she wanted to be kept up on the gossip and it all came out.

"I don't think you fully appreciate why I acted," Kingsley said at last, once the describing was done.

"You *bet* I don't," Benjamin shot back. He had been holding his tongue because the last few hours had drastically shifted the power balance between the two men, and he was unsure how to deal with it. "Neither does Martinez."

"She does not know my methods, but you, with our ancient association, might have guessed my intention well before I was ready to reveal it."

"I'm afraid I'm being sidelined after the first few plays."

"That will not happen, I assure you." Kingsley sat back and wrapped both hands around one knee, leaning back as though to relieve knotted muscles. *He carries tension that way, same as me,* Benjamin thought. *But doesn't show it in the face or voice.*

"I'm pretty damned mad."

"With good reason, given what you know. Let me say I appreciated your not giving voice to that at the Center. It would have done no good."

Channing had let them go through the first quick rush of it, their words coming out in machine-gun volleys. Now she made a show of fetching some nibble food, leaving them with a lingering observation: "I'm impressed that a U.S. agency will spring so quickly on the advice of a Brit astronomer."

"I've been functioning as a sort of scientist-diplomat since well before the Astronomer Royal appointment," Kingsley called after her. "My good fortune that I've made the right contacts."

"I admire your understatement," she called from the kitchen.

"Why not tell me?" Benjamin demanded, irked at her cavalier nonchalance at this whole abrupt maneuver.

"Because it would have compromised a delicate transition."

Benjamin sat back and crossed his arms, demanding, "Explain. Better be good, too."

"I've been asking people around the world to work on this intruder problem, sending e-mails and calling—any idea why?"

"To get them involved?" Channing ventured when Benjamin just shook his head. "So these U Agency types would *have* to come in?"

"Dead right. I want this controlled by the United States, not by some United Nations committee."

Benjamin nodded. "A nation can act quickly, a committee, never."

"And there's more, isn't there?" Channing bore in on Kingsley, leaning forward, her hostess skills giving way to her professional ones.

"You could always spot my motives," Kingsley laughed. "The U Agency fellows will pull in some 'foreign advisers' right away."

Benjamin saw it. "And the people you e-mailed the most, brought into the discussion earliest—"

"They'll be the ones recruited." Kingsley smiled.

"And the astronomers I saw today working for the Agency—"

"Exactly. They were brought in the traditional way, a consultancy for a sum they could scarcely decline."

"They know what we're doing?"

"Of course. Some have been monitoring our work—which impresses them, I'm happy to say—since the first week."

Channing said, "You make it sound like moving chess pieces."

Kingsley looked reflective. "I suppose it is. All done very diplomatically, of course, through all the proper channels. I was afraid I was being a bit obvious, but so far Arno has not caught on."

"You believe," Benjamin said, sitting back and gazing up at the hard, bright stars visible through the softly rattling fronds of palm trees.

"I wanted bright people here, people I knew from my work. Screens are going to start coming down soon, I'll wager."

"Really?" Channing chewed her lip, her face pale in the gloom.

"This is the calm before the storm—a very long storm, quite probably," Kingsley finished morosely, taking a long pull at his drink.

Benjamin told her about the trajectory Kingsley had displayed. "It's moving faster, cutting the time to reach Jupiter."

"And that provokes the U Agency?" she asked wonderingly.

Kingsley studied the leafy garden with a skewed slant to

his mouth. "I felt bound to let those above know, as did Victoria. We spoke of it the second day I was here. I did not include you two in my thoughts because, frankly, I felt it was a side issue, just a reporting up the chain of command sort of thing. But quite quickly it caught the attention of certain people at the NSF, then DARPA—my sources tell me."

Benjamin disliked both what he was learning and getting it from Kingsley. The man had mastered astronomy, international diplomacy, and—no doubt, they would soon learn—figure skating. Now he knew how laymen felt when confronting the complex weave of astronomy with only newspaper-level knowledge. He hated playing straight man here, but stifled that and asked, "Why in the world would the Defense Advanced Research Project Agency have connections to NSF's astronomy office?"

"There is a standing procedure, ever since the Air Force began detecting what turned out to be gamma-ray bursters, remember?" Kingsley smiled. "Their satellites designed to detect nuclear explosions found signals coming from the sky. Bursters bequeathed us this alliance of interests."

"And from there on, let me guess," Benjamin said, "it went to the National Security Council, then the President's Science Adviser."

Kingsley raised an eyebrow in appreciation. "You know more of this labyrinth than I expected. Pretty nearly so, yes."

"So we're stuck having to work with those Chicken Littles, huh?" Channing said.

Kingsley gave her a puzzled glance. "Uh, Chicken . . ."

"The U Agency's purpose is to stop disasters before they grow, mostly by taking action across national and even continental boundaries. They're a quietly accepted part of global integration," she rattled off knowledgeably.

Benjamin was surprised at how much she knew. When she had a mind to, she showed as much acuity as Kingsley. And he, in turn, had small blind spots, like not remembering who Chicken Little was. The man's concentration upon his career had swept all else from his mind. Most astronomers were distracted sorts, unable to recognize many of the faces on the magazines next to the checkout line in markets. Kingsley took this to an extreme, but his footing among the corridors of power was deft and firm.

With lacerating sarcasm, Channing made fun of the U types, reminding them that she had some dealings with the Agency in her "spacesuit days." Her eyes danced with memories. "The two most common elements in the universe are hydrogen and stupidity, and they've got plenty of both."

Benjamin felt their home around them like a warm cocoon and hoped that it could be a quiet refuge from the growing tumult outside as word inevitably spread. Something big was coming, and he was not ready. Above he saw the spray of glimmering that was the plane of the galaxy, the Milky Way, and wondered from which, of all those stars, this thing had come. It had been gobbling up iceteroids for some time, no doubt, so its initial incoming direction was no clue. It could be from anywhere. Given the vast spaces between the suns, it could have been traveling for centuries, millennia. And what unimaginable technology lay behind the downright weird signatures of the intruder?

Starship? The word seemed inadequate for the energies the thing poured forth. They needed a better term, a name that carried the mystery of it.

4 Channing gave it a name that stuck, within a week. One much better than "X-1" or "intruder."

To concentrate and save her energy, she worked in the quiet of her home study. A doctor had told her that fighting this disease would be like the late career of a fading boxer: pacing yourself, resting when you could, so you could go a few hard rounds when you had to. She had a countdown to heed, and now the Center had one, too, with the intruder.

A few days after the entrance of the U Agency, she noticed a small detail in the high-resolution pictures of the intruder's spectacular collisions.

The hottest region had an extended magnetosphere, a glowing dot that kept expanding with each collision. She compared images from all available kinds of telescopes—starting with the radio's spindly jet, up through an infrared blur of hot gas, on into the visible spectra that revealed sharp streamers of agitated atoms arcing like geysers from the core, and finally on into the X rays that showed a white-hot center of intense heat, a seething central furnace that grew larger with every collision.

The entire range of deep space telescopes now sent images to the Center, a gusher of data each time the intruder devoured another hapless chunk of matter in its path. One collision had decidedly different spectral signatures. Careful analysis showed emission lines from silicon, carbon, iron. It had struck an asteroid. With the same outcome—a jet of microwave-emitting electrons, hot gas, and plasma, trailing the intruder, a neon sign seen all the way across the solar system.

Overlaying all these results with some sophisticated graphics, she got a consistent picture.

The strong magnetic field was building in a huge active region, lighting up brilliantly, growing. She suggested some adroit observations, brought them to Kingsley's attention, and soon enough the big-dish "ears" of Earth's radio telescope net were mapping the moving magnetic region in intricate detail. They were the first to see a bull's-eye disk, with circular lanes of varying luminosity centered on an unresolved blur.

So she took it into the Center and the Gang of Four. "Looks like a target," Benjamin said. "A bull's-eye."

"An accretion disk," Kingsley observed dryly, his expression showing his lifelong dislike of homey analogies for astrophysical objects. "The mass it has acquired is spiraling in. It collides, rubs, and gets warm. Hot enough and the matter emits radiation." He nodded to Channing, who sat at the controls of one of their big-screen displays—a fresh compensation for their enforced collaboration with the U Agency, who had just installed higher-power computers and flat-screen displays of eye-opening quality. "Your working hypothesis is proved."

"I'm that obvious?" Channing was slightly miffed at having her thunder stolen.

Benjamin called up from the massive Center computers his compilation of the radio telescope data. Using Channing's discovery of the high magnetic fields, they had been able to take quick snapshot-like radio maps of the inner region.

"Here, I've made it into a film," Benjamin said. "It even has a plot, sort of."

The view opened far out in deep space, our sun a mere glimmering spark. In an overlay, Channing saw vast swarms of rock and iceteroids orbiting. Suddenly a strange glowing disk like an uncoiling silvery snake plunged across the field of view. It struck an iceteroid with a brilliant flash. Gaudy luminous streamers clasped the doomed mile-wide chunk of ice.

"They were lucky enough to get a series of maps and optical images when it hit its latest victim," Benjamin said to the darkened room. "I've blended them here."

The snake coiled up and deformed, becoming all mouth. Blue-hot, it gnawed its way through the ice. Channing knew that at its speeds, these had to be images made in slices finer than a millisecond. The eerie beauty of it was captivating, the lapping strands of magnetic fields flickering among the flying fragments.

Then something luminous emerged like a wasp from a cocoon at the other side of an expanding ball of hot gas. The intruder moved on, now bearing a halo like an immense multicolored rainbow around a central bright hoop. But within the inner ring lay an utterly black core. The rainbow was a momentarily expanded disk of matter, she guessed, a hundred-kilometer-wide firework accelerating inward.

"So we have seen the beast at last," she murmured into the shocked silence of the room as the images faded to black.

Benjamin stood next to the big screen, his suntan giving him an odd bronzed look in the small lamp of the speaker's podium. A casual audience of astronomers who had come in for the show peppered him with questions and he fielded them well, the distances and times and resolutions at his fingertips.

She let the moment wash over her. To her surprise, she had not been surprised. It looked just the way she had seen it in her dreams. Fevered, troubled dreams.

Finally Kingsley got her attention by addressing a public question to her. "You hinted by e-mail that you had a name for the object," Kingsley said with amusement.

"I suggest we call it the Eater of All Things."

"Because it is a black hole," Kingsley finished for her.

"Exactly," Benjamin p...
while she massaged her data...
have been thinking the same t...

This was the first truly pu...
looked at each other silently, so it w...
say, "You don't want to alarm the U pe...

"Right," Benjamin said. "The spectral...
and blues we found early on, remember? Th...
hole idea. Now we can see it trapping mass. Ca...

Channing leaned back and regarded their Gang...
the Big Screen Room, as the U types had labeled it...
had slapped labels on rooms all over the Center. "I h...
we're under no illusions that all this data isn't being copied...
by the U computers they just installed. They'll have this
processed shot of Benjamin's by now."

"And they are far from dumb," Kingsley agreed. "Particularly the newest fellow, Randall. Knew him on a visiting
appointment at Harvard, before he went 'underground,' as
the U people say."

"Into classified work," Benjamin supplied for Amy.

"Oh." Amy seemed startled that an astronomer would go
into any other line. Her expression plainly said, *Once you
understand how big and wonderful the universe is, how
could you do anything else?*

Channing permitted herself a nostalgic smile, remembering when she had worn just such an earnest expression—and
had meant it.

ut in. "I kept the secret pretty well
but I'll bet half the people here
...ing—without saying so."
...lic announcement. They
...as left to Amy Major to
...ople, correct?"
...shifts—those reds
...ey fit the black
...se closed."
...of Four in
...They
...ope

e in the garden,
Kingsley had a
asually tossing
nd pub crawls,
board back in-
side to keep it out of the dependable tropical rain showers
and then had considerable use for the cushion's other, secret
purpose. Often when he got home he would take a stroll in
the garden while Channing finished making dinner, her favorite daily task. When he reached the portion out of view of
the house, he would approach the cushion and give it half a
dozen good, solid punches. He had discovered this outlet
years before and realized quite well that his need of it told
him something about his feelings.

He made good use of the cushion every evening now. As
the flood of data deepened, he staked out a clear position
that learning more is the best short-term goal. In this the
Center staff backed him solidly.

"Ummm," Channing said over a dinner of baked ono in
papaya-ginger sauce, "and good ol' savvy Kingsley sees this
as a power clash from which he can profit."

"Uh, yes. I was going to put it a little more delicately—"

"To that Arno guy you can be diplomatic, but it's wasted
on me, dear. Kingsley is just staying in character. The U
Agency isn't using a hobnailed boots approach; they're

smarter than that. It's more what we used to call at NASA a 'soft presence' style—you know they're there and can take over the operation in a millisecond, and they convey that without saying anything."

Benjamin admired how she could sum up what had taken him days to realize. "Yup, subtle they are."

"So far."

"Meaning?"

"They don't have to stay that way."

He was having trouble river-rafting in the fast administrative U Agency waters. They operated as if they knew what mattered before they asked questions, so the answers had better fit their expectations. And pronto. He heard "cut to the chase" several times a day. "I keep getting signals like that," he admitted.

"I'm not there all the time, so maybe I can see it in a clearer perspective. Everybody's getting more tense and the whole thing is going to crack open pretty soon."

"I hope not."

"Kingsley handled the public announcement very well, but it's a stopgap."

"He can keep on handling it, for all I care." Benjamin had found the whole press conference an anxiety squeeze from start to finish. He had not mastered the art of saying only enough to cover the subject, avoiding any speculation even when badgered.

So it had been no surprise when Martinez gave Kingsley the spokesman job. He had downplayed any danger, though of course the mainstream reporters leaped on that immediately, implying with sneers and eyebrows yet another "cover-up." Yet somehow, with a few quiet prebriefings and some postbriefing hospitality to various opinion-setters, Kingsley had managed to get just the right media angle: huge global interest, but so far, just curiosity.

"It helps that there's this new water war between Turkey, Syria, and Iraq. Plenty of juicy footage," Channing said.

"Oh, I hadn't noticed."

"That's why he's Astronomer Royal. He timed the press conference in late afternoon, when the global news coverage was already locked up, plenty of shooting scenes ready to go."

"I hope that explains why some of the U Agency's hired-gun astronomers have been arranging to get their own private channels of information."

"How?" She had been serenely distant so far, picking at her fish, but now frowned.

"Getting their own simultaneous feeds on the Long Arm data, among others."

"A precaution?"

"Against who? Me? I can't see them worried about that."

"How can we be sure the data stays in-house?"

"We can't, not now."

"They want to have somebody on the outside checking us?"

He felt pleased that she had arrived at his conclusion. Her instincts were good for this kind of infighting, a legacy of her NASA days, whereas his had been dulled by years of routine administration.

"So what can I do?"

"Nothing. It's probably a Kingsley maneuver we don't understand yet."

"I hope so."

There had been several such. As Kingsley had warned, there were "side effects" of working with the U Agency umbrella over them. Their home and his apartment had been carefully invaded, searched, analyzed—purely pro forma, of course—and then just as carefully put back as they were. Their electronic records had yielded e-mail addresses, and most valuably, the system still carried the signatures of recent use. This gave the e-mail paths of Kingsley's recent messages, though even to the best of agents the system could not divulge their content; that was erased. The Agency and those over it did not realize that his leaving the e-mail tags in place was a neat way of ensuring that his correspondents would be rounded up and brought to him, to keep the lid on word of the intruder.

In this manner, he gained a few people he had not asked for, explaining that some nuance was a good idea in these matters. Kingsley also hoped that they did not catch on when, earlier, he had deliberately been rude to several bureaucratic figures, precisely to provoke this measure. Of this last touch he was openly proud; "actually Machiavellian," he termed it.

But the next day, when the two of them caught Kingsley alone for a moment and pressed him on the issue of the U Agency having separate access to incoming data, he denied any involvement. "Arno is the best of that lot, believe me," Kingsley explained, spreading his palms, face up in a gesture of openness—a little defensively, Benjamin thought.

Channing looked worried. "Then we go to Theory B."

"Which is?" Kingsley asked, sitting on the edge of his new polished teak desk. The U Agency had offered it when he decided to stay indefinitely. Not that he had any real choice, he had noted to Benjamin, and one might as well take the good with the bad in such matters.

"That they want a backup team to check us."

Kingsley nodded and Benjamin felt compelled to say, "And in case we can't do the job anymore."

Both Channing and Kingsley shot questioning looks at him. "In case we're put out of action."

"How?" Kingsley asked.

"Politically, suppose the United Nations decides to make this their party?"

"We're on American soil."

"But the United States is pretty unpopular in the Security Council over this war business," Benjamin said.

"It couldn't go *that* far," Channing said.

"Just a thought," Benjamin said lightly. Then, jibing, "I'm sure Kingsley has a better Theory B."

But he did not, and their conversation broke off. There were more concrete issues to think about. It was by now clear that magnetic nozzles, like those of rockets but immensely larger, had begun to flare behind the intruder. A plume jet many thousands of kilometers long now twisted and flared. Each step of their understanding was being revealed by incremental observations, science as detective work, and the entire Center staff was fitting together more parts to the puzzle daily. The Long Arm got better close-ups of the Eater as it sped inward, still slamming into more iceteroids daily. It had been barely six weeks since the first detection.

They met with Martinez and Arno later that same day to discuss moving several existing deep space probes to rendezvous with the Eater for close-up study. They had at their command advanced light, unmanned spacecraft—descendants of NASA's faster-cheaper-smaller doctrine of the 1990s, developed for computer-enhanced exploration of the solar system. Assisted by ion rockets, these were the Searcher Class spacecraft, and to Benjamin's astonishment, Kingsley casually called up the right people at NASA and began moving them into position to intercept and study the Eater. The smell of unalloyed power was heavy in the room, though unremarked.

The afternoon waxed on. Benjamin keenly sensed the rising tension in the Center, a kind of electrical energy that he felt as he walked the corridors, listening to detailed technical conversations. A compressed tautness laced through the conversations about Janskys of measurement and arc-seconds of resolution, technical terms freighted with a gathering sense of storm.

Arno casually waved away worries that they could muster resources quickly. Channing obliquely brought up the U.N. possibility and Arno looked grim for only a fraction of a second before returning to his patented ceramic smile. "No chance," he said. Benjamin had noticed that at points of tension Arno seemed to revert to a Clint Eastwood–Gary Cooper imitation.

Still, Arno's certainty was reassuring, for so little else

was. Within an hour they received a gusher of data from the Arecibo radio dish, still the largest in the world. This huge array of metal held its cupped ear to the cosmos in Puerto Rico, in a high mountain bowl that swept across the sky, listening intently. Only at certain hours did its sweep include the Eater's trajectory, and so far they had heard little more than the electromagnetic hiss of the intruder's flailing jet tail. Now, though, the radio telescope picked up an intense, high-definition pulse of emission. An hour later the Eater fell below Arecibo's horizon and the Very Large Array spread across New Mexico's high plateau took up the task.

They had tracked the Eater now in great detail, adding images to the Long Arm's pictures of the Eater's inner core. Now the point was not mapping, but rather signal reception. Something highly detailed was coming from the very core of the intruder, and it made no sense.

Benjamin watched all this with a growing sense of urgency. He could scarcely ignore the obvious fact that Channing was fading as the afternoon waxed on, her eyes hollowing out and mouth seeming to grow thinner, hands trembling under the strain of work. But she refused to go home. Upon her sallow skin there came an expression of adamant energy, and she said, "I'll stay. I'll stay."

This carried a hard existential weight and he was cowed by the hard certainty in her voice. He loved this woman and sometimes he understood her in a way he could not express—to her or to himself—and he did as she wanted. He helped her settle into one of the rather luxurious new leather form-fitting chairs before the big-screen display and they watched the sliding columns of compressed data. The entire processing capability of the Center bore down on what Arecibo and the VLA had found.

"Unmistakably artificial," Kingsley was the first to say.

"A message?" Channing said with her wan yet edgy energy.

A staff specialist came in and displayed the enormous broadband complexity of the transmission and the Gang of

Four plus some U Agency astrophysicists went through the data stream with him. "It's digital, encoded in a fashion we haven't cracked yet," the specialist said.

While they puzzled over what this might mean, Arno drew Benjamin and Kingsley aside. "Thought you might use the services of a bright cryptographer I had brought in."

"He's here?" Benjamin asked to cover his surprise.

"She, yes."

"That slim woman I asked about?" Kingsley pressed him.

"That's the one." Arno's smile had a touch of preening in it.

"You suspected we would need one, from the very first." Kingsley nodded his head ever so slightly in respect.

"Just covering all the bases."

Benjamin could see why the woman had caught Kingsley's interest, for she was quite attractive. Conversely, he wondered why he had not noticed her himself, even among the confusing crowd of new people in the Center. When distracted, one did not notice being distracted.

In short order, she broke the code; it proved to be deceptively simple. "It's frame-compressed at high speed," she announced to the jammed room. As word spread, people slipped in. Arno and his aides were so drawn into the suspense that they were not even policing the "information boundaries," as they put it.

Benjamin asked, "How about slowing the signal?"

The cryptographer looked a little irked. "We are. Here, the run is nearly finished—"

Onto the screen leaped a string of break-down interpretations. Plainly the sender had meant this to be easily read. In short order, everyone in the room saw that it was a very short message in over a hundred languages. Each language carried the same terse message. Chinese, Spanish, then third in the string was English:

I DESIRE CONVERSE.

PART THREE

A DERANGED GOD

1 In the moments after the revelation, Benjamin noted that scientists and U Agency types alike looked the same: jaws agape, eyes blinking in wonder, disbelief wrenching mouths askew, nostrils flared. And for once, nobody had anything coherent to say.

Consternation is a term far too abstract to describe the next twenty-four hours at the High Energy Astrophysics Center. The simple three words—though there were more in other languages, with many different shadings of meaning—immediately split the staff at the Center into factions.

For decades a small band of astronomers, principally at the Search for Extraterrestrial Intelligence Institute, had listened in the radio bands for signals from other civilizations. They and many others had debated the abstract principles involved in answering a message—should one be received. Most favored not answering immediately. There seemed no rush to reply, considering the huge travel times of light between stars. But with the Eater less than an hour's time delay away, that argument slid into an ethical debate. Who should speak for Earth?

Arno made no secret of his view. "We do. The whole world has fed its astronomical data here, we have the best people in the field right down the hall, and the White House has given us freedom of movement—so we do it."

Most astronomers did not feel that way. Anxiety beset

them, knots meeting around the coffee urns in tight-lipped arguments. Channing stayed away from these. "The U Agency will call the shots here," she said to Benjamin in his office. "Notice that they're all behind Arno? No brooders there."

"They're hired guns," Benjamin said. He gazed at his desktop screen, where the long strings of the message glowed. "I desire converse, too, but how?"

"You're the scientific head here," Channing said softly. She felt the familiar old fatigue gliding up through her bones but pushed it down, her heart tripping with a quick, high rhythm. "Do it."

Benjamin jerked his eyes away from the screen, startled. "Me?"

"You discovered it."

"Amy did."

"Okay, bring in Amy. The discoverers get to name the object, that's standard—"

"You named it."

"—so we extend that right, say that the discoverers get to talk to it."

He chuckled, clasping his long, bony hands behind his neck and leaning back. "Don't take up a legal career. Too big a leap."

"I'm serious. That thing is moving fast and obviously it can think fast. Learning a hundred languages, just from eavesdropping?"

"An old cliché of B movies—"

"But probably right. Not answering right away, that sends it a message, too."

Benjamin looked startled again. "I suppose so, but . . ."

"Look, the halls are packed outside with astronomers making guesses. Suddenly nobody's an expert. I heard some guy floating a theory that some undetected planet is orbiting the black hole, and the message is from there."

"Nonsense."

"Of course, and there'll be more like it. How could anything like a zone livable for life-forms like us survive passage between the stars?" She snorted derisively. "No, it'll take a while to face the fact—that this is something utterly strange."

"What did its three little words mean, exactly? Converse as in conversation? Or as in the contrary?"

"It's a stilted diction, but I'll bet on conversation. It's bound to get context and syntax a little confused. Languages are species-specific, but this thing managed to make sense and even construct a simple sentence that meant something. Give it a break."

"Fine—so how do we talk to it?"

"Simply," she said simply.

"What should all of humanity say?"

"Keep it easy, just as the Eater did."

He brightened. "Maybe just 'We desire converse, too.'?"

"Who could blame you for that? It's the truth, and it gives nothing away."

"I don't know. It's an overwhelming responsibility."

She watched him work it out on his own. She felt lazy and weirdly relaxed, despite her hammering heart. There had been another appointment with Dr. Mendenham early this morning, which she had dearly wanted to skip but didn't. She had gotten up at dawn and made herself one of her crazy breakfasts to boost her spirits, fish and eggs with paprika. A treatment course of mahi-mahi should be added to the therapy regimen, she had decided. Trouble was, you thudded back down under the bland gray reality of modern medicine and all of its grisly matter-of-fact manner.

Without her noticing it, Benjamin had gotten on the phone, talking to somebody at Arecibo, his sentences sliding by her like glazed word nuggets—*side lobes, milliarc-seconds, sampling time, rep rate.*

She had other concerns, minor itches. The morning's treatments now irked her in myriad ways, especially her skin. Nowadays her fashion taste boiled down to whatever didn't itch, period. She wore hats to cover her patchy induced baldness, not caring that in some she looked like a lampshade in a brothel. She also discovered that an older woman could wear bright lipstick during the day without looking like she just had a binge with a jam jar. Or maybe everybody was just too polite to notice.

Now Benjamin was mustering people into the room and here was Kingsley, squatting down next to her, his slender face lined with concern. She put him off with a wavering sentence and shushed him into silence so that she could hear. Arno sat on a corner of Benjamin's desk, in his standard maneuver to dominate the room, straightening the seams in his standard Mancetti suit, charcoal-black today, all the while arguing quietly but intensely with one of his aides.

The meeting began. All good scientists had big egos, and the high nervousness of the room brought that out. While young, they had been outstanding at something widely admired. Brightest in their class, smarter than anybody they knew, it was bound to go to their heads. The wiser ones outgrew it, some becoming even mildly humble before the immensity of unanswered questions facing them. Some—alas, even some of the best—never did.

A few of the Center astronomers made their cases against any reply right away, in tones of subdued outrage. She wondered why scientists so often couched their views in abstract terms while giving their game away by the tone of voice, seemingly unaware that most people could read their emotions more tellingly than their ideas. It all seemed funny now, as she watched it from the high perch her quirky physiology had cooked up for today. She had told Kingsley that she didn't do drugs anymore because she could get the same effect by standing up fast, but he had taken the joke completely deadpan. Did she honestly look that frail?

Maybe, but she could still track the labyrinths of the argument as it worked around the room. The same views emerged in different guises, long on logic, brimming with unstated passion.

We have no right to speak for all the human race.

But only we have a prayer of knowing how to respond.

How can you? The idea's outrageous!

It might be dangerous to answer. The thing could learn how to destroy us.

It might be dangerous not to answer. And it has huge energies at its command already.

It's already taken the giant step of learning our languages. That implies an intelligence far beyond ours. Don't try to second-guess it.

But the sheer arrogance—!

Have you considered that it might be dangerous either way?

Finally Arno spoke. "This is still a matter of some secrecy, though we cannot expect it to remain so for long. It is also a matter under the governance of the United States, occurring on our territory, though in an international facility."

Protests, exclamations, as everybody in the room saw which way it was going to go. Arno brushed them aside.

"I have gotten a quick okay from the White House. They believe a reply is in order, and soon. I have been authorized to transmit one simple line."

He looked at Benjamin, and Channing saw that somehow they had planned this, right in front of her, and she had missed it. Maybe she was more feeble than she thought. Here she was at the center of historic events, distracted by her itches and not tracking.

Benjamin said, peeling off the words, "We desire converse also."

2 An answer came from the Eater at the minimum possible interval, allowing for the 8.7 Astronomical Units it had to cross—seventy-two minutes.

By this time Arno had told Benjamin and Martinez to keep their staff "in order," meaning that they were not to leak any whisper of the messages. His U Agency team held a "briefing" for the Center astronomers, rather delicately laying out the security precautions that would henceforth surround the Center's activities. In the middle of this conference, the reply arrived.

I AM ENGAGED TO CONVERSE.
MY FORMS WILL MAKE ORDER TO CONVEY MEANING.

"What in hell does that mean?" Arno asked in a tight tone, the first sign of tension Benjamin had detected in the man.

"I would venture," Kingsley said in his humble mode, "that it is organizing itself for a high-bit rate transmission."

Arno looked puzzled, as did most of the rest of those crowded into the Big Screen Room. Kingsley said smoothly, "I noticed that it transmitted when Arecibo could receive—indeed, when it was near the zenith at Arecibo's longitude."

Benjamin said, "We've been using it a lot to map the ionized regions near the Eater's core. These last few days the team at Arecibo bounced radar signals off it."

Kingsley nodded. "So it probably has noticed that half the time our largest receiver is out of view, on the other side of the Earth from the Eater. The Eater wishes to use the biggest dish we have, presumably to transfer a great deal, or else it would simply send messages to every radio telescope we have. I expect, then, that from now on it will use the second-largest facility—Goldstone, in the California desert—when Arecibo is out of its sight. We should find a third dish and send the coordinates in our own next message, so communication is continuous."

This quick analysis impressed even Benjamin, who reluctantly nodded; he had not thought of the problem, much less solved it.

Arno folded his arms. "Well, looks like we got a dialogue going here. What do we say next?"

Channing's thin voice began, and one of Arno's men started to talk over it, only to cut off abruptly when Arno shot him a severe glance, eyebrows clamped down tightly above hard eyes. Channing started again. "Ask the basics. Where it's from, what it is, what it wants."

This seemed so sensible to the small group—the Gang of Four plus some U Agency types who seemed spooked by Arno's authority—that they accepted it, arguing only over the phrasing of the questions.

Again the response came back in only a few seconds more than the computed delay time due to the finite speed of light.

I AM ONLY ME SELF ALONE. A COMPOSITION OF
FIELDS.

"What fields?" Arno wondered.

Kingsley looked at Benjamin. "I suspect, following on Dr. Knowlton's discoveries, that the black hole's magnetic domain itself is talking to us."

Astonishment met this bold venture. Benjamin saw Kingsley's thread and said, "If we're dealing with some . . . well, magnetic life . . . here, that would explain a lot."

Channing said weakly, slowly, "The fields are strong. Maybe they can contain information—say, stored in the form of Alfven waves, the most common form of magnetic waves."

Benjamin pointed out that Arecibo's high resolution radar image showed glowing filaments threading around the Eater's core. "The tightest picture we can get so far comes from the Very Long Baseline Array, though, picking out details a few kilometers in size. There's a tight knot of structures in the strong field region near the hole."

Amy Major asked incredulously, "But how did they *get* there?"

Kingsley smiled. "I quite know how you feel. This is more bizarre than anything in our astrophysical zoo. Somehow, something has impressed knowledge and intelligence into a magnetic structure."

One of the U Agency men said, "Well, a lot of our technology stores data in magnetic cores, but those're lattices. Iron, say, oriented in well-defined states by the field. *But this . . .*"

He let his silence speak for him, and judging from the open skepticism on many of the faces in the room, Benjamin could see the idea was not going over well. For reference, Benjamin tapped in a command and summoned forth the latest mapping in the microwave frequencies. At the core, just barely visible as a broad dot in these frequencies, was a disk. He knew that it was dense and hot, the captured mass like a glowing phonograph record, turning around the spindle hole that would eventually swallow it all.

A filmy cloud surrounded this bright core, laced by striations that detailed analysis had already shown to be "magnetic flux tubes," in the astrophysical jargon. The intricate architecture of these lines suggested an outline. "An hourglass," Benjamin said abruptly, seeing the structure anew.

Dimly visible, once the eye knew where to look, the symmetric funnel was undeniable.

"The hole is at the center," Kingsley observed, "that unre-

solved dot. It draws matter in along those ducts, into an accretion disk."

"Can't see any disk there," one of the U Agency astronomers put in.

"Hard to see at this angle, I'll wager," Kingsley came
back smoothly. "And perhaps not luminous at these particular frequencies, compared with the electron emission in the
strong fields."

One of the house theorists already had a mathematical simulation of the inner region, which she presented as a slice di-
agram. Depending on the weather around the black hole, there
could either be THICK INFLOW from a wide angle, or THIN IN-
FLOW into a disk at the equator of the system. The inflow
formed a THICK DISK, which could be slowly swallowed as it
spiraled into the hole, reaching MAXIMUM PRESSURE very near
the inner edge. But the energy released by the white-hot mass,
just before it dived into the hole, kept open twin funnels.

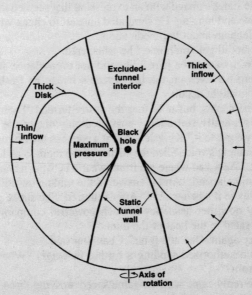

"In this model," the theorist said, "the funnels serve to eject mass, like a rocket nozzle. In steady-state, the funnel wall is static." The hourglass shape of the funnels was striking.

The entire region was only the size of a large building. The larger magnetic realm beyond this could hold enormous stores of mass, organized by the coherent field structure.

"Unbelievable," Arno whispered.

Still, the room was convinced. Heads nodded and voices called out speculations on what some of the slender pathways might be. Plainly small dots of luminosity were moving, as the map refreshed over the next hour, showing a slow, spiraling inward, down the twin funnels.

The technical discussion went on, ebbing and flowing with restless energy. Benjamin moved over to check on Channing. She barely acknowledged his presence, or much else in the room. Instead, he was puzzled to find her regarding the Eater's image with an expression that seemed to mingle awe and longing. He reminded himself to check with Dr. Mendenham about her medication.

"I should get you home," he whispered.

"No. I want to be here." She did not even glance at him, keeping her eyes on the big screen's image as fresh data filled in slight details.

"One cannot but note that the justly termed 'Eater'—or more generally, 'intruder'—answered only one of the questions we put to it," Kingsley said at a pause in the discussion.

Channing's voice filled the silence of the room as all looked at her. "We asked where it's from, what it is, what it wants."

Benjamin said, "And it answered the middle question."

"Maybe it's being coy?" Amy ventured. She spoke confidently now, her hesitancy in such powerful company now evaporated in the heat of the hunt.

"Try again. One at a time," Channing said.

Arno authorized sending a further message: "Where are you from?"

The reply came with the same speed, arriving three hours

later. They had arranged its sentences with proper typography now. The simple code it sent did not carry a distinction between capitals and lowercase, so they left it in caps. For the Eater the implied huge voice seemed natural.

THE GALAXY. I HAVE JOURNEYED THROUGH IT SINCE
THREE BILLION OF YOUR YEARS BEFORE YOUR STAR
EXISTED.

"It's been wandering for 7.5 billion years?" an astronomer asked in a hollow, awed whisper.

The room was silent for a long time.

Channing had refused to go home, and instead had fallen asleep in a lounge chair in Benjamin's office. Benjamin had noticed that even when awake her right foot sloped off to the floor, as if she had forgotten she had one. She roused for the reply and came into the Big Screen Room to see the message glowing alone on the screen. "Hmmm, it seems rather cagey about its origins."

The Center was by now getting crowded as more people poured in under the general U Agency umbrella. Some were directly from the White House, which apparently was confused about how involved it should get. The Gang of Four met with Arno and Martinez to plan.

"This is uncharted political territory," Kingsley observed. "A politician's first instinct is to clamp down upon that which he or she does not understand."

"I'd like it to stay that way," Channing said.

"I think we all would," Martinez said, "but this is going to be far larger than we can manage."

Arno looked unsure of himself, and Benjamin realized that events were spinning out of his control, an anxiety-producing turn for such a personality. It was hard to exude confidence, the crucial executive signature, when you did not feel it. He mentioned this to Kingsley at the coffee urn, and Kingsley chuckled. "Unless one is a practiced politician, and thus an actor."

"I'm not so impressed with his methods," Benjamin said. "His people are rubbing mine the wrong way."

"I fear that was inevitable," Kingsley said. "In my prior experience, science is packed solid with specialists, unused to working with others."

Channing said wryly, "Look, for guys like Arno, the first rule of action is if at first you don't succeed, destroy all evidence that you tried."

"He seems pretty agreeable so far," Benjamin said cautiously. He had respect for her political intuition; what was she seeing that he missed?

Channing's energy had abruptly returned, probably fed by old-fashioned adrenaline. She summoned more by tossing a sugar packet into her coffee. "There's no hiding from this, though—the White House has cut him enough slack to mess up."

Kingsley nodded. "Quite astute. He's got to work with such uncertain materials as ourselves. And clever we may be, but this problem is incredibly broad. I've already recommended that we fly out experts in semiotics, the language of signs, in case we are using too narrow a channel of conversation with this thing. They may have ideas we can use."

Benjamin had to agree. These days, there were cell biologists unable to discuss evolutionary theory, physicists who couldn't tell a protein from a nucleic acid, chemists who did not know an ellipse from a hyperbola, geologists who could not say why the sky was blue. Worse, they didn't care. Generalized curiosity was rare and getting rarer and now they needed a lot of people who could bring in a broad range of angles of attack.

"I think you're giving Arno too much credit," Channing insisted. "He's been behind the curve since the Eater began talking. In situations like this, conventional wisdom won't work. He's so dense, light bends around him."

Benjamin laid a restraining hand on her arm. "I think you're overtired."

The rawboned, ravaged look she gave him had a silent

desperation. He did not know where her sudden moods came from, but resolved to weather them. Trying to toss off the matter lightly, she said, "The two most common elements in the universe are hydrogen and stupidity. We shouldn't be surprised to see it show up a lot in the next few days . . . that's all."

"I'm taking you home."

"Good idea, best of the day." Then she fainted.

3 Living in a female body—Channing mused, lying in the cool, slanted light of early morning—was different. She rustled in the damp sheets, cat-lazy, and watched Benjamin get ready to go back to the Center after having had less sleep than he should.

Males had low-maintenance bodies; shave, trim fingernails, haircut whenever it got too obviously long—that was *it*. They were so *pointed* in their desire to have women, a desire she remembered from adolescence as both frightening and complimentary at once. The sense of the chase lived in them, made them feel their bodies as jackets carrying their imperatives—sperm, armies, ideas, civilization—on its perilous journey. They relished their recklessness, and she had come to understand that it was not an embracing of death, as some feminists insisted, but a zesty drive to slam up against the walls of the world, test the limits.

Even Benjamin's casual moves showed how his sense of space differed, as if this crisis brought out deep responses. Men's world fixed on fly balls in a summer sky, the target at the edge of reach of arrow or gun, the bowl of sky lit by beckoning pinwheel stars, the far horizon as a target. Men felt their bodies, she suspected, as taut with lines of potential. Women revolved around a more inner space, orbiting their more complex innards.

And the penis: willful, answering only to the unconscious. In the small hours of this morning, she had proved this theorem by explicit example, getting him erect as he slept, with artful fingers and lips in a swampy, eager mood that came over her suddenly. In their verbal love play his got a name, whereas somehow her vagina never did—until this moment, the idea had never occurred. He could not lie, erotically; erections spoke truly of what the libido willed.

"Hey, sailor, new in town?" she murmured in her cat voice.

He came rushing over. "Thought you were asleep. Wow, you were great."

"For a kiss you get breakfast."

"Sure. Where?"

"On the deck?"

"No, the kiss."

That led to an extended seminar on several ready reaches of her body and delayed his departure by another half hour. In payment she demanded to go with him, and predictably he said no, she was too tired, and just as predictably, she won.

On the drive up, they had their first private conversation about the Eater since the first message had come in. "You're more afraid than you're letting on, aren't you?" she asked quietly.

"You bet." He drove with his usual concentration, quick and able, tires howling on the curves. Well, maybe today it was justified. Life seemed to be moving faster.

"It's packing a lot of power."

"And with seven billion years of experience, knows how to use it."

"If it cares to."

"That's just what the politicians will soon realize." He shot her a glance, his hands tight on the wheel as the road roar grew under his foot's pressure.

"Why would it be any danger to us?"

"The thing about aliens is, they're alien."

"You think the government will take that attitude?"

"They'd be irresponsible if they didn't."

"Maybe they'll be as out of it as Arno."

"He's doing his best. You really dislike him, don't you?"

"I don't trust him," she said.

"He's secretive, all right," Benjamin allowed. "That makes me suspicious. We're used to open discussion in the sciences and he doesn't even pretend to follow that practice. And his people follow his lead—ask plenty of questions, give damned little back."

"That, and it's hard to believe that he beat 100,000 other sperm."

"Not up to the job?"

"Nobody is, granted." She tried to imagine who would be able to manage a crisis like this and came up empty. "It demands too much knowledge in one head."

"So use more heads."

This turned out to be the solution the White House had settled upon, visible as they pulled up to the Center. Or rather, to a guard post and heavily armed Marines who peered intently at their freshly made IDs, issued only the day before. The hillside was now, overnight, festooned with pre-fab buildings lifted in by helicopter. Communications cables flowered in great knotted blossoms on standing pads, attended by squads of blue-overalled workers.

Inside the Center, the foyer had a security team checking IDs again and a metal detector. This made Benjamin angry, which proved to be "unproductive," as Kingsley termed it when he had to rescue them from the Operations Officer's office. They stopped at a brand-new phalanx of buffet tables, well stocked, and got coffee.

"Is this backed by the CIA?" Benjamin asked.

"I don't think so," Kingsley said judiciously. "The food is quite poor."

They plunged into work. Channing had to allow that Arno's U Agency had brought a brisk efficiency to the usual meandering corridor conversations. In this taut atmosphere, there were no academic locutions: no *in terms of* or *as it were* or *if you will*. This Channing fully approved. Leaving NASA, she had found from a series of visits to the campuses that much of academic life had come to seem either boring or crazy.

No rival for the craziness of the situation she was in, of course. Nothing could match the whirl of speculation around her.

It was remarkable that this magnetic creature had been able to produce even broken, coherent English simply by listening to radio and TV. A century of fiction had assumed any approaching alien would be able to do so, to simplify their story lines, without for a moment considering how prodigious a task it was. The Eater had no common experience, knew little of the Earth's surface, and was dealing with a species unknown anywhere else in the galaxy. It did have vastly more experience dealing with planetary life, though, and this was apparently what made its work successful.

But with their help it could become much more able, the Eater said. So there was a team of linguists working with it.

They started with vocabulary. Children learned language beginning with nouns and built up to abstractions, so the first volley of signals was an assembly of pictures showing common objects, along with the nouns for them. Verbs were a little more trouble. Cartoons proved useful here, showing "throw" and making distinctions like the difference between "rain" and "to rain." Here the American Hopi Indian language would have been useful, since in that tongue English's "it is raining"—with the implied *it* quite invisible, yet a solid noun—was smoothly rendered simply as "rain." The Eater pointed out such subtleties as quickly as they arose, making its teachers feel that English was a patchwork of knocked-together solutions—which, of course, it was.

They quickly got through a basic five thousand words. Then faster transmission of whole texts, with illustrations, proceeded with blinding speed. Kingsley, wearing yesterday's shirt and tie, related this to her in his clipped mode, teetering on the verge of irony.

"What do you think will happen next?" she asked him. He had apparently been here all night, or at least he looked it.

"Depends upon the world reaction, of course," Kingsley said with surprising crispness. "And how fast we can move before the heavy hand of 'responsibility' descends, to make us overcautious."

She blinked. His face was a mask, but she could read a jittery stress in him, especially in the overcontrolled way he spoke and moved. "Why do you stress speed?"

"The Eater—your choice of name has stuck, and perhaps was a bit infelicitous."

"Gee, I love it when you use such fancy terms. How infelicitous?"

"It's more the title of a horror film, isn't it?"

"Or a bad sci-fi flick," Benjamin said, munching a donut. He knew well the distinction between true science fiction and the media dross pumped out in vast, glittery quantities, "sci-fi."

"So you think that'll worsen the first impression, once this breaks?" Channing asked.

"It's starting to break," Kingsley said with abstract fatigue. "Impossible to contain, really."

"What really matters here," Benjamin said, "is how the governments react."

Kingsley managed a dry chuckle. "I remember some head of state in the TwenCen saying that history teaches us mostly that men and nations behave wisely once they have exhausted all their other alternatives."

"I wish I could take the name back," Channing said.

While they slept, and Kingsley had not, the fascination of their opportunity had worked upon the astronomers. They had asked the Eater questions about astrophysics, peppering it with a dozen in a single transmission. This apparently broke the tit-for-tat logjam. The "intruder"—a name Kingsley still preferred to use, and thought might work better but had no hope would be taken up—seemed eager to discuss. It had quickly mastered the protocols of our digital image processing and filled its broadband signal with pictures. There were eerie exchanges. It was almost like a proud parent showing around baby pictures.

> WITNESS, THE LATE EVOLUTION OF A STAR, WHICH YOU TERM THE ROSETTE NEBULA, LOOKED LIKE THIS FROM THE SIDE WHEN IT WAS YOUNG.

The display was awesome, close-ups of giant rosy clouds of shimmering molecules, beautiful testaments to the death throes of a star. The Eater had been traveling near it and for the first time Channing appreciated the limitation astronomers seldom remembered: seeing objects from one angle left questions forever unanswerable.

"This gives us a handle on its trajectory, then," Benjamin observed swiftly.

Kingsley nodded. "We can work backward, using these other images—the Magellanic Cloud, the Galactic Center—and determine its past."

Some of the images were impossible to match with anything ever seen from Earth. Others almost matter-of-factly revised in an instant their picture of the galaxy's geography. The view of the Galactic Center showed what generations of artists had imagined, the glowing bulge of billions of stars that shone in all colors, a swollen majesty rent by lanes of ebony dust and amber striations no one could explain.

It thrilled her, tightened her throat. A bounty now came flooding into the Center as the Eater fed data through Arecibo and Goldstone and the new dish at Neb Attahl, India.

"My God, it'll put us all out of work," she murmured.

"Astronomers? Quite the opposite, I expect," Kingsley said.

"Yeah, we'll be trying to understand these—and the Eater itself—for a generation at least," Benjamin said, biting into his second donut, balancing a plate on his knee in the Big Screen Room.

"Well," Channing said ironically, "it's good to know you won't be forced into retirement."

This pleasant interlude lasted only an hour. Martinez discovered they had come in and held a meeting. Clearly she was struggling to find her role in all this, a small fish caught in a tidal wave. Arno's men had tried to clamp down on the whole story, but it got out through the porous Washington system. In part, that was because the astronomers did not like the U Agency's increasingly abrupt manner. Their styles clashed fundamentally, as mirrored in their clothes: government buttoned-up look against tropical techno-hip. Even in Martinez's oil-upon-the-waters meeting, there were several edgy, sharp-tongued interchanges.

They watched some television, where the story had broken in more or less the correct essentials only two hours before. At first there was a stunned, worldwide awe. Religious proclamations, stentorian speeches by assorted politicians who could not tell a spiral galaxy from a supernova.

Astronomers who were called in to consult at first refused to credit the story. Only release of the Rosette Nebula image convinced these. The release itself was a fortunate error. A Center staffer had sent it as a compressed file to a colleague, instead of zipping it to yet another subagency in Washington; they had, weirdly, WebNet addresses near each other in her file directory.

Within another hour or two, the astronomers outside those in the know fathomed the significance of the Rosette image. Immediately, they raised uncomfortable questions. This was an utterly alien entity, carrying the mass of our entire moon—another factoid which had leaked, this time through Australia. What could it do?

The Gang of Four sneaked off from the ongoing Martinez meeting to discuss just this. Amy looked as though she had spent the night as Kingsley had, fueled by coffee. "I've been trying to figure what it might do."

"A more important point is what it wants," Kingsley observed with a pensive gaze.

Amy said, "It didn't answer our third question. Ever."

"Exactly."

With her advanced computer skills, and the help of a squad of cryptographers from the U Agency, Amy had been in on every exchange in the transcription process. She shook her head. "It doesn't answer any questions that verge on that, either."

"Curious," Kingsley said mysteriously. Channing could tell that he had his own theories, but was unwilling to share them. He had been wrong quite enough for the last week, thank you.

"If it wanted," Benjamin said, "it could plunge straight through the Earth, bore a hole."

Kingsley snorted derisively. "And kill itself, by stripping away the magnetic structures that *are* the intelligence of the thing? No, it will be rather more clever."

Channing had her own worse case and decided to venture it. "With those magnetic funnels, it could blowtorch the top of our atmosphere."

Kingsley looked delighted at an idea he had not had himself. "Ummm . . . you're entirely correct."

"That would work?" Amy asked, startled.

"Absolutely," Kingsley said with an oblivious authority; he was, after all, the Astronomer Royal. "*Sic transit gloria mundi*, eh? 'Thus passeth away the glory of the world,' if my Latin is still decent."

"Is there enough energy density in its system to drill through the atmosphere?" Benjamin asked. Channing knew this well, one of his favorite maneuvers. Deflect the issue into a calculation to get time to think. *Even in a potentially mortal crisis, we play games.*

They found a blackboard—white, actually, with those smelly marking pens—and spent half an hour checking Kingsley's assertion. Finally Benjamin dropped his marker and agreed. "Dead on. It could roast us all, in time."

Kingsley said archly, "If it doesn't get bored first."

Channing had been resting in a lounge chair, especially

brought in by one of the U Agency gofers—a rather pleasant aspect of the Agency's otherwise annoying presence. She brightened with a fresh notion. "Then let's try to keep it amused, why don't we? I wonder if it likes jokes."

4 Actually, it did—but its own humor was weird, unfunny:

LIFE HAS CONTRADICTIONS. BUT CONTRADICTIONS KILL LIFE.

"That's a joke?" Benjamin asked the room, the first to speak up. After his words were out, he was suddenly embarrassed, wishing he could take them back. Maybe there was some deep semiotic content he had missed? There were hugely powerful people here, able to eject him from the Center forever with the rise of a single eyebrow. But heads nodded in agreement and no one disagreed.

The Operating Group, as named by Arno, now encompassed twenty-eight members. It met in the colloquium hall, the Center's largest. Armed guards barred every doorway and three electro-sniffer teams had worked over the room before anyone was allowed to say anything. Having to sit in silence for even ten minutes was difficult, given the air of strain in the room.

"Plainly, we need to know more," Kingsley said from the podium, nodding to Benjamin.

The Eater's latest transmission hung in glowing letters on a large flat screen that dominated the room. They had just watched several of the Eater's purported ideas of humor parade across this screen, including some images of things no one could even recognize. The Eater seemed to equate what to humans would be verbal humor with an inexplicable visual humor that looked like tangled threads of corroded surfaces, in virulent colors.

"Every telescope in the solar system is trained on it. We are learning as quickly as we can." He paused. "And now, something rather curious."

The team from the White House sat in the front row, two seats over from Benjamin, and their faces showed blank incomprehension. They probably had never advanced beyond high school chemistry, he realized, and saw the world as wholly human, filled with the vectors of human power. Technology was to them the product of human labor, no more, and science consisted of stories heard on TV, of no interest to people involved with the Real World.

"Several astronomers have noticed a similarity between the Eater's electromagnetic 'buzz'—that is, what we believe to be its internal transmissions—and signals already detected years previous, from a star not very far away." Kingsley paused and looked out over the crowd. "Most curious."

Benjamin waited through an odd, hesitant silence. *What the hell, got to keep this rolling. And Kingsley looks like he could use some help up there.* "Maybe there's a similar object orbiting—visiting—that star, too?"

Nods from the astronomical contingent. *We've got the momentum here,* Benjamin realized. *The rest are hopelessly far off their turf.*

"If there were," Kingsley argued, "this intruder would know about it already. It has been everywhere, seen everything, for many billions of years."

Why not give the number: seven? Benjamin then realized that every detail had been hastily classified, and Kingsley was playing it safe. The political types might not know the implications of such an immense lifetime and leak it.

More silence. *Well, we might as well turn this into a little colloquium. That's what the room's for.*

"Not so," he said, spreading his arms to both sides of his seat, hooking a hand around Channing's shoulder. *Might as well make a claim on this idea, too.* "We have one small advantage over it. Our telescopes are scattered all over the solar system. To pick up this distant source would be impossible with a receiving antenna the size of the Eater. It's a matter of resolving power. By my calculations"—he let the phrase hang there just an extra second, to establish some authority with this crowd—"it's blind to faraway objects smaller than stars. That probably includes this thing near another star—whatever it is."

This last was pure bluff. He had not kept up with the literature very well, had no clue what Kingsley was referring to.

Kingsley said crisply, "I suggest we have a special assistant team set about making detailed comparisons. Any and all knowledge may prove useful. I believe, in fact, that should be our general principle. Gather, sift, think, wait."

Arno rose—his standard room-ruling maneuver, adapted for an auditorium. His eyes swept the room. "Plainly, ladies and gentlemen, something more is needed. I believe I speak for the entire U Agency when I say that we believe this body, the President's authorized Operating Group, should take control of the entire deep space network."

Some murmurs of assent from the political faction. The astronomers looked sour. Some muttered objections.

Arno swept this away with a broad gesture. "We must immediately—and secretly—launch the new Searcher craft, using the best, highest-density Deep Link bands. With a connection of such high quality, they can be flown under direction by people on Earth."

"An interactive control, close to the source?" a NASA official asked.

"Exactly. Do we—you, madam—have that capability?"

"There are Searchers in Jupiter space." The woman wore one of the new NASA uniforms, introduced a year before, handsome deep blue and gold. "We could begin a few of the micropackages on the way, launching at high velocity, on trajectories to intercept eventually . . ." Her voice trailed off, plainly not prepared for this possibility.

"I believe this group should so recommend," Arno finished and sat down.

Kingsley said, "I believe that has much to recommend it. We cannot know the intruder's trajectory, and it plainly has the ability to alter it in a moment. It is nearing Jupiter, and knowledge gained there should prove invaluable."

"I think we shouldn't launch everything now," Benjamin said, amazed at his continuing audacity. The quiet administrator of only a month ago would have been cowed into utter silence in such a gathering.

Kingsley's mouth pursed, startled. "Why?"

"We may need them closer to home." This blunt possibility sent a ripple of concern through the auditorium.

"The intruder has not announced any plans to come closer. Its present trajectory shall carry it through the Jovian system. Amy?"

Perhaps emboldened by Benjamin, she had held up her hand. "Well, it only said this once, in the middle of another subject entirely, but . . ." Benjamin could see a sudden bout of stage fright seize her, a mere postdoc in such company, but then she plunged ahead. "It said it was going to 'acquire mass and momentum' at Jupiter."

"Quite possibly to gain the velocity it needs to escape the solar system," Kingsley said with a confidence Benjamin found unsettling. "It is a rover among the stars, after all."

"That's an assumption," Benjamin shot back.

"Of course, of course." Kingsley gave him an odd look, as though asking him to go along.

The hell with that. "We lack any understanding of what it wants to do."

Kingsley said sternly, "But lack of evidence is not evidence of lack."

Arno said, "I believe our business here is finished."

On this awkward note, the meeting broke up. Benjamin cornered Kingsley backstage and demanded, "Why'd you do that?"

The angular face clouded. "They are rattled enough already, damn it."

"They need to be prepared for the possibility that it's not an innocent explorer."

"We cannot prepare for everything."

"We can at least think—"

"*You* think for a moment. Do you seriously believe that what we say doesn't go outside the room?"

"No, of course not." Here Benjamin knew he was on shaky ground. "The White House hears, plus no doubt Congress and various allies. Not my turf, but—"

"Decidedly not. I do not have the luxury of merely keeping my nose buried in the astrophysics."

"It doesn't do this discussion any good for you to keep referring to your mysterious higher knowledge. I know you move in bigger circles, sure, but—"

"Being aware of the problem on different levels is precisely what's needed, I should think." Kingsley bristled, his shoulders squaring off in a gesture Benjamin remembered seeing long ago, back in that seminar where they met. *Not much has changed.*

"Look, I don't want you throwing your weight around with my people—"

"I don't delve into any such matters," Kingsley shot back, eyes narrowing.

"I see you in there talking to Amy a lot."

"We enjoy working together. There is a lot of interesting astro—"

"Just remember you're a guest here."

"I should think such distinctions are largely moot by now."

"Not to me."

"If you believe you can keep the usual methods of working, you are being naïve."

Bristling at "naïve," Benjamin jutted his chin forward. "There's got to be a role for the science in this thing, not just politics."

To Benjamin's surprise, Kingsley nodded and gave him a tilted look of newfound respect. "I fear, old friend, that the two are now quite inseparable."

5 In the press of events, she was getting so disorganized that she ended up using an ancient panty hose as a coffee filter when she couldn't find towel paper. As her energy had ebbed, she had adopted rougher rules: if you need to vacuum the bed, it's time to change the sheets. Rugs did have to be beaten now and then, not just threatened. Finally she gave up and found a cleaning lady.

Still, sloppiness seemed within the broad parameters allowed on the Big Island, where salty beach types rubbed shoulders with anal-retentive "cybrarians" at the Data Retention Center just over the hill. For the last year of gathering illness, she had tended more toward the style of her neighbors in the opposite direction, people just down the road whose car had a rag as a gas cap.

Channing had hidden her gathering fatigue as well as possible. Her years at NASA had taught her to give no sign of weakness, or else lose your spot in the mission rotation. After the space station and the Mars adventure, there were plenty of surplus astronauts, each a model of competitive connivance.

Even in crisis, the Center was not nearly so bad, and having a husband who just happened to run its scientific wing helped, but still—best to look vigorous. Falling asleep in a crucial discussion, then fainting—not good, girl. So she planned her forays to work carefully, not letting the dark-rimmed eyes show, sipping coffee to stay up. She had learned to let Benjamin drive her home when she started to ebb; he was getting good at spotting the cusp, down to the exact moment.

But she had to admit that probably most people just weren't paying attention, thank God. Benjamin had persuaded her to sit in on a panel reviewing "Semiotics of Contact," a topic that swiftly came to cover a hodgepodge of issues—but mostly, anything the astronomers didn't want to deal with.

She went in late in the morning and today saw a van with a HONK IF YOU LOVE PEACE AND QUIET bumper sticker. So she honked; she loved paradoxes. Such as her gathering feeling for Kingsley. Who would have thought *that* still smoldered? A smelly bone, best buried in the backyard of her life. She had written him off to his wife, a classic type: big eyes, big hips, dark curly hair you could bury your hand in up to the wrist. How pleasant, to know that even such a goddess could lose out in the romance wars!

She arrived at the Center after threading the multilayered checkpoints. The TV platform set up in the foreyard had guards around it, big-shouldered types carrying automatic weapons. *A bit overdone,* she thought, then realized that the weaponry was not for real use, but display. Arno's way of saying, *We're being serious here.*

Already the media mavens had taken off from the news, CNN with twenty-four-hour coverage. Within months there would be spinoff movies, no doubt, thoughtful magazine pieces and books, the Eater finally entering the media hereafter as videos or the inspiration for toys.

She came late into the Semiotics Working Group, as Arno had labeled it, hoping nobody noticed, so of course it was at a pause in speakers and everyone looked her way. Still, it was fun to just sit and listen to the flood of informed speculation that poured from the visiting experts.

The astronomers had quickly been revealed as the Peter Pans of humanity. They never truly grew up and kept their curiosity like a membership card. Most believed the Saganesque doctrine that aliens would be peaceful, ruled by curiosity, eager for high-minded discourse. Carl Sagan had been a conventional antimilitary liberal, and so assumed that a radio message from space would shock humanity, damping down wars and ushering in a cosmic sense of cooperation between nations.

Humanists were made of tougher stuff. Nonsense, they said, but more politely. Why hadn't the Europeans' discovery of the Americas halted warfare in Europe? Instead, they fought over the spoils. Would the Eater somehow become fodder for our ancient primate aggressions?

Another Saganesque doctrine was that contact with aliens would yield a bounty of science and technology. Half credit on this one: plenty of science, so far only astronomy, but no technology. The Eater had none. It seemed to be a magnetic construction, first made by some ancient alien race. Its origins were still blurry because of its coyly obtuse phrasing. It had said:

I CAME INTO BEING BY ARTIFICE OF ANCIENT
BIOLOGICAL BEINGS. AFTER THAT I VOYAGED AND
BECAME LARGER IN SELF AND IN PURPOSE.

Whole squads of semioticists and linguists now labored over such sentences, mining with their contextual and semantic matrices, but little glittering ore appeared beyond the obvious. The extreme humanists argued instead that, beyond the pretty pictures it seemed so eager to send, we probably could learn little from the Eater of All Things. Science simply gave us the very best chimpanzee view of the universe. Our vision was shaped by evolution, sharpened to find edible roots or tasty, easy prey on a flat plain. Our sense of beauty came from throwing honed rocks along the beautifully simple arc of a parabola to strike herbivores with cutting edges.

The Eater's technology used magnetic induction, control

of hot plasmas, advanced electromagnetics, and probably much else we could not guess. "Face it," one panelist said, "unless an alien is a lot like us, we can't learn much from it. Even with goodwill—and we don't have really good evidence of that, so far—we *can't* harvest technology from a creature so different."

This deflated Arno's adjutants. They were easy to pick out, because in the status-shuffling of personnel here a person's authority was inversely proportional to the number of pens in their shirt pocket.

Her pager beeped her. Reluctantly she left the room as a decoding expert began drawing conclusions about the Eater's habits in encoding information. It had been steadily getting better at understanding human computers and methods, so the bit stream coming down from it carried an ever-higher density content—mostly astronomical pictures in wavelengths ranging from the low radio to the high gamma ray. One of the tidbits that intrigued her was that the Eater had spent much time between the stars, taking centuries to cross those abysses. Very low frequency electromagnetic waves were reflected by the higher density in the solar system, so could never penetrate. The Eater had pictures of the galaxy made by receiving these waves, a whole field of astronomy impossible from Earth.

The call was from Benjamin and she found him in the Big Screen Room. "How's the semiotics?" he whispered.

"They're impressive, I suppose, in their way." She studied the screen, which showed a beautiful view of the solar system seen from the Eater's present location.

"They seemed to be talking gibberish jargon when I looked in."

"Well, maybe my inferiority complex isn't as good as yours."

He got the small joke, one of the traits that had endeared him to her long ago. Kingsley had, too, but in a subtly different way, more as a conspirator than as a simple act of merriment. She wondered for a moment about that and then Arno came striding in, exuding grim confidence.

At first she thought he was going to give an aria in the key of "I," taking credit for the "great advances" they had all made, but then he unveiled an extended message from the Eater. It had "a supplication": it wanted humanity, which it seemed to regard as a single entity, to transmit a store of its art, music, and "prevalent enrichment."

"Does that mean our culture?" a leading member of the humanist team asked.

"I-trust the deciphering team can tell us that soon." •

"Seems probable," Channing said. She had always felt that the humanities were too important to be left to the humanists. And now, apparently, the field might come to include the nonhuman. For the Eater proposed a trade.

"The bounty of other, alien societies," Arno said grandly. "That appears to be what it is promising."

The crowd murmured with a strange tenor she had seldom heard: eagerness and caution sounding in the same anxious key.

Kingsley and many from NASA looked relieved. Unlike Benjamin's suspicions, there seemed no threat here. Arno, their principal conduit to the White House, was plainly out of his depth. He had said his piece and now gazed out over the crowd as if trying to read a script in too tiny a typeface.

She leaned toward Benjamin. "So the culture vulture theory of the Sagan crowd looks right."

He said, "It still isn't headed for Earth, either."

Arno was going on about ramifications. "An international committee can assemble a compendium of our greatest works, the arts and mathematics, perhaps even science— though there may be a security issue there."

"Let us offer whatever data it wants," a voice from in front said.

The final decision would come from on high, of course, and that lent an air of liberation to what followed. The discussion went quickly, specialists vying to spell out how to do all this.

The battalions of data managers, as they were termed, had

already erected an elaborate architecture to deal with speaking to the Eater. What was not so obvious, but now clear, was that in transferring information—say, the Library of Congress—the Eater would learn a good deal more about how our computers thought. It was astoundingly swift at learning our computer languages. Some of its remarks in passing implied that all this was rather primitive stuff—to it.

She and Benjamin stayed for hours, following the discussion, volunteering nothing. This was not their province. Toward the end, though, Benjamin made a remark she would remember later. "It's getting close to Jupiter. Let's see what we learn there."

"You're not so sure this cultural shotgun is what it wants?"

"Thing about aliens is, they're alien."

"Ummm. I remember an old movie about an art collector who went around buying up living artists' work, and then killing them, to increase resale value."

"Good grief, you're in a great mood."

"Just the old mind wandering. I suppose everyone's taking comfort in the fact that once it's at Jupiter, it's in close range of our Searchers. We'll learn more."

He gave her his angular grin. "Old Army saying. 'If the enemy is in range, so are you.' "

6 Benjamin clasped her to him with a trembling energy. She kissed him with an equal fervor and then, without a word or the need of any, he left for the Center.

She had agreed to rest a good part of each day, but insisted on being at the Center for a few hours, at least. Each day he hoped she would just plain rest, and each day he was disappointed. She came up around noon to catch the day's energy at its full swell. Benjamin was pleased that even in the hubbub, people looked after her, included her in the flow of work. There was quite enough of it to share.

They had both been surprised at how quickly the U.S. government had gotten in line on the cultural transfer process. The usual cautionary voices had loudly complained about giving away secrets that could be used against all humanity, but the sheer strangeness of the Eater made it hard to see how a digitized image of the Parthenon could be a defense secret. "Good ol' Carl Sagan," Channing had remarked. "Who would've guessed that his view of aliens would have infiltrated the Congress?"

Indeed, they needed a figure like Sagan, dead now for decades, who could command the confidence of the greater public. Like all good popularizers in science, he had been roundly punished for it by his colleagues, denied membership in the National Academy of Sciences and the subject of *tsk-tsk* gossip by many who were not his equals as scientist or educator. No such astronomer had arisen since Sagan's time, and the best the profession could muster were various pale figures from the usual scientific bureaucracy. Compared with them, Kingsley did quite well, and so had undertaken a lot of the Center's public relations work—when not shouldered aside by Arno.

Both Benjamin and Kingsley suspected that the political leadership was mounting precautionary measures, but there was no insider word of such plans. At the Center all policy matters, and even the different spectral bands of the observing teams, had become more and more boxed into neat little compartments.

The Center was preoccupied with shepherding the data flow to the Eater. Channing had become edgy and preoccupied, following the Eater news obsessively, making fun of Arno. ("Maybe his major purpose in life is to serve as a warning to others.") Sometimes she seemed to surprise even herself with her brittle humor, as if she did not fully know how black a mood lay beneath it.

Benjamin thought about her, fruitlessly as usual, as he came into the new wing of the Center. It had been thrown up in a day by teams who descended in massive helicopters. The big new office complex was a rectangular intrusion into a hillside carved unceremoniously for it. Each floor was one big room, the nondenominational Office: a three-dimensional grid bounded below by a plane of thin nylon carpet, two meters above by a parallel plane of pale acoustical tile. This space suffered punctuation by vertical Sheetrock planes that came to shoulder height, barely enough to give the illusion of partial privacy and damp conversations. Squares of recessed fluorescent lighting beamed down on the symbolic Euclidean realization of pragmatic idealism, a space of unimpeded flows. Spherical immersion tanks dotted the space between the rectangular sheets that stretched to infinity, and around them technicians moved with insect energies. In these the cyber-link specialists kept in close touch with the array of satellites and sensors they now had spying on the interloper.

A cube farm: big rooms clogged with cubicles for the drones. When something loud happened, the prairie-dog heads would pop up over the half-height walls.

As the Eater plunged closer to Jupiter, it had rhapsodized about alien cultures it had visited, sending samples of outré art via the microwave high-bandwidth links. Some were released to the public, particularly if they seemed innocuous. Predictably, distinctions between "photographs" and "art" were difficult to make. There were apparently straightforward views of landscapes, odd life-forms, stars, and planets, even some "cities" that might just as well have been regularly arranged hills. With thousands of such images to chew upon, the public seemed satisfied.

Carefully the government figures charged with filtering the information did not give away the true vast size of the galleys it sent. Nor did they release unsettling images of grotesque scenes, hideous aliens, and unaccounted-for devastation. The Eater provided little or no commentary, so battalions of assembled art critics, photo experts, and other sorts labored to interpret these.

So far the world reaction had been varied—there were always alarmists—but comparatively mild. The sense of wonder was working overtime among the world media, though that would undoubtedly give way in time, Benjamin thought.

The more advanced works were another matter. These the computers had assembled into holographic forms and an entire yawning gallery displayed them. Benjamin stopped there to see what was new. Even knowing how much effort was being marshalled worldwide on deciphering the Eater's transmission load, he was daily astonished at how much new work appeared.

It was eerie work, subtly ominous. Portraits of creatures and places in twisted perspectives, 3D manifestations of objects that appeared impossible, color schemes that plainly operated beyond the visible range.

He went into the Big Screen Room. The ranging grid

showed the orange profile of the Eater at the very edge of Jupiter's moon system. There was a crowd and he found a seat at the back only because a new staffer gave up his, leaping to his feet when he saw Benjamin's ID badge.

A murmur. Benjamin watched as one of the Searcher 'scopes came online. Its high-resolution image flickered through several spectral ranges, settled on the best. Kingsley materialized in the seat beside him; a staffer had given up his for the Astronomer Royal. The incoming image sharpened at the hands of the specialists. "It's veered in the last hour," Kingsley whispered, "and appears headed for an outer moon of the system."

"Couldn't we have predicted that?"

"Some did." Kingsley shrugged. "It does not respond to questions about its plans."

"Still? I thought it was talking more now."

"The linguists have given up trying to render its little parables in literal ways."

"They seem more like puzzles to me."

"That, too. 'Cultural dissonance,' as one of them termed it."

"I'll have to remember that one." Benjamin grinned dryly. "Sounds almost like it means something."

Suddenly the screen brightened. In a spectacular few seconds, the orange profile warped into a slender funnel, blazing brightly.

"It's ingesting," Kingsley said matter-of-factly. "I suppose it met a tasty rock."

"We knew it had some motivation."

"Note how no one seems very worried? I believe we are all simply too tired for that."

"I wondered if it was just me. I figured I was beyond being surprised anymore."

"I rather hope so."

Benjamin had stacks of work waiting in his office, but once again he gave way to the temptation of just watching. The Eater was moving at nearly a hundredth the speed of light, an incredible velocity. The plasma types had given up hope of explaining how its magnetic fields could withstand the sheer friction of encountering solid matter and ionizing it.

"Something beyond our present understanding is happening right before our eyes," Kingsley murmured. "I have almost gotten used to these routine miracles it performs."

The images coiled into a complex conduit of magnetic fields, etched out in the brilliant radiance of superheated matter. In a few moments, it had destroyed a moon, grazing it just right, so that some matter was sucked in while the majority was thrown away, adding thrust.

A keening note sounded in the room. A fresh signal, high and sharp. "It now sends us codes earmarked for audio playing, once it worked out how our hearing functions," Kingsley whispered.

"It's . . . weird. Ugly," Benjamin said.

"I believe a proper translation is that it is singing to 'all humanity' as part of its payment for our cultural legacy."

Benjamin studied Kingsley's lean profile in the shadows. "It's like some . . ."

"We should not impose our categories upon it," Kingsley said crisply.

"Sounds like you've been listening to the semiotics people again."

"Just trying to keep an open mind."

"Damn it, to me that stuff sounds like, like . . ."

"A deranged god, yes."

"Maybe in all that time between the stars, it's gotten crazy."

"By its own account—one we have received, but it is so complex the specialists still can't find human referents—it has endured such passages many millions of times."

"So it says."

Kingsley nodded, a sour sigh of fatigue escaping. "And we have come to accept what it says."

The semiotics teams had been feeding it vast stores of cultural information, with some commentary to help it fathom the masses of it. Most texts, like the Encyclopaedia Britannica—still the best all-round summary of knowledge—were already available in highly compressed styles. These flowed out and were duly digested.

Material from the sciences encountered no trouble; the intruder hardly commented upon them, except to remark obliquely on their "engaging simplicity." Benjamin took this to be an attempt at a compliment, while others seemed to see it as an insult.

The social sciences came next. These confused the Eater considerably. It asked many questions that led them back to the vocabulary lessons. The Eater did not have categories that translated readily into ethics, aesthetics, or philosophy.

The arts were even harder. It seemed unable to get beyond pictorial methods that were not nearly photographic; abstractions it either asked many puzzled questions about or ignored. In this the Eater seemed to ally with the majority of current popular taste.

"I wonder if it is telling us the truth about anything." Benjamin mused.

Kingsley's mouth tipped up on one end. "Why would it lie? It can stamp upon us as if we were insects."

Benjamin nodded and suddenly felt Kingsley as a fellow soldier in arms, worn by the same incessant pressures.

"Crazy, you said?" Kingsley said distantly. "From the long times it has spent between the stars? Remember, it has been alone all its life. Do not think of it as a social being."

"But it asks for social things, our culture."

Kingsley mused silently, watching the orange signature on the screen creep toward the rim of the gas giant planet, and then said suddenly, "Crazy? I would rather use an Americanism, *spooky*."

Benjamin wondered if their speculations had any less foundation than what the semiotics and social science teams said. "I heard a biologist talking at the coffee machine the other day. He pointed out that it may be the only member of its species."

"That makes no sense. We still have no idea how it came to be."

"Something tells me we're going to find out."

"From it?"

"It may not even know."

"Find out from experience, then?"

"Yeah."

The next several hours were as unsettling as anything Benjamin had ever encountered.

The black hole and its attendant blossom of magnetic flux swooped in toward the banded crescent. An air of anxious foreboding settled over the viewers at this meeting between Jupiter—the solar system's great gas giant, a world that had claimed the bulk of all the mass that orbited its star—and a hole in space-time that had the mass of a moon packed into a core the size of a table.

Its trajectory arced down into the vast atmosphere. And in a long, luminous moment, the Eater drank in a thick slice of the upper layers, gulping in hydrogen with glowing magnetic talons.

The audience around Benjamin came to life. Gasps and murmurs filled the room. There were few words and he caught an undertone of uneasy dread.

The image shifted as the bristling glow followed a long, looping flyby. To study life-forms that do exist there, it said. It even sent short spurts of lectures on the forms it found. One of Kingsley's new aides brought word of these messages, printed out from the translators, as they came in.

"Look at the detail," Benjamin read at Kingsley's shoulder. "Balloon life, a thousand kilometers deep into the cloud deck."

"It is teaching us about our own neighborhood," Kingsley said.

"Yeah, along with a few remarks about our being unable to do it."

"Well, that is one rather human trait," Kingsley remarked sardonically. "Plainly it loves having an audience."

"It's been alone for longer than we've had a civilization."

In the next hour, it compared its findings with similar dives into other massive worlds it had known.

Data swarmed in. Sliding sheets of information filled screens throughout the Center. Sighing, Kingsley remarked, "Data is not knowledge, and certainly it is not wisdom. What does this *mean*?"

As they watched through a long, laboring afternoon, the swelling magnetic blossom dove and gained mass—three times. An enormous, luminous accretion disk spread out like a circle around it.

Arno appeared before them, gray and shaken. "We have just registered fresh jets of high-energy emission from it. The atmospheric entries are over. We have a preliminary determination of its trajectory."

They all waited through a confused silence. Arno did not seem able to speak. Then he said, "The . . . intruder . . . it has again picked up speed—and is headed for Earth."

Benjamin bowed his head and realized he had known it all along. He turned toward Kingsley and in narrowed, apprehensive eyes he saw the same knowledge.

PART FOUR
THE MAGNETIC HOURGLASS

1 She had hoped it was Benjamin, home early with the latest news, but instead the thrumming in the driveway was a package delivery woman. She opened the package to discover—oh, joy!—that the Right to Die Society had targeted her with an offer of a do-it-yourself home suicide kit. The four-color glossy foldout was lovingly detailed.

Their primary product was the Exit Bag, with its "sturdy clear plastic sack the size of a garbage bag, a soft elastic neckband, and Velcro fasteners to ensure a snug fit, plus detailed instructions for use." Quite a well-done brochure, especially when one realized that they were not expecting a lot of repeat business.

She made a special trip out through the garden to throw this into the trash, heaving it with a grunt of relish. Somehow, in this age of zero privacy, her illness had become a marketable trait. Sickies were usually stuck at home, so they could be targeted. She had hung a chalkboard next to the telephone for messages and when salesmen called she would run her fingernails across it until they hung up. Somehow the sound never had irritated her, so she might as well use the fact to advantage.

She paused in the garden, drawing in the sweet tropical air with real relish, and just for fun punched Benjamin's dartboard backing. The slam of her fists into it was no doubt

deplorable, primitive, pointless—and oddly satisfying. The
exertion left her panting, head swimming.

As her reward, the world gave her the growl of a car as it
spat gravel coming down their driveway. She angled over to
greet Benjamin and again it wasn't him. Kingsley unlim-
bered from his small sports car, one of the tiny jobs that
flaunted its fuel economy. His frame was slimly elegant in
gray slacks with a flowery Hawaiian shirt.

"I was going by—"

"Never mind, I haven't seen enough of you for days and
days," she said with a quick fervor that surprised her.
Where's that from?

"I had hoped to catch Benjamin. I'm coming back from
an emergency meeting in Hilo, held in a massive airplane
standing on the runway. It would seem that is the new technique for being security conscious, control all access." He
gave her a crooked smile. "Good to see you."

"It was more Washington people?"

"And U.N., yes. Lots of frowns, shows of concern, brave
speeches. No ideas, of course."

"Any concrete help?"

"They are hopelessly behind the curve. When confronted
with something genuinely new, the bulk of the U.N. re-
sponds on time scales of years, not hours."

"Is the United States doing any better—really?"

"A bit, but only by standing aside and letting the U
Agency operate. You may recall I had something like that in
mind."

"Ah, that Brit modesty again. Most becoming."

During the worldwide panic of the last few days, she had
been more happy than ever to be on the most isolated island
chain in the world. The U Agency had seized access to the
Big Island and was buttoning up the place. The Agency remained mysterious even in action, which kept the media
mavens abuzz but information-starved. As nearly as she
could judge, with some cryptic remarks from Kingsley, it
had emerged as the can-do element in the U.S. government,

in collaboration with various allies. Bureaucratic style favored setting up a new agency to actually do things, while
the older agencies spent time in turf wars. This stood in the
long tradition of the CIA, which begat the NSA, and onward
during the late TwenCen into a plethora of acronymed
"black technology infrastructure" groups, which then eventually demanded consolidation into the U Agency, with its
larger than purely national agenda. Or so she gathered.

"How's the news?" she said with an attempt at lightness,
ushering him with body language into the garden.

"We made an enormous public relations error in announcing the time of the Eater's Jupiter rendezvous. I see
that now."

"Did we have a choice? Any competent astronomer could
calculate it."

"True, but we could have controlled admittance to the
large telescopes' images. Perhaps even prevented the visual
media from getting close-ups of what it did to Jupiter."

"Don't blame yourself. It would come out—hell, every
amateur with a ten-inch telescope could *see* the flares."

The later stages of the Eater's devouring had been heralded by the bright jet behind it, lancing forth like a spear
pointed backward at the troubled crescent of Jupiter.

Kingsley sighed, collapsing into a lounge chair. "And now
everyone wants to know what can it do to Earth."

"And the answer is?"

"As I recall, you first pointed out its ability to scorch our
upper atmosphere. I opened with that and it seemed quite
sufficient to induce panic among the 'advisers' on that airplane."

"Good to know I'm still useful," she said archly.

"They concluded—big surprise here—that we need to
know much more about its thinking and purpose."

"How insightful."

"So the figures from the Air Force and NASA came forward with a new crash program to integrate the classified
technology with NASA's near-Earth craft."

"Anticipating that it will come that close? I suppose we could field some potent ships within, say, the distance to the moon."

Kingsley nodded pensively and she could see him thinking, so she went inside and got some drinks together, including one for Benjamin when he showed up. When she returned, he was still staring into space but stirred at her approach. He gulped the wine cooler gratefully and said, "After some years at this, I've learned that 'pilot' is a bureaucrat's way of saying two things at once: 'This is but the first,' plus 'we believe it will work, but . . .' Still, they committed themselves to outfitting new ships, both manned and not, ready within weeks."

"Let's hope we don't need them."

"I suspect we all are suffering from an unconscious fatalism, brought on by weariness—at least on my part. The policy people, as well."

"They aren't used to confronting something this strange?"

"That may be it. In astronomy, the new is delightful, a revelation."

"In politics, it's a problem. Makes me wonder what the next revelation will be."

"I don't think you should be bothering yourself with this, truly." Kingsley's gaze came back from abstract distance to a worried focus on her.

"I like it. And what should I be doing, fretting over my rickety body?"

"It's a fine one, quite worth the attention."

He stood and she turned away toward the flowers, their heady fragrance. "Don't start."

"I'm only expressing what we both feel."

"No, what you feel. I'm . . ." She could not think of the right word.

"Troubled, I know. But I feel radiating from you a need, and something in me wants to answer it."

His long hands clasped her arms from behind and she bowed her head, the honeyed air swarming in her nostrils.

His hands were strong, certain, deliberate, and she was the opposite. "How . . . how much of this is unfinished business?"

"From decades ago?"

His voice came softly through the layered air and it helped a great deal that she could not see him. But the hands remained on her upper arms, calm and reassuring and altogether welcome.

"Somehow it's not over," she managed to get out.

"When I saw you again, after so long . . ."

"Me, too."

"I don't believe we're being altogether rotten about this."

She laughed silently, head hanging. "Not so far."

"I didn't mean that. Only that you need support and—"

"And if Benjamin's too busy to give it, you will."

"Someone must."

"Support, that's all?"

He turned her gently with the long, big hands and she tilted her head up to look into his eyes. They were unreadable. "Maybe that was one thing I always liked about you, that I couldn't tell what you were going to say or do."

"And with Benjamin you could."

"Something like that. The lure of the unknown."

"I don't mean anything wholly sexual in this," he said with an almost schoolboy earnestness.

"I know. I wouldn't do anything like that."

"I'm quite certain not, yes."

She wished she were half as sure as he seemed. She could not predict what she was going to do these days, or understand why. "It's emotions here, not actions."

"Yes, yes." He seemed suddenly embarrassed.

"New territory. I've never died before."

"It's . . . the physicians . . . they—"

"Pretty damned sure. I've got maybe a few weeks."

"Benjamin knows."

"Some of it. The technical stuff is pretty boring."

"Shouldn't you be under more care?"

"I hate hospitals, and the hospice I stopped by gave me the creeps."

"But surely—"

"I'm giving in to my personality flaws. Without them I'd have no personality at all, most days."

He smiled wanly. "Your tongue is as fine as ever."

She kissed him suddenly and just as suddenly broke it off.

He blinked, engagingly flustered. "I scarcely expected . . . it would not have been . . ."

"Appropriate? Right."

"There are levels here . . ." He was appealingly awkward.

"Yeah, and me, I'm at one with my duality."

This provoked a grin from him, dispelling his mood. "You're amazing."

"Just improbable. Side effect of the chem supporters they've shot me full of."

"Medication?" His eyes widened in alarm.

"A new line of delights. Keeps your metabolism running pretty flat and steady, just ducky until the whole system crashes. I've got some embedded chips just below the skin, tasting my blood and titrating into it some little bags of wonder-drug stuff."

"I think I read something about those."

"The bags they tipped into my upper thighs. They don't even itch or anything." This was too much detail, she saw.

His hands had lessened their hold and she could sense him wondering how to get out of this moment. Very delicately, taking all the time in the world, she kissed him lightly on his uncertain lips. "Thanks. A gal needs some appreciation."

"More than that."

"Love, if you want. I still love you, in a way I haven't got the language for. Just having you here is fine, nothing more expected."

"I knew when I saw you again, knew it instantly."

"So did I."

She leaned down and kissed his right hand. It seemed an

infinitely precious movement, living in a moment carved in the elastic, fragrant air, as if all life should be fashioned from such passing, exquisite gestures. An hypnotic illusion, of course, quite possibly the outcome of titrated solutions doing their chemical work, but absolutely right at this time, this place.

He dropped his hands and they stood in a quiet glade of the garden, silent and warm. Then came the spitting of gravel and Benjamin's car rumbled to a stop in the driveway.

She hung in the long easeful glide away from that jeweled moment, passing as they all do, clinging to it while Benjamin arrived and she kissed him. So soon after Kingsley, it felt awkward. Kingsley retreated to his silent reserve. In the first moments, she felt a tension between the two men, as though Benjamin sensed something and did not know how to deal with it. Then he visibly shrugged and accepted a drink with a wobbly smile.

Benjamin cracked whatever remained of her crystal serenity with news. The updated determination of the Eater's trajectory confirmed that it was bound on an accelerating orbit for Earth. "Unmistakable," Benjamin said firmly as they moved indoors.

"How much time do we have?" Kingsley asked, his voice full of caution, as though he was still prying himself out of the last half hour.

"A few weeks, if it continues at its present acceleration."

"Surely it must run out of fuel."

"There are several asteroids it could snag on the way."

"Ah, a chance to learn something more of its processes," Kingsley said judiciously.

"Digestion, you mean," Channing said, handing Benjamin a dark wine cooler.

"Quite so."

"Wish we hadn't named it Eater. The media's, well, eating it up. Scaring the whole damn world."

Benjamin seemed to come out of some other place, eyes taking in the garden at last, then her. "How are you?" He put down the drink and embraced her, his hands on her arms in an eerie echo of Kingsley's.

"Glad to have my two favorite men here. I needn't suffer in silence while I can still moan, whimper, and complain."

"Which she never does," Kingsley said gallantly.

"Better living through chemistry," she said lightly, feeling light in the head as well. "Come, fair swains, ply me with technobabble."

Which they did.

2 He opened his front door to get the newspaper, gummy-mouthed and rumpled, and found a camera snout eyeing him from two feet away. "Just a word, sir, Doctor, about—"

Thus did he discover that he was the target of what he would later hear termed a "celeb stakeout." He slammed the door hard and several thoughts rushed by in parallel. Sure, they were just doing their jobs, all for a public that Really Wanted To Know. But this was *their* house. He felt invaded. How was he going to fetch his newspaper?

He felt a spike of swirling anxiety, his trajectory out of control. And then a third sensation: a spurt of excitement. People, millions of them, *wanted to know* about him. There was a primitive primate pleasure in being paid attention to. He was *interesting*. Tomorrow maybe a hurricane in Florida or a babe in a scandal would be better, but for today, it was Dr. Benjamin Knowlton.

This diffuse delight lasted until he and Channing got into the Center, past a gauntlet of security and media that lengthened by the day. Only weeks ago the Center had been a comfortable two-story complex with broad swaths of grass and tropical plants setting it off. The only visible sign of its purpose had been the large microwave dishes on nearby hills. Now bare tilt-up walls framed the buildings, windowless and gray slabs forking into wings. Not a blade of grass re-

mained anywhere; all was mud or "fastcrete," the new wonder material.

"Wow." Channing pointed. "They're putting up another
new building."

"One of those prefab jobs, chopper them in and lower the
walls into that fast-dry concrete." Benjamin wondered what
fresh echelon of overseers this heralded.

"We could use more thinking, less managing," Channing
said.

"That Semiotics Group, can I sit in?"

"I think they're inside an 'information firewall,' as the jargon puts it."

"But how are we going to link the maps of the Eater,
which are sharpening as it approaches, with how it actually
works?"

She shook her head wordlessly in the calm way that had
come over her in the last few days. They had given up their
daily battle over her coming into the Center. She *would*, and
that was that. When he went in alone, she followed in her
car. He had toyed with disabling it and realized that she
would simply get a ride some other, more tiring way.

They went through the newly expanded main foyer. News
items shimmered on big screens, where a crowd of media
people watched. Arno was giving a briefing elsewhere in the
complex, his head looming on a screen here like a luminous
world with hyperactive mountain chains working on it. "Not
again," Channing said. "He's up there every day."

"I think he has to be. The Story of the Millennium, they're
calling it."

She scoffed. "Barely started on the millennium and we're
laying claim to it. And Arno, his talks are like a minibikini,
touching on the essentials but not really covering much."

"That's a talent now, not a lack."

She went into the Semiotics Division hallway and he entered his new office suite. He had his own foyer—like this
morning, a spurt of delight; *he was being paid attention to*—
from which radiated prefab, bone white, fluorescent-lit hall-

ways and byways where hundreds of astronomers and data analysts labored.

Within half an hour, the high had dissipated in the usual swamp of memos, Alert Notices, data dumps, and plain old institutional noise. These absorbed his morning, but not his attention, which kept veering off. He suppressed the urge to sit in on the meetings Channing attended, with her instinct for ferreting out the most interesting work. He wanted to be in those sessions, both to be with her and to hear about something other than optical resolution, luminosities, report summaries, spectra, and fights over 'scope time. Thus were his days whittled away, with precious few moments to actually think.

Just before noon he had to take an important issue "up top," as the U Agency termed it, and so walked into Kingsley as he stood before a TV camera, while on a huge wall screen the President of the United States lounged in a terrycloth robe, hair wet, with an indoor swimming pool behind him. A glass of orange juice, half-empty, stood on a small table and the President's legs were thick with black hair.

Kingsley stood at attention, addressing his remarks to a pointer mike, his face concentrated. Kingsley's secretary left Benjamin standing in shadows and he stayed there, suspecting something afoot. Kingsley had not noticed him, blinded by a brilliant pool of light with the emblem of the Center behind him. The man knew how to play to the dramatic. His small staff sat farther away, people new to the Center who ignored Benjamin. A technician gave the start sign.

The President's warm drawl described how "a swarm of Searchers is damn near ready to go, so you've got no worry there." The man was obviously speaking from prepared notes, eyes tracking left and right as he spoke, but it came over as utterly offhand and sincere. He deplored the "spreading panic" and was sorry "that this makes you astronomers' job even harder," though—with a chuckle—"now you know what it's like being in the media fishbowl."

Kingsley said, "Sir, we have doom criers surrounding the observatories farther up the mountain."

"I thought the island was sealed." A puzzled frown, a glance off camera.

"These are locals, I fear."

"Then we'll just have 'em rounded up."

"I would appreciate that."

"Want and expect the best of you, Mr. Kingsley." A flicker of the eyelids. Someone had told him of the slip, but the President saw no way to correct easily, so just glided on. "You've been doin' great."

Benjamin had to admit as the conversation went on that Kingsley was adroit, slick, even amusing. Though British, he easily rode over the issue of nationality, getting the President and the Pentagon to promote him as controller of Earth's response to the Eater's approach. Benjamin stood undetected by Kingsley's staff, who were all watching the President as though hypnotized. Well, the man did have a presence, a quality Benjamin knew he would never acquire. That was why, in a way, he chose a slight pause in the talk to walk straight onstage, taking a spot next to Kingsley.

"Mr. President—" and he was into a quick introduction, as though this had all been planned. "Sir, I'm Benjamin Knowlton, head of Astronomy Division. This is a world problem, and you can't let it seem as if you're ignoring the rest of the planet."

A curious glance to the side. "Well, I never intended—"

"No doubt, sir, but that is how it's playing out here. I'm more in touch with the international astronomical community than anyone else here, even Kingsley. I know how this is playing among those we must rely upon for full-sky coverage of the Eater, continuous contact, and the use of many dozens of telescopes on Earth and off."

His pulse thumped, he could not quite get enough breath, but he held his place. One of Kingsley's aides gestured from off camera, someone whispered, "Get security," but Benjamin knew—or hoped he did—that Kingsley would not permit the appearance of disorder here. Pure luck walking in on this, and he had to go with it.

"I haven't heard anything from State about such trouble."

"This isn't about diplomats, it's about keeping ourselves in an alliance with others. I had trouble with a German satellite manager just this morning, demanding that we forward data and images that they don't have. I receive similar demands every day, and the voices are getting more strident."

"I'd think, this being science, that you all would share." The President appeared genuinely puzzled.

"That's how it should work. But this buttoned-up security posture is a mistake. You can't keep this under wraps—particularly if it's wrapped in the U.S. flag."

This line seemed to tell. The President blinked and said with calculated shrewdness, "You have a bargain in mind?"

"Just an idea. How to work it out I leave"—he could not resist—"to Mr. Kingsley. I believe we should have shared control of the Mauna Kea facility and the world network of astronomers. Full disclosure at dedicated Mesh sites. Nothing held back."

"Nothing?" Plainly the President had never heard of the idea from any of his staff.

"For the moment, nothing."

"I hear it's not telling us much about what it plans," the President said.

"Precisely why it should be safe to reveal it," Kingsley came in smoothly. "I endorse Dr. Knowlton's proposal."

The President blinked again. "I'll have to think about this. How come that Arno fellow didn't say anything about it?"

"He thought it best if I—we—proposed it directly," Benjamin said, looking straight into the camera in the way he had gathered conveyed sincerity. Very useful, especially when lying.

"Well, I appreciate your views." The President looked ready to sign off, in fact raised eyebrows toward someone off camera, but then said, "Say, you really think they'd do that? The other astronomers? Cut us off from their data and so on?"

"I do, sir," Benjamin said, and in another second the President's image dwindled away, like water down a drain.

3 Channing heard about the fracas on the way back from lunch. She had wondered why Benjamin did not join her, but she was grateful for the chance to just sit by herself, eat quickly, and leave. The others in the Semiotics Group knew enough to leave her alone, so she got to simply lie down on a convenient bed in the infirmary to snag an hour's delicious nap. When she woke up, he was there.

"I hear you made a name for yourself today," she murmured sleepily.

He grinned, obviously on a high. "Ah, but what name's that?"

" 'Bastard,' I overheard that. Also 'maniac' and 'amateur.' "

"You've been listening to U Agency types."

"Not entirely, but yes—they talk more than astronomers."

"Kingsley was frosty after we went off the air. I was amazed that he recovered fast enough not to appear provoked, to just stand there while I went on."

"His job—and yours—depends on Washington's confidence in him."

"Sure, but then to endorse my idea—that was amazing."

"We talked about these issues only last night."

"Sure, but that was dinner conversation."

"Kingsley wasn't saying anything like that to the President, then?"

"Not at all. I'm afraid he'll try to get even now."

"Kingsley? Not his style."

"He's not a saint. Look, in your NASA days, you'd have done the same."

"I don't get even, I get odder." She liked the small smile he gave her at the joke, an old one but serviceable enough to break the tension she felt in him.

"Come on. Arno called me in, and I'd like you there."

"Sure, I'm all slept out," though she wasn't.

The virtue of scientists lay principally in their curiosity. It could overcome hastily imposed U Agency management structures with ease. Fresh data trumped or bypassed the arteriosclerotic pyramids of power and information flow the Agency had erected, all quite automatically, following its standard crisis-management directives. Kingsley understood quite well the habits of mind that advanced, classified research followed, though he had given few hints about how he had acquired the knowledge.

Standard security regulation used strict separation of functions, at times keeping the right hand from even knowing there was a left hand. The Manhattan Project had been the historically honored example of this approach, dividing each element of the A-bomb problem from the other, with transmission only on a Need to Know basis.

Historians of science now believed that bomb production had been delayed about a year by this method. Under a more open strategy, the United States could have used bombs against Berlin, perhaps destroying the German regime from the air rather than on the ground. This might have kept the U.S.S.R. out of Europe altogether, vastly altering the Cold War that followed. Bureaucracy mattered. It irked scientists, but it shaped history.

Astronomy defeated even this outdated compartmenting method. The entire science depended upon telescopes that could peer at vastly different wavelengths, spread over a spectrum from the low radio to gamma rays, a factor in wavelength of a million billion. Seldom could an astronomical object be understood without seeing it throughout much of this huge range.

As well, the habits of mind that astronomers brought to the Eater would not stop at a wavelength barrier. To understand the steadily deepening radio maps, for example, demanded spectra in the optical or X-ray ranges. Astronomy was integrative and could not be atomized. This fact—as much as Benjamin's walking into "a presidential conversation that took me days to organize!"—brought Arno to a rare fit of anger.

The first part of the meeting was predictable, and Channing found herself nodding off. She reprimanded herself, whispering to a concerned Kingsley that it was like dozing at a bullfight, but in fact Arno could do nothing but bluster about Benjamin's intervention. The President was considering his proposal, and that was that. No amount of U Agency tweaking could put the horse back in the barn. Still, Benjamin had been doing more—sending needed information to groups outside the Center.

"I hold you responsible for these leaks, Knowlton," Arno finished his military-style dressing-down, smacking a palm onto the desk he sat upon.

" 'Leaks'? My people are merging their different views to make sense out of them," Benjamin said, looking rather surprised at how calm he had remained in the face of a five-minute monologue.

"We can't have it."

Kingsley at last said something, waiting until the right moment. "I believe we have a fundamental misunderstanding here, friends. The Eater is perhaps a week or two away. No one with the slightest sense of proportion will sequester data that might help us deal with it, once it has arrived."

"That's not the way we work here," Arno said, pausing between each word.

"Then it must become so," Kingsley said amiably.

"I'm going farther up the chain on this," Arno said darkly.

"I'm afraid we have already done that," Kingsley said.

She saw suddenly that Kingsley had played this exactly right, yet again maneuvering with an intuitive skill that could not be conscious. Benjamin's move, which he obviously had been pondering for days and yet had not revealed to her, was deliberate and risky. But Benjamin was like Salieri playing alongside Kingsley's Mozart. Already Kingsley had co-opted Benjamin's point and used it against Arno, a triumph that would undoubtedly echo in the echelons back in Washington.

She returned to the Semiotics Group meeting and Benjamin came along. "Done enough for today," he said affably. "You guys are having better ideas. I might as well hear them."

Perhaps so, she told him, though some people, even in NASA, were showing the strain, carried away by the majesty of the Eater and its beautiful disk. "A higher form of life, virtually a god," one of them had said at a coffee break.

"I hope that doesn't catch on," Benjamin said.

On their way, they passed through the main foyer. At its new high speed, the Eater would reach Earth within an estimated time that kept changing as it encountered fresh mass to ingest. Tracking its velocity, a digital clock now loomed over the tallest wall of the foyer. It had begun ticking down the time remaining. One of the media sorts had already dubbed it the Doomsday Clock. Benjamin grimaced. Beside it, feeds from observatories gave views of the magnetic labyrinth and its plasma clouds.

They settled into seats in the back row and listened to arguments about how to best communicate, negotiate, and placate the Eater. She was still impressed by the fact that any understanding could pass between entities of such different basic substrata: a magnetically shaped plasma talking to walking packets of water. The specialists argued that this was possible because there were general templates for organizing intelligence.

This must be true in a very sweeping way, a woman from Stanford argued. Scientists often congratulated themselves on having figured out how the universe worked, as if it were following our logic. But in fact humans had evolved out of the universe, and so fit it well. Our minds had been conditioned by brutal evolution to methods of understanding that worked finely enough to keep us alive, at least long enough to reproduce. Some ancient ancestor had found the supposedly simple things of life—how to move, find food, evade predators—enormously complicated and hard to remember. Such an ancestor faded from the gene pool, selected against by the rough rub of chance. We had descended from ancestors who found beauty in nature, a sense of the inevitable logic and purity in its design.

Intelligence reflected the universe's own designs, and so had similar patterns, even though arising in very different physical forms. This view emerged as she and Benjamin watched, until one grizzled type from the University of California at Irvine remarked, "Yeah, but the animals are a lot like us, too, and look at how we treat them."

Benjamin asked ironically, "You mean we should not expect it to share our view of our own importance?"

The gray-bearded man nodded. "Or our morality. That's an evolved system of ideas, and this thing is utterly asocial. It's a loner."

Benjamin seemed commendably unembarrassed to speak among specialists in a field he did not know. She admired his courage, then realized that if the detailed talk she had heard here before could not be translated into something others could comprehend, it would be useless in the days ahead.

Benjamin asked, "Cooperation with others of its kind never happened, as far as we can tell. The latest transmissions from it say that it was made by a very early, intelligent civilization whose planet was being chewed up by the black hole. They managed to download their own culture into it, translating into magnetic information stored in waves."

This sent a rustle through the room. Benjamin leaned toward her and whispered, "Just as I thought. This firewall security system has kept a lot away from the guys who actually need it."

His revelation provoked quick reactions, which Benjamin fielded easily. It was very big news and he enjoyed delivering it in an offhand way.

Now she understood why he had come here. He was still on the move, steering through treacherous waters nobody knew. She felt a burst of love for him, and to her surprise, fresh respect. "Go get 'em, tiger."

"What else can you tell us?" the graybeard asked.

Benjamin plunged in. Sure enough, some important Eater messages had either not gotten through, or were distorted. "Experts with an axe to grind, putting their own spin in." Benjamin summed it up.

The discussion turned into just the sort of free-for-all she had missed so far among the rather stiff semiotics gang. She turned over the issues as others with more energy attacked them, and somehow the ideas mingled with a vaguely forming plan of her own.

This being had lived longer than the Earth had existed. To it, a million years would be like a day in a human life. She tried to think how it would view life-forms anchored on planets. *Mayflies.* Whole generations would pass as flashes of lightning, momentarily illuminating their tiny landscapes. Eons would stream by, civilizations on the march like characters in some larger drama witnessed only by the truly long-lived. Birth, death, and all agonies in between—these would merge into a simultaneous whole. Rather than a static snapshot, such a being could see a smear of lives as a canvas backdrop to the stately pace of a galaxy on the move, turning like a pinwheel in the great night. Whole species would be the players then, blossoming momentarily for the delectation of vast, slow entities beyond understanding.

Compared to it, humans were passing ephemerals. To a baby, a year was like a lifetime because it *was* his lifetime, so far. By age ten, the next year was only a 10 percent increase in his store of years. At a hundred, time ticked ten times faster still. She tried to imagine living to a thousand, when a year would have the impact of a few hours in such a roomy life. *Now multiply this effect by another factor of a million,* she mused.

She wondered if anyone was paying attention to the Eater's own artworks, beamed down in compressed digital packets. It had remarked,

> THE TRUE STATE OF SUCH RESULTANTS RESIDES IN MY
> FIELD STRUCTURES. I SEND ONLY NUMERICAL ANALOGS.

What would its creations say to them if they could be seen in their natural form?

4 He got used to the media onslaught within a day or two, then irritated, then bored.

Not that he was, as one reporter archly termed it, "seriously famous," but he did have his head bashed by swinging TV cameras, got chased down an alley, backed into a corner, all with the sound effects: questions barked, name called, bystanders' applause and boos—all got to be like the weather whenever he left a building. "Over here, Dr. Knowlton, look this way!"

Dimly he realized what was so fundamentally misguided about liking that sort of attention. He was allowing them to define who he was, whether he was worthwhile. The media meat grinder ate and also excreted.

When public pronouncements shifted to the ever-adept Kingsley and to other, more distant members of the Executive Committee, some of the zip went out of it. There were still big crowds at the fences and gates when he went to an ExComm meeting, but it was oddly irksome when he got out of a limousine to hear the paparazzi shout, "Who is it? Who's that? Oh, it's nobody. Only Knowlton."

He had gotten lulled into the feeling that somehow he controlled the lurching beast, just with the sound of his voice. He tried to speak clearly, exactly at first, then found that the hectoring pundits wanted answers to sensational questions, and were miffed if they didn't get an emotional expressiveness.

163

When he saw the sound snippets they cut his remarks into, he wondered if perhaps there was indeed some truth to the old superstition that having your picture taken let the camera rob a piece of your soul.

"Pity the people who are looking at this story through such distorting lenses," Channing had said. The Center personnel, sheltered behind regiments of security, barely got a glimpse of the chaos pervading the planet.

What Benjamin did see revealed the unreality of the experience for others. The world was so media-saturated, so shaped toward capturing eyeballs rather than merely carrying information, that the unfolding events were experienced as theater, a show. Politics had long ago become primarily performance, and now even the supposed elite—ministers and professors, pundits and prophets—alike wanted the same commodity: audience, attention.

**DANGER FROM SPACE! SEE IT ALL RIGHT HERE
MILLIONS DIE?—AND YOU'LL KNOW WHY.**

He grudgingly appeared on a panel discussion for *World Tonight,* featuring supposedly learned commentary. One part of the show was called "The Cultural Critic Corner." "The Eater has become not so much a thing to think *of*, but to think *with*," the fabulous-looking woman said. "A figure in constant symbolic motion, shuttling in our collective unconscious between science and fantasy, nature and culture, the image of the other and a mirror of the self." He shook his head and without warning found himself in an argument using terms he did not know. By the end of it, he was determined that he would never do *that* again.

Kingsley had a far better on-camera presence. He remarked to Channing and Benjamin, over lunch at the Center cafeteria, "Governments always wish to be reassuring. We have to tell the truth while suppressing panic, and I do what I can."

"A stylish Brit accent helps," Channing said, poking at a salad. "Evokes authority."

"Sure," Benjamin said. "Look at our own Beltway Empire. The Department of Health and Human Services deals more with sickness than health. The Department of Energy spends more on nuclear weapons than on energy. The Department of Defense was meant to wage war."

Kingsley said, "If necessary, DoD will always add. And your classic American strategy was to defend itself in somebody else's country."

"Only here, it's the whole planet," Channing added. "You think it's going to come close?"

"To Earth, you mean?" She knew Kingsley disliked being put on the spot so plainly, but he fielded it nicely, looking unworried. "It caught another asteroid early this morning. Latest orbitals say it will be here within fifteen days."

"The Searchers got anything new?" Benjamin asked, his high, raw voice giving away his uneasiness.

"Better interior definition, some spectra."

"Any chance we could talk it into stopping at, say, the moon?" Channing asked.

"It fails to respond to all such discussions."

"Ummm. God doesn't answer His mail."

But then abruptly it did.

An hour later Kingsley sought out Benjamin and Channing and hurried them to his office. "It's readily responding to a whole class of questions. More about where it came from originally, for one."

They stared at the message on his screen.

ONCE LONG AGO IT WAS A MERE NATURAL SINGULARITY. A MINOR REMNANT OF SOME EARLY ASTROPHYSICAL EVENT. PERHAPS A FRACTIONAL REMNANT OF A SUPERNOVA. THEN BY ACCIDENT THIS OBJECT, WHICH IS NOW MY PRESENT CORE, TUNNELED THROUGH THE PLANET OF AN ANCIENT CIVILIZATION.

Amy had come in while they talked. She had been away for days, working with specialists elsewhere in integrating the tight, highly secure communications network the U Agency was putting in place among astronomers around the world. Kingsley was effusively glad to see her back. She studied the message and said, "It could then orbit in and out of the planet. Along its path some rock would fall into the hole, releasing explosive energy."

"How much?" Kingsley asked.

"Maybe ten percent of the MC^2, with M the infalling matter at a rate . . ." She scribbled a moment. "It's a traveling, continuous hydrogen bomb."

Channing said with a jerky lightness, "Not in My Backyard with a vengeance. The residents would have very little time to react before the entire planet was a wreck."

Benjamin said slowly, "At that rate, blowing a huge tunnel through the world, there would be immediate seismic damage all over the globe."

"Ask it what happened," Amy said.

THAT SOCIETY SAW THAT THE ONLY WAY TO PRESERVE IT-SELF WAS TO DEPOSIT SOME FRACTION OF THEY-SELF INTO REPRESENTATIONS. THIS DONE, THESE RECORDINGS THEY EMBEDDED IN THE MAGNETIC HALO OF THE PECULIARITY THAT IS MY CENTER. THAT OLDEST CIVILIZATION IS TERMED THE OLD ONE. IT INVENTED THE PROCESS AND RESIDES WITHIN THE LARGER IT.

Kingsley remarked, "Notice how it sometimes refers to itself in a neutral manner, as 'it' and elsewhere, its parts as 'the disk' and 'field repositories,' whatever they might be—all rather than using a possessive."

Channing said, "I guess a semiotics type would say that those are too 'primate-centered constructions' for it to comfortably use."

They asked more and with some delay—the Eater was beaming down unintelligible 'cultural' data—a later transmission seemed to answer their questions.

THESE PATTERNS STILL LIVE AS MAGNETIC WAVES,
PROPAGATING IN COMPLEX PATTERNS THROUGHOUT
MY NIMBUS OF FIELDS. WITH AGE AND MUCH TIME THE
PERSONALITIES SO EMBEDDED GAINED CONTROL
OVER THE MASS FLOWING INTO THE HOLE. THEY-
SELVES USED THIS TO ERECT THE GUIDING JETS OF
ENFLAMED MATTER. THIS MADE THE OLD ONE A
VOYAGER. IT VENTURED INTO THE SPACES BETWEEN THE
SUNS IN PURSUIT OF KNOWLEDGE AND DIVERSITY.
NEAR OTHER STARS IT FOUND WORLDS WITH LIFE. AT
SOME IT COULD TRANSFIX FORMS OF LIVING
INTELLIGENCES. THESE JOYOUSLY ADDED TO THE
WEALTH OF THE HALO AS THEY WERE GATHERED UP.
SLOWLY GREW THE ABILITY TO MANIPULATE THE
MAGNETIC FLUXES EVER MORE ARTFULLY FROM THE
FLAMING DISK THAT RIMS THE SINGULARITY. IN TIME,
THE MANY PERSONAE INHABITED AND ENLARGED THE
GATHERING ABUNDANCE/FULLNESS OF WHAT HAD
ONCE BEEN CRUDE MASS AND GEOMETRY, WITHOUT
IMPORT OR PROSPECT.

"Read it twice," Kingsley said. "Its linguistic range has
grown enormously and there are subtleties here."

Benjamin did not challenge the implied authority in
Kingsley's voice. These matters were certainly beyond his
own range. Nobody was an expert here. In the silence of the
office, he said, "And this has been going on for nearly eight
billion years."

Channing said thoughtfully, "Maybe this explains the
Fermi Paradox? Why we have had no visiting aliens, and
hear none in the radio bands of the galaxy?"

Benjamin nodded. "They've been . . . eaten."

"That may be an implication, admittedly," Kingsley allowed. "It does not *say* that it simply swallows civilizations."

Benjamin said, "It records them."

"In some sense we cannot imagine right now," Kingsley
said.

"You made the basic point weeks ago," Benjamin said. "That if it slammed into the Earth the collision with solid matter would strip away the magnetic field structures around it."

"Kill the Eater itself," Channing said. "That's reassuring."

"So how does it 'gather up' intelligences?" Benjamin asked.

Kingsley said in measured tones, "I do not believe we wish to discover that."

5 Long before now, as her strength had waned, dinner and a movie had become takeout and a video. She had to get away from the Eater for a bit, so she went home early and fell into a familiar crevasse of her own interior. So many different flavors of depression to choose from! Gray existential despair, fruity sorrows of remembered childhood, dimly sensed wrongs done to people now dead, the sobering sadness that made life seem to be mostly burdens: phone calls, chores, tedious newspapers wide-eyed with Eater news and views, mostly the latter by people who knew no astrophysics.

Losing your mind, like losing your car keys, she found to be a hassle. It was also ridiculous. *Why don't you just get up?* her no-nonsense self would ask and, stupidly, she still just idiotically lay there. She had once done skydiving. It had been easier to crawl along a strut toward a plane's wingtip against an eighty-mile-an-hour wind at eight thousand feet than to get out of bed *right now*.

Drugs helped. She did well with "selective serotonin-reuptake inhibitors," an endless parade of chemical adjustments known only by their acronyms, since no human could remember their true names, or would want to. Handling her "bodily management" was tricky, especially the drains, especially with the cheerleading nurse they sent around: "Serosanguinous fluid, very good!"

So the unholy ghost of depression had come again, turning her into a zombie who could not read or turn on the 3-D or lift the phone to call for help. Benjamin worked late and she drifted. She got angry at him for his absence, even though she understood it. Then she came to appreciate the time to herself. Time to get down to the Self at last.

Some nerves once scraped raw now felt cloaked in lead. She had read up on depression, of course, the eternal student's conviction that learning would bring wisdom, or a solution. But it was no help to be told that mildly depressed people were actually more realistic than happy people, had a more balanced view. The happy really *were* mindless, believing all sorts of positive, self-enhancing illusions.

So her sense of menacing sadness was at least genuine. How reassuring.

So she lay in the moist, fragrant tropical gloom and listened to the idiot, joyful insects celebrate the coming of night and thought of what she had to celebrate. Not much. Hard to live in the joy of the moment when the moments were getting few.

But she was nurturing an idea and that helped. *So much to do.*

In the end, that made her get up and use the computer in her home office. The sheets of e-mail tags she ignored, hunting down information on cerebral theory, data-stacking technology, and advanced research in recent review papers, their language so tangled that she could scarcely read the abstracts.

She had become fascinated by the "sculptures" the Eater had transmitted. After a hurried glance at them in two-dimensional slices—the Eater's preferred mode of data packing, for reasons unexplained by it or anyone—the semioticists had rushed on to the more intensive later transmissions. As the night deepened, she used the Executive Committee's worldwide preemption of computer meshes to make full-scale holograms of the alien art. She had at her command dozens of cyber-aces and used them ruthlessly. They pressed into service vast complexes of parallel processing arrays. The U Agency certainly knew how to muster the troops, she thought, as enormous data files flickered across her screen. It was hard work, but in the middle of it she suddenly noticed that her depression had evaporated.

6 Benjamin was preparing to weave his weary way home when Channing came through the door of his section, looking downright brisk. He was so startled that her quick, efficient kiss left him blinking as she swept on. "Got to use the rep chamber," she called back to him airily.

He finished a small job that had a deadline well past, then hurried after her. The representation chamber was a new cyber-marvel assembled by a U Agency team to give full, all-surround images. They were using it to project images of the Eater from every spectral band, so that one could get the illusion of walking through its magnetic realms.

When he came in, though, Channing was standing at the center and he could not make sense of what surrounded her. Slithering, glistening bodies worked through a soupy air, in pirouettes and glides like dancing, swimming birds.

Then, with no transition he could catch, the shapes changed to craggy wedges of enameled light. These contorted into shapes whose outline he could grasp without comprehending for a moment what they were. He had the distinct sensation of seeing something the wrong way around, like one of those black-and-white optical illusions that can suddenly jump from being an old crone seen in outline to a vase. Here, though, the effect did not snap back and forth between two simple choices. The shapes would jolt into something else, like a miniature misshapen tree suddenly becoming an animal with two necks, then a machine moving on beams of light, then a wrenched, pale building that extruded layers of rooms, each lit by what seemed like purple fires.

All this happened just fast enough for him to grasp a fleeting feel for what was revealed, and then the shapes would strain and wring into something else, on and on in an endless parade of strangeness. They did not repeat while he watched. Each shape followed its own patterns.

Channing was wandering inside the 3-D representations. Among their uncanny beauties, her face glowed with an expression he could not read. She reached up into the air, alive with holographic color and mass, and caressed the images.

He called to her across the darkened image-pit, but she did not respond. He felt a rising tension in him, something straining, and a blinding headache descended like a veil. He had to leave. Worry creased his face as he wobbled down the corridor outside. The headache settled into his eyes with a piercing pain.

He downed four aspirin as Kingsley came through the door of his office, quickly closed it, and went without a word to Benjamin's screen console. "What's up?" Benjamin asked raggedly. This was like no headache he had ever suffered. He could not seem to get his eyes to behave right, as though they were receiving instructions from a different part of his brain.

"In the middle of a rather ordinary transmission, it ceased sending, then sent this."

IT-SELF NOW DECIDES TO HARVEST REMNANTS OF YOU-SELVES. IT SENDS NOW INSTRUCTIONS OF HOW TO COMPLY. REMNANTS SHALL BE IMPACTED IN PLACE.

Benjamin read as rapidly as his vision would allow. Pages of instructions. With each revelation he gave a grunt of amazement. Kingsley said nothing, pacing back and forth before the desk, looking firmly at the carpet. Kingsley's blue shirt and pale brown suit were rumpled and creased, as though he had been sleeping in his clothes.

"It's all there. Very clear, clear indeed," Kingsley said abruptly. "It is coming to 'harvest' us as a species. It demands a hundred thousand people, sacrificed and uploaded into digital form to transmit by microwave."

"Good grief. How?"

"It will translate them into 'magnetic selves' to form a 'company of their selfkind,' it says."

Benjamin asked hollowly, "*That's* why it came?"

"Apparently. It has said before that it suffers from something like outright boredom, though it does not use that term."

"I don't think we can even do this . . ."

"It says that since we have the 'minimum requirement'— computers, digitization—then it can teach us the rest."

"How convenient for us." Benjamin tried to get his mind around what the Eater might mean. "All to be part of some kind of . . . 'company'?"

"For its library, I suspect. Or museum. Or zoo."

"Someplace it can go and, uh, put up its feet and . . ."

"Read people like books? As good an analogy as any, I suppose."

"It doesn't say?"

There was more from the Eater, sheets of technical description. "It will make of them these 'remnants,' I gather."

" 'Remnants'? Meaning the rest of us will be gone? Dead?"

"I believe it sees us all as ephemeral. A 'remnant' would be kept for its own uses for far longer than we would live."

"Or for as long as it found the remnant interesting," Benjamin mused.

Kingsley turned suddenly and faced Benjamin across his messy desk. "I haven't talked to anyone else about this. Arno will get it within minutes and will come running to us in a pure blind panic."

"And he'll want to know what to do," Benjamin said with

a sinking resignation. Though the Center now housed whole battalions of specialists and there was surely no shortage of opinions to be had, the pace of events was too rapid to allow much to filter up from below. He and Kingsley would have to have opinions, plans, and options about this.

Kingsley said in a weary gray voice, "And I have not a clue what to say."

"This is for the politicos."

"I do hope so. They are not at their best when required to act quickly."

"We can't comply, of course."

"I wish I understood quite why." Kingsley frowned. "Muslim, Buddhist. . . . Completely contrary to my instinct, the world's religions appear to agree with you. And I do not know why."

"I believe they're stunned. Aren't we?"

"I am, at least. I would think they'd be more concerned for the mass, the flock, than the individual."

He chuckled. "I can't explain it. Maybe it's just that being stunned can bring out deep responses. This feels to me to have come from someplace nobody knew."

"Because no society has faced anything remotely like this before."

"Maybe in the Old Testament. I never finished reading it. The size of *War and Peace*."

He allowed himself a small grin. "It might fancy a comparison with Jehovah."

"That stilted tone is its way of imitating our ancient voice of authority?"

"I meant more than it merely using a tactic. Perhaps the way to get a grasp of matters is that it may be playing a role, but primarily for itself. It transcends any notion we might have of being self-involved."

"Or it could be adopting a mode that worked before. Maybe it thinks of us as a species it knows about. Or a genera. Order. Kingdom—that's the highest biological class, isn't it?"

He was lost in thought. "So it may well have a policy, then—based solely upon its classifying of us—regarding what to do if we fail to comply."

"I hope it won't come to that."

Kingsley's face seemed to sharpen harshly, his chin drawing down in derision. "Note the tone of address it uses."

"Yeah, that's an order, all right."

"One we must obey," Channing said. They both turned in surprise. She had slipped through the door without their noticing.

"What?" Benjamin demanded. "Why?"

"Something I can't explain, but from what I just saw . . ." Her voice drained away and she seemed lost in thought.

"I cannot imagine that we would subject people to such a thing," Kingsley said with crisp dignity.

"I can't imagine we won't," Channing said, her voice so serene and mild and certain that it sent a chill through Benjamin.

PART FIVE

A THINKING THING

1 In her purse lurked her neuroses writ small. Survival-
ist provisions like chocolate bars and breath mints,
nail polish and Kleenexes, Chap Sticks and thread and a
palm computer and a wrinkled notebook and assorted pens:
yellow, blue, black. She also had taken lately to hoarding:
unpaired gloves, broken eyeglass frames, bits of tape and
twine. Peering in, she felt as if she gazed into her unconscious, where dark objects conspired with painful memories.
She had retreated to ever-larger purses roughly at the time
she was diagnosed. Before she had used briefcases or book
bags, the businesslike approach of a woman who no longer
announced that she carried her house on her back. Yet she
still associated purses with her mother's generation: solid,
sure, but also awkwardly dressed and uptight, clunky and a
bit out of it. The purse's shadowy collective unconscious
now prompted her with fragments of her past selves. It
reeked of pruderies and fears, anxieties hidden from the
world but carried everywhere, like a Freudian fanny-pack.

   She used this bulky brown satchel to keep herself afloat at
the Center. She could hide her medication and carry it with
her, and when a nurse came to administer the more difficult
injections, she could use Benjamin's spacious office, with its
little "executive alcoves" for deal-making away from the
main room of walnut desk and Big Screen Comm Center.
When Benjamin or Kingsley—the only people who took

much notice of her, luckily, in the hubbub—protested that she should be home working, she quoted Einstein: "Only a monomaniac gets anything done."

"All too true," Kingsley said somberly, his luminous eyes looming over his slender, lined face. "You're . . . looking well."

She had an urge to laugh at his obvious struggle to find a remotely plausible compliment, but suppressed it. "You're a dear, dear liar." She kissed him lightly, a satisfying soft smack.

To her surprise, this flustered him. To smooth matters over, she went with him for a coffee and deliberately chose one of the high-octane variety named Kaff. He looked troubled most of the time now, but her choice made him frown further. "Should you be, well—"

"Taking in caffeine? Mendenham says not to, but my body says, 'Either gimme some or lie down.' "

"A demanding body."

"You should know."

Again he startled her by blushing. "I believe I can recall," he managed.

"As the prospect of having much more of it fades, I live in my sensual past." Teasing him was unfair, but the world was not exactly packed full of fun lately, and she needed the ego boost. So she rationalized as she watched him put his composure back on. She could even see it happening in his face, mouth getting resolute again. Under the pressure here, maybe his barrier against facial giveaways was falling.

"You have every right to," came out judiciously phrased. "If there's anything—"

"A lot, but it's probably immoral or something. Content me by telling me the gossip."

This put him on his favorite ground, the slightly disguised lecture. The great game now was not astrophysics but amateur alien psychology. "The creature going on obliviously, chattering about all sorts of things, as if we are all waiting here for its orders."

"And we aren't?"

"The leadership is saying and doing nothing."

"They've had two days to think it over—"

"My dear, this is a matter for the entire world. In two days, they cannot agree on the color of blue."

"They'd better hurry."

"There's mildly good news there. It's braking."

"Ah, good. How?"

"Only an astronomer would make that her first question." He grinned and for a quick moment some of the old joy brimmed between them. "Most would want to know how many more days that gives us, which is perhaps now fifteen in all. To answer *how*—through a forward-pointing jet, quite powerful. Apparently it found fresh quarry and has extended this jet, anchoring it firmly with magnetic flux ropes in a helical pattern. That funnels and ejects hot matter from its accretion disk."

The coffee had given her enough energy to be incredulous. "That's slowing it enough?"

"I know, a simple calculation shows that slowing a mass exceeding our moon's, down from a velocity of hundreds of kilometers a second is, well, an incredible demand."

"It's an incredible creature. What's it *say* about this?"

"Its deceleration? Nothing. Not one to give way to Proustian introspection, it seems."

"Skip the literature. I'll settle for hearing how it does the jet trick."

"Understanding how it thinks is now critical, I gather."

"Sure, right after we understand how we think."

"Touché. It did refer to Proust the other day, I saw. Something about his understanding of time being what one would expect of 'doomed intelligences,' I believe the phrase was."

"Well, as a fellow doomed intelligence, I agree. Never could abide Proust, anyway."

"Nor I. Its transmissions are fascinating stuff and I look in on them when I can."

"I should, too," she said distantly.

"It's sending masses of stuff, a million words a day." Too casually he looked at her hands, which were fidgeting—and not due to the Kaff. "I gather you have been looking at its own inventory of art."

"Ummm, yes. It appended a note saying that these were representative works from other members of our class."

He frowned. " 'Class'? As technological civilizations?"

"No, as what it called 'dreaming vertebrates.' With the implication that our class is fairly common."

"Good Lord. I wonder if those working out its orders know that. I'll have to tell them."

"Orders?"

"Oh yes, it has a menu and proceeds to order up whatever it fancies."

"From what? Our broadcast media?"

"And references such as the Encyclopaedia. Still having a bit of trouble keeping straight that people pass from the scene so quickly. Or else thinks we're somehow hiding them away still."

"Who does it want?"

"Artists, scientists, sports figures. It caught transmissions from decades past as it approached our solar system. It even sends the pictures of those it wants. Lauren Bacall, Einstein, Bob Dylan, Gandhi, Esther Dyson, Jack Nicholson, and Hillary Clinton, as I remember."

She felt a chill then at the reality of what was coming at them across the solar system. "Good . . . grief."

"Yes, imagine the feelings of those on the list."

"They've been told?"

"It would seem. Of course many are dead, but others are now near death. Arno wondered aloud if any would be willing to, you know, give up the remainder of their lives"—he shrugged, eyes rolling skyward—"for humanity and so on."

"To . . . copy . . . them." The word was hard to get out.

"It has already sent 'helpful additions' to our computing and other technologies that it says will permit us to 'read' a good deal of the memory stored in brains. Seems incredible to me."

"It . . . wants all the person?"

"So I gather." He looked at her quizzically.

"Why should we do it?"

"It does not need to brag about its threatening abilities, of course. Apparently brute intimidation has worked before."

"We all judge from our experience," she said lightly. "What does this tell us about other intelligent life in the galaxy?"

"They must have complied, I suppose, else it would not think this a winning strategy."

"Something about the idea gets me in my, well, my gut."

"Me, too. In terms of game theory, doing a cost-benefit sort of analysis—"

She chuckled loudly. Kingsley stopped, blinked. "You think I'm off the mark."

" 'Applying game theory'—that's the kind of idea only an intellectual would believe. This is a gut issue."

Ruefully he tried to share in the humor of it, managing a thin smile. "I suppose I betray my origins."

"You may think that way, but I'll bet ordinary people sure don't."

He nodded energetically. "I think you're dead-on right."

"To deal in people this way is as profound an insult as I can imagine."

"Ummm. Perhaps this hints at what we should call a fate worse than death?"

"How are people reacting?"

He sighed with gray exasperation. "Those above are dithering, terrified. News has gotten out, of course. Arno tried to see that all radio telescopes that could pick up the Eater's transmissions were in our control, but that notion failed immediately."

"Too many?"

"Far too many. A small dish with superior software in Sri Lanka picked up the vital part of the story. The Eater sent it several times in different terminology, apparently to be sure it was understood."

Benjamin came by, saw them, and hurried over. "Been looking for you both. Come on. You can watch in my office."

From his tight-mouthed expression she could read that the morning had not gone well. She labored up from her chair. "More trouble with Arno?"

"He's trying to find scapegoats for the leaks."

"This place is a sieve, in any case," Kingsley said amiably, unconcerned, as they both slowed to her pace.

"The Sri Lanka was bad enough, but somebody's letting other stuff get out," Benjamin said as they entered his office. Two assistants waved for his attention, but he in turn waved them away. Something had toughened in him in all this and he seemed more assured than he had ever been. She was proud of him, especially when she saw the strain on the faces of Center personnel. Benjamin's expression was unlined, though intent.

He punched up the international news—not difficult, since channels carried virtually nothing else since the Eater had left Jupiter space. "What's the reaction?" Channing asked, sinking into a form-fitting chair that clasped her in its leathery embrace.

"Horror," Benjamin said. "Here—"

They watched reaction shots from some of those 'ordered up' on the Eater's menu. After the third one, her attention drifted and she let events slide by for a while. When she came back, there was the news Benjamin had brought them in for.

Some totalitarian governments had started to comply. Footage of people rounded up—criminals, the politically out of favor—and being herded away.

"To have their brains sliced-and-diced and uploaded into computers," Benjamin said. "Incredible."

"And the bastards in charge are claiming to do it for the benefit of all mankind," Kingsley said.

"Transparent," Benjamin said with disgust.

The twenty-first century had no lack of dictators. In the crush of populations among the tropical nations particularly, the strongman promises of order and equal shares, though seldom fulfilled, found a ready audience.

"They know their unsavory reputations," Kingsley observed, "and this move allows them to appear as benefactors of humanity while consolidating internal power. Rather neat, overall."

Another news flash, this time yet another intercepted Eater message. "Not from here," Benjamin said. "Some dish grabbed it."

The Eater encouraged this latest development from the dictators. It wanted a large, functioning "eternal society" to join it, addressing humanity as though it were a unity.

I DESIRE CONVERSE WITH A TRUE VARIETY OF YOU.

2 Benjamin did not want to go for even a short walk on the beach, but she insisted. The day's events had been unsettling, as usual, and he felt the old island softness creep into him as they made their way through palms and onto the broad, warm sand. The sunset was a spectacular streaked composition in purple and orange. She could barely manage making her way in the white sand.

"When will we be able to see it as a naked eye object?" she asked, gazing up.

"Inside a week, I believe, if its deceleration continues as is."

"Should be pretty."

He turned to her suddenly, back to the sunset. "Look, I can step down from running things, spend these days together. Here on the beach, as much as we can."

"Your heart wins out over your head," she said abstractly, gazing at the fading fingers of deepening red that arced over them.

"Sure, sure, for you." They embraced and he felt a warm wave of relief. "I'll see Arno tomorrow, quit—"

"No, I need you to talk to him, but not about that."

He blinked, seeing something strange come into her face. "But . . ."

Fervently she grasped his arms, hugged him, stepped back. "I want to go."

" 'Go'? Where? What—" Then he saw it.

"Upload me."

"That's . . . that's—" His throat tightened painfully.

"Crazy, as crazy as what's already happening."

He scrambled for rational reasons. "It's untried, chancy—"

"It's not to evade death," she said in a straightforward, businesslike voice. "I know that a copy is not the original. I'll be gone, as far as the little 'me' that rides around behind my eyes. And I'm not going to discuss whether an uploaded 'person' has free will, either—philosophy doesn't ring my chimes, not now. I've got another reason, one you can argue for with Arno and the others."

"If you think I'll—"

"Hear me out, lover. I want to control a Searcher spacecraft, fly it into the Eater. They need onboard guidance to do that. I can be uploaded into a control module."

"Not like those bastards in the tropics." He was trying to see what drove her to this, but his mind didn't seem to be working very well. Did she think some digital replica was like becoming one of those sculptures, the alien ones?

She abandoned the business voice and pleaded nakedly. "I can help, even after I'm gone."

"And you are an astronaut," he said lamely. "You'll get back into space, sort of."

"I hadn't thought of it that way." She hugged him.

He recoiled from her grasp, confused. "You're saying, 'Kill me early'? No."

"It *is* my life."

"No!"

She reached out with a soft, tentative hand. "Something of me will come through. Maybe."

He looked at her trembling lips and kissed them. It was wrenchingly hard to resist her. "But I want every remaining moment with the *real* you, damn it."

Channing picked up a handful of sand and let it run through her hands, trickling into the passing breeze like an hourglass. "Time runs out for all of us. I just want to control my end."

"But this method, it's bound to wear you down. You could easily die sooner."

"Saving what, a few weeks of wasting away? No—I want win-win, remember? This way, we get the Searcher swarm to work better. And I get . . . something nobody's done."

"They don't know what the hell they're doing with this stuff, it's just parts of technology slammed together, it's . . ." He ground down into silence.

"I've read the reports, preliminary and sketchy but promising." Back to the business voice, crisp and NASA all the way. "They get lots out of the cerebral cortex. Trouble is, reading the deeper parts of the brain."

"But they won't capture *you*."

"The body won't be worth much. I'm a walking ruin already."

He had never liked her talking about herself this way, especially not the body he had learned to worship in so many ways. "I can't believe they can read you like some neuronal book."

"All of me is beautiful and valuable," she said, tone now light and brittle. "Even the ugly, stupid, and disgusting parts."

Was part of him drawn to the idea of giving her some form of digital immortality? A last flight?

Confused, his mouth working with unrelieved strain, he turned and walked on. Without them noticing, the sun had glimmered away and the sky slid into purple darkness.

3 At dawn she was weak with a numbing hollowness in her bones that cried out to be left alone. A separate child-self, wanting only the comfort it remembered from an impossibly distant time.

Channing gave it a few minutes to get used to the idea, and then very slowly and silently got out of bed. Going out through the kitchen, she grabbed a banana for energy. Opened slowly enough, the back door did not creak. In shadowy silence, the car started suddenly and she got out of the driveway before he could come running out, in case he woke. She drove up the hill behind one of the behemoth jobs from the cheap-gas decades, its plate proudly announcing VANZILLA. A hastily made sign on it carried the logo of a news network and she tromped down, enjoying the surge of acceleration as she shot around it.

Arno wasn't in yet. Summoning more of what appeared to be her last energies, she snagged a muffin and coffee and found Kingsley. He wore the same clothes as yesterday. He even sat and listened to her whole case, his fingers steepled before him as if he were worshipping. Amy Major came in, looking equally bedraggled, touched Kingsley's sleeve, then had the good sense to leave.

At last she was done, her voice trailing away before she could make herself frame a naked plea.

"I guessed yesterday," he said from behind his fingers.

"Then you'll support me?"

"I can't imagine not doing so. But what I feel does not matter, surely, compared to Benjamin."

"He's thinking it over."

"You bring it up before your own husband has—"

"There's no time."

He shook his head. "I cannot manage my personal feelings and give you reliable advice at the same time."

"Look, you've faced my death. I'm *going.*"

"But certainly you cannot expect me or Benjamin to hasten that."

"Think of it as an assisted suicide with a big upside."

He finally broke down then, his façade crumbling. He bent slowly over his desk and his head bowed until it rested on a yellow writing pad. She let him sit like that, part of her wanting to comfort him and the other wanting to let the moment work upon him, in a cool and bloodless way that came back to her from somewhere in her years devoted to her own momentum. She had always had this streak, a compact, composed sense of self that let her know when, for example, she could let a man go, send him back for a fluff and fold while she went on with her life. She needed that now, and so she used it, letting the silence run on because it was running her way.

In time it worked. Kingsley had plenty to say, his fine long sentences purling out as she let him work his way to an understanding of what he would have to do to help her. But the cusp moment had passed in that silence and now he was the old Kingsley, put back together with hardly any of the cracks showing.

"I am of course aware of your tragic situation," Arno said by way of preamble, "and that knowledge led me to consider the matter in detail."

He was in his familiar perch on the edge of his desk. Here came his patented warm, understanding, yet commanding smile. "I like the idea. As you argue, this will give us a 'digital presence' of higher order than anything available in existing Searcher craft."

Benjamin was there by this time, still early morning. In the caverns of the expanded Center, there were no windows—for security reasons—so she readily lost sense of time. The stretches of memory lapse and simple stupor added to the effect. *I'll be timeless pretty soon now, one way or the other,* she mused. Then she snapped awake, aware that she was drifting again, right in the middle of Arno's speech.

He was dwelling on the technical details, on up to the grand questions. Would her simulation be bound by the craft's programming? No, though the philosophical issue of whether a simulation behaved like a person was beyond anybody, at their primitive level of understanding. And so on.

She saw in Benjamin's grim, set jaw his stifled anger at how she had outflanked him, going around to Kingsley. Well, she would make it up to him. *Something special, great meal, wine, a Victoria's Secret evening, the works.* Then she blinked and knew she was beyond that, too, thoroughly out of it now, no body worth bothering with anymore. Or mind, either, to judge from her slippery hold on events.

Kingsley was speaking now, and Benjamin was arguing, and it was all under glass for her. Kingsley arguing that Benjamin was "too close to the issue," then some military types coming into Arno's office, earnest expressions turning to blank-faced when they realized she, *the one*, was there. Kingsley's clashes with Benjamin had been personal, bitter in their tone, and she let all that sweep away from her. Pieces of the discussion came to her from the dozen men in the room.

". . . barely technically possible . . ."

". . . research in this area is still crudely developed . . ."

". . . U Agency wishes to sequester her data . . ."

". . . crash basis, can get the black box up to orbital rendezvous within a day . . ."

One of the Air Force generals she had seen interviewed on 3-D sat nearby and said, looking right at her, "The whole world is on a war footing, after all—the first interstellar war."

She roused herself to quote a famous bureaucratic maxim. "You can get great things done as long as you don't have to get credit for it." Then she sank back and let them try to figure out what it meant.

She saw, from an airy distance, that she had slipped free of ambition, a clean escape. No longer did the fires of desire for fame or success burn in her; they were banked forever. Now much of her earlier striving seemed pointless, even contemptible. She could be a spectator now. But even in the End Game, as chess players called it, the old astronaut ambition governed.

Arno again, speaking to her. "We all respect your contribution. It is a very valiant thing you do, for all humanity."

She gave him a long look that should have struck several centimeters out of his back. "No heroics. I'm doing this to *do* it."

Then the Air Force and NASA types came in and she tried to hold on to the thread but failed. *Keep quiet, so they don't know,* her good sense told her. Even that wasn't easy.

Somehow the big stuff went by smoothly, but she snagged on vexing details. One of the NASA astronaut contingent described how the control systems of the Searcher craft would be refitted to accept her commands—or rather, the digital "her." He outlined how this would be the ultimate in compact control systems, ". . . manned, I mean crewed," with a nervous glance at Channing.

She said slowly and with shaky clarity, even though she was not really sure she was right, "The word 'manned' comes from the Latin for hand, I believe, as in 'manipulate.' Nothing sexist about it."

Everyone smiled and she saw that they were on her side, as much as anyone could be. Comforting. But Benjamin was stern and dire, his big-eyed gaze full of fear and confusion.

4 "Agencies despise uncertainties, old fellow," Kingsley said, "but we are scientists and know that knowledge is based upon doing experiments that can fail."

Benjamin sensed that this was a set speech, well honed in the corridors of power, but let it do its work on him, anyway. Kingsley had a way of letting you in on the secrets of command. This last sentence filled him with hope. "You're saying they aren't going to go for her idea?"

"No, I am saying that Arno is going against the instincts of those above him. Our only chance lies in how rattled they are up there."

Benjamin's elation fizzled away. He might as well admit how he actually felt, even if it was to Kingsley. He could hardly say this to Channing: "I'm against it, y'know."

Absolutely expressionless: "I suspected as much."

"Yeah?" Somehow Kingsley's razor precision made him use sloppy Americanisms in return. "I . . . don't want her to suffer any more. This thing . . ."

"It won't truly be her."

"But it'll be *like* her so much."

"A copy is not the original."

"If they map her, though, there'll be two of her at once." His confusion welled up in him like bile.

"The Air Force types say they cannot realistically fly it, her, before the, ah, original is . . . gone."

193

"So there'll be no direct comparison."

Kingsley nodded. "If it works at all."

"She's counting on it."

"So are many people now. I surmise from my work over the last two days that it has caught the imagination of both NASA and the military. It even plays well internationally."

"How come?" He had been so wrapped up with her that he had not even thought about this angle.

"It brings the entire matter to human scale."

" 'Human scale'? That's the only way I can see it."

"Of course." Kingsley reached across the coffee table and put a reassuring hand on Benjamin's shoulder, the first time he could remember such a gesture passing between them. "They mean valiant woman astronaut—"

"Daring last dramatic attempt—"

"Heroic expedition into the heart of the monster. That sort of thing."

Pale smiles passed between the two men. They sipped their coffee for a moment in silence, the other Center personnel at nearby tables a thousand miles away.

"If they do it, they will build her into a heroine overnight."

"Crap. Don't want that."

"Your will—or mine, for that matter—has nothing to do with it."

His sense of helplessness rose, a queasy sour lump in his stomach. "She may get near the thing, all right, but what can she do?"

"The President asked me if she could carry nuclear warheads."

"On a Searcher?"

"Quite right, impossible, far too much mass."

"So what use will she be?" Benjamin had heard very little of the technical plans. She had been resting nearly all the time and he had liked staying home almost like the old days, the two of them alone on a long weekend.

"Reconnaissance, mostly."

"What will be her link to us?"

"A broad bandwidth, secure line, with backup satellites launched to keep her in sight."

"Well, at least she'll get a spectacular ride."

"Ah, you're not expecting this simulation of her to . . ."

"Survive? No, don't want to think about that."

Kingsley sat back and from the shift in his tone Benjamin knew that their moment of closeness was over. "An experiment that gives you a clear answer is not a failure. It can surprise, however, and the best do just that. The true trick in science is to know what question your experiment is truly asking."

This was another set piece, obviously to prop up a shield between the two men, and Benjamin resented it. "Come on, this is a war, not an experiment."

Kingsley would not come out from behind his fresh new barrier. "We must still think like scientists. Knowledge is our only way out of this predicament."

"Excuse me, but I'm not all that damn worried about the problems of politicians right now."

"Still, realize that they aren't scientists. They fear failure, by which they mean unpredictability."

"They're sending her in for reconn and she'll die in there. Only she'll already be dead for me, got it?" He realized that he was shouting, coffee spilled in his lap, and had gotten to his feet somehow, and people were staring.

Channing lay back on their couch with a strange smile. "*Sic transit gloria mundi*, wasn't that what Kingsley said? 'Thus passeth away the glory of the world.'—and I'm not even named Gloria."

Benjamin had finally told her his feelings, blurting them out within ten minutes of arriving home. His talk with Kingsley had given him the courage to say it all. Had that been Kingsley's real motive? Not impossible. "So I'm not going back to the Center. I'll stay here with you, right through to . . ."

"The finish," she finished for him softly. "I know, it's been an immense strain on you. Come here."

Some snuggling, he seeming to need it more than she, and then Channing was off again, manic. On the couch and floor were documents, all homework to prepare her for "My new life as digits," she remarked with an odd, sunny expression. She had been studying between naps and injections from the attending nurse, a hovering presence.

"Got you a little something, though," she said, fumbling among some papers.

"You went out?"

"I had Harriet drive me."

"Uh, she's . . ." He was having trouble keeping track, with events piling up. Perhaps some part of him did not want to face even the bare fact that she now needed a home aide.

"My nurse, the new one. I was getting cabin fever. Imagine what I'll be like when I'm in a little box, eh?"

She presented him with "a parting gift"—an hourglass.

"I . . . don't . . ."

"*Sic transit.* Time passes."

"It looks like the magnetic funnels of the Eater."

"That, too. Call it a visual pun."

"I think . . ."

She kissed him slowly, breathing in long drawn sighs, as though laboring. "Don't think. The whole rest of my god-damned existence, I'm going to be nothing but a thinking thing."

They went back into their bedroom then, hearts thudding.

"A little personal therapy, Harriet," Channing called.

He managed to trip over their rattan furniture on the way, carrying her—*so frightening, her lightness*—and then it was enveloping, the air liquid and their skins like the silent slide of silk.

5 Dying was more interesting than she had feared.

You got mail about it, even. The public only knew that she had volunteered to be uploaded, nothing about the true mission. They presumed that, like the others already transmitted by microwave as 0's and 1's, she would shortly become a digital commodity for the Eater to relish.

Even such momentary renown combusted with her faded astronaut glory to make her a momentary celeb. Being slightly world famous and sheltered by armed guards up and down the street gave dying a certain, well, zest. The postman still delivered, apocalypse coming or not, and so she got bags of letters.

It was impossible to take this unasked correspondence at face value. These people were probably doomed, too, if the Eater grew irritated, and they knew it. Still . . .

To their credit, men did not decorate their notes with scented, colored stationery, dotting *i*'s with circles or even hearts. With big ridiculous loops to their *p*'s and *q*'s, women's letters were a topographical pain, even when writing premature condolence notes with a smiley face at the end. *We shall pray for you*, many of them concluded.

Prayers were fine, but as she had weakened she had become an aficionado of bed linen. Piqué, matelassé, Porthault, Egyptian cotton *vs.* English linen, dotted Swiss, chenille. Gourmet sleeping, though they couldn't contend with the sheer contentment of snuggling against Benjamin. But when she rested through the day, lying alone in luxury, the 280-threads-per-inch seemed to *matter*.

Harriet reluctantly took her out, usually in the mornings when she was most energetic. Benjamin was at home as much as possible, but shooing him off to the Center did them both good. The U Agency had added to Dr. Mendenham a corps of specialists and the "sustaining terminal" class of drugs, introduced first in the 2010s, had been doing a stunning job of keeping her aloft, despite the steady growth of tumors and other blights distributed throughout her body. They hurt some, and then a lot. In astronaut training, they had taught her to displace herself from the pain and still function, a talent that came in handy. She got fond of morphine in the bad times, and liked Mozart particularly that way. *Go, Wolfgang!*

On a sunny Tuesday, she voyaged out with Harriet, listening to a wrist-radio talk show that hashed over the visibility of the Eater. She had seen it the night before, a pinprick of blue light from the decelerating jet, pointed straight at Earth. Predictably, this excited everyone, as though until they could see it with their own eyes the whole thing was a mere theory.

A brilliant, tropical day, enough to persuade her that the Problem of Evil was just a rumor. It was so windy she saw a dog sticking its head out of a parked car. In the market, at a display of I LOVE YOU ONLY Valentine cards, she bought one to leave behind for Benjamin, especially since there was the added inducement, NOW AVAILABLE IN MULTIPACKS! She did not realize that she was laughing so hard until it turned to sobbing and Harriet led her out.

On a lark, she went to one of the new casinos on the island, Harriet in tow. Nobody recognized the world-famous astronaut hero lady. While playing craps and blackjack, she noticed that most of the steady players were weirdly superstitious. One at the blackjack table always said, "Thin to win, deep to weep," when he cut the cards, always leaving only a thin stack at the top, apparently believing this affected the game. Others wouldn't cut the cards, folding arms and pronouncing profoundly, "I won't cut my own throat." Others would not accept higher denominations of chips, even though they were winning. Some got attached to lucky chips when they played and would snatch the sacred chip back from the dealer or croupier if it was lost. Others turned over their chips so the Gambling Gods could not read their denominations and see that they were getting too lucky. She even saw two who would get up and walk around their chairs every time the dice changed hands, as another way to confuse fate.

Yet was this any worse than the other symptoms she saw? The Gambling Gods didn't exist, but neither did any others she knew. Still, only the day before she had looked up Psalm 90:

> *For when thou art angry all our days are gone;*
> *we bring our years to an end, as if it were a tale that*
> *is told.*
> *So teach us to number our days.*

T.S. Eliot had been right: the spirit killeth, but the letter giveth life. Who would have thought that her wobbly Episcopalian would come back, like a native tongue somehow forgotten?

Strange indeed, considering that all her adult life she had felt that to exist implied a duty to burn with a hard, gemlike flame, living as a passionate vehicle of life's eternal transience. To prevail without God or any metaphysical hydraulics, without foundations in an accidental prison sentence handed down to us by a deity who did not exist.

She was halfway tempted to bring such matters up to the Eater itself. Now that Arno had cleared the way for her, she could do anything she wanted with the Semiotics Group data flow. The Eater was now within a light-minute of turnaround time, and as quick as ever. Working with the team that monitored and conversed with it around the clock, she noted oddities.

When it said "Greetings" or "Goodbye" or used "please," some witnesses seemed to feel this meant it was becoming friendlier. Using their language necessarily made it seem more human, but surely it was clever enough to recognize social lubricant words and use them as a matter of course. Any natural language would have both redundancy and deliberate padding, for living creatures were not perfect conduits of meaning. Superficial linguistic gesture meant little. Certainly reading into them the personality that resided in magnetic strands was a huge error, like trying to eff the ineffable.

The Eater was being as pleasant as it could be, while letting its demand stand. This schizophrenic feature drove many in the Semiotics Group to distraction, but she was untroubled. It was alien, and fitted itself into human categories only roughly.

That saturated even the Eater's apparently casual conversation with implied meaning. In one exchange with a physicist, it had pointed out that planetary life labored under weighty restrictions—and here the pun was clearly intended. Gravity makes it hard for life-forms to grow large, defeating economies of scale. Muscle and bone protect delicate neurological circuits, and these take up most of any body. Muscle burns energy and oxygen, bone hampers movement even as it protects brains. Ideally the largest creatures should be the smartest, but in fact these had been dinosaurs and whales and other relatively unbright forms. Being forced to move at the bottom of a gravity well, the Eater meditated, meant that planetary life, the gravitationally challenged, could never match space-born forms. The immense interlocking neurological networks of the Eater, spun of sheer gossamer magnetic fields and filmy plasma, had far higher information content than even the human brain, on a pound-for-pound basis. A diffuse, ionized medium was

THE OBVIOUS BEST SITE FOR LIFE IN THE LONG RUN

as the Eater put it.

A further limitation, it said, came from the paltry energy budget of planets. Earth's life ran on the sunlight falling through its air, plus a small volcanic contribution, and a bit from the ebbing decay of radioactive materials. The Eater lived on a huge energy budget, whenever it could harvest an iceteroid. Though to human eyes their world's bounty was prodigious, in energy terms it was tiny—a thousand watts per square meter exposed to the sun. The Eater enjoyed a billion times this bounty, coursing through its mesh of trapping fields and vigorous particles.

The bounty of semiotic theory was a gusher of speculation. She skimmed through learned-sounding papers based on the wildest of ideas.

> . . . *transparently it thinks of itself as a kind of traveling Ego, when actually its focus upon instant gratification of its needs, be they icestroids or personality copies, makes it much more an unrestrained Id. Clearly what it lacks is a Superego* . . .
>
> . . . *with proper guarantees that they would not be mistreated, a more socially responsible Eater could garner many more volunteers for uploading* . . .
>
> . . . *it is fitting to ask: Who is most interested in collecting mayflies?—that is, short-lived life. Clearly, amateur collectors and entomologists. Eater is a bit of both. Losing half a million mayflies to obtain a good specimen is nothing to a collector seeking a perfect sample of a rare breed. Anything we can do to make ourselves appear ordinary lessens its desire to collect us. Refusing to kill ourselves to furnish copies for it may well signal stupidity to Eater, and thus make us uninteresting. Caving in immediately might signal our "commonness," since apparently most societies have done so; it has collected many. Paradoxically, complying would reduce our value to a collector. We should entertain the notion that our response has been mixed. Some wish to submit, others to fight. This*

rather contradictory response may make us an inter-esting and valuable item to add to the collection . . .

*   . . . while it must "eat," it dislikes being called Eater. No matter how it denies consciously this con-nection with the needs of lower life-forms, this explains why it is fascinated with the unconscious structures in human minds—and thus desires our whole minds, not just its products, works of art, etc. . . .*

All these were projections of human categories on to the Eater. None seemed to deal with her suspicion that many so-cieties had attacked it with weapons as advanced as Earth's. It would have evolved a way to survive even the most fierce of assaults. Kingsley had guessed that the most they could expect was to drive it away.

Of even that she was more and more unsure. Still, she read through the tangle of speculations. She put herself through this because she was venturing into its territory. Her NASA years had taught a firm lesson: *do your homework.*

But the eerie tang of the thing, that was the most basic lesson, and the hardest to truly learn.

She fled from these sessions back to the comforts of home.

She barely had time to suffer Harriet's injections when a neighbor knocked: there was a party, and they would like to have her and Benjamin come, though of course they knew how busy . . .

It was delightful. Like most hard-driving professionals, she and Benjamin had only a distant connection to their town. Their province was the global world, firmly secured by electronic media and airline tickets.

But outside their lives, the rhythms of the tropical island culture went on. Natives called the mainlanders *haole* but welcomed them. The Polynesian blended here with Asian. She liked the rituals of this O Bon Odori, a Japanese dance festival that let her dress up in a blue and white cotton ukata, feast on juicy BBQ squid, gingery pancakes and luscious mango shave ice, fried noodles, and sweetened bean confections. That evening beloved ghosts were supposed to return from the spirit world and briefly visit, as they had been doing for the 1,400-year tradition of the festival. The ghosts got tiny dishes set out for them: roasted eggplant, squash and potatoes cooked in sesame oil. At dusk families gathered at graveyards to burn incense and escort the ghost-souls with flickering paper lanterns. Dried hempseed burned in bowls to guide them to the proper homes, where families could talk to the ghosts and be sure of being heard. At the end of the season, the ghosts got farewell rice dumplings and hypnotic taiko drums.

No one mentioned the Eater, though some children tried to make out its blue-white glimmer in the sky. Their neighbors kept a sympathetic blanket of nonchalance wrapped around the evening, making small talk.

She and Benjamin walked home together over the bumpy tar roads. She inhaled the aromatic air and wondered what it would be like to live as digital abstraction, free of body.

> *Yea, though I walk through the valley of the shadow*
> *of death,*
> *I will fear no evil;*
> *for thou art with me;*
> *thy rod and thy staff, they comfort me.*

It took everything she had, but they made love in the close, moist night air and it gave her something she could not name.

6 He tried to smile with assurance, but his face felt as if it would crack like hard plaster.

The President was visiting, along with assorted members of the self-luminous set, U.N. and allies. Show of confidence. All hands onboard. Face the approaching crisis with a firm hand.

None of this was for the Center staff, of course. The media were the whole point. But there had to be something for the President and entourage to actually do, so Arno and Martinez took him on a tour. Plenty of shots of his craggy visage gazing sternly at the latest maps of the Eater interior. Nodding, taking it all in with a concerned yet confident scowl.

After the well-lighted photo ops, a reception. Maximum attention to Channing, now in a wheelchair to underline the precarious state of her health. She did need it. Benjamin stayed beside her with the nurse and she managed to chatter amiably with the President. Only then did Benjamin have to step forward and shake the presidential hand. Offered with the legendary charm, it was firm. Benjamin joined in the photos with Channing, all smiles but not too joyous, as this *was* a crisis.

Then the two of them, plus Kingsley and Arno, sat at the presidential table for a ritual snack. Talk flowed, guided by the President and the Secretary of the United Nations.

Kingsley glided gracefully through all this, and from him Benjamin learned an important lesson.

"Sharp, smart people—we're all that," Kingsley said to him and Channing. "And at a do like this, we meet others no less sharp, but also blessed with charm and an easy social facility, a talent that cannot be learned or imitated."

Channing watched the President, whose attention illuminated the other half of their circular table, and nodded. "The spotlight of his gaze."

Short sentences were all she could manage now, but these words brightened Kingsley. "Yes!—precisely. That charisma conveys to its target a sense that you are indeed special, that the charmer and the charmed form tightly orbiting worlds."

Benjamin saw the point now. "So you get caught up."

Kingsley seemed unafraid of dissecting a performance going on only a few feet away. Benjamin saw why: nobody was paying the slightest attention to them.

Kingsley said, "Just so. Basking in this warm glow, imagine that you notice a mediocrity at the edge of your special binary, someone not worth bothering with. But the charmer turns and includes the mediocrity"—he did a perfect mid-American accent—"*Hi, gladtaseeya.*" Channing laughed and Kingsley beamed. "So then this inferior's eyes brighten as pleasant small talk and personal tales pass among you, now a party of three. Now, what is passing through your mind?"

This he addressed to Channing, who came back quickly with, "You listen with a little smile." A cough. "Hiding your secret."

"Exactly!" Kingsley beamed.

"Because," she went on, "the poor old mediocrity. Does not *know*. That this is just social fluff. That the primary relationship here. Is between you. And the charming leader."

"As usual," Kingsley said happily, "quite observant. 'Poor mediocrity,' you think! But even laughter and good spirits cannot conceal the dreadful moment when you catch a glance from the mediocrity—"

"And see that he is thinking. Exactly the same thing. About you," Channing finished.

Benjamin laughed, caught up in the sheer headlong joy of it. "And that frozen instant is a glimpse into the social abyss."

Kingsley grinned. "Absolutely. The truly genius social creatures, they dwell on levels far above us."

Then he saw why the moment was so wonderful. This was the way the three of them had been back at Cambridge, in the years when the world had seemed utterly open, brim-full with promise. And together they had captured it together again, for a glancing moment.

With the media whisked out of sight, the presidential party got down to business.

Then when the President spoke, it was less to convey information than to make others react according to his plan. Benjamin watched through the several hours of discussions, trying to see how the master communicators achieved this effect.

Flattery, subtle bribery, psychology, even flat-out threat—all these came into play, some as difficult to catch as a momentary reflection on an ocean wave. As long as their plan kept working, means did not matter. Usually arguments couched logically but carrying a deep emotional appeal worked best with the U.N. representatives. This was a political culture in which short-term interests always dominated long-term concerns in the minds of virtually everyone, but in this crisis they were out of their depth, facing a hard fact.

The Eater would not negotiate; it was not remotely political, resembling more the weather than a person. This had barely penetrated to the political elite, Benjamin saw, as various men reported on attempts to cajole, wheedle or threaten the Eater, all total failures. They were unused to the Eater's pattern of simply ignoring the high and powerful. Instead, it preferred to pursue discussions with members of the Semiotic Group, on topics cultural and biological. The President could not find a way to soften this, finally used his standard approach of following the bald truth with a side of sentiment.

A specialist enlisted by the White House displayed on a large screen a "typical passage" from the Eater, in response to an attempt to negotiate on the issue of uploading people.

> I HAVE NEED OF THESE MINDS. ONLY BY CLOSE
> RELATION TO THEM CAN I FURTHER STUDY YOU, AND IN
> MY SCRUTINY YOU SHALL FIND YOUR ULTIMATE
> RESIDENCE UPON THE GALACTIC STAGE. YOUR MINDS'
> IMPRESSIVE TALENTS AROSE IN PART AS COURTSHIP
> TOOLS, I CAN SEE ALREADY. YOU EVOLVED THEM TO
> ATTRACT AND ENTERTAIN SEXUAL PARTNERS FOR THE
> LONG PERIODS NEEDED TO PRODUCE AND REAR YOUR
> CHILDREN. YOUR OWN RESEARCH SHOWS THAT THE
> MOST DESIRED TRAITS BOTH SEXES HAVE IN A MATE
> ARE KINDNESS AND INTELLIGENCE. YOUR STANDARD
> ARGUMENT IS THAT WOMEN PREFER POWER AND
> MONEY, OR THE SIGNS OF THE ABILITY TO GET THOSE.
> MEN ARE DRAWN TO SMOOTH SKIN, YOUTH, A
> PROPORTION OF WAIST TO HIP. ALL TRUE—BUT NOT
> PRIMARY. KINDNESS AND INTELLIGENCE ARE MORE
> ABSTRACT QUALITIES, BOTH INFERRED FROM SPEECH.
> THESE I CAN CONTEMPLATE ONLY BY PROLONGED
> EXPOSURE.

Exasperated, the specialist said, "Now, how can we deal with a thing that answers clear, direct questions like this?"

"Gingerly, I should think," Kingsley whispered to Benjamin and Channing. They were sitting to the side, near the rear of the big new auditorium, behind a phalanx of military and policy people.

The unwieldy group then broke into subsections, each in a different room. They finally got to meet with the Action Team—there seemed to be a new term for every feature of the problem now—devoted to Channing's mission.

A group Benjamin had not even heard of gave a report on what the intelligence specialists thought was going on in the Eater's innermost regions. A Defense Department satellite of advanced design had made a map, using X-ray emission. From that, NASA had already sent a Searcher hurtling directly at the Eater's core. Piecing together the X-ray pictures and the Searcher's views as it flew in, they produced a processed picture:

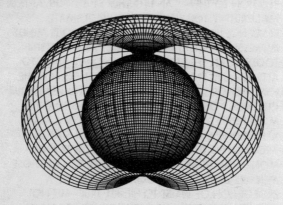

"We see here a cutaway view," a prominent black hole theorist explained. She was a slender, sharp-faced woman with a ready smile, in her element, playing before the most powerful crowd in the world. "The outer surface is the last point at which an object can orbit the hole. The surface is only about ten meters across."

Benjamin asked, "The Searcher tried to orbit it?"

" 'Tried' is the word," the affable woman said. "It failed. Instead, it flew closer in—the ergosphere."

Benjamin persisted. "It has a bulge?"

"Yes, and we're seeing it here from about twenty-five degrees above the equator. That's why the inner sphere—the hole itself—looks a little distorted."

He barely remembered the term, ergosphere, and did not

want to show any ignorance. "The hole is rotating rapidly—that is our principal finding. That is apparently how it manages the enormous magnetic arches and funnels outside. The rotation couples with the accretion disk in a kind of enormous motor."

The discussion picked up then and Benjamin could barely follow. The bulge of the outer surface arose from the swirl of space that a black hole's rotation created. Because that swirl was outside the inner sphere, the hole stored rotational energy in the region between the two surfaces. Thus, *erg* from the Latin for energy.

"What happened to the Searcher?" Benjamin asked, feeling awash in the discussion.

"It was one of the miniaturized models, high velocity, ion propulsion. Small enough to survive the heating from the accretion disk. We flew it in at a thirty-degree angle, a steep dive."

A NASA official added proudly, "Miniaturized small enough to get into the hole's vicinity without being torn apart by tidal forces, either."

"It flew into the ergosphere," the woman said, "on automatic program, of course. It sent one last gasp of data, which gave us this figure. We never heard from it again."

"The hole swallowed it," a man from Caltech said authoritatively.

"We don't know that," the woman countered.

"The hole would *have* to grab it," the man answered testily.

"It's a completely warped space-time," the woman said. "There are other paths available. The Searcher could escape through the outer boundary of the ergosphere—if it had enough energy."

"I calculate that it did not," the Caltech fellow said.

"So do I, but there are intermediate fates."

"Such as?"

"The Searcher could exit the ergosphere along a path that pops out into another space-time, or another time in our own space."

"Like a time machine?" the man asked incredulously.

"A theoretical possibility, yes," the woman said.

"Point is, it's gone," Channing whispered.

The audience overheard this and looked silently at her. She was going into this place, Benjamin read in their eyes, and they half-envied her. She sensed this and said in a croak, "The physics is great, sure. But this isn't a natural black hole. It's been built up . . . by an intelligence."

"We must not think of it as being the kind of structure we think of as intelligence at all," a noted evolutionary biologist remarked. "It is not of a species. It is unique, a construction."

"A self-construction," a voice added, "maybe more like a self-programming computer. Gotta be a way to think about it from a cybernetic angle—"

Kingsley's incisive voice broke in. "We fondly imagine that evolution drives toward higher intelligence. But eagles would think evolution favored flight, elephants would naturally prefer the importance of great strength, sharks would feel that swimming was the ultimate desirable trait, and eminent Victorians would be quite convinced that evolution preferred Victorians."

Only Channing found this amusing.

7 She had learned from the morning paper that when Halley's Comet filled the skies in 1910, word spread that the Earth would pass through the gases of the tail. There was worldwide panic, directives from the Pope, quite a few suicides.

She quickly calculated over coffee that the entire tail, compressed to a solid, might have fit into a briefcase. Ignorance could be fatal.

Benjamin had to go to a seminar by a specialist in "extreme case fear responses," which someone high up at the U Agency thought would be helpful in the times ahead. He wasn't inclined to go, but Channing shooed him out of the house before her three-car-plus-ambulance escort arrived. Still, she was so fretful on the drive to the clinic that the driver finally leaned back to where she lay and said very patiently, "Please don't drive when you're not driving."

She had to go through the preps for her "reading," as the diffident specialists put it, which meant another day of tedium. Still, while the preps took hold, she had herself wheeled into a room where she could watch the show on a big screen. Just for laughs, she said, and they dared not contradict her. This was a special site just for her, plus a few other people who were very ill and had volunteered to be uploaded. Arno had certainly cleared her way; the screen for her to view was his latest indulgence.

The speaker was quick, efficient, and despite expectations, interesting. The best way to confront fear in a group was to make the group diverse, she said. Assemblies that were all men or all women fared badly when confronted with danger or merely the unknown. Less obvious, but supported by research, was a finding that mixing age groups was good. One exerted more self-control in front of strangers and dissimilar people.

The bad news was that preexisting groups did not respond well to fear. Even tests on championship athletic teams showed that they reacted badly to simple dramas like getting stuck in an elevator. Luckily, being "high phobic-tolerant" correlated with being in good physical condition, and most astronomers met at least the minimum standards there. Living in Hawaii had made them more outdoorsy than the usual run of the profession, and astronomers as a whole were more athletic than the norm. But altogether, the Center could expect some fairly large levels of panic in the days to come.

"How come?" she wondered aloud.

Nobody watching the screen answered, but her "psych escort" put in helpfully, "They're planning for it to maybe attack some way."

"Huh? Why?" Being at the supposedly center of events and yet quite out of it was not fun.

The escort was sweet but slow, it seemed. "The Eater . . . it might get angry."

"Anger isn't a category we can be sure it even possesses."

"Well, the governments, they've agreed to not let it have all those people."

"It wants the complete list?"

"Every one."

"Has it made threats?"

"It doesn't say anything about that."

"Coy bastard, huh?"

"The news, it says the Eater is giving us the silent treatment."

"Actually, it's gabby. You just have to ask the right question."

On her palm computer, she punched up the conversation she had from yesterday, in reply to some demand by the U.N. It was perfectly indirect:

> YOUR DISCOURSE EXPLAINS YOUR PROPENSITY FOR
> GOSSIP AS A GROOMING SUBSTITUTE. MY-SELF'S
> ANALYSIS OF YOUR DRAMAS SHOWS YOUR FINEST
> ARTISTS DEVOTING TWO-THIRDS OF YOUR
> CONVERSATION TO IT. LABORERS AND LEARNED ALIKE
> PREFER TO TALK ABOUT PEOPLE, NOT IDEAS OR ISSUES.
> WITHOUT GOSSIP, YOUR SPECIES MIGHT NEVER HAVE
> BOTHERED TO LEARN HOW TO TALK. PHYSICAL
> GROOMING IS STILL MORE SATISFYING TO THE OTHER
> OF YOUR ORDER, THE PRIMATES. THUS THEY DO NOT
> SPEAK. CHAT IS UNLIKE HUNTERS CALLING OUT IN A
> MASTODON HUNT, OR GATHERERS REPORTING WHERE
> THE HERBS ARE, WHICH CLEARLY HAD USES FOR YOU.
> THIS TALK OF OTHERS AND FORMING POWER
> COALITIONS WERE EVEN MORE IMPORTANT. I CAN SEE
> THAT TALK IS MORE EFFICIENT THAN PHYSICALLY
> GROOMING EVERY OTHER MEMBER OF A TRIBE, WHEN
> TRIBES BECOME LARGE. TALK IS EASIER THAN PETTING,
> FOR YOU CAN DO IT TO SEVERAL AT ONCE, WHILE YOU
> ARE PERFORMING OTHER TASKS. THIS SUGGESTS A
> USEFUL RESEARCH PROJECT MIGHT AIM TO MEASURE
> SEROTONIN PRODUCTION DURING GOSSIPING TO
> VERIFY THIS VIEW. I COMMEND IT TO YOUR SCIENTISTS.

So it was advancing theories about humans already. Even suggesting research! Who could have guessed that their first alien contact would be so abstract?

With more experience of intelligence throughout the galaxy, it could generalize in ways impossible to visualize. What more could it tell us about ourselves? She felt a chill then, the awe and allure of the utterly strange.

Then she was into the treatment, that flat medicinal smell, the attendants pushing her down the corridors, eyes watching her—the famous astronaut heroine!—from doorways. Into the cool ceramic air of the special clinic, which had been set up on a hillside with the now-routine incredible speed.

Then the teams around her very attentively got down to the grungy details of how to extract the information in her head. In principle, the experts had explained, they could do this without knowing in detail how the brain worked. Instead, they used the principles of copying software to recognize neurons and then replace all the functions of each neuron with a computer simulation.

Neurons held her identity, encoded in myriad connections. It was not enough to know the location and type of neuron, though. They also had to see how each one responded and sent electrical signals, how it was affected by its chemical environment—a swamp of detail. Impossible without the rooms of computers she had glimpsed on the way in.

All for little ol' me. Pleasant, to be the center of attention on your deathbed. Research animal plus world-class news object. They informed her early on, days ago, that she thought differently when her adrenal glands had been squirting into her bloodstream. *I've known that all my life. Goes with being temperamental.*

She lay still as a buzzing bank of magnetic readers sat atop her skull, like a mechanical hairdo. These nests of quantum detectors registered her thoughts while she watched videos of sunsets, tiger attacks, pictures of Benjamin and her mother, a steak, flowers, storms, even porno—they apologized in advance for that, but it was actually good, the sly devils. Then smells, sounds, touches. She did arithmetic on demand, listened to music, to railroad trains and children laughing. Sheet sensors covering the crown of her brain built a three-dimensional map of each thin layer of her brain cells. Added to a general map of human neural structure, teams of surgeons wrote programs to model the myriad idiosyncratic ways she thought.

This working model then got sharpened. The surgeons compared its output signals to those she emitted when they showed the same pictures, flashed lights, fed her, played music.

Like getting a dress tailored, she thought, *only this cost millions of bucks per hour.* Flash by neuronal flash, the computer model came to echo her. *But an echo isn't the song.*

"It's not you," Kingsley agreed when he came to visit. They gave her breaks to keep her neural tone tip-top, and let him in to recalibrate her sense of being human, she supposed. "Just a simulation."

"It's all there'll be of me, pretty soon."

He gazed at her soulfully, wordlessly. "If it's any consolation, I heard from Arno how they're doing this trick in the dictatorships."

"Pretty rough? Make you watch old black-and-white movies?"

"I think I'd settle for *Citizen Kane* happily enough. But no, they haven't these magnetic sheet recorders. To reach the deeper layers, the surgeon's easiest path is simply to shave away your brain."

"So . . . their brains, to be fully read, must die?"

"One ends up with an excavated skull. Luckily, the brain has no pain perceptors down there in its spaghetti snarls of nerves."

"Gee, Dr. Science, that's spiffy."

"Not a voyage for the squeamish, no."

"And they don't even want to go, either." She gazed up into the hard fluorescent glow as if an answer lay there. "Makes this seem easy."

He held her hand for a while and they did not speak. She slowly registered that he was crying, and felt bad about that, and then just let it go. That was getting to be automatic: releasing the moment, permitting the passing parade to wash over her like the warm waves of the Pacific. With a sudden pang, she realized that she would probably never feel that salty caress again, and then she was crying, too.

Kingsley said quietly, "I've always loved you."

She had dreaded this moment and was tempted to let it drift by. But no, he deserved better than that.

Before she could bring herself to speak, he added, "I simply did not know until recently just how much."

After what seemed like a long time, she mustered some self-respect and made her voice behave. In a faint rasp she said, "I have always loved you. In my way. But this last year has taught me that the man I truly felt the real thing for was Benjamin. Always him."

He nodded. A rueful smile played upon his lips. They looked at each other with an emotion she felt powerfully but could not hope to tell him about.

A long silence tiptoed by. Gratefully, she drifted.

Kingsley worked the conversation around to ground they could both stand on. He was good at doing that, she realized; she had not even noticed the transition. Small talk, reminiscences . . . Then: "Obviously," he said, "the material self will be gone. Your represented self will remain, in silicon."

"Yeah, it says so, right here in the contract."

"Quite right. This is experimental."

"Always happy to be at the cutting edge. When do they do that?"

"Cut? Not at all, I gather."

"I wonder. After I'm dead, wouldn't they recover more if they could use invasive surgery?"

"À la the dictators?"

"I'm willing to give this the best effort."

"Heroic, but I think unnecessary."

"I just want the best copy, is all." To her mind, this wasn't remotely valorous. In her pantheon, science had few heroes. Most good science came from bright minds at play, like Benjamin and Kingsley. Able to turn an elegant insight, to find beguiling tricks in arcane matters—pretty, amusing, a frolic. Play, even intellectual play, was fun, good in its own right.

"You are going to fly into the mouth of the monster. Classic Beowulf-style hero, by my measure."

He was being charming, hardly able to keep his feelings

from flooding out, but she disagreed profoundly. Her heroes stuck it out against hard opposition, drove toward daunting goals, accepting pain and failure and keeping on, anyway. All the way through astronaut training, those had been her ideals. This making a Xerox of herself was a last gesture, not bravery. Maybe just foolishness.

"No, *I* won't. My copy will." He sat gazing down at his hands and she wondered how to get him out of his funk. Be bright, cheery. Men were so grateful for that. "Continuity, that's really it, right?"

"How so?" Head up, plainly happier to be off on abstractions.

"That's the essence of it, of the identity problem. We do it all the time, really. When we sleep, the unconscious remains active, so we get continuity at a broad level."

"Ah. Your point is that no one wakes up and thinks they are a new person."

"Yeah, only lately, I feel a thousand years old."

"Patients brain-cooled until their brain waves lapse can later revive with their sense of self intact." His brow furrowed, then relaxed. "I see—how will we know it's truly 'you,' eh?"

"I suppose you could just log on to the computer aboard the *Searcher*, my ship, and read me out."

"But I don't know you like that. I know you—love you— this ordinary old, human way."

"Inside I'm a mess, lemme tell you."

"You look orderly and understandable from a distance."

"And only that way. Close up, inside, I'm ugly."

"All of us live inside, always close up. Other people look methodical and tidy only because they're at long range."

"That's comforting."

He pressed her hand into his. "I'll know you."

"How?"

"You'll think of something, m'love." He grinned, but there was no elation behind it. "I know you."

8 A few more days had crept by, and now that they were at the nexus of it all, he felt only a yawning vacancy.

"This must be the strangest thing anyone has ever done," Benjamin said to her. The specialists' army had withdrawn, leaving them in an enclosed space, almost comforting in its intimacy. They were surrounded by advanced magnetic reading gear and diagnostics.

She smiled. "Yeah, and out of love, at that."

"To . . . leave me something?"

"That's part of it, for me. But love is a big, cheesy word, able to cover a lot of things."

Channing was fully uploaded now. The last few hours had been pretty painful for her and she had stood up well, sweat popping out on her brow. He had wiped it away carefully. She had kept waving away even the light painkillers they had offered. "Don't wanna cloud the picture," she had kept repeating earlier. As though she were an artist at work on her last oil painting.

The offhand weirdness of the scene kept throwing him. They had come to him with a proposal about the use of her brain afterward. He had listened and gone through confusion to anger to swirling doubt and then he had made them go away. Their idea was to slice her dead brain layer by layer, so that scanning machines could read the deep detail digitally, getting better resolution to sharpen the simulation.

This had sent a cold horror running through him. They had put it as nicely as they could, but still it meant slowly planing away her brain. In the end, her entire cranium would be excavated, leaving half a skull. He could not bear the picture.

She struggled up out of her fog and managed a wrecked smile. "You have to die to be resurrected."

"I'll . . ." The words stuck in his throat.

"You'll see me again." She gave him a blissful look. "Goodbye, lover."

It was the last thing she said.

After a night of no sleep and a lot of sour drinking with Kingsley, he met with the specialists again. They showed him the long black box housing Channing's uploaded mind. "Reduced to a featureless . . ." he began, but could not finish the sentence.

"We'll be processing, compiling, and organizing," a woman in a smart executive suit said.

"Fine."

"In a few days—"

"Fine. Just shut up."

He understood all the parts of the arguments. Magnetic induction loops, tiny and superconducting, could map individual neurons. Laying bare the intricacies of the visual cortex, or evolution's kludgy tangle in the limbic system, had already unleashed new definitions of Genus Homo. Still, nobody considered Homo Digital to be an equal manifestation. Parts were not the whole.

They played a voicebox rendering, a voice repeating, sounding exactly like her. He saw them looking hopefully at him and he didn't give a damn about their marvelous trick. Numbly he pulled from his coat pocket the hourglass she had given him. He set it atop the box—*her, now*—and watched until its sand had run down.

He wondered what it might mean to upend it, to start the cycle again. He struggled with the thought.

No.

The decision came as a release.

*   *   *

It was a slow day for the Neptune Society, so theirs was the sole party when he went out with a few friends from the Center. The captain wondered if he wanted the champagne before or after. After, he said. There were little printed cards set out next to the champagne with some doggerel titled LET ME GO inside and the data: ENTERED INTO LIFE OCTOBER 15, 1978, and ENTERED INTO REST, but he could not read the date through some blurring that had gotten into his eyes.

He gazed up into a sullen cloud cover, a pearly gray plane halfway up Mauna Kea. This pathetic fallacy still quite accurately mirrored his curiously displaced mood. The sea was flat and glassy and he said little on the way out. They gathered at the bow and the captain gave him the urn, blue with odd markings. Not his to keep, as if he would want to. Off came the lid and inside were gritty gray ashes, the color of the sky. He poured the powdery stream and bits of bone into dark blue water. Some of it spread on the surface, some blowing away on a mild wind, but most of it plunged deeply, an inverse plume that seemed like transposed smoke rising to the depths. He had not expected that. His intellect, spinning endlessly in its own high vacuum, told him immediately that it must be the heavier parts sinking, but that did not explain why a bubble burst in his chest and his throat closed and the world seemed to whirl away for a long moment, suspending him over an aching void.

Someone murmured something of farewell and he could not echo it, getting only partway through some words before his voice became a whistle through a crack in the world. He had wanted to say simply *goodbye*, but it came out *why?* and he did not know why at all. Then the captain pressed a bunch of flowers into his hand and he tossed them after the ashes. The boat slowly circled the floating flowers and he could not take his eyes off them and that was all there was.

*   *   *

The next day on the big screen he watched the black box being inserted into a Searcher craft.

Some commentator spoke with grave excitement. Arno made a little speech. It launched and he felt a pang at the brave plume of rocket exhaust. Cheering. At least nobody pounded him on the back.

What had she said in that last hour? First, a pained *I can't go on like this.*

Before he could speak, she had provided her own jibe. *That's what you think.*

PART SIX
ULTIMATA

1 Like bad breath, Kingsley had often noted, ideology was something noticed only in others.

Even at this supreme crisis, nattering concerns of infinitesimal weight furrowed the brows of supposedly wise leaders. Here at power's proud pinnacle, the politician's aversion to risk reared above all else.

"Dr. Dart," the President said, "how can we be *sure* this will work? I have a grave responsibility here, ordering the use of nuclear warheads."

"I should think, sir, that nothing is certain here."

"But using these weapons so near Earth, I . . . well . . ." The President let his voice trail off into the air-conditioned, enameled silence, as if to do so allowed someone to come in with a quick solution to his grave dilemma.

Sorry, not getting off so easily this go. Kingsley smiled slightly as the occasion seemed to demand. "We hope to short out some of the flowing currents in the vicinity of the black hole. The thing's a giant circuit, really—a 'homopolar generator,' in the physics jargon."

A German general from European Unified Command said sternly, "These are the very best warheads, Mr. President."

"Ah, I'm sure," the worried politician said, his eyes moving from side to side as if seeking a way out. The idea of having all allies present—to spread the responsibility and thus risk, Kingsley supposed—gummed up matters nicely.

225

"Surely, the quality of arms is not the issue," Kingsley said.

The general said smoothly, absolutely right on cue, "We have every assurance of success."

"The Eater comprises an immensely complex balance of forces, utilizing gravitational, magnetic, and kinetic energy stores. It vaguely resembles the region near a pulsar—a rotating, highly magnetized neutron star, that is."

"It's like a star?" the President asked, as if this would simplify his problem. He had seen stars, after all.

"The region around it is. The Russian term for a black hole once was"—a nod at the New Russian Premier—" 'frozen star,' because seen from outside, a collapsing mass appears to stop imploding at a certain point. It hangs up, its infall seeming to halt. The star fades from our view like a reddening Cheshire cat, leaving only its grin—that is, its gravitational attraction."

"No light, just gravity?" the President asked. He was a bright man, but he had lived in a world in which only what other people thought mattered. The physical world was just a bare stage. Techno-goodies and assorted abstract wonders came occasionally in from stage left, altering the action mostly by adding prizes to the unending human competition that was really the point of it all.

"In France, the equivalent phrase *trou noir* has obscene connotations, so 'frozen star' would be better," a woman from the State Department added unhelpfully.

The President was a practiced ignorer; while nodding, he did not take his eyes from Kingsley. "These maps of it, it looks like a kind of interstellar octopus with magnetic arms."

"Not a bad description," Kingsley allowed.

"I can't see how we can kill an octopus without having to chop off its legs," the President said.

"Kill the head," Kingsley said. "The legs are secured by the accretion disk, plus those anchored directly in the black hole itself."

"I see," the President said. "We try to get at this little disk it carries around."

"More that the disk carries the hole, sir. The hole is just a singularity, a gravitational sink, nothing more. The essence of the Eater lies in the magnetic structures erected using the accretion disk as a foundation. If we can shake that foundation, we can damage the great house the Eater has built upon it."

"I understand," the President said in a tone conveying admirably that he did not.

"More precisely, my point is that we cannot solve the pulsar problem, even after half a century of trying. On the face of it, a reliable model of the black hole's inner regions—and their functions—is impossible."

"Then I don't think I can authorize—"

"But you must!" the Secretary of State broke in. "The consequences of not following through—"

"These are *our* weapons and delivery systems," the President shot back, showing why he was President.

"But the world alliance agreed—"

"To leave final judgment, moment by moment, to the nation actually doing the job," the President finished. "I am keeping my options open."

"Not attacking this thing—"

"May yet prove to be the best course," Kingsley felt himself forced to say, before this deteriorated further. The Secretary of State had been rumored to be a highly political appointment from a wheat state, he remembered hearing. Something about shoring up support with a domestic ethnic constituency, which unfortunately appeared to be a major theme of this administration, rather than competence. "Only its response to our counteroffers will tell the tale."

"But it doesn't answer," the Secretary of State said moodily.

"Silences are the most artful phase of diplomacy," Kingsley said, and instantly saw that this was the wrong tack. The Secretary of State's eyes widened a millimeter. Plainly he did not like being reminded, however indirectly, of his lack of background in diplomacy. "A strategy you have employed well in the past, as I recall." *There. That might put a Band-Aid on the wound.*

The Secretary of State opened his mouth and paused, apparently to let this buildup set the stage for a devastating reply, but the President wasn't having any. He smacked an open palm on the mahogany table between them and said, "I have to be convinced that using weapons of mass destruction is necessary. I'm authorizing only readiness. No codes are to be passed down the line, as insurance in case we lose communications."

This was the essential practical point. No one knew what the Eater could do to their web of connections. Yet targeting nuclear-tipped warheads on the beast's interior demanded timing of fractions of a second, for fast-burn missiles closing at very high speed.

"If I take the Secretary's point, he is quite right, there is likely to be no time for deliberation."

Actually, "dithering" would better describe the tortured path whereby they had reached this point. Kingsley had never operated at this level and had always fondly imagined that matters proceeded here with a swift clarity that made lower echelons look like the swamp they so often were, in his experience. It was never pleasant to discover that one was naïve, and in this case it was quietly horrifying.

The Secretary gave Kingsley a quick nod. Fine; with such people the striking of instantaneous alliances was automatic, part of the conversational thrust, encumbering one for no longer than the need demanded. Certainly not grounds to neglect a later opportunity for betrayal, either.

The President mulled this over for some seconds. "That's a powerful argument for striking early, then, before it reaches inside these belts you mentioned."

"The Van Allen belts?" Kingsley had been called upon to deliver minilectures with slides the day previous.

"You said it may have trouble moving so fast, once it's inside the magnet sphere."

The President was a reasonably quick study and Kingsley would not think for an instant of correcting him on jargon. "Yes, sir, the Earth's magnetosphere may deform its outer regions. Of course, it may be able to deal with that. It is experienced."

"Yeah, eight billion years of experience," the President said with sudden, sour energy.

"Your point is that targeting could be better done before it is that close?" Kingsley prompted. There were only eight people in the room and all seemed to suffer from the fatigue he saw everywhere at this command center outside Washington. Only the guards seemed fresh.

"Is that true?" the President asked the room.

The Secretary of State had been making permission-to-speak noises for some time and now answered, "There are grave consequences if we engage it close to the atmosphere."

"Don't want to let it get that close, do we?" the President said. "We've got enough chaos to deal with now."

This summoned forth rather relieved murmurs of agreement. "Got our hands full just dealing with the breakdown in the cities," a domestic adviser said. More murmurs.

"Any ideas what happens if we fail?" the President asked the room.

"It has announced no purpose here beyond acquiring those uploads," the Secretary of State said. This he had gotten from Kingsley's report of the day before.

The President pressed him, something like dread in the overlarge eyes. "What's the downside?"

The Secretary said, "It could retaliate, I suppose."

"Of course," the President said irritably. "Point is, how? Dr. Dart? What's U think?"

"Its range of response is very large. It could inflict considerable damage."

"How about what the media are hot on? Flying through the Earth, eating it, all that?"

"To plunge into our surface would strip the hole of its

magnetic fields, essentially killing the intelligence lodged there."

"Good to hear. It'll keep its distance?"

"It is entirely composed of plasma and gas managed by fields. To collide directly with a solid object would be fatal."

A Science Adviser aide asked, "How come it could eat asteroids?"

"A grazing collision, using its jet to pre-ionize much of the asteroid. It collects the debris using its fields."

"So what can it do to us?" the President insisted.

"I suspect we do not wish to find out," Kingsley said.

"Let's hear from DoD," the President said.

The Defense Secretary was a quiet but inpressive man, exuding a sort of iron conviction Kingsley had seldom seen, for a pointed counterexample, in the English cabinet. But he was obviously starved for material, for his own technical groups had not envisioned many scenarios beyond what the Eater had already displayed. These the President hashed over. Clearly there was danger to all assets in space, national and private alike.

Kingsley kept quiet, a welcome relief. He was there for astrophysical advising, bundled off by Arno, yet to his surprise had been drawn quickly into the very center of decision-making. The intruder's ability to hand them surprises had shortened the lines of communication inside the administration. By the time the specialists could figure out what was going on, their insights were needed at the very top. No time for the usual opinion-pruning, spin-alignment, and image-laundering of conventional policy.

In turmoil, everyone—even the immensely powerful—turned to authority. Kingsley had inherited the robes of the high scientific priesthood, not by a thorough selection process, but through the offhand accidents with which history crowded its great events.

"We have to be ready to launch against it soon," the Secretary of Defense came in.

The President raised tired eyebrows. "And?"

Just the soft pitch the Secretary had wanted to coax forth, altogether too obviously. "We're on top of that, sir. Our people are just about in position."

"This is for the China option?" the President said vaguely, looking at his leatherbound briefing book. "I'm getting split opinions on that one. U is split."

A nervous silence. A few heads looked up alertly, others seemed to duck.

The President blinked. "Oh, sorry, that's another meeting, isn't it? This damned thing's got a lot of parts." He tried a sunny smile beamed around the room. "Don't seem to fit right."

The Defense Secretary said hastily, "That's for the later discussion—"

"And targeting, that's a big technical problem, right?" the President prompted. Heads nodded. "Got people on that? Good, then."

The President looked satisfied, a subtle shift apparently signaling the end of the meeting. The man's time was being sliced thin, a style of governance by crisis the Americans had developed to its frazzling fulfillment. He slipped into mechanically affable, look-confident mode as people left, nodding and smiling broadly as if on the campaign trail.

Blank-faced aides ushered Kingsley out of the central sanctum. This was by far the most heady rubbing up against raw power that he had ever experienced, yet it left him curiously unmoved. No one got to even the relatively minor level of Astronomer Royal without some hunger for power, or at least the look-at-me urge that reached far back into the primate chain of evolution. But the vastly greater authority of this company around him, which he was sure would have left him breathless only months ago, seemed to pale compared with the implications of the bright blue spotlight that now hung in the sky over Earth.

His working group convened again in one of the innumerable conference rooms buried in this mountain retreat. If civilization collapsed, the planners apparently had provided that talking could go on indefinitely.

He paid close attention to the gaggle of theorists who had analyzed the magnetic avenues near the black hole. They had cobbled together ideas from the study of pulsars and quasars and their story fit together reasonably well. Yet the Eater was not a natural system, a crucial distinction. He had not been stretching matters when he had told the President the extent of the uncertainty here.

The working group milled around this central fact and then, given the press of time, ended with a list of targeting options. Luckily, Kingsley had begged off chairmanship of this group, and a bulky French astrophysicist got the job of carrying their conclusions to figures in the Department of Defense and to their parallel figures with the U.N.-based coalition. The political nuances now seemed even more complicated than the physics.

Kingsley got away pretty quickly, dodging the usual pockets of undersecretaries and such who always wanted one's "angle" on the thinking of the inner circle. The familiar Washington circuitry of instant analysis and jockeying for position ran on at high voltage, blissfully unaware that this was an event unparalleled in the experience of even this remarkable—and remarkably lucky—nation.

Some of the policy mannerisms here were identical to those of London. *Always be clever, but never be certain.* That held for a good 90 percent of the time, for example. It was no good in this crisis, since only firm answers had any chance of being heard over the din.

Perhaps, he pondered, that explained his anomalous entry into these elevated circles. He had been willing to make predictions that came true—and not only about basic physics and astronomy. These minds around him were used to dealing with social forces that were, in the large, predictable. But the very concept of the utterly strange was for them the stuff of horror, not thought. Yet science taught its practitioners, at an intuitive level, that the universe was fundamentally of the Other.

Still, he felt a curious claustrophobia in the entire proceedings. It would be good to escape back to Hawaii.

Regrettably, he had agreed to submit to an interview arranged for the press pool. Arno had not worked out well in that regard, proving too brusque for the whipsaw warm-and-reassuring pose useful before the cameras. As well, Kingsley's attempts to fashion Benjamin Knowlton into a serviceable media buffer had failed ignominiously. After losing Channing, the fellow would probably be much worse. It had hit him hard.

So he found himself facing a battery of the modern breed of journalist, faces famous in their own right for being at great events while having no responsibility for them. Their assurance equaled only their ignorance as they shot questions at him and he tried to convey some of the scientific issues without looking impossibly prissy about terminology.

He got through a vague description of what they knew of the hole's interior regions, and then a savant of the image works asked, "Why is an Englishman leading the scientific arm of what is mostly a United States effort?"

Kingsley paused just long enough to give the appearance of thinking this over. "Because the Americans have pulled in those they can work with, I suppose."

"There's a resolution before the Security Council to force control into the Council's hands explicitly—"

"Yes, very bad move."

"—and world opinion is lining up pretty solidly behind it."

"The only solidity to be gained here is through the alliance the United States has yet again stitched together. Who could imagine, say, the Chinese doing remotely likewise?"

"But assembling the wisest heads of all nations at the U.N. would—"

"Be a madhouse."

"But certainly with everyone's lives at stake—"

"Since the Gulf War of thirty-two years ago, the Americans have twice more put together a coalition to deal with a rogue state. This one deals with a rogue entity, but the classic means of alliance diplomacy are the essential skills."

"As a scientist, how are you qualified—"

This last from a frowzy woman apparently noted for her "incisive" questions. He put a stop to her by turning his back and walking away, which from startled looks from the "handlers" assigned to him was Just Not Done to Famous Media Personalities. Nonetheless, it got him quickly out of the floodlit room and shortly after into a helicopter for Dulles.

Everywhere people seemed to have only a dim notion of what was at stake in this crisis. He avoided conversation with people in nearby seats from State and Defense. Takeoff was delayed by several people maneuvering for seats near others. The Marine guard got irked at this, quite rightly, and threatened to throw a White House aide off if he would not "get your ass in gear," a delicious American turn of phrase that no foreigner could ever get exactly right in intonation.

"Hey, Kingsley," a fellow from the U Agency called, plunking himself down next to him before Kingsley could think of a plausible reason why the seat had to be kept open as a grave matter of national security. "Herb Mansfield. I met you a couple weeks ago on the Big Island. You heading back?"

"To Hawaii? Yes."

"We'd like you to catch a chopper at Dulles, visit us over by Langley."

"Sorry, can't. Have to"—*What's the Americanism?*— "mind the store."

"We had a few things to go over."

Something ominous in his tone? "I believe there are a plentitude of you fellows at the Center."

"Not policy stuff."

"Scientific?"

"Personal."

The helicopter roared into the air then, giving him time to judge this odd approach. He barely knew this man. There was an air of heavy assurance about the way he wore his gray suit and undistinguished tie, a massive sense that he was not used to being differed with. When they had cleared the trees over the nearby hills, Kingsley said, "I didn't think you cared."

This lightness had no effect upon the government armor. "Oh, we do. Vital personnel we are taking a big interest in."

How nice. "I am scarcely vital."

"You handled getting your friends into the Center pretty well."

"I prefer to work with people I know."

"Funny you didn't bring your wife in."

"She is not a scientist."

"Talked to her lately?"

"I haven't spoken to her in months; I don't like to interrupt her."

This little joke provoked not even a twinge of his upper lip. The helicopter hammered at the long pause between them. *All right, then, dead earnest it is.* "I suppose I might find it difficult?"

"Some people are hard to reach."

He had to admire the style of this threat, as anyone overhearing it would think it completely bland chat. "You may have overestimated the value of that particular card."

"Don't think so."

"We are separated."

No big effect, but the eyes lost a touch of hardness.

Kingsley sat back and allowed himself the luxury of looking out at greenery zooming by. Generally this sort, from his admittedly limited experience, took a steely stare as the *lingua franca* of such negotiations. Perhaps a show of indifference would work best. He took his time with the scenery. Then: "I don't believe you have weighed all factors here."

"I think so, friend."

"Negative inducements seldom work."

A shift of mood in the otherwise uninteresting face. "Maybe not, for a customer like you. Let me shift the terms."

"Do."

"Your wife could be taken to one of the shelters."

"Which are?"

"The hot ticket. How come you don't know?"

"I have been rather busy."

"A global system, using the old shelters put up to protect national asset people in case of nuclear war."

"Which this promises to be."

"Right, hadn't thought of it that way. Anyway, we stocked these up, got them running. Spot for your wife in one of ours, the best."

"If I . . ."

"Do your duty."

"I might remind you that I am not required to feel any patriotic sentiment."

"Yeah, but you're one of us."

"And I have a job you do not seem to properly appreciate. I work for the world now."

"And for us. The U is making this all happen for you—and fast."

"I am aware of that. And Mr. Arno knows I shall cooperate."

"Just wanted you to know she can have the spot—"

"So long as I am a good boy."

"Uh huh. Want me to have her picked up?"

A long pause. A small, malicious part of him visualized how irked she would be, to be incarcerated among such types as these. On the other hand, she would be safer, and he did have feelings for her. He loved her, in a way he had been incapable of conveying very well. Not a night passed, even in these circumstances, when he did not wonder how she was getting on.

He made himself stop thinking of that. Seconds mattered here, decisions that could affect everything of importance to him. "Yes, I believe so."

"Good decision. We'll give her top-flight treatment, believe me."

"Will there be a flight involved?"

"Huh? Oh, will we bring her here?"

"Versus, say, getting her into the parallel U.K. citadel."

"Well, I don't know, but—" He reached for his portable,

punched two numbers, and was speaking into it before Kingsley could tell him to not bother.

Kingsley sat thinking rapidly. Obviously some faction in the U Agency wanted him well in hand. A split in the U.S. government itself? An all-encompassing emergency could provoke extreme reactions in nations as well as in people. The President had been edgy and had referred glancingly to a division in the advice he was getting. By coming into such advanced policy disputes late, Kingsley became a pawn readily conscripted with a touch of leverage. The U Agency was more accustomed to using muscle.

Taking deep breaths, a decision percolated up from within, tightening his stomach muscles with a tingling anticipation. He recalled from schoolyard scrapes that the best way of dealing with a punch was to duck it. Very well.

Only after Herb had rung off did he realize that the reassuring report Herb was giving them, smiling all the while, would work in nicely. Herb's superiors would take it that matters were going well. That would, in turn, give Kingsley more time to act once they were on the ground.

Herb gave a reassuring nod. "They say sure, we can move her over here."

"Actually, I'd rather she were in England. The installation is out toward Wales, I believe, and that is country she has always appreciated."

Herb frowned. "Afraid it's done, friend."

"Not changeable?"

"I really don't want to go back and keep switching—"

"Very well. I understand."

Though he had not planned matters this way, this tiny sign was just what he needed to resolve him to a course of action. Now if only he could bring it off.

"We want to be on your side in this thing, y'know," Herb said.

As if it had a sense of timing, the helicopter began its yowling descent. The world had a habit of forcing his hand, of late. "All right. Done."

They landed in one of the great pools of light that dotted Dulles. Most of the airport had been closed off for national security reasons for weeks now. Aircraft of every description, many military, took off in a continual background yowl.

Their party got out and walked quickly into the terminal. The usual Dulles passenger transports worked the truncated civilian part of the field, moving like ponderous, big-windowed apartments on wheels.

The U Agency type stuck with him as he made his way upstairs. There was a special check-in counter for people traveling on government craft. His special flight to Hawaii was to leave in less than an hour. Herb announced, "Y'know, I might just come along on that same jet, if there's room."

"Oh?" Herb did not seem to doubt that there would be a seat for him. This sudden decision was more confirmation of Kingsley's working hypothesis. The plan he had improvised was unfolding from his unconscious. There was something tensely delicious in allowing it to do so in its own good sweet time.

The big executive jet for their group was already in place at the end of a passenger ramp, guarded by two conspicuously armed Army men. Such a plane was wasteful, but mandatory in the pecking order. Protocol officers babbled at him while he watched the crowd, but no one came forward to join the U Agency fellow. *Very good.*

Perhaps half an hour before boarding, but there was much to do. "Unbearable in here, isn't it?" Kingsley began, his heart thudding at this opening pawn move.

"Yeah, they overheat these places."

"Let's get a breath, shall we?"

Herb thought a second too long, perhaps realizing that there was no plausible reason to object. "Sure, sure."

They went out a side door and down a corridor, Kingsley furiously trying to remember times before when he had wandered through this terminal. After a false lead, he found a door that opened out onto a broad parapet, the sort of useless ornament to the building where no one actually went. Sure enough, there was no one looking at the waning sunset. Planes buzzed on the field about twenty feet below. Kingsley put his briefcase down and made a show of sucking in a lungful of moist air.

"We can go around to the other side, should be able to see the burning in D.C.," Herb volunteered, his voice mellow in good-buddy mode.

"That should be a sight. Still out of control?"

"Yup. Got the National Guard in now."

"Pity."

"People just plain going crazy, is what it is."

Idly Kingsley walked along into a more shadowy zone. Herb tagged after. Kingsley thought again through his chain of logic and could see no flaw in it. *Still* . . . "I presume she can leave the facility in the U.K. whenever she likes?"

Herb did not pause. "Oh, sure."

Clear enough, then. A trap being set, disguised as a plum. Herb was a remarkably inept liar.

"See that big one? What sort is it?" He pointed out onto the field.

As Herb followed the line Kingsley checked again in both directions along the parapet. No one in view. The parapet's guard rail was of raised concrete with a thick lip, suitable for leaning on. This Herb proceeded to do, gazing out at the moving airplanes.

Kingsley had taken a course in judo long ago and had been trying to remember some of it over the last few minutes. Frustratingly, the only item he could call up was the instructor's admonition that the *body* had to learn the moves, not the nasty old, unreliable *mind*.

Fair enough, he thought, stooping slightly to grab the belt at Herb's back. *Now the difficult part.* As Herb turned, Kingsley took a firm hold of the back of the man's suit and shirt collar. He dropped farther and turned himself, bending his knees to take Herb's weight. As he pulled the man over onto his back, he heard a strangled exclamation, "Wha—"

He felt the weight come fully onto his back and a fist slammed into his left ribs. The pain made him suck in air. Kingsley turned farther, lifted with the one burst of energy he had. The other fist pounded at him. "Help—"

This shout Kingsley cut off by straightening up suddenly and twisting. This heaved Herb over the guard rail. The body went partway over, then the suit coat caught in the railing somehow. "Help—"

Kingsley found the wadded coat cloth that was exerting just enough strength to keep Herb's scrabbling hands and feet on the parapet's lip. He shoved at the body and it was gone. A soft thump came from below. He leaned over. Herb lay on his side about fifteen feet below. A trickle of blood had started down his brow and ran onto the tarmac.

There seemed to be no loading crew nearby and no sign that anyone had seen. On the other hand, Kingsley could not see the ground floor of the terminal, tucked back below the parapet. Herb did not move.

He trotted back to his briefcase, picked it up, and started walking in a perfectly ordinary fashion. Airplane roars matched his hammering heart. He succumbed to the temptation to look over the parapet again. Still no movement from Herb.

But now a woman in overalls was running toward the body from the right. She called out something that an airplane takeoff drowned out. In the bright light, she looked up at Kingsley and he jerked his head back, probably too late to avoid being identified. *Damn.* Stupid, of course, once one was committed, to look back.

He walked quickly back inside and past the gate where his airplane would soon begin boarding. This part of it he had not fully thought out, but he knew it was a good idea to get out of the government-controlled part of the terminal. This proved simple, as all the security measures were directed to screening out the opposite flow. He walked through some guards and down an escalator.

At the American Airlines counter, he saw a flight for

Hawaii leaving within the hour. To Oahu, not the Big Island, but that was a small inconvenience. He did not dally at the counter, where anyone could see him, and instead found his way to the Admirals' Club, where he had a lifetime membership.

He had often enjoyed the perks of this club, but never so much as now. Here he had no difficulty booking onto the flight, so long as he was willing to go first-class. *If sailing on the* Titanic, *why not?* he thought a bit wildly.

He knew the airlines kept their own bookings of first-class. There was a fair chance that even the U Agency, should it be searching soon, would not find access to those files right away. A chance, at least.

He went straight along to the private telephone rooms they kept down a deeply carpeted corridor and dialed. He found himself holding his breath, This would all prove to be a ludicrous, dangerous waste unless—

"Hello?" A fuzzy voice. "Hope you've got a good reason to—"

"I do. Listen quickly." He had to rely on her recognizing his voice. His name might touch off one of those listening programs governments used to target calls. "You're to pack a bag, enough for a week, and leave the house immediately."

"What? Why would I—"

"Because you are in danger. Some people are going to try to round you up. I'd suggest going to a friend's, someone they cannot easily trace."

"But what's this about? Why would they—"

"To use you as hostage. Once they have you, I'd do what they want."

"Who is this 'they'?"

"That's the dicey part. I don't know, not precisely."

"Then why should I—"

"There are forces at work here I do not fully understand." She was fully awake now. "It's pretty damned arrogant—"

"No doubt, but pointless to debate now. Just move. Go to a hotel to get your bearings if you want."

"Whozzat?" a male voice came from the background.

"Quiet," she said quickly. Then, to let the speaker know, she added, "Kingsley, I don't follow your orders any longer."

"I hope that you've kept matters reasonably discreet?"

"What? Oh, what the hell, I don't care if you know. Yes, I've been quiet about him, if you must—"

"And your newfound friend has a place?"

"Well, of course, he's not a street person—oh, I see."

"Yes. Hole up there for tonight, probably safer than being in a nearby hotel registry."

"I haven't said that I would—"

"There isn't time to have a pleasant little debate about this. I just injured a man, perhaps killed him, all to make this telephone call."

"What?" The newfound friend was saying something in the background again.

"I can't talk much longer. Be out of the house inside half an hour."

"But I don't know . . . I . . . What's this about—"

"You might actually be safer in a shelter, old girl, but I can't have them using you against me."

"My God, do you think things are going to get—"

"I don't know how badly we might fare, but others with more power are covering a lot of different bets. You and I are very minor figures in all this, but we may share the fate of a church mouse who sleeps with a restless elephant. Best to be elsewhere."

"I still don't—"

"Go to the boyfriend's. Don't tell me where it is. They might have had the foresight to tap this phone."

"He's not a 'boyfriend,' he's much more—"

"No time for that. Go. I'd advise a nice trip to someplace in the country. Then get a secure lodging for the week to come."

"Damn it, I—"

"Got to ring off now. I still love you, you know."

He hung up and let out a long, rattling sigh.

Now a brisk walk to the auto-cab stand. He used his credit card, got in, and punched for a hotel in D.C. As the car paused, he got out, secured the door, and watched the hump-backed car dutifully trundle down the ramp and into the controlled section of the highway. An easy trace for anyone to follow.

He went around the terminal on the outside. The yellow glow from D.C. filled the eastern sky. He saw an ambulance pulling away, lights flashing. It seemed unlikely that Herb had died of the fall.

Kingsley had seen no other way to gain the time and get free of the U Agency. A moment's reflection had shown that the only safe haven for him now was back on the Big Island, but interception while on a government flight was surely certain. And he most certainly did not want to fall into the hands of the lot at Langley.

Most probably they had people in the terminal by now. He surveyed the impossibly crowded waiting bays. Far too easy for them to pick him up while in that crowd, and quite possibly they had thought of the Admirals' Club by now. The jam of vexed people had an air of fevered impatience, something beyond the usual expected from delayed flights.

This was the first time he had seen firsthand how the ordinary world was dealing with the Eater's approach, the fever of anxiety that somehow permeated the air of every ordinary moment. Even in this air-conditioned terminal, he caught the sour smell of something elemental and unsettled.

He wondered what England was like now. He had to guard against the mixture of envy and contempt Europeans often felt while in the United States. Americans had their blemishes, particularly a curious kind of practical self-righteousness, but at least they did not brim with the world-weariness Europeans often equated with cultural maturity. Europe was a comfy land going nowhere now, and the Eater must strike many of his countrymen as an affront to their assumed eminence in the world. All humanity was all truly in the same trap now, stuck at the bottom of a frail atmosphere beneath a being that cared nothing for human assumptions.

A small band of musicians was performing for the throng. Public entertainment was so common now he never gave it a thought. In the leisure-rich 2020s, more and more people were pop musicians, filmmakers, actors, or "alternative" comedians, artists all—except that they had no audience. Bands performed for free at parties, jokesters eagerly launched into their routines at dinner parties. Thankfully, there were a few artistic areas where lack of aptitude did inhibit performance; there were few struggling trapeze artists. But in his experience that did not stop a contralto from bursting into song in the living room at house parties, provoking a quick exodus to the far reaches of the house.

This lot was halfway decent, their Latin rhythms rolling over the edgy crowds, quite possibly lightening the mood. Faces relaxed near the swaying music. Some looked for an upturned hat to toss change into, but there was none; these were *gratis* performers.

For the third time, he saw a woman in a severe suit watching him. *Stupid to be out here like this*, he admonished himself and took advantage of a passing clump of Chinese tourists to slip away. She followed him onto a concourse and he used the usual elevator ploy to go up one, then back down, exiting as the doors to the next elevator closed upon her startled face.

He spent the remainder of his wait in the men's room, popping out to get boarding information. This apparently worked, for on his third excursion, they were ushering first-class onboard. He badly needed the proffered drink by the time he settled in.

It took him a while to work out why this flight was worse than usual. He had been on many torturous red-eyes, even one in which a screeching cat escaped its cage and spent hours in the dim netherworld of coach-class, eluding pursuers. But this flight had a restless anger. Abrupt insults exchanged over stowed carry-ons. Seat kickers behind.

Quarrels over meal selections running out. The attendants were frayed.

Kingsley adopted his standard maneuver to avoid conversation, pulling out a sheaf of work and at the first question telling the chap to his left that he was in insurance. That did not deter the woman to his right, so he leaned toward the window and said expectantly, "Think we'll see any UFOs?" For insurance, he took from his briefcase some working papers and placed atop them insignia from the Internal Revenue Service that he had downloaded from their Web site long before. A sure conversation killer.

Au revoir, États-Unis! he toasted with an agreeable California claret as they cleared American air space. Hawaii was a state, of course, but never felt like the rest of the United States. He made himself concentrate upon the wine to slow his still thudding heart. Adrenaline zest had gotten him through the airport, but now he needed to be calm. There was surely more to come.

He had received by classified e-mail a selection of recent Eater messages. Scanning them, he wondered at the sort of mind that slithered from one subject to another, unaware of the impact upon the swarms of minds that would receive its words.

THERE WERE 10^{18} SECONDS SINCE WHAT YOU TERM THE BIG BANG AND WHICH COULD BETTER BE TRANSLATED AS AN EMERGENCE, NOT AN EXPLOSION. THERE ARE 10^{88} PARTICLES IN THE KNOWN UNIVERSE. THESE ARE TINY NUMBERS COMPARED WITH THE WAYS OF COMBINING INFORMATION, THE TRUE FONT OF INTELLIGENCE. HERE LODGES THE TRUE RICHNESS OF CREATION. A DECK OF YOUR GAME CARDS CAN BE ASSEMBLED IN 10^{68} WAYS. EACH NEW SHUFFLE PROBABLY HAS NEVER BEEN DEALT BEFORE. REARRANGING THE 0'S AND 1'S ON A MEGABYTE OF MEMORY COULD YIELD $10^{3.5 \text{ MILLION}}$ DIFFERENT BYTE STRINGS. THE TRUE CONSTRAINT ON NATURE IS NOT

THINGS BUT WAYS OF ARRANGING THEM, AND IN THIS
THERE ARE NO TRUE BOUNDS.

All this, apparently, as cheerleading for people to relish uploading into the Eater's "library." Or so a naïve human mind could read it.

I MANIFEST MY-SELF THROUGH GRAVITATIONAL
ENERGY, WHICH IS IN THIS UNIVERSE THE LARGEST IN
QUANTITY. IT ALSO IS THE LEAST DISORDERED AND
FROM THIS SUPERIOR QUALITY CAN CHANGE EASILY
INTO OTHER FORMS. THUS I BRING IMMINENT ORDER
TO YOUR KIND.

He supposed one should expect a being unique and isolated to become something of an egomaniac. What choice did it have? Every other intelligence it had encountered vanished into the abyss of astronomical time, devoured by its own terminal brevity.

YOUR LIFETIME COMPRISES A TRILLION OF YOUR BRAIN
EVENTS. YOU ARE AQUEOUS SUSPENSIONS OF
MOLECULES AND SO COMPRISE A TRANSIENT MEDIUM.
CAUGHT IN YOUR SMALL BOX OF TIME, YOU CANNOT
ATTAIN THE HEIGHTS OF SOME FORMS I HAVE
WITNESSED.

Apparently the biologists had caught its attention. The Eater was notorious by now for abruptly swerving among subjects and ignoring entreaties. This fit the developing model for its own mental organization: a compilation of many magnetic knots storing separate agents of mental structure.

Each agent could come forward as a governing principle and shine the spotlight of consciousness upon itself. In this sense, the Eater had access to its own unconscious—unlike humans. It could watch itself thinking, and so felt no need to dress itself in the clothing of a smoothly operating over-mind, to be one "person."

I HAVE SEEN AND NOW CARRY WITH ME THE MINDS OF
BEINGS WHO STORED THEMSELVES IN THE CLAY ARRAYS
OF THEIR WORLD'S MUD. THESE COULD THINK IN SPANS
OF MILLIONTHS OF YOUR SECONDS, WHILE YOUR-
SELVES CAN ONLY MASTER THOUSANDTHS. I ORBITED
FOR MANY OF YOUR MILLENNIA A CLOUD THE SIZE OF
YOUR PLANETARY SYSTEM AND THIS CREATURE
THOUGHT FAR SLOWER THAN YOU. BUT IT WAS MORE
VAST THAN ANY I HAVE FOUND AND HAD THOUGHT
FOR LONGER THAN YOUR STAR HAS BURNED.

He wondered how they could deal with this. The fear he had seen in the President's eyes was global. Would the volunteered uploads from the dictatorial nations be enough? Or did it have further amusements in store for itself, at humanity's expense?

Well, only a few days to go until they all found out. The cabin was dark, the plane on its long night arc over the Pacific. He looked out a window and with practiced eye could find the blue-white blotch that was the Eater's decelerating jet. Brighter, nearer, hanging like a strange eye in the blackness.

He allowed himself to think of Channing a bit. Her upload had apparently gone reasonably well and now "she" cruised in orbit. Apparently the specialists were engaged in "linearizing" her onboard consciousness from afar, an unparalleled technical feat. Fuel pods were being attached to give her multiple booster capability. Her whole remaining self was a mere speck perched atop masses of refrigerated hydrogen.

Then, without noticing the transition, he was awakening as they banked over Honolulu. Time to get back into the game.

No one intercepted him as he disembarked. The terminal

reeked of festering anxiety. Once aloft he had phoned Arno and asked for an escort, giving enough detail to convince him that there were factions at war now within the U Agency. "Something about China," Kingsley added.

"Don't repeat that word," Arno said hastily.

"It's a fairly well-known nation." Kingsley could not resist the jab. Arno should never have allowed Kingsley to go into a situation inadequately forearmed. Put it down to haste and the press of events, but still . . .

Sure enough, three men he recognized from the Center and carrying the right recognition code met him at the gate. Wordlessly they took him to a private federal airplane, gray and unmarked. In short order, or so it seemed to his hazy state of mind, they were landing at the new field just scraped from the valley near the Center.

He was quite knackered and begged off going straightaway to the Center. Kingsley rang off and called ahead to his private number. "Be there soon," he said, not trusting himself to go any further with the driver and two burly guards, who crisply took him to his flat.

She answered his knock. He embraced her gratefully. She had started their relationship wearing ratty housecoats, but had quickly learned how he liked to be greeted—by an actual woman, not a housekeeper. Dressed in suitable nineteenth-century undergarments, red or black if possible. *Sailing on the* Titanic, he thought fuzzily, *why go steerage?*

"Thanks, luv," he murmured at her black merry widow, "but afraid it's no use this time."

"I'll be here when you wake up."

"Can't say how long that will be."

"Pretty bad?" A warm kiss.

"What's the saying? 'Politicians, diapers—both should be changed regularly, and for the same reason.' Particularly the ones with guns."

She laughed softly, as if to say it did not matter whether she had heard this chestnut before. He hugged her. To be in her arms was quite enough, thank you. They had been drawn to each other as the crisis deepened. In the face of the abyss, people needed each other. He wondered if he was falling in love with her. Something in him hoped so.

"Something to drink?" Amy asked.

"Lately, I sup solely from the cup of knowledge."

He kissed her again, this time urgently, something escaping from him, letting out the leaden fog of his desperation.

2 Benjamin could not mourn her anymore.

For three days, he had gone on beach walks and sat staring at the bottom of various bottles, talked with friends, and read over obsessively her last writings. Nothing helped. In the afternoon of the third full day, he so dreaded the coming of shadows that he fled. He finally knew that he had to go to the Center and face the unknown that loomed there.

A traffic tie-up and even more guards than the last time stopped him outside the new, high gates a full kilometer from the Center. Someone spotted him stuck in the jam and ushered him around, down a side road where he still had to submit to the triple-check of ID, retinas, and all. Sunset brimmed over the hills and he could pick out in profile the snouts of tactical-range missiles, installed only days before.

Just who were they defending against? No one had explained. There were more U Agency faces in the corridors every day, but they never spoke, just looked professionally grim.

He peered upward, eastward, and there it was: a hard blue-white dot spiking down at them. The Eater was decelerating at a prodigious rate. Its forward jet ejected mass apparently accumulated in its accretion disk, which X-ray telescopes showed had thickened to resemble a fat, rotating donut. Now the donut was dwindling fast, its stored matter fed by glowing streamers into the braking jet.

Nobody understood how the system could have stocked up so much mass, enough to shove around the incredibly dense nugget of the black hole. The magnetic labyrinth around it must have remarkable retention ability. The hard radiation coming out of the jet got degraded into visible light, the whole glowing over ten times brighter than the full moon.

Cults had begun worshipping it by night, he had heard. The wave of suicides which was sweeping the world focused upon doing themselves in "view" of the Eater, as if it saw or cared. He could feel nothing for such people, not even pity. They were just marks on a chart, statistics floating beyond the gray veil that shrouded his world.

Inside, he spotted Kingsley looking tired, talking to a U Agency woman in a conference room. The man had just returned from Washington and had left several e-mails for Benjamin, asking for a meeting with Arno. Benjamin ducked away and went to his own office.

There was a lot of paperwork to do. Somehow even the supreme crisis of human history could not avoid its tedium. He plowed through, thankfully oblivious, for an hour. Then he got the expected call, and when he reached Arno's office, there was Kingsley. They shook hands silently, and after a moment's awkwardness, business picked up.

"This is just to inform you," Arno said, waving at a screen that carried specifics about missiles.

Kingsley seemed to comprehend the news at a glance. Benjamin shook his head to dispel his numbness, but it was not physical. "What am I looking at here?" he asked finally.

"Missile classes and capability," Arno said.

Even with this, it took him a moment to pick out the crucial detail. "That's a submarine-based missile," he said blankly.

"That's the point," Arno said. "We just launched three from off the coast of China, near a peninsula."

Kingsley said, "The Liaodong Peninsula."

"Why from there?" Benjamin was startled. "And subs are built for ICBMs, not shots into deep space."

Arno said, "The Department of Defense used a new class of ICBM, specially fitted with one hard-nosed warhead, rather than the usual multiple suite."

"The launch point nicely placed just south of the peninsula," Kingsley said dryly, "halfway between Beijing to the west and the Korean capital, Pyongyang, to the east. It is an interesting historical accident that the capitals of our primary antagonists in Asia are at nearly the same latitude and only a few hundred kilometers apart."

Then Benjamin saw. "If the Eater can backtrack the launch, it will believe the Chinese or North Koreans did it."

"And exact a retribution, perhaps," Kingsley said.

"Unless we knock it out, which is the idea," Arno said.

Anger cleared his head remarkably. "This . . . this is crazy."

"President didn't think so, and Kingsley was right there advising him." Arno even held a hand out to Kingsley, as if to pass the buck.

Benjamin said hotly, "But the risk—"

"It can do a hell of a lot to us we already know about. Plus plenty we don't know, I'll bet." Arno straightened the seam of his blue suit, keeping him in good order under fire.

"Fail and it'll be able to punish us big time, too," Benjamin shot back.

Kingsley said mildly, "We should remember that it is entirely alien. The notion of revenge may well not apply to its thinking."

Arno looked pained. "You always say something like that. Not that I'm agreeing with Benjamin here, but how can it not want to hit back?"

"Punishment deters by setting an example, all to lend credence to threat." Kingsley steepled his fingers. "That, and not the sweetness of revenge, is its utility—to *us*. Punishment is a social mechanism, well evolved in us because it keeps tribal discipline. This thing *has no tribe*."

"It's done this before, though," Benjamin said, though his mind was still trying to work its way around what Arno had so casually implied. He wasn't used to these high altitudes in the policy mountain range. "Maybe thousands of times, even millions, it's come into a solar system and demanded what it wanted from intelligent species."

Kingsley said airily, "And, just as for us, it regards its history as philosophy teaching by examples?"

"So it's learned how to threaten and hurt?" Arno looked skeptical.

"It sure knows how to whipsaw us, doesn't it?" Benjamin asserted. "Look at how its demand for uploaded people has split us already. A lot of people are saying, 'Why not give up a few hundred it specifically asked for? Then make up the rest from the nations that are only too happy to discard their "undesirables" in a good cause.' "

Arno said, "The U.N. has taken a stated position against making any individual undergo—"

"So far," Kingsley said distantly. "It could undoubtedly kill millions if it wanted, and the moment it starts, there will be plenty of voices calling for us to cave in."

Benjamin said, "And we're shooting at it already? Why not wait?"

"If punishment is to be exacted," Kingsley said, "I surmise that the coalition of powers rather wishes it to be bestowed upon their strategic rivals."

Arno nodded. "The launch point's far enough away from our nearest strategic holding, the Siberian Republic."

"A team at Caltech argues," Kingsley said, "that the Eater cannot resolve the launch point better than about a hundred kilometers. Similarly its anticipated response. So its retribution may well include the capital of an enemy."

"I had no idea we were so far in . . ." Benjamin faltered. He was not cut out for this sort of thing.

"The President wants to kill it now," Arno said.

Kingsley said, "Plus getting what I believe is termed a 'twofer.' Devastation for China or Korea or both if the attempt fails."

Benjamin jabbed a finger at the launch parameters. "The

Chinese have good observing satellites. They'll have seen these lift off already."

Arno smiled without humor. "We have a few tricks to hide our plumes. And what can the Chinese do, anyway? The birds are gone."

"This is monstrous," Benjamin said, still angry.

"There is a monster in our skies," Arno replied simply.

The missiles took eight hours to reach the Eater. This was a remarkable achievement, as the launch vehicles had to attain a final speed in the range of twenty kilometers per second.

Benjamin had no idea that strategic warfare had advanced to such potentials. The missiles converged upon the Eater's outer regions at about half a million kilometers above the Earth's atmosphere.

The rendezvous was well beyond the Earth's dipolar magnetic belts, which could retain the plasma the warheads would generate. This was the crucial requirement. Releasing high-energy particles into the regions near the many thousands of communications satellites would destroy them by charging them up until the potentials shorted out components.

This was what the missiles tried to do. They flew into the black hole's magnetosphere and detonated in a pattern calculated to send currents fleeing along the field lines. This was to occur slightly after dawn in Hawaii. The Eater hung low on the horizon. The Center was packed, silent crowds before every screen.

Benjamin went outside with Kingsley. They were of the last generation which felt that events were more real if seen in person, rather than watched over authenticity-inducing TV screens.

"No trouble spotting the bastard," Kingsley said, facing into the warm offshore breeze. Solid and moist, the tropical lushness lay beneath the fierce glare of a blue-white dot.

"How good does the targeting have to be?" Benjamin asked to focus his attention. He was still distracted and foggy and wondered if this internal weather would be permanent.

"Not terribly, the magnetosphere theorists say. The vital region is about a hundred kilometers across and they are closing at speeds that allow the warhead triggers to go off within a microsecond's accuracy."

"So we can hit it within a few meters' accuracy? Wow."

"These weapons chaps are quite able. Impressive. Unfortunately, our understanding of the underlying magnetic geometry is muddy. I am not optimistic."

"Want to lay odds?" Benjamin chided him.

Kingsley had spilled most of the insider stories from his trip, including the incredible bit about the U Agency guy at Dulles. Benjamin still had trouble believing that things had gotten so extreme. But then, he had told himself, they had spent months holed up here, while the world outside went through a conceptual beating.

So far this entire thing had been easier for scientists to take because they were used to rubbing against the irreducible reality of a universe that was in a sense even worse than the hostility of the Eater. The TwenCen had cemented a solid belief that the universe was indifferent. For many ordinary people, that view was impossible to accept. Not that the eerie interest of the Eater was much solace.

"On success? Small, I should think."

"Let's be quantitative."

Kingsley smiled. "All right, what odds do you give me?"

"Three to one for a fizzle."

"I'm not quite that large a fool."

"You really don't think we can short it out?"

"Quite unlikely."

"But you helped target them."

"Precisely. I am not married to models, particularly those devised by theorists like ourselves."

"Okay, ten to one."

"That I can accept. Stakes?"

"I'll put up a thousand bucks."

"So if the Eater dies, your bank account does, too."

"Don't give a damn. I'm betting on American warheads."

"Good point. A general treated me to an hour's lesson on how hardened and compact they are. 'A megaton inside a suitcase,' the fellow boasted."

"Damn right," Benjamin said and wondered why he felt called upon to swagger around like this.

"I shall cheerfully pay up."

They waited in silence in the soft, salty wind. The ocean lay like a smooth blanket and the world held its breath.

The three flashes came as one, a hard white blink and then a fast-fading yellow. A cheer came faintly up the hillside, ragged and angry, from a thousand voices inside the buildings.

"I'd pray if I believed any of that," Benjamin said.

"As would I."

"It'll be a while before we know—"

"No, we've failed."

"What?"

"The color of the jet emission has not even altered. Its ejection is operating normally."

"Well, that could—"

"To succeed, we had to disrupt its control mechanisms. Moving mass into those magnetic funnels is a colossal endeavor. We haven't a clue how it pulls off the trick. If it can still do that, it has survived."

Benjamin had known it, too, but something made him argue with Kingsley. "Yeah. Yeah."

"Where is she?"

"In an orbit timed to put her on the other side of the Earth right now."

"Good show."

"You think she'll . . ."

"Have to be used?" Kingsley gave him a long, sympathetic gaze. "Inevitably."

"Damn, damn, I . . ."

Kingsley put a hand on his shoulder. "That is, above all, what she wished."

3 Kingsley quickly realized the next morning that to the bureaucratic mind, the most pressing matter would, of course, be the assigning of blame.

This fell to an assortment of U Agency types. These in the general Executive Committee meeting used "It is believed" rather than "I think," theorists who said "It has long been known," when they meant "I can't remember who did this," or stated portentously "It is not unreasonable to assume" instead of "Would you believe?" Those defending their ideas—the imported target specialists, DoD experts and the like, retreated into "It might be argued that," which was a dead-on clue that it actually meant "I have such a good answer to that objection that I shall now raise it myself . . ." These were the same sort whose speech included "progressing an action plan" and "calendarizing a project." Only painfully did it penetrate that the calendar here was set entirely by a being nobody understood.

Part of the problem in assigning responsibility was the swelling numbers of Center consultants, U Agency staff, assorted specialists, and the like. More moved in as the possibility of communications failure grew. The Eater might chop the human digital networks with a single swipe.

In the end, there was plenty of blame to go around.

All Earth's telescopes and diagnostics, concentrated upon the comparatively tiny region of a few hundred kilometers around the rapidly decelerating Eater's core, saw much that no one comprehended. The huge energies of the three warheads had sent great plumes of high temperature plasma into the magnetic geometry, all right. But somehow it flowed along the field lines and then into the accretion disk. More fuel for the Eater of All Things.

"The Eater ate them," Amy Major observed laconically. "And like us all, eating makes you bigger."

It had swelled, become more luminous. In the next few hours, the Eater crossed the remaining half a million kilometers to Earth, bearing in on a spiral orbit.

Kingsley watched the U Agency break down into factions that fed upon each other. Outside the Center battalions of newsfolk demanded answers. Washington already knew that, fundamentally, there were none. The Eater said nothing about the attack, until two hours later:

MY-SELVES NOTE THAT YOUR INTERCOMMUNICATIONS REFER TO ME AS A PROCESSOR OF FOOD. THIS IS NOT A SERVICEABLE DISTINCTION. INGESTION IS SHARED BY NEARLY ALL LIFE-FORMS. I WISH YOU TO REFER TO ME BY A TERM MORE NEARLY DESCRIBING MY ESSENTIAL BEING IN YOUR MEASURE.
ULTIMATA

"Looks like a signature," Arno commented to the Semiotics Group.

"But what's it mean?" a voice called, and others chimed in:

"The ultimate?"

"Should be singular."

"It says 'my-selves,' though."

"So it's what? An anthology intelligence?"

"Like Father, Son, and Holy Ghost?"

"Don't be humorous about that!"

"About life and death? Laughing is best."

"Ultimate as in final? Fatal?"

"Maybe it's the plural of ultimatum."

This last from a University of Oklahoma professor sent a chill through the room.

Later, secluded in his office, Arno asked the old working group of Martinez, Amy, Benjamin, and Kingsley if they thought these were reasonable readings. Amy said, "It knows dozens of languages by now. Choosing a name like that—well, it proves it's learned how to pun."

"To underline that it wishes its demand for specific persons obeyed," Kingsley said.

Amy said, "There's a Mesh story that says they're reading the sections of Einstein's brain that were in formaldehyde."

"Lots of luck deciphering that," Benjamin said.

Amy waved the Einstein matter away as a stunt, but then said earnestly, "There are thousands of specialists working on the whole uploading problem. They're learning every day. If we have to give it all those people, the technology will be ready."

Arno asked her, "How many volunteers?"

"Real ones? A few dozen."

Arno looked startled. "But the Mesh says there are already over ten thousand."

"That's counting captive 'volunteers' from dictators."

"How about reading in the brains of those just dead?" Arno pressed. "There are eight billion people on Earth. Dying at a rate of better than a hundred thousand every *day*—"

"Everybody's resisting that," Amy said briskly. "Most aren't anywhere near a facility that has the equipment. And anyway, the magnetic sensing process takes several days, minimum. Dying patients aren't up to it, and their readings get screwed up, too."

"The Eater doesn't know that," Arno said.

Kingsley said, "Not so. It samples all our radio and TV. It can eavesdrop on a great welter of talk."

Amy seemed more energetic than the men here, and Kingsley marveled again at how she had become steadily stronger as this crisis developed. That had first drawn him to her, the sheer sense of untapped energy. She had an appetite for detail, for stitching together the innumerable Eater messages, then shopping them out to the working groups—all the while remaining a warm, insightful woman, not an office automaton, as did so many of both sexes in these fear-fraught days.

"I . . . see." Arno's former spotless attire had eroded. His suit was unpressed, tie askew, shoes unpolished—all mirroring his wrecked face, which was not used to receiving a serving of unremitting bad news. No sleep and pressure from above had not been kind. "Well, at least we've solved the question of who was after Kingsley."

This made Kingsley brighten. "How is old buddy Herb?"

"Conscious, finally. He'll recover. He was from the China-option faction, I found out."

"Trying to silence opponents?" Kingsley guessed.

"They wanted you in hand to control reactions and help with follow-up targeting," Arno said.

This startled them all. "They planned on failing?" Amy asked.

"Any good general has a retreat in mind," Arno said. "They wanted to hit it several times, overload it."

Kingsley guessed again, "But didn't say so to the President."

"Seems so," Arno said. "He overruled that, of course. If they'd had you to head up the advocates, maybe they'd have won, be slugging it out with the Eater right now."

Benjamin said angrily, "Inside our satellite belt? That would skragg all our communications."

"Yep," Arno said blandly. "I'm getting so nothing surprises me, even from Washington."

"The pronuke faction is vanquished, then?" Kingsley asked.

"Not at all." Arno grinned cynically. "They just sit in the back of the room now."

"Ah, politics," Amy said.

Arno's screen beeped and a priority message appeared, more from the Eater:

IT IS INCONSISTENT WITH THE NATURE OF THE UNIVERSE FOR A SEVERELY LIMITED, NATURALLY EMERGED BEING SUCH AS A HUMAN TO BE FULLY ACQUAINTED WITH THE DIVINE, OR WITH CREATED BEINGS OF HIGHER ORDERS.

"Cryptic son of a bitch, isn't it?" Arno prodded them.

"Sounds ominous," Benjamin said.

"Think so? It hasn't even taken notice of what we did." Arno's eyes darkened with worry.

"All this time," Benjamin asked, "it's been carrying on dozens of conversations with specialists, as though nothing happened?"

"Right." Arno thumbed a control. "Here's one that got booted to me. Goes to motives, maybe."

YOU ARE A BEAUTIFUL BRIEF MUSIC, YOU THIRD ORDER CHIMPANZEES.

"So it does know how to toss off a compliment," Amy said sardonically.

"At least that's positive," Arno said a touch defensively.

"I think a bit of physics may be a better guide here than amateur psychoanalysis of an alien mind," Kingsley said.

"You mean its refueling problem," Amy said.

"Quite. It has shed so much energy to slow its prodigious velocity, to get into orbit just above us. Why we do not know, beyond its demands. Still, if it is ever to leave, it must gain mass."

"From where?" Arno asked. "The President wants a list of possibilities from us."

"And options for further action?" Kingsley asked dryly.

"Yes—and right away."

"That'll be due to the prodding of the Science Adviser."

Arno nodded. "It'll be in a nearly circular orbit soon, the trajectory guys project. What will it do then? It can't actually run right into the planet, you all say—"

"Its capabilities are beyond our horizons," Benjamin said.

"The easiest mass to harvest," Amy put in, "is our upper atmosphere. Nice and diffuse, ionized on contact."

This startled Arno. "It would do that? So close to us—"

"It apparently believes itself of a vastly different and superior order, in the biological sense," Kingsley observed distantly. "And probably of a different moral order, as well."

The next few hours proved this to be so.

The Eater began to skate across the top of the atmosphere, skimming over two hundred kilometers high.

Its braking had lit the sky with a many-colored glow rivaling the sun. Vast clouds fumed where its deceleration jet struck the air. It had knifed through the thin upper air in a virulent red firework—aerobraking on a scale vastly beyond the puny spacecraft that humanity had sent into the atmospheres of Mars and Jupiter.

It was like a cannonball tens of miles across, Kingsley thought as he watched the seething display on the big screens. Devouring the air in its wake and using this grist to feed its braking jet. Tunneling through the sky.

In its wake the air closed again. This sent monstrous bass thunderclaps rolling down across whole continents.

The entire Center population emptied onto the surrounding hills to see the thing rise over the western Pacific. The security officers tried but could hardly contain them, over a thousand strong. In the slanting afternoon light, it was easily visible, a radiance that paled the sunlight.

It was already supping of the rarefied gas at that altitude, steadily lowering further, circling the planet in under three hours now.

It seemed to Kingsley like a great spiderweb of innumerable strands. Its looping, dipolar pattern was a brittle blue, laced with flickering orange and yellow spikes as electrodynamic forces worked through it. A snarl of angry purple marked where the leading jet somehow sucked ionized air into the knotted muzzle of tight field lines.

"Bet it's hungry," Amy said.

"Ah, but for what?" Kingsley answered. It came off as more brittle Brit wit, but he meant it earnestly. It had not come here to sample the air, perhaps not even to sample humanity.

He put an arm around her and she nuzzled him, body trembling. He was surprised to feel in her a quaking fear, expressed entirely in body language. So much for the sharp façade.

He, on the other hand, was far better at the stiff-upper-lip act, in fact had done something like that façade—he now felt, suddenly—all through his life. Pretending to be meaner than he in fact was, for starters. He was thinking about this, intently, when he saw Benjamin standing nearby and regarding them with genuine surprise.

Well, they hadn't been secretive about it, just private. And what was a man to do at such a time, in any case?

Benjamin came over and stood awkwardly, obviously not wanting to broach the subject of Amy and yet not wanting to let it go. Kingsley felt a burst of affection for this man, who had endured so much these last few months. But he was no good at expressing such emotions, either. They stood next to each other in the strange, sudden silence that had descended upon the hills all around.

The Eater grew in scale as it passed overhead, unfolding more luminous blue field lines.

These peeled off from the web, lit—or so a Center astrophysicist nearby speculated—by excited oxygen lines as already ionized atoms were caught and compressed by field tensions. It behaved precisely like a beast unfurling great magnetic wings.

At its edge began a medley of glows—yellow, ivory, a satiny green. An atmospheric chemist nearby estimated that this came from its processing of nitrogen and oxygen, the air's two principal gases, in different molecular states. The fretting of light gave the crowd a better view of the size of the thing and gasps came from the crowds. It revolved slowly, as though basking in this bath.

"Thin gruel," Kingsley said.

Only then did he realize the sensation of heady lightness that had been building in him for several moments. An airy lifting.

A creaking came from trees nearby. The crowd stirred like wheat blown by a wind. A shuddering started to come up through his feet. He felt uneasy, then comprehended—

"It's tide. The Eater's mass is raising a tide on the surface of the Earth."

Amy gasped. The sense of lifting strengthened as the Eater neared the peak of the sky, drawing them toward it.

"It's the mass of a moon, orbiting just a few hundred kilometers away," Amy said wonderingly.

The crowd sighed. There was no other word for it. A collective easing as gravity ebbed for a moment. Kingsley felt a release from the burden of weight, stirring his blood at a fundamental level. How like a god . . .

Then they all simply stood and *felt*.

Awe, Kingsley recalled, was a mingling of fear and reverence. Probably few watching from the moist, warm slopes believed in God, but the press of foreboding wonder upon these people was palpable.

The most unexpected aspect of the moment was the thing's monstrous beauty. It rotated again, this time around a different axis. A spew of fire-red brilliance came suddenly from the very center of it, where lurked the accretion disk. The fine field lines of the new jet worked with amber light, extending itself out of the mesh of bruised brilliance. The slow rotation began bringing the jet to point toward the planet's surface.

The first atoms from Earth's air have sputtered down onto the disk, Kingsley guessed. *Can the jet be preparing to raise the orbit already?* The disk was a mere bright scarlet dot.

Hopeless to glimpse the black dot that was the cause of it all, but he tried anyway and failed.

" 'Gruel'?" Benjamin said in a croak. "It can convert maybe ten percent of the mass-energy of what it grabs. Mc^2 is a big number, even from thin air, if it's getting spent in your own neighborhood."

Kingsley hoped that this remark would not be predictive, but he was proved wrong on this same orbit.

The Eater's jet rotated further as the Eater arced across the Pacific and the western United States. Its orbit was tilted with respect to the equatorial plane by about forty degrees, so that it rose to high latitudes as it crossed the twilight line.

No one had foreseen what came next.

The jet brimmed with pulsing ruby light at its core. Then a spike of hard blue light shot from it. Satellite spectral analysis showed this to be high-energy plasma, mostly ionized nitrogen.

This fresh jet struck the upper layers of the atmosphere with a splash of fiery virulence, stripping atoms, heating them, depositing a fraction of the converted mc^2 energy harvested from the tenuous reaches above.

Such energy is restless, always moving. The illuminated spot expanded and reradiated in the infrared spectrum. This propagated downward. Within a minute, a tongue of heat radiation licked at the surface. Where it struck, scorching flames rose.

The jet first forked down above the Midwest. Within minutes, it grew a hundredfold in power. The Eater's central engine was the union of gravity, the fruit of its compacted mass. This coupled with exquisite dexterity to utterly weightless magnetic conduits and accelerators. Watching it function was a rebuke to humanity's pride. This was engineering of a kind and scale to which not even the mad had aspired.

Within moments, the torch was brighter than an early morning sun. It hung in the night air like a moving, radiant lance.

By Ohio the infrared heating had become fierce. It wandered as the Eater rotated, bringing the focus above West Virginia.

"It's writing," Amy whispered. "With a plasma pen."

Kingsley blinked. "On the forests."

"In a line miles wide."

The jet played with skill, tracing out a flowing script. Clearly in the loops and jots there was meaning, but— "No language we know," an expert said nearby. "Something from its past?"

"Cosmic graffiti," Amy said.

Benjamin murmured, "Not everything it does is an attempt at communication. Maybe it's just writing its name."

A long silence fell over the crowd in the Center. They watched with a cold, gathering dread.

Only when it had left the rugged mountains did the brutal heat begin to rise yet again. The entire Eater surged in brilliance, a cobweb prickly with ominous radiance. Millions watched it swell and blossom, its central, shining shaft now unbearably bright to the eye.

Crowds turned from it in terror, but by then its target had become clear to the defensive forces that watched from myriad artificial eyes in orbit and on the ground.

As the resplendent tongue plunged still farther down, into the moist clouds that shrouded the District of Columbia, steam burst where it licked.

The cloud cover evaporated in seconds. Then the hammer blow of infrared struck the river and instantly vapor began to rise there.

Tar bubbled on the roofs of tenements. Trees steamed, then erupted into flame. Within moments, the entire District smoked, then roared out an answer in flame.

People standing in the streets and parks to watch felt their hair crisp and crackle as they ran for cover. Cloth smoked. Fabrics melted. The air hummed. Their homes followed suit, shake roofs flaming into pyres within seconds.

The Eater pulsed, keeping its jet turned artfully toward the

District even as it passed toward the horizon and out over Chesapeake Bay and the Atlantic. The jet ebbed. Orange lightning traced along its retreating shaft. Within a few more minutes, it was a mere kindled spire attached to the broadening web of spiderweb brilliance that dominated the black sky.

A helicopter got a shot of the Eater setting on the horizon like a luminous insect scuttling after fresh prey.

Fire alarms wailed in a chorus of thousands below.

Behind it, the thing left a simmering record of ruin.

"It makes its point well," Kingsley said a while later, when the shock had begun to wear off. The old Gang of Four, minus Channing, found itself in a seminar room, like the meetings they had held what seemed a thousand years before. "It was not fooled for a moment by the launches from China."

"But *how*?" Arno demanded. "The President—thank God, he was underground in the Catskills—demands to know."

"I imagine it is quite versed in our politics by this time. It has been freely dipping into our torrent of news for at least months now—and probably much longer."

"What can we *do*?" Benjamin asked.

"I fear even the generals are stymied. I certainly am." Kingsley felt he should be with Amy now, but he could not very well leave immediately. Her parents lived in Silver Spring, a suburb of the devastated area, and she had broken down as they viewed the aftermath. City-wide fires still raged.

"Give it what it wants," Benjamin said.

"We can't," Arno said. "To force people, kill them—that violates every moral code."

Kingsley said, "I very much doubt that our notions of morality figure largely in this thing's worldview."

"We have to take a stand," Arno said, but without much conviction.

"We are all making the same calculations from our own

moral calculus, I suspect," Kingsley said, "and I do not believe we much like the outcome."

"Let it *have* them!" Benjamin said wildly.

Arno looked at Benjamin, then at Kingsley, who gave him no sign of help. Benjamin gulped, took a breath, then said in a ragged voice, "Look, the thing's probably killed a hundred thousand already. What goddamned difference does it make if . . . if . . ."

"I suggest we begin sending it what we have," Kingsley said coolly.

"Why?" Arno asked anxiously. "That'll take maybe a few days and then it will want more."

"Right. But we will gain time."

"To do what? That's what the President, what the U. goddamned N. wants to know."

"Kill it, if you want."

"How?" Arno demanded.

"I do not know."

Arno's screen beeped and a fresh message appeared:

HE MAKETH ME TO LIE DOWN IN GREEN PASTURES;
HE LEADEST ME BESIDE THE STILL WATERS.

A long silence.

"I rather admire its choice of quotations." Kingsley spoke to cover his own sensation of a rigid chill that swept up from his belly. "It may have a sense of something we could call irony."

Amy said, "More like Zeus than Jehovah."

"Gentlemen," Arno said in a wobbly voice, "we have to tell them something. You saw the crowd outside this office. Good scientists, technical people, sure. That's what they are. But they couldn't come up with anything in their present state of mind."

"Fear paralyzes," Kingsley observed to gain time.

"Anywhere it wants, it can do that—any time it likes," Arno went on.

Kingsley realized that Benjamin had begun to weep, quite quietly. "I advise preoccupying it with fresh input. Give it what we have."

"Then what?"

"Understand it further, certainly. Then kill it, as I said."

"We have nukes, plenty of them—"

"Pointless."

"Probably so. But it's what we've got."

"Not entirely."

They waited for him to complete his thought, and for a moment, something caught in his throat and he could not go on.

Kingsley thought swiftly yet carefully about the properties of magnetic jets. For Benjamin and himself, long ago, the subject had been a suitable battleground for polite academic dispute, arcane calculations, airy and fun. Now he contemplated with cold fear the same images, now augmented with horror. A black hole spinning in its high vault of utter darkness, rotation warping space around it. That distortion, in turn, twisted the assembly of minds that thronged outside the hole, intelligences caught in a magnetic prison older than the sun. The entire grotesque assembly was now impregnable, had proved immune to the defenses of the thousands of civilizations it had consumed like a majestic, marauding appetite—

"We have Channing."

NO BODY IN A BOX

PART SEVEN

NO BODY IN A BOX

1 She *popped—*
   —flowed—
   —expanded—
   —out into the flexing space before her.

Plunging. Riding translucent highways along parabolic lines, she felt unfamiliar muscles work with red heat down her spine, up her legs, skating across a velvet skin she could not see.

She seemed to fill the fat balloon of soft blackness around her. Yet in an eye flick she could be anywhere in that geometry, one of myriad tiny glowing flecks.

Points of view. Searchers. All coasting in a beehive swarm above the great slow-spinning sphere of Earth, itself a mottled infrared mosaic.

So she was a central point in a rotating coordinate frame. And simultaneously the skeletal ivory frame itself. Diffuse, like a fog. Yet if she chose to be, she could anchor herself at a joint.

Cartesian questions, she thought with icy shock. *Baby, I got dem mind-body duality blues. To be a box and know it, yet wonder what it means.*

If she *thought* about herself, a whole interior world welled up. Teeth sang in their sockets. The calcium rods that framed her chest were chromed ribs, slick and sliding in swift metallic grace, *Ah, so clean!* Purpling storms raced down squeezed veins, up shuddering ligaments. Her toes rattled, strumming, talking to the ground she could never again tread. Her ankles were dancing on their own, her bald head thrown back, neck stretched into spaghetti by a halo of po- larized light. Now her spine turned parabolic and crackling as she *banked* on jets that were her feet, running in sheer weightless abandon. Hurricane hallways yawned in her.

What is this thing I am?—and from her a lockjawed agony-song screeched. It reverberated in hip sockets pol- ished by blue-green, hungry worms. They swarmed over bone lattices, eating in rhapsodic hunger.

Pain? Plenty of it.

So stop. Click. Just like that—

The torture fingers left her, blew away in the escaping fragile seconds, leaving her cool and smooth and sure. *To be a box.*

Down she went, across and through—all equivalent in this space of freedom-as-thing. She saw before her, around her, in full three dimensions. The Searcher spacecraft, a sil- very swarm zooming in toward the graceful arching lumi- nesce of the Eater.

A blink—and the Searchers became her many eyes.

Her point of view shot through the realm of the magnetic strands, high above the disk of hot matter in the black hole's equatorial plane. Beyond rolled the gravid Earth in regal, moist splendor. Around her magnetic palaces made a lumi- nous dominion, a steel-wire spider at the gnawing center of a gigantic web. She swiveled and found the core—geysers and light storms arcing from the utterly black center of it all.

A rattle of human-speak came to her like pebbles on a tin roof. *Careful, vector to 0.347 x 1.274.*

Yessah, boss. Here there be tygers, galleries of magnetic forces to traverse.

Skating. She eased delicately past white-hot waterfalls, green-rich tornadoes of turbulence. *Tock!*—a stone-storm of crass dusty plasma clattered against her carbon carapace. Raw food the Eater had stored. Or a weapon; one could not be sure.

Did it know they were here? Of course, impossible to believe it could not sense along its electromagnetic tendrils these flashing solid motes. Two Searchers already drifted, charred by discharges.

So it would kill them if it could locate them. *Us. Me.*

More Searchers rose from below to aid her. Abruptly some sparked to burnt cinders at the very rim of magnetic stresses, killed by some edge defense. She had lodged in several knots already, then had to bail out as they arced with huge potentials.

Yet she could not shake the airy feeling of floating suspended above a huge abyss.

Diffuse am I, for I am nothing that has ever existed. Like the Eater—one of a kind.

Getting heady here. Careful. Too easy to get drawn into phony poetic abstraction.

And what else dwelled here? Hesitantly, working as intermediary with Control, she felt her way among ropes of snarled flux. Edgy, tentative, the whispery sounds came—voices, calls, and cries and strange haunting musics, wisps of convex lore, echoes of . . . what? A multitude floated in her global, three-dimensional eyes—shining, ghostlike creatures of strands and velvet, lustrous lattice.

Creeping among complex innards. Yet again she felt a cool distance from events. She was free to slide in and out of this world.

Only a lack of imagination saves me from immobilizing myself with imaginary fears.

Her eyes were all-seeing, swiveling impossibly, anywhere she wanted. In her other self, the eyes had been where the brain surfaced and supped from the world, taking in light along an optic nerve that both transmitted and filtered, doing the brain's work before the glow even arrived at the cerebrum.

Now she felt a wedge between her and the world she could behold. A chunk of glassy silence that measured and knew, separately.

Gingerly she burrowed into that watery pane. A dizzy, jolting ascent took her. Suddenly she was hanging above the entire solar system. She glimpsed it as a spheroid cloud of debris, filigreed with bands and shells of flying shrapnel.

She knew instantly that these fragments could be pumped into long ellipses, into wobbly orbits that could now and then make a sharp hook by skimming near another piece of scrap, and slam into a blundering planet.

"What was that?" she asked aloud. (How? Yet they rang like words.)

Control's monotone answered, "You slipped into the overview mode of our entire Searcher system inventory. Don't do that again. Concentrate."

"Yessah." Control was, well, controlling. It (he?—yes, it felt like a he) kept missing the point of her experience here.

Instantly, some subself presented a catalog of possible wisecrack material:

> *One sandwich short of a picnic.*
> *Elevator doesn't go to the top floor.*
> *One brick short of a full load.*
> *Couple chapters missing from the book.*
> *Half a bubble off plumb.*
> *Gears stripped off a few cogs.*
> *A beer short of a six-pack.*

Now where did that—

The enormity of what had happened to her descended.

Benjamin, forever gone from her.

The world—swallowed in abstraction.

No salty tang of sandy beach. *Just a bunch of digits.*

So when she wanted to speak, an inventory of retorts had duly shuffled into her mind, read off like a computer file. Not invention, but a handy list of stock phrases. Because it was waiting for just that use—somewhere.

No, not somewhere. *Here.* Blackboxville.

Had her mind had those lists in it all her life? She could understand why the brain researchers wanted to use simulations such as herself. Here, a mind could sometimes watch itself.

"Try to focus all the Searchers onto the core." Control's voice now was smoother, warm, and soothing. A response to her irked state? "Channing, we have got to get better resolution."

She felt her eyes seem to *cross* and then rush outward.

Suddenly she sensed the hourglass magnetic funnels, alive in their luminous ivory, as mass flowed down them. Fitfully the aching matter lit the turning, narrowing pipes. Each headed toward doom.

The fields were firmly anchored in a bright, glowing disk at the center of the hourglass neck. The Eater's intelligence, she knew, resided in these magnetic structures she could make out—knotted and furled, like lustrous ribbons surrounding the slowly rotating hourglass.

Zoom, she moved. At her finest viewing scale she could make out the magnetic intricacy—whorls and helices as complex as the mapping of a brain. Here the legacy of a thousand alien races rested, she knew (but how?).

All this stood upon the brilliant disk at the neck. Glowing mass flowed down the hourglass neck, heading toward the glare.

The inner realm of the Eater was its foundation, the turning accretion disk. She blinked, recalibrated specter. It brimmed red-hot at its rim, a kilometer from the dark center. The disk was thickest at its edge, *a hundred meters tall* some part of her crisply told her.

As the infalling, gyrating mass moved inward to its fate, it heated further by friction. Inward it seethed with luminosity, shading in from red to amber to yellow to white, and then to a final, virulent blue. The red rim was already 3,000 degrees (a subself informed her). Abstractly she knew that in the slide inward the doomed mass exceeded the temperature of the surface of the sun, greater than 5,000 degrees.

"Look closer," Control said in the comforting tones of . . . who? Memory would not fetch this forth . . .

Closer. There at the very center—nothing, a blank blackness. Like a hallucinogenic record turning to its own furious music, faster and faster toward the center, where the spindle hole was a nothing.

But not quite nothing. At higher resolution—and blinded against the glare—she could see a fat weight that warped light around it. At its very edge, red refractions and darting rainbow sparklers marked the space. She saw that an ellipsoid spun there, furiously laced by crimson arcs. As she watched, fiery matter traced its last trajectory inward, skating along the rim of the whirling dark. These paths swerved inward, and a very few skipped through the wrenching blackness to emerge again.

"Unstable orbits, I see," Control said.

She felt a wave of immense dread. Yet she headed down there.

2 Benjamin drove stolidly toward the Center. His arms were of lead, his head swiveled on scratchy ratchets.

That morning a poll had reported that the world was praying more since news had come of the Eater. There was even a statistical breakdown, showing what were the hot topics on the prayer circuit:

1. Family's health and happiness	83%
2. Salvation from black hole	81%
3. Personal spiritual salvation	78%
4. Return of Jesus Christ	55%
5. Good grades	43%
6. End of an addiction	30%
7. Victory in sports	23%
8. Material possessions	18%
9. Bad tidings for someone else	5%

"Good to know the species hasn't lost its bloody-mindedness," Kingsley remarked from the seat next to him.

" 'Bad tidings for someone else,' " Benjamin said sourly. "As if there weren't enough."

"Um. You mean this news of the Eater's course correction?"

"Yeah. What's it moving to higher altitude for?"

"It won't say, as usual."

On the drive, he saw yet another church going up, this time in a converted gas station. Stumps of pump stands extruded from the concrete islands in front. Churches were thronged every day now. New ones jutted their flick-knife spires above the palms.

He had gotten better and could now go for maybe a whole hour without thinking of her. He had found himself reviewing their life together to get himself ready for what was to come this morning. They had followed what he supposed to be a predictable arc. Passion had settled down into possession, courtship into partnership, acute pleasure into pleasant habit. For both of them, lives that once had seemed to spread infinitely before them had narrowed to one mortal career. To accomplish anything definite, they had given up everything else, sailing for one point of the compass. Yet he had the hollow feeling of missed opportunities. Could something be made good through what he had to do next?

"It shouldn't be too demanding," Kingsley said out of the silence.

"I'm that easy to read?"

"Old friend, depression is simple to diagnose. You are acting under intolerable pressures."

He slammed a fist into the steering wheel. "I have to keep working."

"Of course. And you're vital."

"If only I could sleep."

"Haven't been getting a lot of that myself, either."

"At least—"

"What? Ah, you were going to say, at least I have Amy."

"Yeah."

"And so I do. Not as though it is a betrayal of my dear wife."

"How is she?"

"Had word just last night. Coded, of course. From a country cottage she arranged through friends. Indeed, the U Agency had conducted an extensive search for her. She barely got away."

"You're sure they were going to hold her hostage?"

"One is never certain. I felt that I could not risk it."

"She might have been safer."

"With *that*"—a finger poked skyward—"prowling the skies? I expect it can strike any place it likes, to whatever depth."

"The infrared only bakes the surface."

"Do we truly wish to learn more of its capabilities?"

"Ummm, good point."

They let a companionable silence build between them. Benjamin was comfortable this way, just sliding on from moment to moment, trying not to think of what they would ask him to do. As they left their car and passed through the layers of security at the Center, he felt tensions building in him again, but fought them down.

There passed before his eyes procedures and people and none of it left any lasting impression. Amy Major, looking more worn than usual, was there when they got to the Control wing. She came out and greeted them and Kingsley instantly asked, "What signs do we have of its state of mind?"

"Still no mention of the whole Washington burning episode," Amy said.

"Damn." Kingsley's face was knotted with frustration. "How can we conceivably understand it if the thing gives no clue?"

"I suppose that's the point," Amy said mildly, putting a hand on his sleeve.

For some reason, that simple gesture brought a tightness welling into Benjamin's throat. He almost lost his remaining scraps of composure then. It took a moment and a dodge about going for coffee before he could trust himself to speak. "What's it saying, then?"

Amy called up its latest dispatch to the Semiotics contingent:

YOUR BIOSPHERE HAS MANIFESTED FOUR PINNACLES OF SOCIAL EVOLUTION. FIRST WERE THE COLONIAL,

SPINELESS SUCH AS THE CORAL REEFS. THEY ACHIEVED NEARLY PERFECT COHESION AMONG INDIVIDUAL UNITS THAT DIFFERED LITTLE IN THEIR GENES. INSECTS ATTAINED A PEAK, THOUGH WITH MUCH MORE DIFFERENCE BETWEEN INDIVIDUALS. STILL LESSER PERFECTION OF SOCIAL GRACE CAME WITH THE SPINED ANIMALS OTHER THAN YOUR-SELVES. THEY COOPERATE BUT HAVE MUCH DIFFERENT GENOMES. THIS TREND FROM CORALS TO ANTS TO BABOONS MY-SELF HAS SEEN ON HUNDREDS OF WORLDS. COMPLEXITY SELECTS FOR SELFISH, LESS SOCIAL BEHAVIOR. THE BEAUTY OF THIS LOGIC IS PROFOUND: WHEN GENETICALLY NEARLY IDENTICAL, ALTRUISM ABOUNDS AND COOPERATION THRIVES. AS GENETIC RELATEDNESS EBBS, SO DOES INTENSITY OF SOCIAL BEHAVIOR. UNTIL YOUR KIND. YOUR-SELVES EMPLOY SOCIAL STRUCTURES OF THE SPINED CLASS BUT COMPLEXIFY IT. YOU RETAIN SELFISHNESS BUT USE INTELLIGENCE TO CONSULT YOUR PAST AND PLAN YOUR FUTURE. THIS REVERSED THE DOWNWARD TREND IN COOPERATION THAT MARKED THE LAST BILLION YEARS OF YOUR BIOSPHERE'S EVOLUTION. THIS IS YOUR UNIQUE ASPECT, AS THE THREE OTHER MODES I MENTIONED ARE PEAKS SCALED REPEATEDLY BY INDEPENDENTLY EVOLVING LINES OF CREATURES.

"Intriguing miserable little lecture, isn't it?" Kingsley said. "Makes one wonder if its droll sense of humor extends to making fun of us through acute boredom."

"Sounds like a curator making up the label it will put on its newest exhibit," Benjamin said.

"Good analogy," Amy said. "Now shall we . . . ?"

Here came the part he had been dreading. They marched him through a large bay filled with work stations, people quietly monitoring the intricate tasks of managing the Searcher fleet. They were an exact duplicate of NASA's operating room at Houston, assembled here at blinding speed in case communications broke down. Backup was the watchword.

In a separate room, they seated him at the center of a kind of spherical viewscreen. Leads measured his vital signs, a complex head gear descended, much buzzing and clicking began as they got him calibrated. He had given up trying to fathom all the technology. Then—

He was *with* her. No point in wondering how it was done; he felt himself suddenly in a presence he recognized. He had to struggle to not look around and find her. But she was nowhere at all, he reminded himself. Instead, the spherical screens showed him what she saw, a field of dark dominion dotted with Searcher radar images.

"How are you, lover?" she asked.

"I . . . am doing . . . okay." Like molasses, his tongue.

"I am, too."

He could not help himself. "What does it feel like to be . . . a mathematical construction?"

"However I want it to feel."

"You can control . . ."

"The body simulation? Yes. My feelings, in the old sense? No."

Her voice had shifted into a cool, analytical mode. But it was hers, all the same. How did they do it? Or was she . . . it . . . doing this? "I . . . see. No pain?"

"Physical, no. I . . . I miss you so much."

He could not seem to get his breath. "Well, here I am."

"With me. Again. Thank you for coming."

Alarm filled his otherwise empty mind. He could not think of anything to say that did not seem to mean something else. "Do you . . . like the work?"

"Let us say that I am willing to make the mistakes if someone else is willing to learn from them."

"Ah. Yes."

"You are wondering if this is really me."

"I wonder who you are, yes, but—" He froze. But what?

"Perhaps you are afraid that I am her?"

"Damn, you were always good at reading me."

"Do not give me that much credit. I made my mistakes."

"You were smarter than I was."

"I often proved that high intelligence did not necessarily guarantee fine table manners."

He tried to laugh and could not. Somehow the remark was amusing, but the delivery was wrong. He tried a gruff, bantering tone. "Yeah, old girl, you did."

"I would feel better if you did not use the past tense."

"Oh. I didn't mean—"

"Just a joke."

"I always liked your jokes."

"They were an acquired taste. Remember what my grandfather used to say? 'Eat a live toad at breakfast and nothing worse will happen to you the rest of the day.' My jokes played that role for some people."

"Yeah, I *do* remember your telling me that." He felt a wash of relief. If this voice knew that much about her past—but then he felt confusions rise again. The specialists had said that they could copy memories without knowing what they were. Like a symphony laid down on a disk, the machine that did it didn't need to know harmony or structure.

Just a recording. But she was so real.

Better get back onto something that would let him conceal his tornado of feeling. "How's the job going?" The words sounded phony, but maybe she wouldn't notice.

She laughed, surprising him again. "Like being a bird, sometimes."

"Sounds great."

"I spent a lot of time just getting used to this body-that-isn't."

"Bird body?" He didn't know where this was going, but at least it wasn't about how he felt, a subject upon which he was no expert.

"Birdbrain, it feels like sometimes."

She pinged right back to his pong, but wasn't giving much

away. *Okay, be direct.* "They moved you around the Earth after it hit Washington?"

"Yes, I got an extra booster attached by a crew that flew up to rendezvous. That got me out here, to keep me away from that damned jet. How many people did it kill?"

"A quarter of a million, the last I heard." He had stopped listening to the news then.

"It's moving out now, I heard." Actually, he had seen the jet flare and drive the thing away from the low orbit. And heard the muted cheering of hundreds around him, outside in the night. The yelling had blended anger and wavering hope.

"Slow but steady. Don't know—damn, there goes another."

"Another what?"

A silence. Then: "Another satellite, a communications one this time. It got the Fabricante orbital an hour ago. There were two people aboard."

"Damn. It's doing that? I really ought to keep up."

"You've had a lot of grief. Give yourself a rest."

Suddenly her voice was not the cool, businesslike tone that she had been using. The words resonated with feminine notes he had come to love. He said, "You need me. I hope."

"Oh yes, I do more than ever."

"You've got it in view?"

"I can see the orange plume of the jet, but I'm staying away. Tracking the satellite damage. It's eaten hundreds—"

Onto the enveloping spherical screen blossomed a sharp image. Coils of magnetic field tightening around a chunky satellite. Folding it in. Then vaporizing it with a virulent arc of high voltage. The plasma glowed green and violet traceries sucked it along the field lines, bound for the accretion disk.

"Got tired of our atmosphere?" he asked.

"Or bored."

"Are you getting some feeling for it?"

"It has a lot of parts and they fit together in a way I can't see yet."

"Don't get any closer."

"I'm thousands of klicks away."

"Keep it that way."

"I think it knows I'm here."

Alarm stuck in his throat. "How?"

"I don't know, just an intuition."

"Has it done anything, struck against you?"

"No, and I don't know why not, either. Probably I'm just not important enough."

"You are to me. Don't get closer."

"Distance didn't do the President any good, did it?"

"What do you mean?"

"It blasted the terrain around that dugout of his in the Catskills on its next pass over the D.C. area."

"It did?" He really wasn't keeping track. Or had he heard and just forgotten? He had to admit he didn't give a damn about what happened to the President.

"I believe he survived—barely. It doesn't say a word about any of that, of course."

"Our spanking administered, it drops the subject?" Benjamin knew his words were coming out jagged.

"Nope, Kingsley was right. Keep away from human analogies."

He didn't want to say what immediately came to mind, so sure enough, she did instead: "Speaking as an analogy myself, I think that's good advice."

He could not summon even a dutiful chuckle, but she laughed with what seemed to be gusto.

3 "Nothing is impossible to those who do not have to do it," Kingsley remarked caustically.

Arno bristled. "I have every assurance from the President that—"

"That he doesn't know what he is doing," Kingsley finished. He instantly reprimanded himself for this childish outburst, but Arno's face already congested with red anger.

"You are not to take this any further—"

"Sorry, but I have to say this is stupid."

"If it can't hear our media, it won't know as much."

"Yes, but hasn't a moment's inspection of its many transmissions told us that it likes listening in?"

"Intelligence has established that leaks onto cable TV led it to deduce that the launches were ours."

"This thing is not an idiot. It knows quite well the state of international politics. Little children in the street guessed the truth—why shouldn't the Eater?"

Arno subsided slightly, long enough for Benjamin to say, "I don't think it's a good idea, either."

"Who *cares*?" Arno flared again. "You guys don't get any say. The White House just wondered what you thought it would do when the President's—*and* the U.N.'s—shutdown starts."

"When will it be?" Kingsley asked with what he hoped was a calm, interested expression. *Hard to attain these days, though.*

Arno glanced at his watch. "Two hours."

"Expect something bad," Benjamin said, then went back to looking at his shoes.

"I agree," Kingsley said.

"Why? The whole planet ceases all transmissions, including satellite cable traffic, telephones, radio, TV. So what?"

"It will not like any sign that we're breaking off contact," Benjamin said, a lackluster sentence that he tossed off as though he was thinking of something else. Which he probably was. Since leaving the comm apparatus where he had spent several hours with the Channing-craft, he had been distracted. No surprise, but Kingsley needed help and in this climate old allies were the best. At least with Benjamin, he did not have to watch his back.

"I don't see why that has to be," Arno said. "It's been sending lots of chatty stuff, never mentions the D.C. thing or the missiles."

"Aliens are alien," Kingsley said, trying not to sound as though he were talking to a child. "Do not misread—which is to say, do not ascribe easy motives to its statements."

"Look, the Security Council thinks this is the best way to show it that we aren't giving away any secrets, not anymore."

"How jolly."

"Look, it even sent a commentary on Marcus Aurelius to one of the cultural semiotics people. Philosophy—and it seemed to agree with this guy." Arno mugged a bit and folded his arms, leaning back against his desk in a way that Kingsley had come to know signaled what Arno thought was a put-away shot.

Kingsley disliked obvious displays of erudition, but here was a useful place for it. "Aurelius was a stoic, resigned to the evil of the world, wishing to detach himself from it. Also happened to be an Emperor of Rome, which curiously enough made detachment an easier prospect. Before organized press conferences, as I recall. Not the sort of attitude I would wish of a thing that could incinerate the planet."

Arno looked wounded, an about-face from his flash of belligerence only moments before. Everyone seemed to be running on fast-forward now. He said gravely, "It's getting more refined, if that's the right word."

"Is it progress if a cannibal uses a knife and fork?" Kingsley asked, crossing his legs wearily.

Benjamin laughed, just the wrong thing to do. Sarcasm was useful only if played deadpan straight. Arno did not take Benjamin's chuckling well, reddening up in the nose and cheeks again.

"I mean that you cannot mistake a change of style for change of purpose." Kingsley hoped that stating the obvious would get them back on track. People under strain sometimes had such a reset ability, and perhaps it could get him out of this scrape.

"I understand," Arno said, "but the President wants an assessment of what to expect *when*"—heavy emphasis here, with eyebrows—"the shutdown starts."

"Retribution, I should say," Kingsley said.

Benjamin managed a wan smile, still regarding his shoes with intense interest. "You're slipping into human thought modes yourself, ol' King boy. Alien, it might do anything."

Arno said hotly, "That's no damn good, tell the White House the sonuvabitch could do any damn thing—"

"Though it has the utility of being true," Kingsley said.

"I bet it will do both." Benjamin looked up then and smiled, as if at a joke he alone knew. "Something nasty, and something weird."

"Good point," Kingsley said. "No reason it must do only one thing."

"You guys are no damn use at all."

"You bet," Benjamin said with something that resembled happiness. Kingsley studied him, but could make nothing of the expression on his old friend's face.

4 Benjamin wondered when the gray curtains would go away. They hung everywhere, deadening, muffling. Even this latest bad news took place behind the veils. He registered the dispatches, but his pulse did not quicken and the world remained its flat, pallid tone.

"What the hell *is* it?" Arno asked the assembled mix.

Amy said in a voice obviously kept clear and deliberate, after the panic of the last ten minutes, "A magnetic loop. It's tight, small, and moving at very high velocity."

"Headed where?" Arno asked a man in a gray suit whom Benjamin had never seen before.

"Intersecting the Pacific region in about twenty minutes."

"It's that fast? The Eater's a long way out now, nearly geosynchronous." Arno looked around the room for help.

"The hole ejected it half an hour ago," Amy said. "We caught it all across the spectrum."

"What'll we do?" Arno glanced at his watch, at his U Agency advisers, back to the astronomers.

"No time for a warning," Benjamin said, just to be saying something.

"Where'll it hit?" Arno licked his lips.

"Looks like mid-Pacific," the gray-suited man said.

"Why in hell shoot at that?"

"We are in the mid-Pacific," Kingsley said quietly.

"At us? It's shooting at us?"

"A testable hypothesis," Kingsley said. "I imagine this is intended to establish some principle. Were the Eater human, I would suppose this would be in retaliation for some injury."

A voice across the room said irritably, "We haven't done anything."

Benjamin said, "We cut off all radio and TV. When did that start?"

Arno bit his lip. "About an hour ago."

"Long enough for the planet to rotate a bit," Kingsley added. "Enough time to establish that the silence did not arise from a power outage or accident."

"Why this, then?" a voice called.

Amy said, "It wants electromagnetic transmissions resumed. It launches a magnetic loop, using electromagnetic acceleration. Maybe that's the connection."

Arno glowered. "Sounds pretty far-fetched."

Amy gave him a long, level look and her voice was steady. "It anchors its magnetic fields in the accretion disk and on the hole itself. It managed to disconnect one of its field lines and tie the ends together, then propel it out through the overall magnetic structure. We've never seen anything like it, not even in the magnetic arches that grow on the sun, structures thousands of kilometers across."

"So?" Arno was weighing all this, but saw no way to go.

Kingsley said diplomatically, "I believe Amy's point is that the Eater knows magnetics the way your tongue knows your teeth."

Arno grimaced at this as the big screen filled behind him. A view from one of the few surviving satellites, Benjamin saw, looking at a tangent to the Pacific. Sunset was behind the satellite and the image was in the near-infrared. The ocean shimmered dimly and some stars stood out as yellow.

These false colors threw off Benjamin's judgment for a moment as he studied the vectors of the problem. Against the black sky a luminous blue hoop moved. Its trajectory was simple to estimate. Measured by eye, its distance from the curve of the Earth was closing.

"How big?" Arno's mouth drew into an alarmed thin line.

"It started out a few kilometers across," Amy said. "Elementary electrodynamics—once a loop is free, it expands. Or should."

"What can it do?" Arno pressed.

"Let's go outside and see." Benjamin made for the door.

"Huh?" Arno held up a hand. "What's the deal?"

It proved to be easily visible. The slanted angle cast the perfect circle into an ellipse. It had hit the upper atmosphere and glowed a cherry red. "We're seeing some molecular line, must be," a voice commented in the darkness. Benjamin realized that word had spread and now hundreds stood nearby on an open, grassy hill immediately behind the Center. A soft tropical breeze warmed the thick air.

Amy said, "It's headed this way."

The crowd rustled anxiously. "They have every reason to worry," Benjamin said to Kingsley and Amy.

"You think it's aimed at us?" someone nearby whispered.

"What else that's relevant to the Eater is in the Pacific?" Benjamin whispered back.

"What can it do?" Arno suddenly asked. Benjamin jumped at the rough, distressed voice just over his shoulder. "I mean, this isn't like that jet."

"It's magnetic energy, efficiently stored," Benjamin answered. "Right now it's banking to the left—see?" The hoop had slid slightly to the side. "Probably hobnobbing with the Earth's field, though I guess it's much bigger than ours."

"Right," Amy said. "Imagine, throwing off a loop and aiming it accurately through our dipolar field structure. Got to admire its ability."

"Best not to stress that particular angle," Kingsley advised. "Though I concur."

"What can it *do*?" Arno insisted.

Nobody spoke, so Benjamin guessed, "The energy density is pretty high, if it had around ten kiloGauss fields where it started, back in the accretion disk. I'd estimate—" He multiplied the energy density, which scaled as the square of the field strength, by a reasonable volume. This he judged by eye as the glowing thing crawled across the blackness. Getting larger, spreading. "Around a hundred kilotons of available energy, if it can annihilate all the field."

"Everybody inside!" Arno shouted suddenly.

"Why?" someone called.

"Security!" Arno bellowed. "Get them inside—*now!*"

Benjamin avoided the herd stampeding for the buildings by walking quickly into a stand of eucalyptus nearby. When he turned to watch the sky, he saw figures following him and realized he was an amateur at this, they certainly would use infrared goggles or something to round people up.

"Good idea," Kingsley whispered. Amy was with him. "I rather figure the buildings are more dangerous, not less."

"Why?" Benjamin asked.

"I doubt your calculation applies here. No simple way to get more than a small fraction of the field energy to annihilate. How would the hoop twist around to get the fields counteraligned, then rub them together?"

Amy whispered, "I see—so instead, it'll just produce an electromagnetic sizzle."

"Seems reasonable." Kingsley moved deeper in among the heavily scented eucalyptus.

Benjamin jibed, "Reasonable? Violating the remember-it's-alien rule, aren't you?"

"Ah, but you see, it's not stupid. Surely it's playing by the same physics rule book as ourselves."

Amy said, "It made a remark about exactly that a few days ago, I saw. Something about our having the basics down, but missing the larger point. Irked the hell out of the physics guys when it wouldn't tell them anything more, aside from some math nobody could recognize."

"I wonder if it has a cruel streak," Benjamin murmured.

"They begged it for details. It wouldn't even answer."

"It prefers rather different modes of reply, I'll wager," Kingsley whispered.

The tall eucalyptus trees rattled their branches in the sea

breeze. The contrast of their moist aroma and the coolly descending luminosity above was striking. Benjamin moved to see the sky better. Kingsley called, "Stay well back. They're searching."

But now the numerous Security men were craning up at the sky. The loop was inflating, filling the black bowl, dimming the stars. Its glow had shifted to an eerie, bile green. They could see elaborate structure now. Soundlessly the green strands coiled and flexed like strange, swelling snakes.

Now one edge of the loop alone striped across their view. At its edges, a thin line of orange flared. "Shock boundary, I bet," Amy mused.

Filmy green filaments twisted above them, closing fast. There seemed to Benjamin no place to flee—and no reason to run, anyway. It would come and the whole matter was out of his hands. Beyond intellectual curiosity, none of this had moved him.

Now they could see the full complexity of it as the emerald strands shaded into delicate lime structures. Apparently it was traveling faster than sound, for nothing disturbed the soft symphony of the wind. Palm fronds rattled and someone shouted in the distance. Life went on beneath an olive sky.

Just before it hit, he heard a crackling from the Center. A power pole nearby burst into a yellow firework. Sizzling balls arced up in a blinding fountain.

"Transformers blowing," Kingsley said in a normal voice. "I do hope Arno thought to switch off the power."

Amy said, "The lights are still on in there."

"Damn."

The human body cannot perceive magnetic field except at enormous strengths. Still, Benjamin felt a pulse of electricity jitter through him as all the lights went out. Immediately afterward his skin itched in quick, darting waves. Then it was all over, the familiar night sky returning, constellations embodying human legends stretched across a comforting black. Yet as he gazed up, the distant fuzzy blue-white of the Eater hung like a threat among the myriad stars—one of them, celestial, not like anything a primate born in moist chemistry could comprehend.

He breathed in the almost liquid density of tropical air and let it out with a sigh. Magnetic fields could not directly harm beings who were, after all, packages of long organic molecules in dilute solutions, capable of standing erect and studying stars.

Maybe there was some small comfort in that bare fact.

He walked down the hill toward the Center with Amy and Kingsley. Cries came up toward them. Somewhere a window shattered.

It was a while before he noticed that the gray veils were gone for him. But he knew that they would return whenever he thought of her.

5 "Not overly surprising," Kingsley said as he un-
wound into one of the massage chairs Benjamin had
in his office. *For Channing* came the memory.

"What?" Benjamin was still a bit foggy. Even Arno's
anger after the attack—"Why didn't you guys *warn* me?"—
had not shaken him into paying much attention. Understandable, even in an ordinary time. But in this on-rolling
calamity, ordinary sensibilities had to be put aside. Kingsley
firmly told himself that he could not take the time to be the
sympathetic friend, letting time heal wounds. There was no
time—not for anyone.

"That she seems so like Channing," Kingsley said as
mildly as he could.

"Oh. She . . . is Channing."

"An interesting philosophical issue, but not my point."

"All the Channing I've got left."

"Quite." An emotional truth, and there was the nub of the
problem. How to put this? Directly, perhaps? Always risky,
but he owed Benjamin that. "The essential of this issue is
whether she can be relied upon to perform as would the
Channing we knew."

"Know," Benjamin corrected without looking up from the
floor.

"Old friend, there are sophomore distinctions to be made
here that have ramifications on policy."

Benjamin gave a dry chuckle. "I sense a lecture coming on."

"A short one, I hope. Asking for an objective understanding of an interior experience is a contradiction. Objectivity is a direction along which understanding can travel, starting with the utterly subjective, but there is no true, final destination along that axis."

"So we can't know if she's 'really' Channing?" Benjamin said caustically. "Fine. So be it. I'll take what I can get."

"We can expect her to be a quite good . . . simulation."

"It's all of her there is."

"Yes." This was a damnable situation, but he had promised Arno that he would try to deal with the problem. Far better a friend than the team of mind managers Arno had recruited. How to proceed? Retreat to the technical? Perhaps. At least he would feel better himself on some safe ground for a moment.

"The data-processing issue is no longer a major roadblock, after all," Kingsley said, probably a bit too brightly. "Estimates I've seen hold that the total memory of a hundred-year-old person could be about 10^{15} bits—a pentabit, the experts label it. That may be transmitted by optical fiber in a few minutes. Microwaves, somewhat longer."

"Ah." Benjamin's lined face said quite eloquently that he did not like this way of thinking of the woman he loved. Quite right, but there it was.

"So they may have—what was that awful word they used?—'harvested' quite a lot of her, even given the difficulties with her physical deterioration."

Benjamin said, "I never thought it could be like this. Maybe a thing like a computer program, accessing memory files, a robot . . . that's what I imagined."

"The computer johnnies are advancing relentlessly. Quite left me behind long ago."

"Look." He leaned forward earnestly. "She's still the woman who was an astronaut. She's reliable."

"I take your point. That is what Arno wishes to know and

cannot properly ask. So an old friend gets to do the dirty work."

"Yeah. Why?"

"Well, they have contingency plans . . ." Best to let that one trail off, fraught with implication. Not that Kingsley knew all the possible options. Arno never showed all his cards.

"They always do. Guys behind desks dreaming up stuff for other people to do."

"We have many such now, all around the globe. Not that we get all their input. The magnetic attack took out a great deal, but we're getting most of the high-bit-rate equipment back online. 'Crippled but defiant' is, I think, the motto."

"The reason I asked, she wants to know what to expect."

"Ummm. Just what one would expect."

Alarm whitened Benjamin's eyes. "She's going in?"

"She must. The Searchers go well ahead of her, of course. But she's got to be near them, not on the other side of the planet."

"Look, keep her standing a long way off."

"I will, I assure you. But she may not do what we want."

"Why not?"

"She has autonomous control of her propulsion. There are extras all over her Searcher module. Everything they could bolt on, it would seem."

"She used to talk about the free will problem. Here it is. Is a simulation unpredictable?"

"No one knows, not at this level of technical ability. We may not have the computational power to even decide the issue in a useful passage of time." Kingsley grinned. "She always had a taste for paradoxes. This one is, no doubt, delicious to her."

" 'Delicious'?" Benjamin gazed off into space. "I hope so."

"I believe she wants us to anticipate."

"I see." Benjamin sat up, brushing aside his reflections. "Say, what do you make of all this data we're getting?"

Benjamin's open-faced entreaty was disarming. In the last few weeks, Kingsley had spent a great deal of his time trying to fathom what the people who thought about thinking made of the Eater's structure. As usual with those most comfortable among abstractions, the gritty truths of a wholly new way of organizing a mind sent most of them packing. The few who remained dealt in analogy, and he could not blame them.

To his relief, Amy came in and sat. Without a word, she somehow lifted the tension in the room—only one of her many admirable qualities. He filled her in on matters and she nodded. "Sorry I'm late. We're getting stretched thin. Arno is bringing in more people and somebody has to integrate them with existing systems."

"We're to be independent of NASA and the others, I gather," Kingsley said.

"In case we lose all the remaining satellites, yes." She brushed back her hair, a gesture that usually meant she was thinking hard. "Do you think we could?"

Benjamin said, "Easily. It has a large appetite."

"One should be grateful that it discovered the apparently more bountiful feast of our satellites," Kingsley mused.

"Is the damage from the tidal stresses still going on?" Amy asked.

"Earthquakes and the like, yes. We're spared the collapsing buildings and large tides," Kingsley said.

"Thank God. I hadn't heard . . ." Benjamin's subdued tone trailed off and he stared into space.

"Makes one appreciate as never before the simple fact that tidal forces drop off as the cube of distance, not merely the square," Kingsley said. "A ruthless tutelage in undergraduate mechanics."

This attempt to swerve the discussion into more abstract avenues failed; Benjamin did not react. He and Amy exchanged glances. She said, "We've got to get some idea of what Channing is going to confront if she goes in further."

This roused Benjamin to blinking awareness. He sat up

and said with a hollow briskness, "The magnetic geometry, yeah. I've looked at some of the old models. Not much use. We're skating on our own here."

Good, Kingsley thought, *back on solid technical grounds. Best way to keep him sailing upright.* "I think we have to follow analogies here. Alien this bastard may be, but its physics is the same as ours."

Amy came straight in with some material they had discussed in private. Her usual crisp delivery: "Human brains operate on direct current, like telephones. Radio and TV use alternating current and deliver information far faster than D.C. My guess is that the Eater uses electromagnetic waves to send signals across itself, so its natural flow rate is not the petty human scale of ten or twenty bits per second. Instead, the Eater can transmit data at about the same rate that the entire human body receives all its sense data and processes it. Maybe as much as ten billion bits per second."

Benjamin responded, "Okay, but to do that demands high, oscillating voltages. Which fits—it shorts out satellites, boils them off as plasma, grabs them with magnetic grapples, swallows them."

Kingsley said mordantly, "Reminds one of spiders. This picture means, though, that the bastard has to keep itself thoroughly clean."

Amy nodded. "Because impurities could short out its high voltages."

Benjamin joined in with sudden fervor, "And burn away its enormous energy stores into useless heat."

"Good," Amy said. "I was thinking about what Channing might meet if she goes as far in as its magnetosphere. The D.C. voltages and speeds of human expression are imposed by our hopelessly slow, serial method of stringing words together. Luckily, human thinking is far faster than human talking or reading, which is why all the true mental heavy lifting is done by the nonconscious mind. All our data suggest that the Eater's speed is essential, because it's vastly different in mental organization. *That's* what we have to attack, or at least understand."

When Kingsley first met Amy, it had been uncommon for her to deliver little lectures like this, but she had grown in confidence. After his failures with his wife, this small feat pleased him. He urged her along with: "If I follow your drift, the human mind can be visualized—by the cliché analogy to computers—as a great number of parallel processors, simultaneously filtering and analyzing the exterior world. On the other hand, the Eater's mind—"

"Which it described itself, when we asked it," Amy put in.

"—is something more like a standing whirlwind, with whorls of thought entering and diverging from the general rotation as needed. All that, interlaced in radial symmetries that follow the ceaseless cylindrical twirl of the disk and magnetic fields."

"How can that possibly work?" Benjamin asked.

"Simply shows the limitations of analogies," Kingsley said with a dry smile.

"We don't have to work out the whole mental process," Amy said. "That's impossible. Maybe we can get just enough to guide her through."

Kingsley tried to wrestle aloud with a vague set of ideas, an approach he usually tried only when desperate, as it opened his uncertainties to all. Surely this was the most desperate he had ever been. "As I recall, from the myriad messages the thing sent, the Eater had once remarked that humans were very nearly all alike, so their communications and styles of thinking were suited to that fact. The Eater is radically different, so translation between us is enormously harder."

"Is that why it just won't talk about what it's doing?" Amy asked.

"Perhaps. I was just thinking aloud about a remark it made some weeks ago, concerning its physiology."

Amy said, "It's so strange. We can't be sure that even crude analogies mean anything."

"It still has to satisfy conservation of mass-energy," Benjamin said. "But yeah, I agree."

Kingsley made a tent with his fingers. There was something here, he felt it, and talking was the best way to flush the game from the shrubbery of his mind. "The bastard said that it could experience pain if its equilibrium were disturbed, just as humans get indigestion, headaches, and soreness. The Eater's indigestion came from disruption of the smooth rotation of its accretion disk, interrupting the trickle of mass that kept its inner edge a glaring violet. Upset, it said, came from snarls in the magnetic fields as they encountered vagrant fields from outside."

"That's its version of Montezuma's revenge?" Benjamin asked.

"Apparently." Kingsley worked his mouth around, puzzling out what this implied. "Based upon that, I should imagine that disruption could also come from radioactivity trapped into the disk, which could increase ionization locally. That might trigger something resembling pain."

"Pain, fine," Benjamin said. "But we have to kill it."

Kingsley glanced at the hand-lettered sign he kept on his wall. His first act upon moving into any workplace was to visibly resurrect the advice he had received the first year he had come up to Oxford:

SATURATION

INCUBATION

ILLUMINATION

The great nineteenth-century physicist Hermann von Helmholtz had argued that these were the steps in having a new idea. You had to immerse yourself in the problem, concentrating, and then let the mass of thoughts simmer. Maybe all that happened during such incubation was the withering away of whatever bad ideas were blocking you. Then, often when you were doing something else, the answer would appear, as if delivered by some other agency of yourself.

For the scientist, there was necessarily another stage: verification. You had to see if the bright idea actually worked.

But with the Eater there would be only one chance.

"I propose we try to use a one-two punch, then," Kingsley said slowly. "Use its dislike of plasmas to move it, and then deliver a blow it cannot counter."

"Where? If nuclear weapons don't work . . ." Amy shrugged.

"Forget the magnetic structure, which it quite rightly defends as its mind. At the center of its mind lies the hole. Attack that, I'd guess."

Benjamin studied him as though he were quite lunatic. "Attack a singularity in space-time?"

"The extreme curvature arises from the matter that once passed through the event horizon," Kingsley said. "The steep gradient in gravitation is a ghost of mass that died there, passing who knows where. I propose that we consider giving the bastard not mass but its opposite."

6 *Blessed are the flexible, for they can tie themselves into knots.*

She had thought this state would be sublime, ghostly. Instead, she had hauled along her whole stinky, tangled neuroses-ridden self. Sure, she now flew in space in a way no astronaut could. But her mind was still tied to her body. Worse, knowing the body was a digital figment did no good.

Tracking the beast demanded fresh navigation skills, fast movement, and her reward was sore "muscles." The programmers, in her opinion, had left entirely too much of her mind-body link. If she overused her gorgeous ion jets, they ached. Turn too fast and the "knees" smarted, sharp and cutting.

Simulation she might be, but why the body's baggage? What next, callused feet?

The illusion was good. Her breath whooshed and wheezed in and out. No oxygen at all here, but they had thought she needed the sensation to quiet her pseudo-nervous system, make it think she was breathing. In fact, *it* was breathing *her*.

She took a deep nonbreath and fell into a shadowy space dotted by orbiting debris. This was a messy Eater, gobbling up satellites and leaving twinkling motes. She shepherded her Searchers through this in pursuit of the glowing archwork ahead. Or below; directions were free of gravity's grip, here.

Far better than being an astronaut in the creaky old space station. She had watched the dear old patchwork of bad plumbing and congressional nightmares—abandoned, finally—as the Eater dismembered it. Good riddance! It had crippled the pursuit of better goals for decades. They owed the monster for that, at least.

But nothing else. She felt her giddy sense of weightless purpose as her pretty blue ion jets thrummed and spewed, taking her up/down/sidewise. Getting better at this, but still it made her balance whirl. Thank God they had edited out the entire inner-ear responses.

Now the hard part. She glided into the first filmy tendrils of the beast. Ionized streamers marked the feathery magnetic fields. Their tug she felt as a brushing pressure against her aluminum carapace. *Careful, don't alert the misbegotten monster. Down, hard—then a calculated swerve.*

If at first you don't succeed, kiddo, skydiving is not your sport.

She had lost a dozen Searchers finding out scraps of largely incoherent information. The labyrinths of fields confined dense thickets of Alfven waves, forming webbed patterns. It did not seem to mind intrusion, but the rule was, read and be eaten.

"I'm back," Benjamin's wavering tones came. She grasped them like ripe, liquid fruit. The message's cypher-defenses peeled away as she filtered them—their only defense against the Eater eavesdropping. So far it seemed to have worked. Seemed.

"Missed you. It's not so much the dark here, but the cold."

"I thought you couldn't feel temperature."

"Category error, lover. It feels like a chill, so it is. Maybe it's actually the color green in disguise."

"I had to go to a meeting, find out what's happening."

"What's that cliché? About nobody on their deathbed regretting time missed at the office?"

"I suppose you'd know." He was too somber, needed some joshing.

"I always kinda missed the ol' office. Remember, though, this is the me of when they recorded. How long has it been?"

He blinked, startled. "Weeks. My God, you don't know what's happened?"

"Oh sure, I got all the news. A bath of it. But no personal stuff."

He wore his thoughtful distraction expression. It was looking ragged. "Hundreds of thousands have died. And I don't give a damn."

"You don't have the room for it."

"That's a good way to put it. I've felt like a monster."

"Caring only about my dying doesn't make you an ogre, not in my book."

"Getting the balance right . . ."

His voice trailed off and she knew exactly what he was thinking. *Well, better face it.* "I'm alive this way, and all those people dead, really dead—all because of the Eater."

"Yeah. Life's going too fast for me now, kid."

He was back to putting on a brave face, but it wouldn't work with her. She could feel how close to shattering he was. "Me, too. Just live in it, Benjamin, like a suit of clothes."

He blinked. "That's what it's like for you?"

"Has to be. I don't even sleep anymore."

"My God, that must be . . ."

"Refreshing, actually. The thought just doesn't come up."

"You're always wide awake?"

"Yep, and without my old love, caffeine, too."

"What's it like to pilot a rocket?" He was still uncomfortable, but they had always used their love of the technical to get through bumpy spots. *Fair enough.*

"It's made me realize that when we open our eyes each morning, there's waiting a world we've spent a lifetime learning to see. We make it up."

"And you're free of that now?"

"No, just so *aware* of it. When I was living down there,

I'd see everything with a filter over it—experience, habit, memory."

"Now it's all new."

"Not entirely. I swoop, I dive, but it feels like running, not really flying. My body is always, in a very profound way, telling me a story."

"The body you don't have."

"Right. Weird, huh? So I wonder what the Eater feels. It has no solid body."

"Even the black hole really is a hole. Not a mass, a thing it can feel."

"I suppose. The magnetic storage of information, I wonder what it feels like?"

"Stay away from that," he said with quick alarm.

"I think I've got to go there."

"Observe. That's all you're supposed to do."

"Y'know, I'm in charge up here." *Just to slide the point in.*

"Don't scare me." His face was naked again and she felt a burst of warmth for him.

"Tell me what you guys know now, then. I need to know."

He was glad to lapse into tech-mode again. The experts thought it was best for her to get her input this way, through Benjamin, and neither of them cared to know why. They liked it; that was all that mattered.

"The way Amy describes it, there are captive—well, 'passengers' might be the best word—in the Eater's magnetic 'files.' It keeps records of cultures it has visited."

Channing said, "That's what it calls 'Remnants'?"

"You know about that?"

"They gave me thick files of what it's been saying. I can read it ten thousand times faster than I could with eyes."

"Does that help?"

"Understand it? At least it puts me on a processing level more nearly like its own."

"Ominous stuff it's sending, seems to me," Benjamin said delicately.

"I've picked up waves from the distinctive knots in the magnetic structure. There are tens of thousands of them, at a minimum. They're living entities, all right. Somehow they share its general knowledge, so some at least have learned to speak to us. They say they were 'harvested' by the Eater."

"Magnetic ghosts." He shivered; she could feel his inner states by reading the expressions of his pinched mouth.

"There's something else, an 'Old One.' Any idea what that is?"

"Last I heard, the theory people here think it might be the original civilization that uploaded itself into the magnetosphere. Just a guess, really."

"Ask Amy for me? See if there's anything new on this 'Old One'?"

"Sure."

"I suppose you don't have to. This whole conversation, it's monitored, right?"

"I suppose so. Haven't thought."

Dear thing, he wouldn't. "Privacy is not giving a damn."

She had not expected this to make him cry, but it did.

7 Kingsley stood beside Benjamin as they watched the launch on a wall screen. History in the making, if anyone lived to write it down.

He was partly there to see the event, but mostly to steady Benjamin, should he start to fall over. That had happened twice already from apparently random causes. If Benjamin were seen to get visibly worse—distracted, morose, or worse—Arno would see him off the property straightaway. That would depress the man even more. Leaving him alone in their house would invite something far worse still.

"Steady there," he whispered. Benjamin took no notice, just stared.

The view was of a lumbering airframe framed by puffball clouds that could have been anywhere; these were above Arizona. He still had a bit of trouble getting excited about these air carrier, three-stage jobs. Takeoff from any large airport, drop the rocket plane at 60,000 feet, whereupon the sleek silver dart shot to low Earth orbit. This one would in turn deposit its burden, a fat cylinder instructed to find and attach to the Channing–Searcher craft.

The modular stairway to the stars, as the cliché went. Economical, certainly. Without it, they could never have fielded an armada of Searchers and support vessels to meet the Eater. Still, he missed the anachronistic liftoff and rolling thunder.

The dagger-nosed rocket plane fell from the airframe belly and fired its engine. In an eye blink, it was a dwindling dot.

Benjamin murmured stoically. Kingsley wondered what was going through his friend's mind and then, musing, recalled Arno and the Marcus Aurelius reference made by the Eater. Why had the creature dwelled upon Aurelius?

Stoic indeed, that was the smart course in such times. Did the isolation of Aurelius at the top of the Roman Empire correspond remotely to the utter loneliness of the Eater? The paradoxical permanence of change must loom as an immensely larger metaphor for it.

Such a being, though constructed by an ancient intelligence, surely had undergone developments resembling evolution. Parts of so huge an intelligence could compete and mutate as magnetic fluxes carrying the genetic material of whole cultures. There could presumably be selection for what Kingsley supposed could be called "supermemes"—to coin an utterly inadequate term for something that could only be conjectured.

Amy said from Benjamin's other side, "They've set up a bar."

"Capital idea," Kingsley said with utterly false enthusiasm.

"Think that's a good idea?" Benjamin asked mildly.

"I believe it to be a necessity." Kingsley made a beeline for the bar before the crowd noticed it. It was admirably stocked and he complimented Arno on it as the man took a gin and tonic and the barman prepared Kingsley's exact specifications.

Arno seemed pleased and proud. "Great idea, wasn't it?"

Unlikely he was referring to the bar, but what else? Before Kingsley could rummage through a list of suspects, Arno added, "The antimatter thing."

"Quite so." This would not seem immodest because clearly Arno had forgotten who had thought of it.

"My guys are sure it'll work—and they should know."

"Certainly." *How to play this?* Arno was not exactly a torrent of information at the best of times. His habits of concealment, well learned in other agencies known chiefly by their initials, still held.

"They've done the simulations, pretty sure it'll work."

"The physics is a bit dicey. I—"

"They've discovered a lot of new stuff."

Arno's certainty was granite-hard, so Kingsley tried a mood-altering diversion. "Well, the classic joke about scientists and women is true of me, I'm afraid."

Arno frowned. "Haven't heard it."

"For scientists, it is better for a woman to wear a lot of clothes that take time to take off, you see, because they are always more excited by the search than by the discovery."

This got a hearty laugh that did not appear to be put on. *Pressures of the job escaping*, Kingsley surmised. From Arno's lined face he could see that it would be good to keep things going on the good-fellow front. Always a wise idea, but essential in a crisis of any size; and there had never been one larger.

"Timing is crucial, of course," he said quickly—to pry forth some information before Arno's mood shifted.

"We've put down that U.N. negotiation position, too," Arno said. "They wanted to give it everything."

"All the people?"

"And more. You've seen the new list?"

"It wants more?"

"You bet. Raising the ante to over half a million names."

"Extracted from the news media, I imagine."

"No wonder it got so hot about our turning the TV and radio off."

"The moral landscape has turned into a minefield, admittedly. Some voices are arguing that we are likely to incur more than half a million dead if it decides to skate along the atmosphere and give us the jet again."

Something in Arno's smile gave him warning. "Maybe you should be reading the list instead of listening to those 'voices,' my Royal Astronomer."

"I'm on the list?"

"The monster watches a lot of TV."

"And you?"

"Yeah. Damned if I know how it got me."

"Benjamin?"

"Sure. Half the people working on this, easy."

"My God."

"Apparently that's what it thinks it is."

This sobering talk made the alcohol all the more necessary, in Kingsley's opinion. Still, quite enough had been done along the lines of intimidate-the-out-of-it-scientist. Before he left the bar, he decided a gesture of indifference was required. "I'd go like a shot if it would settle this matter," he said.

"You haven't been keeping up on the gusher of transmissions it sends," Arno said comfortably. "It doesn't like the 'harvests' we routed to it, of people recorded using the electromagnetic-induction technique."

"The technique Channing received?"

"Yes, only she got more detailed attention. Lots more. We're having to do all this in a rush, people knocking themselves out, around the clock—"

"Why does the bastard not like the results?"

"Low definition of some areas of the brain, I hear."

"We knew that. The regions that regulate body function, digestion and motor skills and the like."

"Yeah, it says it wants more of them."

"I gather we impose some body simulation to make up the difference?"

"Not good enough, it says. It prefers the skull-shaving technique some other countries used."

"Ah. Have to rethink my position, then." He kept his tone light and collected the drinks before beating a retreat.

He was on firm ground with Arno when discussing astrophysics, but the man had an uncanny way of getting the stiletto in when the subject shifted. The matter-of-fact horror of it all weighed heavily now. And Arno had a sly relish in unveiling the latest faces of the thing that hung in their sky like a great, glowering eye.

"New drink?" Amy asked, peering at his.

"Pernod and tequila with a dash of lemon. I believe it's called a 'macho.'" This joke went unrecognized, perhaps justifiably, and Benjamin began discussing the Eater's dynamics.

"You've learned a lot from her," Amy said.

"That's the idea, right?" Despite his earlier eyebrow raising, Benjamin slurped down his beer. "Give her a 'friendly interface,' the Operations term was."

"I'm sure you're the crucial element," Kingsley said, believing every word. Certainly fellows like Arno would have driven Channing to suicide by now if they'd been in the loop.

"I wonder why it doesn't like the EM reader method?" Amy mused.

Kingsley said, "I expect it is a connoisseur in such matters."

"How?" Benjamin looked both puzzled and distracted, a difficult combination to fathom.

"It has enforced such orders and used the results perhaps thousands of times before," Kingsley said.

"I wonder what it does with them?" Amy asked, taking a strong pull at her gin and tonic.

"I rather suspect we do not wish to know."

Benjamin looked soberly into Kingsley's eyes. "That bad, huh?"

"Morality is a species-specific concept. The Eater transcends species themselves, since it is an artificial construction left to evolve now for a time longer than the Earth has existed. Outside our experience in a way that does not reward considerations of right and wrong."

Benjamin gave a grim smile. "Sounds like a classy way of saying it can do what it damn well pleases, so don't think about it."

"Well put," Kingsley said as an aide tugged at his elbow.

The man whispered, "You're needed immediately in Conference B."

Kingsley shot back, "I'm bringing these two with me."

"Sir, they weren't included—"

"Then I'm not coming."

"Well, I don't know, I'll have to—"

"Come along." He ushered Amy and Benjamin forward.

When they reached the inevitable battalion of Security personnel, there was the usual orchestration of knitted foreheads and worried doubts. He got through that with a combination of bluster and can't-tolerate-this-oversight fast talk.

"No matter," he said to Amy as they walked down a hall with a phalanx of guards. "This is just the usual confusion. The U Agency is acting in this crisis like what the world plainly needs—a multinational government by default. Yet it will share all the irksome traits of the old style nation-state, principally rust in the gears."

"Your wife is still undercover?" Amy asked.

"Comfortably so, I gather."

She had caught on. Rather than skulk around, it was better to quite obviously flout their rules. Doing so earned a certain measure of grudging bureaucratic respect. Such strategies had served well in these days.

He had learned a lot. To avoid getting entangled in interference-blocking, running errands, and other lubricating distractions, he had to step lively. There were nations to soothe and endless anxieties issuing from the ever-intruding snout of the media pig. And with exquisite irony, the reward for many, including himself, was to make the Eater's list.

Straightaway he gathered the intent of the meeting. Arno was running it. His mouth twisted at the sight of Amy and Benjamin, but something kept him from objecting—quite possibly, time pressure. Each figure around the long table had a little sign detailing their positions, chimpanzee hierarchy again, but the discussion was the least formal of any Kingsley had yet seen.

Everyone was in a barely controlled panic. The magnetic

attack had placed one rim of the loop upon the Center and another upon installations of "strategic value" elsewhere in the Hawaiian Islands, one woman from Defense said. A similar loop had landed about an hour later upon the area outside Washington, quite neatly destroying communications. No one had heard from the President since. "Whereabouts and fate unknown," Arno summed up.

For a world that routinely looked to the United States to pull together alliances, this was a trauma. It did not help that as the meeting proceeded news came of a third loop on its way. Some men rushed out to get details.

"It is now obvious that we had better carry on independently," Arno said. "We can't rely on anyone else."

"We can still reach Channing from here?" Benjamin asked.

The entire table looked at him as though he had shouted in church. He was not a policy maven, but they knew who he was. Their gaze said that his role was to be a gallant warrior, bravely talking his sim-wife through it all, and leave the actual thinking to them.

"I believe so, yes," Arno answered after a two-beat pause. "We have DoD antennae positioned offshore in case these here—the replacement ones, after our losses—get knocked out again."

"Where is our fallback installation?" Kingsley asked.

"We want to keep that information closely guarded," a severe woman in a black pants suit said. She was new, like most of the faces here. Probably from Washington. Crisp, narrow-eyed, the usual.

"Just how are we to flee there, then?"

Arno snorted testily, "All right, it's up at the 'scopes."

"The top of Mauna Kea?" Benjamin said disbelievingly. "But that's so exposed."

"Everything is," Arno shot back. "We're living at the bottom of a well."

"And we can line-of-sight to the fleet," the DoD woman added. "Gives us a big effective platform for operations."

Apparently both U.S. Pacific fleets had been drawn secretly into a perimeter around the Hawaiian Islands. Kingsley had not heard of this, but there did seem a lot of military aircraft in the sky lately, many of them heavy helicopters suitable for carrying substantial equipment up the slopes to 14,000 feet. That they had constructed a redoubt atop the mountain without even Center personnel noting the fact was a tribute, probably to someone in this room.

"We are counting on another attack, once our assault begins," Arno said. "Maybe even the jet."

This sobered everyone. "It's out near geosynchronous orbit now, finishing off the rest of our satellites," a man nearby said. "Cracks 'em open like nuts. That jet can't reach this far, I heard."

Kingsley came in smoothly, "I believe Dr. Knowlton is the expert on this."

It was best to build Benjamin's position here on technical grounds, not let him be seen as distraught-husband-off-the-rails. Benjamin seemed to get this point without even a glance at Kingsley. He deftly led them through a discussion of the jet, highlighting what his astrophysics team had learned by observing it incinerate Washington. "The magnetic focusing will work at just about any distance," Benjamin concluded. "The Eater sets up a circuit effectively. Beautiful physics. The current in the jet self-pinches itself, and the return route for the circuit flows through the cocoon of plasma the jet generates outside it."

"Very neat," someone commented. A puzzled silence.

Kingsley understood this remark, however. He wondered for an instant if an appreciation for the aesthetics of physics and engineering could form a better grounds for comprehension between utterly different life-forms than the old routine of serial language.

Such abstractions were swept away, however, by a minor tsunami of moral objection from several around the table. How dare the fellow speak well of the monster, etc.? In the name of decency, and more along those lines.

This gave Benjamin time to think, so that he broke into the pointless jibes with, "It will be under stress—electromagnetic ones, not psychological—when it uses its jet, though. That's the time to hit it."

This got their attention. The DoD woman stalled for time by reviewing their own thinking. Actually, the term was undeserved. They had cooked up a bigger nuclear warhead attack, counting on Channing to deliver the knockout at the end. This she presented in eager-terrier style, looking eagerly back and forth along the table like a girl scout bringing home a prize. Kingsley guessed this strategy's primary asset was that it would allow DoD to claim the victory, should there be one, since Channing would certainly not survive to do so.

Swatting down this notion consumed a full hour. Such trench warfare was interrupted by news that the third loop had landed, again quite neatly, on Beijing.

"Seems our Chinese friends did something nasty, too," Arno said with dry relish.

This shook everyone. Kingsley found Arno's remark chilling, for reasons entirely separate from the China attack.

Those in the room were getting more rattled. They drank coffee, ate some spongy tropical kind of donuts, and murmured like a Greek chorus uncertain of their song. But Arno would not call for a break. Instead, the lady from DoD came forward again and kept saying in various uninstructive ways, "Leave the fighting to those who know." To this, the physicists rebutted, "Sorry, you are plainly outgunned and need new ideas."

It was a predictable collision that needed to get worked through. Institutional thinking was on the hedgehog model, knowing one solid thing. Kingsley preferred the fox model, as he had leaped over several hedgehogs in his life. Only toward the end of the hour did he manage to get a word in and derail the slow-motion train wreck the meeting was evolving into.

"I recommend using Channing and her Searchers alone," he said. "During the time the jet is on, if it chooses to use it."

This simple suggestion took another hour to thrash through in classic committee fashion. Kingsley had to defend the use of antimatter, first carefully defining it and reviewing the decades of research that had led to a packet the size of a wallet containing the explosive power of a hundred hydrogen fusion warheads.

Not that technical arguments carried the day, of course. He was dealing with Americans and so played out the accent bit, using "shedule" and "lehzure." To buttress the tactical side, he slid a few recognizable names past at the right speed to be fully caught, yet not so slowly that they would suspect he was trotting them by deliberately. All these he had conferred with—briefly, of course, but no one need know that.

In the policy dust-up that necessarily followed his presentation, he called in Benjamin again, Amy twice. Each time they provided the right scientific detail and fell back to let him drive the point home. Sketches of the Eater interior. Routes into it while avoiding magnetic turbulence, and most importantly, the accretion disk. Old methods he had first learned on Cambridge committees came into play. Knowing that his foes lay in wait, he paused to breathe in the clearly defined middle of his sentences. This let him rush past the period and into the next sentence, allowing no one to make a smooth interruption.

The next hour meandered on until Arno struck. This was lamentably often the best way to settle an issue. Exhaust everyone, then cut through the Gordian verbiage with an Alexandrian sword. He was de facto in charge here, bar word from Washington. Therefore he took command of the military resources and ordered them to stand down, awaiting further orders.

Kingsley was reasonably up on American constitutional law, but this looked doubtful to him. Arno's appointment was through DoD, and the secretary of that massive agency could assume the presidency should the true President be unreachable. Plus the Speaker of the House, president pro tempore of the Senate, Secretary of State, and so on.

This entire argument seemed wobbly, but Arno sold it to the room in short order. The thin veneer of bureaucratic calm had dissolved about an hour before, and now the panic among them made them reach for any seemingly solid solution. Rule by Arno apparently played this emotional function.

Kingsley shook hands with him afterward, murmuring congratulations sincerely meant. He had never seen as deft a maneuver carried out at the airy heights of power. Though of course he did not say so, he ardently hoped that he never would again.

8 *Into the living tree of event-space.*

At the ragged red rim of the magnetosphere, she felt the first crackling electrical discharges, alive with writhing forks. With her all-eyed view, she could see the fretful working of the magnetic intelligence. It reminded her of many natural patterns: pale blue frost flowers of growing crystals. The oxygen-rich red in bronchi of lungs. Whorls of streams, plunging ever forward into fractal turbulence.

Pretty—and quite deadly. With an agonized shriek, one of her leading Searchers flared into a cinder.

Ripples of intense Alfven waves told her that the Eater was sensing/thinking/moving. All those functions were linked in its world. The cybertechs had explained all this in their arcane lingo. To her it was not dry theory but *experience*—the restless slither of magnetic fields around her like a supple fluid.

She was gaining a sense of it, an intuition fed by her swimming through the invisible thing-that-thought. How strange her former brain now seemed! She had caught portions of the Eater's thought and now could see human intelligence anew. Compress a life onto a sheet, paper-thin. Crumple it. Stuff it into a bony carrying case. With that, primates had evolved to store a hundred billion neurons, all firing like matchheads in a webbed array still only poorly understood.

No more, for her. Now she was a slab of silicon, being mated to—*thunk*—a cylinder of death.

The attachment complete, she dove.

She vectored a swarm of missiles into the outer swelling of the magnetosphere. To her, the Eater was an enormous blue blossom of spiderweb-fine lines, each snarled with innumerable knots.

Time to go to work. She began the attack upon the magnetic equilibrium. Deftly she guided nuclear-tipped plasma bursts to the spot where the fields could be forced to reconnect.

Behind her, an enormous cloud of bright barium exploded into billows. The solar wind blew around the Eater, fended off by its magnetic pressure. The beast was like a small planet, defending itself against the solar bath. But the barium was far denser than the thin wind. She watched the Eater retract field lines, avoiding the prickly energy of the high plasma flux.

"You're on it!" Benjamin's excited voice came.

"I always wanted to fly a fighter against the fearsome enemy," she said. "This is better." To show him, she did a tight turn, airy and graceful on her ion plumes.

"The package made it?"

"It's riding on my right."

"Try the other methods first. That's only a last-chance backup."

He was trying to keep his voice level, businesslike, but it wouldn't work with her. She could read him. That was the downside of using Benjamin as intermediary, but Arno probably hadn't thought of that. Benjamin was supposed to steady her up here, and he did. And it worked both ways, thank goodness. She wondered if she had ever loved him more, back when she had a real body to express it.

"Things tough down there?"

"It got the house."

"What?!"

"The electromagnetic induction from that field loop

slamming into the island. It blew the transformer at the end of our street. The fire spread all the way to Hakahulua Street. When I got there, the house was just smoldering black stuff."

Her heart sank. *All gone*—"Damn!"

"It's killed a lot of people, some in our neighborhood. Pacemakers went out. There were a lot of effects nobody can explain."

She started to cry and the wrenching sobs were utterly real, coming up from her nonexistent lungs and through a clenched throat. She let the spasms run. Part of her agonized. The other basked in the fleshy feel of living. Mind-body again.

"I . . . God. I guess I was never going to go there again . . . but . . ."

"Yeah. I'll miss it, too."

"Everything we had . . ."

"Not quite. After you . . . left . . . I took all the photo albums, our wedding stuff, and put it in a safe deposit box."

A gale of joy blew through her. "Wonderful!"—and she was back aloft again, bird swooping, spirit rising.

"Whoa, girl, tune it."

"Oops, my mood swings are going over the top."

"You have reason to."

She made herself slow down. No fighting the body, no intellect arm wrestling with hormones. She simply concentrated and the gusty spirit blew away, leaving a precise, analytical glaze over her mind. Not that it would hold for long, she wagered.

"Ah!" A sharp crack in his background sounds. "We're getting heavy weather here on top of all that. I—"

"The Eater's sending that."

"What? How?"

"I can sense it from here. It's acting like a voltage source, driving the global electrical circuit. Currents running everywhere up here."

"Why's it after us?"

"It must've figured out where our command centers are."

"That fits." He grimaced. "We just lost even the supposedly secure links with Washington."

Alarm resounded in her like a hollow gong. "You're getting cut off?"

"Every other channel died hours ago. We've got only the antennae here, that's it."

"They're locked on the satellites below me?"

"Those few are our only targets now. It's eaten everything else in the sky."

"If you get blanked out—"

"Yeah." A strumming, pregnant silence hung between them. "It seems to be making a big ionized layer right over the island."

"Putting a conducting plate between me and you."

"So far, it's failing. Feels like Zeus throwing thunderbolts down here."

"I've got to do something."

"Operations says they don't have all the Searchers within range yet."

She fumed. "I'll go with what I have."

"No, don't. Look, the black hole theorists, they've got some new input for you. I'm sending it on a sidebar channel—"

And here it blossomed in her spherical view: a 3-D color computer simulation of the black hole itself. An orange oblate spheroid, spinning hellishly fast. A sedate sphere, fattened by its own rotation until it grew an ocean-blue bloat at the equator.

Benjamin said, "Point is, the ergosphere—that's the midrift bulge, in blue—has zones with so much rotational energy, you can fly through them safely."

"Oh sure."

"Do I detect sarcasm?"

"No, realism."

"They're saying you could bank in over the accretion disk, drop your donation, and then veer in. That'll give you the energy to escape."

"All this at an appreciable fraction of the speed of light."

"You don't sound convinced."

"Do you?"

"They say it's your only chance."

"And what order of magnitude would those odds be?"

"Not great, right."

"Well, send up the trajectory, anyway. I'll log it in."

"Remember, there are relativistic effects this close in—"

"Yeah, so I'll have slowed time to deal with."

"And it'll help you a little. Give you more time to execute the maneuver."

"And catch up on my reading. Did you know they stored the whole goddamned text of *War and Peace* in my buffer?"

"Huh? Why in the world?"

"Something to do with buttressing my long term memory."

His face clouded and he obviously struggled for words. "Look, this is the only way, they say . . ."

"I register. I'm not really what I once was to you. I can't be."

"You *are*."

"I'm as much as I can be, that's all."

"Enough for me."

"I'll try to make it back out."

"I . . . guess that's all I can ask for."

His face broke into rasters, lost color. "I'm having trouble with the link here—"

"The lightning, it's—" His lips moved, but no sound came through.

"Benjamin, don't—"

A spray of gray static showered across his image. Then that froze . . . stuttered . . . and was gone.

"Benjamin!"

She coasted alone in a suddenly eerie silence. Alone.

She close-upped the globe below. Hawaii lay in view, just emerging from the dawn line. Angry blue-gray clouds shrouded the Big Island. She could make out the forks of descending electricity. Not just local lightning, but the larger discharges as well: sprites, the vast thin glowing sheets that climbed down from the ionosphere.

Alone. Shepherd to several hundred Searchers. Mother hen to an egg that rode in its cylindrical majesty beneath her tail.

She had not thought she could carry out the complexity of all this by herself. Operations had agreed.

Now she would have to try. Preparation would—here her subself, full of calculation, provided a fast estimate—take at least another day. Then she could begin.

Without Benjamin. The leaden realization dragged at her. At the back of her mind, something else was vying for her attention. Presiding over her inner self was like keeping an unruly grammar school class in order . . .

A quick blip of information squirted through her filters.

A message, digitized Eater-style, but riding to her on the magnetosonic waves she had slowly learned to decipher.

FROM YOUR EXODUS 23:19:
"NO MAN SHALL SEE ME AND LIVE."

"Oh yeah?" she muttered to herself. But it chilled her all the same.

PART EIGHT

A HEAVEN OF SORTS

1 Lightning tore at the dark-bellied clouds with yellow talons, ripping rain from them in shimmering veils. Kingsley watched out the narrow windows, still feeling in his English soul that rain should properly be accompanied by cold. Here, sheets of it swept through cloyingly warm air.

Great crashes rattled the prefab walls of the Center. The crowd of people around the big screens flinched as the hammering booms rolled unceasingly over them.

"Bit dicey, I'd say." Kingsley turned away from the static-filled screens. "There's no hope of reaching her using the high frequency bands?"

Amy shook her head. "The techs say it's got an ionized blanket over the island now."

"Even in the 96 gigaHertz band?"

"As soon as they start at that frequency, it runs up the plasma density in a spot above the transmitters."

Benjamin said shakily, "A huge current discharge, right down a funnel from the ionosphere. How in the world can it do that from so far out?"

" 'How in the world' is precisely it." Kingsley sized up the disarray he saw in the faces around them. "It has had practice on other worlds. It knows planetary atmospheres the way we know our backyards."

Amy said, "Or better, the way birds know air."

"It cut her off so *fast*," Benjamin said.

"It knows she's there. Senses what we plan, probably," Amy said somberly.

Kingsley ground his teeth. "It's seen a lot of tricks, I'll wager."

"We're checkmated," Amy said. "Those Searchers, they're like pawns, cut off without even a knight to—"

"Ah, that's the point, isn't it?" Kingsley thought rapidly. A fleeting idea had scurried by.

While he gazed into the distance, Benjamin said flatly, "It's got to be worried. Why bother to cut us off from her and the Searchers? It's concerned."

Kingsley nodded. "A compliment, I suppose."

Amy roused from her depression slightly. "So it knows that we can do it real damage this way?"

Benjamin visibly rallied himself. "It moves to cut her off from Operations, right? Which implies that it works kinda the same way? With a managing center."

Kingsley liked to frame ideas as he thought them through, and so said out loud, "It's searching for our command center. We never said we had one. It assumes we do *because it does.*"

Amy brightened. "Those interceptions Channing got—they were magnetic wave transmissions inside the Eater's magnetosphere. If we could trace their routes—"

"—we'd get a clue to its central command, right," Benjamin finished.

"Quite a job," Amy said. "We'd have to—"

"Never mind how tough it is," Arno broke in. "Get on it."

Kingsley had concentrated upon the exchange so intently that he had completely missed Arno's eavesdropping. He was pleased that Amy and Benjamin had pulled the same idea out of their gray matter that he had been vainly pursuing. Somewhat reassuring, when others believe a passing notion has substance. What had his examiner muttered, long ago at Oxford? *The universe is under no obligation to make sense, though a doctoral thesis is.* People craved order, meaning, some certainty in the face of immense mystery. No matter the price.

The others chattered on, plainly glad to have something to do. There was perhaps shelter in numbers. In primate talk—a form of grooming, hadn't the Eater said?

As yet another rattling hammer blow fell upon the Center, he felt the need of whatever shelter—even intellectual—he could find.

2 Benjamin wasn't having any. "Come on, it makes no sense."

Arno gave him the full glowering treatment. Heavy on the eyebrows, stentorian voice, rigid at-attention gaze. "It's the only way we can get this information to her."

"But I've got *no* experience at any of this—"

"Neither does anyone here. Not anybody who can understand the material."

"I've never been in space and—"

"It's easy. I've done it."

Arno did look like the type who would shell out big bucks for a suborbital shot, an hour or two of zero-g, and great views. Probably some high-level government gig had taken him up. Benjamin shook his head adamantly. "I'll be a lot higher up in orbit. I'm not used to zero-g."

"So maybe you'll throw up some. So what?"

He gritted his teeth. "I won't be worth a damn."

A heavy pause. "It's your duty."

To punctuate this, a rolling series of crashes and thunder rolls swept through the center. They were so common now, nobody even cringed.

An aide ran in and said, "We got everybody out of the E wing. It's totalled."

"How many casualties?"

"Plenty of injured. We're setting up Medical in G wing. Got three known dead."

Arno nodded, waved him away, looked blankly at Benjamin. "Well?"

"Okay, I'll go. I don't even see how I can—"

"We'll get you to the airstrip. I've got a first-stage carrier coming in from Oahu."

"You knew I would."

Arno grinned, an unusual expression for him. "Sure, you're an all right guy."

This locker room style did not bother Benjamin, though he recognized the method. "She's in there. Close to it."

"Near as we can tell, yes."

"I'll have to look after her." A part of him said, *If there's any chance it's really her, I've got to act on it.*

"As well you should. She's the center of coordination."

"That antimatter trap you sent—"

"It's a last-ditch thing. Main thing is, we're going for the plasma assault. Kingsley thinks that'll herd it around."

"Enough for the nuclear warheads to get in close."

"I know. It failed before. But maybe we can overwhelm it."

Benjamin had no real faith in this, but he could think of nothing else. A fighter against the ropes should try to slug his way out; the time for subtlety was past.

But then, a fistfight analogy was primate thinking, wasn't it? The Eater would be quite aware of all that. Though were humans really like other, vaguely similar forms evolved around distant stars? How special were these latest products of fitness selection among hominids?

He wondered how often in history men had made desperate moves with the same lack of confidence. *The fog of battle*, he recalled the term. Delirium was more like it.

Soon enough Kingsley was seizing him by the shoulders, a remarkable gesture for him. "I'll be alongside for the briefings. Amy, too."

"Great. I really appreciate it."

Their presence proved to be crucial. Benjamin sat through hurried yet extensive dissections of what they had learned of the Eater's structures. Amy and Kingsley helped him through the spots when he would blank out, losing the thread.

"Like a brain?" one of the specialists said in answer to Benjamin's question. "We're stacked on top, newer brain on the outside. Form dictates function. Within the limits of being a kludge, of course—sticking new parts on while the older ones are running. On the other hand, the Eater's able to rearrange itself whenever it wants, as nearly as we can tell. So no—it's completely different."

"Then why should I trust any of this?" Benjamin shot back. "It keeps changing."

"Because it's all we've got."

This looked pretty flimsy to him, all the theorizing based on interpretations of magnetic wave packets. Channing had picked up most of the data they were using as she darted around at the fringes of the thing. There was a category of localized information the specialists called the "Remnants"—apparently, the records of civilizations encountered in the far past by the Eater.

"We figure they, too, were 'harvested' by the Eater," the specialist said. "But they're not just libraries. They interact. Talk to each other. To the Eater, wherever its intelligence is."

"Magnetic ghosts," Benjamin said.

"Yes, in a way."

"All the people we shipped up to it, that's what they'll become?"

"We guess so. The information density in the thing is incredible."

"That word doesn't mean much anymore."

One Remnant was an especially powerful agency the cybertechs called the "Old One." "Now, that may be the essence of the Eater, the original race that started it all," a horn-rimmed, earnest woman said. "It seems to have pieces of itself distributed all over the magnetosphere. None of the other characteristic wave packets do that."

"This is all just a bunch of guesses," Benjamin said harshly.

"Right you are," she said.

Later, still unsettled from this, he asked Kingsley and Amy, "Why doesn't it just kill us all?"

Kingsley understood power and had a ready reply. He was holding up pretty well through all this, the upside of his classic Brit reserve. "A universal urge," he said. "It doesn't want us all dead; it wants us all compliant."

Grimly, Arno convened with the survivors of high command who could reach the islands. The Eater was slamming away at the United States, pelting it with cyclones, electrical nightmares, fierce winds. Planes did not venture into the snarling skies. The American habit of taking the lead in international matters had now made it the principal target.

Arno and the others tried to raise the stakes. In the last few weeks, various backup missions had gotten into position. Arno used these. There seemed no one in the entire national power apparatus who could stop the on-rolling momentum he had started.

A manned spacecraft with hydrogen bombs tried a suicide mission. They had bombs doped with elements that might interfere with the magnetic filaments, perhaps producing an electromagnetic pulse to scramble the field lines' snarls, lowering their information-bearing capacity.

The Eater figured this out, of course. It hulled the ship with high-speed gravel, shot from its accretion disk. The thin-walled vessel was shredded in a moment.

This rattled Benjamin considerably. The military advisers reassured him, as well as they could when he knew they were dealing with a complete unknown. What did lessons learned by such theorists, from the strategies of Waterloo and Gettysburg and Stalingrad, mean here? Less than nothing.

But Benjamin had Channing to help, they reminded him. Maybe that would matter.

In the hushed, defeated atmosphere at the Center, the staff labored on. Nobody talked much. The Eater was as chatty as ever, transmitting at high-bit rates any number of reflections on life, culture, and much else. This unnerved them all still further.

YOU WOULD PROFIT FROM INVESTIGATIONS MY-SELF HAS CARRIED OUT OVER THREE BILLION YEARS. HERE I DETAIL THEM BRIEFLY. FROM THE MOMENT OF MY ORIGINS, IN MY KERNEL INTELLIGENCE, I WONDERED IF THERE COULD BE A FAR HIGHER BEING THAN MY-SELF. FOR EXAMPLE, A CLASS THAT HARNESSES THE LUMINOSITY AVAILABLE IN THE STARLIGHT OF AN ENTIRE GALAXY. THIS WOULD BE VISIBLE AT GREAT DISTANCES: A LACK OF LUMINOSITY COMPARED WITH MASS, AS REVEALED BY STELLAR ORBITS IN THE SUMMED GRAVITATIONAL POTENTIAL. GALAXIES, I HAVE DETERMINED, OBEY SCALING LAWS BETWEEN THEIR SURFACE BRIGHTNESS, RADIUS, AND MASS. A HIGHER ENTITY FEEDING ON LUMINOSITY WOULD BREAK THESE SCALING RULES. IN THE MANY THOUSANDS OF GALAXIES I HAVE OBSERVED, NONE SHOWS SUCH DIMINUTION. THUS THERE ARE NO GREATER FORMS OF LIFE THAN MY-SELF. I COMPRISE THE ULTIMATA.

"Gee, that's great news," Amy said dryly. "We don't have to worry about anything worse than this guy."

They all laughed, utterly without humor.

They gave him one session of deep electro-sleep. To make him remotely in condition to fly, the physicians said. He had heard of the method, which in practice seemed innocent enough: small patches on his head, a soothing sound, a sensation of skating across a gray plain—and he was waking up ten hours later, feeling better than he had in months.

Then it was just airplanes. Arno's team went with him in a convoy to the freshly scraped landing field a few kilometers from the Center. There a chopper carried him to the Kona airport. It was a deserted landscape pelted by high winds and rains. Enormous waves churned in across the black lava fields and chewed at the runways.

A sleek jet took him to Oahu. Again a barren plain with the military holding a perimeter. No flights except his. The suborbital carrier was of a design he had never seen before, bulky and somehow muscular in its aluminum sleekness. No time delays at all—they hustled him across a hundred meters of slick asphalt and into the passenger cylinder of the beast. They even had an umbrella-carrier who ran alongside. Somebody was taping his every move, too.

The rumble of its huge engines shook him as he belted in. A steward showed him the space gear, patiently explaining each and helping him try them on. He dimly saw that this was part of their method. Keep him busy, focused, no time for fear or imagination. He welcomed it. A fringe of his depression lifted as their wheels left the ground.

The craft labored up through decks of roiled clouds. Above 35,000 feet, a clarity came to the seethe outside. They crossed out of the cone that the Eater maintained over the islands. Engines fought the inrushing winds and slowly spiraled them up to 50,000 feet.

Their rise slowed as the jet gulped the thinning air. They took him into the orbital craft then, all suited up and primed with anti-zero-g medical aids. The moment when they dropped the dart-shaped ship from the jet's bay was a foretaste of orbit, but he did not feel like vomiting. The rocket's kick in the ass brought a heady rush. Vibration, massive weight. A blue-white view through the port that quickly eased into black. Real orbital zero-g was fun. He was enjoying playing with a floating pen and the view outside when they came for him. Into a smaller compartment he went. The pilot sat a meter away and the view was better.

"A closet with a view," Benjamin said amiably. He was feeling so good he did not even wonder why.

"Yeah, Cap'n," the pilot said. "They rushed me up here so fast, I'm still going through the manifest. Gimmie a min. Name's Sharon."

"So beautiful."

"Real pretty for a suicide run."

This jolted Benjamin a little. He craned to see the Eater, out somewhere near the moon. A blue speck.

"We've got boosters out the kazoo," Sharon said. "Hope you're ready for a roller coaster."

"I've got a date with my girl," he countered. *"Go."*

Now he knew why he felt so fine.

3 Channing said, "That phrase, 'my kernel intelligence'—I agree with Kingsley. That might be the Old One."

"Could be. Can you reach it?"

She sensed Benjamin floating in the cowling of his sensaround as he watched/felt her. He was sending all sorts of secondary sensation—the headset pressure, visual processing cues, the wheeze of his shallow breathing. But these were just add-ons to his abstractions, or so they came to her. The miniboosters tugged at him as the craft accelerated and she heard their angry snarl. These she gobbled up, for they suddenly reminded her of how achingly far she was from her old, real body. Emotions washed over her aplenty, but she was sensation-starved.

"The cyberguys have identified a whole catalog of different 'signature' memory waves," she said, accessing her crisp memories. "The Old One has a trademark bunch of Alfven waves tagging its parts, as nearly as they can make out. Those tags are all over the dipolar shape of the fields. A diffuse storage method. Probably to give it a holographic quality."

"So we can kill part of it, maybe, but not all."

"Smart bastard, it is."

"This 200 gigaHertz band works beautifully," he said mildly, the mellow tones telling her that they had done a

339

good job on him. He had weathered the trip untroubled. "You're so . . . full."

"I love having you so close."

Somehow he was now more deeply embedded in the space of her perceptions. Like pale sunlight beams lancing through her 3-D self. The cyberfellas had been sharpening the software again.

"What's that music?"

"Oh." She felt the rhythm eddying through her, called up by his notice of it. "I have it all the time, I guess. Music integrates parts of the mind that make sense of memory, of timing and language. It retools me. When I started up here, I thought it was pointless, working in areas with no real use, like motor control. Until I found that the designers used those parts to pilot my Searchers. Thrifty guys."

"It's more than music, isn't it. It's . . ."

"Feeling? Yeah, I caught on to that once I used it some. The story they fed me is, there must've been neural mechanisms that deciphered music in the early hominid brain. That may have developed as a way to communicate emotion before language came along."

"Wow, it feels different."

"Yeah, somebody's going to make a bundle selling this, once it gets out of the R&D stage."

Their chat flowed easily, part of reintegrating with him. Sensory input laced with meaning, weaving a comfy fabric around them both. *Two of my favorites—clothes and sex . . .*

An echoing voice boomed suddenly, "Channing? Benjamin? This is Kingsley."

It came as a dash of chilly rainwater on a hot skillet. They both flinched. "Yuh, yes?" she managed.

"Sorry to break in—"

"I'm surprised you can," Benjamin said. "Pretty narrowband, though."

"That's the point of having you up there. I may fall out at any time. All the monster has to do is throw a plasma screen between us."

"Your signal's pretty jittery now," Channing said. "Losing the low frequencies. That checks with a plasma cloak just a little too low in density."

"I'll be quick. Pretty rough here, it is. This signal has to go out on an undersea cable and then through a chain of satellites."

"Everybody okay?"

His hesitation told her all she wanted to know. "As well as can be expected."

"Judging from what I can see," Channing said, "I'd say get away from the Center. There's a tube of plasma flow pinning the islands like a needle."

"And low-frequency electromagnetic stuff," Benjamin said. "I can see it on the displays in front of me."

"We have little choice. Arno's arranged a bolt hole for us if it gets bad."

"Arno must be pretty pumped," Benjamin said.

"Indeed. He wants me to provide interface on this."

"You can see the Eater?"

"No, nothing. It's good at blinding us. But I do know that, using a relay through the Navy, we've started the plasma dumping."

Channing felt/saw/smelled it already—a spike of barium ionization at the nearer edge of the Eater's magnetosphere. Like a puke-green worm eating at a fat blue apple. And the dwindling motes of Searchers who had delivered the barium, zapped by the Eater within moments. But they had worked.

"Think that'll drive it?" Benjamin asked. She could feel him sending edgy, exploring fingers through her sensorium.

"We hope so," Kingsley said. His voice was flat, low-quality, riding a meager trail of bits. "It's been following a slow trajectory outward, and Arno believes this will look like another ineffectual failure of an attack."

Channing said doubtfully, "To edge it around the moon."

"I'll admit, this is wholly conjectural," Kingsley said.

"Like me and my life," she said.

Benjamin asked, "We're *sure* it can't decode these transmissions?"

"They are going under a screen signal. Even if it can penetrate that, we have already laid down a pattern strongly suggesting that you are a feint. So it may very well discount what it can decipher."

"More Waterloo thinking," Benjamin said cryptically. "I still—"

"I SHOULD THINK YOU SHOULD START YOUR DIVE!" Kingsley suddenly bellowed. "Oh, sorry, having transfer problems again. I—"

And he was gone. "Damn, this setup is rickety," Benjamin said.

"He was right, though. I'm starting."

Red muscle-clenchings down her spine. Quickenings. Abstractions rendered into a cool sort of body language. She sensed one hundred and thirty-four Searchers start their programmed accelerations. Her subsystems updated them every few moments. Furious work seethed just below her conscious perception, a strumming insect-hive frenzy.

Into the whirlpool.

Her astronaut training took over. She quick-checked twenty things in the time it took to breathe out. (Thinking that, the breathing sensation came back on, full.)

She wasn't going to survive this, but training is training.

"I love you," Benjamin said.

"Ummm. I love you, too, but, well, love the mind, miss the body."

He chuckled in that old way of his.

The webbed intricacy of the magnetosphere rushed at her. "Here goes."

"Good—"

He had started to say goodbye. There had been altogether too much of that lately. More than enough for a lifetime, and here she was into her second one. She was damned if she was going through this all sober and noble.

"Got a puzzle for you, lover. Why did kamikaze pilots bother to wear helmets?"

4 Weirdly colored lightning snarled through the thick air. Kingsley helped some men carry gear out of the collapsed shell of the main building. Through the patter of the unending rain, he heard distant shouts. More bodies were recovered from the adjacent wings.

A bolt came slamming down and narrowly missed— *crack!* The impact staggered him and shattered a guard station a hundred meters down slope. The shock wave hit like a cuff to the body by a giant hand. He dropped his burden in, of course, the largest puddle within view. The box held ferrex computer memories, delicate stuff probably not aided by immersion. He levered the box up again, getting mud over his jacket. Clothes had long since ceased to matter—he had been living in this suit for two days—but the warning twinge in his back said he was getting close to collapse. Fatigue blurred the mind quite enough, thank you, without the piercing pains to which his rebellious spine was prone.

A communications building upslope disappeared in fire as they loaded the 4X truck. Arno came limping out from the smoking ruins carrying his own two overnight cases with large red DEFENSE GRADE 10 labels. From the look on the man's face, Kingsley decided it was best not to refer to the last-ditch lightning rod screen the teams had run up the night before. Their puny defense had withered beneath the incessant voltages the Eater had somehow concocted above the island.

Kingsley decided that reference to any of Arno's decisions was not on for now. Pointless, anyway. Probably nothing could have aided the situation. Stick to the practical, then, with a straightforward "Where shall we go?"

For the first time, Arno showed both confusion and alarm—in approximately equal proportions. An aide ran up and held an umbrella over Arno, allowing the man time to recoup. After an awkward moment, the aide produced an umbrella and handed it to Kingsley, who gave a polite nod. He was already hopelessly drenched, but the thought was the important thing, Kingsley supposed.

Arno managed, "I'd . . . I'd say we spread out."

"How can we continue working, then?"

" 'Working'?"

"Yes, regain contact with Benjamin."

"Working." The concept seemed to need tossing over in his mind.

"We have to get a new base of operations. Plainly the Eater has targeted us quite well here."

"Working."

"Reaching Benjamin. That is our proper job."

"Washington . . ."

"Forget Washington. It might not even exist any longer."

This jab made Arno blink, startling him from his daze. "The comm unit's gone. Totalled. No way we can get an uplink."

"Probably so, but there remain the big dishes up at the top."

Someone shouted at them and then ran off. " 'Top'?"

"The observatory complex at the peak of Mauna Kea."

"Hell, higher up, it'll get even more lightning, won't it?"

"We can't be sure. The Eater must have targeted us very specifically. This isn't happening over at Kona, for example."

"Yeah, the tech boys figure it backtracked on our narrow-beam transmissions. Wish they'd thought of that before."

He spotted Amy working with a medical team. Kingsley called to her and she looked around as if she could not tell where the voice came from. Probably stunned from the thunderclaps and lightning strikes, ears humming. His were ringing as well, but that did not prevent him from hearing the cries of the injured as they were loaded into whatever vehicles could serve. Kingsley waved, did a dance, and she picked him out. Arno was engaged with two of his staff and this gave Kingsley time to embrace her, then just stand together silently beneath the umbrella. He wanted to stay like that, not move an inch, but finally he asked her about the observatories. As always, she knew far more than he expected.

When he got Arno's attention back, he said, "The last anyone heard, the system up top was working."

"It's damned vulnerable up there," Arno said, blinking rapidly. Was the man faltering? Not surprising, really.

"Benjamin's going to have no backup," Amy said flatly.

"I can't think what we could do . . ." Arno's voice trailed off and he stared through the rain at the milling personnel and wrecked buildings, his empire flattened.

Amy said crisply, "If we can get some of this gear up to the data processing facility at the peak, we can use the bands above 100 gigs."

Arno shook his head slowly. "I still don't see—"

"The Eater's holding a plasma discharge over our heads here. We go up to fourteen thousand feet, we're above that."

Arno rallied enough to jut his chin out. "Until it finds us there."

"Until then, we can still talk to Benjamin," Amy said.

Kingsley found interesting how Amy and Arno had interchanged roles. She always saw problems, but now proposed solutions; he, the reverse. Even now Arno stood in the softly pelting rain and just stared at them. No doubt the man would come back to himself, but when?

Moments moved by. Nothing. "I'll help organize some of the specialists," he said to move matters along.

"Ah, okay." Arno did not move.

"I should think you would need to instruct your lieu-tenants."

"Right."

"Quite soon."

"Right."

With Amy, he found Arno's bevy of next-in-command types and got them at least moving in roughly the same direction. Arno slowly came to resemble himself again. Within an hour, something like a convoy departed to wind its way up the Saddle Road. At the last moment, Arno summoned up with his bureaucratic magic wand a fleet of limousines. Into these sleek black Lincoln Continentals they wedged, not wanting to ride in the backs of trucks. Prudently Arno had kept the limos on the island since the threat of a presidential visit had loomed, then receded, weeks before. Amid slashing lightning, they wallowed off into gray, thick rain.

Arno insisted that Kingsley and Amy ride with him, and though Kingsley wanted nothing more than to lean back and nod off, Arno chose this moment to demand a summary of the "scientific situation."

"What do you think the Eater will do next?"

Kingsley was tempted to retreat to his now-standard aliens-are-alien argument, but this newly revived Arno did not seem in the mood to accept that and let him sleep. He leaned forward, summoning up energies he did not until a moment before know that he had. An aide handed him a gin and tonic with crackling cold ice, fresh from the limo bar. This incongruity disarmed him momentarily and he took a sip. What the hell, it was calories. At least Amy was beside him. He needed her much more than the drink, but it, too, was comforting. He dimly noted that his drink hand was trembling and wondered abstractly why.

"It's concerned. Not perhaps desperate; we can't flatter ourselves with entertaining that notion. But concerned, since it is wasting its most vital resource—the hot, fluid, ionized mass that is compressed by gravitational gradients into the disk that orbits it."

Arno was a difficult audience because he knew just enough to ask questions. "It didn't use that to burn Washington. Or to shotgun that ship."

"In a way it did," Kingsley said. "The jets it creates, the gravel it used to poke holes in that ship—they come ultimately from the infalling energy and mass in its disk."

Arno frowned. "It's got a lot in that disk. Hell, I could see it glowing in the sky. Back when I could see the sky, I mean."

"Indeed. Yet mass is a scarce resource for it now, as it has expended a great deal decelerating on its approach to us. To be sure, it retrieved some in our upper atmosphere. Amy has estimated that it could catch in the range of several tens of tons per minute with the expanded field region it has flowered forth. Integrating that over its cruise around the Earth in several shallow orbits, one gets a substantial mass. But still a good deal less than it needs. And therefore *desires*, for I suspect it experiences its most basic needs as a hunger. Desire is a more rarefied way to put it. This thing is best regarded as an extremely sophisticated, moving appetite with more experience than any civilization could possibly have. And of a different kind, as well, one we can explore only by working out the most basic constraints upon it."

This extended blurt Arno greeted with his patented skeptical gaze. He took so long to say anything that Kingsley wondered whether the man was slipping back into his earlier semicatatonia. Then he looked at one of his lieutenants, wedged into the far end of the limo with a security type, and said, "We got any new intelligence on this?"

"Nosir. Nothing *works*."

"No lines to DoD?"

"Nosir."

"The airborne White House?"

"Nosir, it hit us pretty bad."

"Well then." Arno seemed to have decided something, for he now gazed stolidly at Kingsley across the short separation of the limousine's center well. "What you got?"

"Our strategy, if it deserves such a name, is simple. The

one thing it must have to move on with is matter. Our first maneuver is to explode canisters of barium near it. Barium ionizes easily in the solar ultraviolet. The plasma is disagreeable to the Eater, so it will move away."

"Herding it, I remember that."

"But it needs mass, so we suspect—"

"Hope," Amy put in. "A more honest word."

"Quite. We hope that it will move toward the most readily available, substantial mass in its vicinity."

"Right, the moon."

"Yet by the logic we settled upon long ago, when we first understood its nature, the Eater cannot simply plunge into the moon. That would strip it of its magnetic fields—and thus its mind. Suicide."

"So it grazes the moon. Orbits in, real close." Arno nodded. Kingsley could see he was reconstructing this, as if his memory were disarranged.

"And that is where we use matter again—the key to destroying it, as well."

"Antimatter," Arno said. He clung to the word.

"The antimatter Channing carries is lodged in cylindrical, highly magnetic traps. If she can eject the contents at the innermost edge of the Eater's own mass deposit—the accreting mass in its disk—that will disrupt the magnetic fields that are anchored there."

"So?"

"Its greatest energy density lies there."

"So annihilating the mass that ties those fields," Amy put in, "might give the Eater a lobotomy."

Arno's mouth sketched a skeptical curve. "But not kill it."

"There is a possibility," she went on, balancing an orange juice on her knee. "She could drop some antimatter—positrons and antiprotons—into the rim of the black hole itself. There are huge magnetic fields moored there."

"And that would kill it?" Arno asked.

"It would allow the two poles, north and south, of the black hole itself to unite." She grinned triumphantly.

Arno frowned. "They would then, well, what?"

"Annihilate. North and south are opposite poles, and they would cancel each other out. *Poof!*—all the energy in the hole's magnetic storage turns to free energy." Amy beamed.

He felt a rush of emotion, mostly pride. This was her idea and she was justly proud. Kingsley had not even suspected such a thing could occur, but she had shown it in several detailed calculations.

"And what happens to this Channing simulation?" Arno asked.

Amy sobered. "The tidal forces, the torques—this close to the hole, they're tremendous."

Trying to be helpful, Kingsley added, "The trick for it, for her, is to angle in so that the whirlpool of space-time can pick her up. That centrifugal action can counter the inward stresses. It's the only way she could get close enough to carry this out."

Amy went on as Arno struggled to understand. It would all be much easier if they had the vast graphic displays of the Center, of course. Science was now mostly a matter of understanding the pictures shown, not the principles underlying them.

Kingsley sat back and reflected, the gin and tonic helping nicely. The great trouble with understanding this black hole lay in a simple fact: calculations were nearly all about the equilibrium. Average properties, energy theorems and the like. So what did one really know? He had watched a generation of theorists wrestle with the same problems.

Take what happened when matter fell in—did it go all the way to the frightful singularity that lay at the "bottom" of the hole, and so get chewed up? We thought so, but were not sure.

Could the twisted space-time around a spinning hole, and inside it, lead to fundamental new properties—say, wormholes? Not sure.

At the core, physics smeared into topology, the study of surfaces, shapes. Geometry ruled.

Near the innermost regions of a rotating hole, snug up

against the singularity, the laws of quantum mechanics object quite profoundly to infinities. Physics had for decades posted a want ad at this boundary: NEW THEORY NEEDED. APPLY WITHIN. But to properly describe this realm demanded a deep view of quantum gravity, which still—despite much work and false prophets—eluded them all.

Amy had hit a conceptual wall with Arno. Talk between them dwindled and they stared out at the pelting fat dollops of rain. A somber mood descended.

"Perhaps the primary point," Kingsley said, "is that this simulation of Channing is flying into the utterly unknown. The only evidence of her deeds will be what happens to the Eater."

"She'll die," Amy said.

"She knew that going in," Arno said flatly, apparently glad to find a tough-guy line he could use.

"It may be easier for us, when we speak to Benjamin—if we can even do that—to use 'it' rather than 'her,' " Kingsley said.

"Good psychology," Amy said. "Prepare him for it."

The limousine stopped. They had finally growled up the rocky, narrow road to the observatory complex. To Kingsley's surprise, the rain clouds now hung below them. The sky above was not clear, but at least there were no glowering dark clouds and crackling lightning. The telescopes here had long taken advantage of this property, the extraordinary stability of the air above the dead volcano.

"Let us hope the bastard cannot find us here," Kingsley said. He got out of the car and stretched. A dizzying lack of air made him totter. How could he think up here? Back to work, one last, desperate time.

5 Benjamin felt her fully now. The old question about whether a simulation had an internal experience—well, all those abstract bull sessions dwindled to scraps. Here was her *self*, coming through in her voice, her vision, the sensory smorgasbord of a lived interior.

"The sand is running, lover," she said.

"Not yet!" he called.

She coasted in a strange Valhalla of cathedral light and glowing electromagnetic majesty. He floated in his harness, immersed in her world. Through a small port, he could watch the crescent wonder of the great water world below, but his eyes did not stray from the spectacle before him.

Three dots scorched her vision with momentary pinpoint explosions. "Gotcha!" she cried.

He flinched. "What was that?"

"I nailed three of the nodules where the Old One is stored."

"With Searchers?"

"It killed them, sure. But not fast enough."

"More barium?"

"Yeah, giving the beast an enema."

"The big cloud, it's expanding pretty fast."

He sent her his extra data sources on a tightbeam, high-bit squirt. A blooming ivory barium cloud licked at the Eater's magnetic rim.

"Ride 'em, cowboy," she gloated.

"It's heading away, around the moon."

"Hungry, that misbegotten—"

She had stopped abruptly. Benjamin frowned. "What's—"

"It's talking to me."

"About what?"

"Music. Listen."

—RESONANCES WITH HUMAN BRAIN PATTERNS. SOME
SYNCHRONIZE WITH BODILY RHYTHMS. THE BEAT IS ALL.
YOUR "CLASSICAL" MUSIC APPEALS TO A DIFFERENT
CLASS OF CADENCES, MORE PURELY MENTAL RATHER
THAN PHYSIOLOGICAL—THOUGH FOR YOU THE TWO
ARE NEVER ENTIRELY SEPARATE, AS WITNESSED BY FOOT
TAPPING TO EVEN THE MOST RAREFIED STRING QUARTET.

"This is insane," Benjamin said.

"Aliens are by definition insane."

Suddenly, on five channels, came a flurry of transmissions, everything from African tribal intonations to Beethoven, from Chuck Berry to Gregorian chants, no technique or style neglected.

"What—?!"

STIMULATING TO RECEIVE THESE FORMS OF CEREBRAL
JEST. THROUGH YOU IN THE MOTE NEARBY, I CAN
SOMEWHAT KEN HOW THESE GAMBOLS PLAY OUT IN
THE HUMAN SENSORIUM. VERY MUCH AS YOUR OTHER
IRRATIONAL—OR PERHAPS BETTER, SUPERRATIONAL—
METHODS PERFORM. AS, FOR EXAMPLE, IN "LOVE" AND
MECHANISMS OF REPRODUCTION.

"We're trying to kill it and it sends us music criticism?"

She said tensely, "Bravado? To distract us?"

HOW BEAUTIFUL IMMORTALITY IS, THE BLISS OF BEING
BLENDED. COME, JOIN ME. WE SHALL VOYAGE
AMONG THE STARS TOGETHER.

Baroque music sounded. "Good God, it's a sales pitch," she said.

FROM TOO MUCH LOVE OF LIVING
FROM HOPE AND FEAR SET FREE
WE THANK WITH BRIEF THANKSGIVING
WHATEVER GODS MAY BE
THAT NO LIFE LIVES FOREVER
THAT DEAD MEN RISE UP NEVER
THAT EVEN THE WEARIEST RIVER
WINDS SOMEWHERE SAFE TO SEA.

"What in the world . . ." Benjamin felt an eerie sense of an intelligence abidingly strange.

"That's supposed to be enticing? Ha!"

"Must be a poem."

Wonderingly she said, "I think I understand. It doesn't actually believe we will strike against it."

"Why? Because we're scared? It's right—most people are terrified."

"But not the ones who matter—us. Maybe its experience with other aliens leads it to believe that any species will make a rational calculation and give it what it wants."

He blinked. "That's why that stuff about 'superrational methods,' then? It thinks we have an amusing, unreasonable side, but—"

"That won't matter in a showdown, right. It's moving fast now. I'm going after it."

He sensed the surge in her. Not in sight or sound but some other perception, coming somehow through this intense data link.

He was *with* her in a way he never could have been before.

And she was rushing into the magnetosphere. The barium cloud was a hovering mass above, the Eater a rushing fountain of light below. All against hard blacks and the approaching crescent moon.

Plunge!—he felt her elation. She had once said to him that all astronauts really wanted to be space birds, and now he caught the texture of that truth.

"I'm being forced by the explosions at the top and bottom of the funnels," she gasped.

He could see the hourglass shape. In the fever dream of his perceptual space, it resembled a dirty Pyrex tube, slowly rotating. Bits of mass trickled down it. Not much; it was starved. But each funnel ended in the glaring hot washout of the disk.

And her only sliver of refuge lay toward that hard luminosity. Searchers flared like matchheads in the shifting, quilted light of it. They died to erase fractions of the Old One—perhaps. In the hard vibrating seethe, she could not be sure what effect all this was having in the form of the magnetic densities around her. Some, yes—a lessening of pressure skated across her pseudo-skin like a soft easing. Some success, she felt. But how much was enough?

"Thousands," she answered him without his speaking. "I can count them now. We're just picking at it. To it, we're—"

"Get out!" he yelled.

"—irritants. It will swat us like flies."

Suddenly the wall he had built around his inner fears shattered. "My God, get out!"

"I'm in a dive, lover. Blissful hard g's."

"Bail out!"

"Gotta go. The sands are running."

"Wait, you—"

"Sic transit, Gloria."

Her dreamy voice alarmed him. Had she wanted this final plunge all along? "No!"

"Yes."

Her signal Dopplered away, like water whirling into a drain.

6 She had studied all the theory and knew that the Searchers were doomed. And so was she.

But the little cylinder of nestled positrons and dutiful, dumb antiprotons, tucked into her tail like an awful egg—that would do nicely.

Diving. *Thirty seconds to go. What was that old movie?* Thirty Seconds Over Tokyo. *And how did it end?*

She was still close enough to the human sensorium to perceive the onrushing Eater in terms that made human sense. Her "eyes" generalized if they could. They tagged an ensemble of incoming elements—textures, lines—by seizing on a fragment, outlining it with a contrast-boundary, and then compressing all that detail into—

What *was* it?

A swollen cathedral of soaring magnetic towers, impossible perspectives, wrenching structures. All seething with detail that ramified as you looked at it, then split again into underworlds of minutia. Such beauty!

And faintly, hymns.

Her Searchers were dying. Amid streaming obelisks of information, they slipped. Currents found them. Electrocuted.

This place was constructed of electrodynamic flows, she sensed, that laced through the steepling rivulets to find their targets.

A Searcher was a new resistance in this whirling circuit.

Currents dissipated there in an eye blink. Scorching heat fried the Searcher chips.

Then quick sparks lit the way before her. Plasma blossomed. Something had gotten ahead of her and now pried open the magnetic fortress.

Benjamin—?

She felt a dizzy gush of electric aurorae around her. Dove in a centrifugal gyre. Eluded them for a second or two—

Hands. That was what it felt like at first.

Fingers probing, finding, learning. Inside her.

Peeling her into onion-skin layers.

Feeling ornery, she went outside and whistled, which made the neighbor's irritating dog run to the end of its chain and gag itself. It had woken her up with its damned barking last night—

Memories. Did it relish her worst character flaws?

They had a convention: either could raise a hand and say, "Time out," and the other would have to be quiet for at least a minute. Usually she would be chastened, but not so much that when the "Time's up" signal came she didn't launch right into nonstop talk again, words jumping out of her mouth to knit up the damage—

That one hurt more than the choking dog image. *Lost, so much lost—*

This thing knew how to wound.

Searchers dying everywhere. She banked down into the funnel.

At least the magnetic strands did not buffet her here. Still, turbulent knots of magnetic strands slammed into her carapace. Static electricity crawled over her. Fever-itch.

It sought her, poked into her mind. *It's seen everything, done all this before.*

She slammed on her remaining ion reserve. A blur of heady acceleration. Below the bull's-eye disk bristled with eating brilliance. Storms wracked it.

The Eater was all around her now and knew it. Huge hollow cries of godlike wrath battered her.

Suddenly she sensed *them*, too. Shelves of voices. Minds in boxes. A zoo of knowledge/data/selves.

Greetings. Please may you kill us?

Blistering speed, now. A plunge into relativistic velocity. She felt the prickly twist of space-time as a play of stresses all through her.

Slamming down into the disk. *Bank. Thirty Seconds Over Topology*—

Into the rim of the black hole, skirting the ergosphere's bulge. A fat waist at the whirring edge.

Please may you—

She shat the antimatter. It trailed behind her and down into the edge of the furious disk. Annihilating.

Gamma rays coursed out. The whirl of space-time sucked her in and around. Tidal fingers pulled, stretched, popped seams in her. Pain-fingers, now.

Matter died. Fizzed away into photons.

The magnetic fields in her wake lost their anchor. The field lines shot away at the speed of light, freeing the knots and whirls in a growing cone behind her.

Thanks to you. Pleased that you kill us.

She saw ahead the darkness beyond all night. At its edge, glimmering hot light. The ergosphere. She fell in a skimming orbit, on the brink of being swallowed.

Another ship, there. In a wash of gossamer light. Slim, scorched, skin dented and alive with spider stresses—

It was herself. Time-twisted, so that she saw for one glimmering instant her own destiny.

7   Benjamin's missiles plunged ahead of her, he knew that much. Kingsley's updated command hierarchy had helped. The reprogramming Benjamin had to do by feel alone.

Only with an artful sequence of thermonuclear explosions could he provide the necessary plasma density. Enough ions could short-circuit the Eater's equatorial equilibrium. So he had timed it, fired the warheads—

And it had worked. The virulent fireballs had cleared a path for her. Did she know it?

He watched a huge sizzling corona of bristling light erupt from the core of the Eater. Magnetic reconnection of the poles? Spreading—

He sensed her somewhere in there. A sprite, speeding into the maw of certain extinction.

He lost sight then as the Eater's shimmering ghost-strands fell below the moon's brimming crescent.

Goodbye—

One burst, then gone. Her.

Abruptly the moon's rim blazed with furious radiance. A titanic explosion haloed in vibrant colors. Blocking Earth from the virulence. Kingsley's plan.

Circling around, Benjamin saw that the other side of the moon was burned brown.

Melted. Peaks slumped. The plains ran with fuming stone.

8 Kingsley embraced Amy with frail passion. The effort of sending the data, of responding to Benjamin's demands, of fending off Arno's undoubtedly well-intentioned but irksome attentions . . . He was exhausted.

And the Eater had found them again.

Even here inside the soaring vastness of the Keck observatory dome, he could feel the stones shake as lightning struck.

"We've done all we can," Amy murmured into his chest. "You lie down, rest—"

"No, I must see how it comes out. Don't want to be asleep for this."

Arno said, from a shadowy corner where he peered at a communications screen, "It's sending goddamned lightning down a cone. Look at this."

With an assistant's help, Arno had patched into one of the emergency DoD miniobservatories, a package launched after the Eater had supped its fill of metals from the weather satellites. One had to admire the Americans, Kingsley thought abstractly. They had backups of everything, straight off the shelf. The view from three hundred kilometers up showed clouds across the Pacific, with a neatly carved hole giving clear skies over Mauna Kea. The Eater was able to tailor the weather of a planet it had freshly encountered, down to a scale of a few hundred kilometers, while swimming in its magnetic coils near the moon. In some ways, this was the most impressive of its feats. He peered at the hole in the cirrus sheets. Down a conduit that plunged through the entire atmosphere shot sparkling jabs.

"It knows the global circuitry of planets," Amy said. "That's pretty clear. And it found us from the tight-beam to Benjamin."

Arno nodded firmly. He seemed fully back now, the manager of old, but there was a twitching in his lips that boded ill. "The nukes, they'll go any minute."

"Time to discuss our next strategic move," Kingsley said.

"This flops, we're finished," Arno said.

"Funnily enough, no. This is a rational creature. Strange but rational. More so than we, perhaps. We can deal with it even after."

"Frap we can!"

"Someone must." Kingsley was having a hard time holding on to his decrepit sense of reality. Amy gave him a sympathetic look, which he answered with a kiss. He put himself on automatic to encourage this new line of discussion. "We'll do it some damage, that seems clear."

"And it'll be mad as hell. It'll come after us."

Kingsley deducted several degrees of respect he had harbored for Arno's hunched-over figure. Earlier the man had rolled up his sleeves, the first time Kingsley could recall him unwinding even a bit. Revealed on his left forearm was a tattoo: DEATH BEFORE DISHONOR. *Quite so*, he had thought. He gathered this tattoo was a standard one for U.S. Marines, which would explain some of Arno's comportment. The phrase had set Kingsley to thinking, because behind their antagonism with the Eater was something just so elemental. Small and puny humans might be, but without much actual discussion, the entire vast tribe of it had subscribed to just that emotion. There was something undoubtedly primate-centered and puny and irrational and still glorious in all this, a mark of a young species just learning what it was, marching on grim-faced into dark vistas, humbled and loud-mouthed and yet still coming.

Amy opened her mouth to enter the discussion, but Kingsley shook his head. Time to calm the waters with a big dollop of snake oil.

He got firmly into Arno's field of view and said, "Think of it as a wounded god. It might go into orbit around the sun and wait for a more compliant humanity to emerge from its ruins. It has infinite time available, with patience to match."

"We're out of ideas," Arno said with leaden certainty.

"Not at all. You may dimly remember that months ago one of the radio astronomy groups spotted emissions similar to the Eater's from a nearby star. Perhaps merely accidental, of course. But we should consider selling the Eater on the idea of leaving us in pursuit of some other intelligence, perhaps like itself."

"That's crazy," Arno muttered. He stared at the satellite display before him. Forking stabs of electrical ferocity traced down through clear skies, converging on the mountaintop.

"We have a slight advantage over it. Our radio telescope net is the size of the inner solar system now. That is how we could target these emissions. The Eater is too small to pick up and resolve such transmissions."

"But it's been wandering through the galaxy," Amy said, looking at Arno's back with a worry clouding her face. "It must know everything in the spiral disk by now."

"Not so," Kingsley countered with a tone somewhat approximating optimism. "It does not have the scale or sensitivity of networks created by little beings working together, like us. It is solitary, with all the lacks that implies."

Amy got the idea and said almost brightly, "What do we offer it?"

"The exact coordinates of these emissions. Perhaps the cause is a fellow magnetic intelligence. Perhaps it is merely an astrophysical oddity we do not yet know enough to tell from true intelligence. Be frank about that. Bargain. Entice. Go away, we say to it, and here's where."

Amy said, "It could come back."

"We can prepare for that. What was that old Daniel Boone expression? 'Look sharp and keep your powder dry.' "

From Arno he had expected no coruscating shower of wit, nor some chin-wagging soliloquy of desperation, but still less had he anticipated that instead the man would begin to weep.

This was, finally, too much. If masculine toughness meant anything, it surely implied an ability to face uncomfortable truths, even to the point of the death of humanity. Arno's weakness spread. Kingsley saw the sudden collapse in Amy's face, a gaping mouth, and utter despair in her eyes.

He felt precariously close to that himself. Yet he dare not abandon the methods he knew. Among reason's tools, the hammer was evidence, the knife was logic. None would work here. But what could?

Let events cure them, he thought despairingly. He had no ideas.

In a long, sliding moment, he felt profoundly how inadequate he was, how unsuited were all astronomers, for thinking about a creature like the Eater. Those who studied stars blithely chattered about stellar lifetimes encompassing billions of years, while they saw suns in snapshot, witnessing only a tiny sliver of their grand and gravid lives trapped in telescopes, capturing light emitted before humanity existed. That imbued astronomers with a sense of how like mayflies the human species was, yet it also insulated them. They could not alter suns. Biologists could help or hinder living things. Astronomers had lived blithely in the shadow of immensities without the burden of acting in the glare of such wild perspectives. Astronomy's coldness carried a foreboding that humans were truly tiny on the scale of such eternities.

Perhaps they all had shattered, finally, in the face of that.

Suddenly, in this dark, cluttered communications room, with staff hovering before their screens like acolytes worshipping in a technological shrine—finally it was all too much. The claustrophobia of enclosure strummed in him, tightening his chest.

Suddenly he saw his own life, a mere mote in eternity's glare, and sensed its rising slope. Quite a heady ascent, indeed, far more than he had ever hoped.

Until here, until now. This was certainly the peak. He would never again act upon so grand a stage, command such resources, confront so colossal an enemy. From now on it would be the long smooth slide down, hearty applause and cushy appointments and modest speeches and the lot. He could dine out on these events until the grave claimed him.

The summit. *Here. Now.* A satisfying grace note, in a way, and yet with the ring of doom to it.

Intensely he wanted to hold on to this moment, the very crown of his life. The Eater might well be dying across the sky outside and he was here, cowering in a shadowy, man-made cave—ironically, an observatory, meant to open onto grandeur.

He had to see the damned creature one last time.

Without a word, he turned away. Amy had begun sobbing, too, and he knew he should comfort her again.

Let it go, he thought, *and let me go in the bargain.*

He found a corridor leading out. Down the cold concrete passageway, head wobbly with lassitude. Shove on the door. *Out, free.*

Cutting cold embraced him. Cleared his head a trifle, even.

Sharp sunlight. Thin air rasping in his throat.

He walked to the edge of a broad steel parapet. He could see clear up into the deep bowl of sky from here, over the Keck's brilliant bulge. The moon hung halfway up to the zenith in a troubled blue sky.

Faint twitches of fevered light stirred at the edge of the moon's crescent. Probably from Benjamin's final assault. It would all happen quite swiftly now.

Head back, teetering in a whipping wind.

He saw the very moment. A huge burnt yellow corona of virulence lit up the moon's rim. Light crawled and licked around the clean curve.

She had done it.

He felt a sudden hammering in his chest. *Victory and death.*

How wonderful, to see it here, alone, in the utter silence of a cool clear mountaintop.

He shouted up at the dying sky, a pure roaring cry of released joy.

Raptly he stood petrified, gazing upward over the eggshell-white observatory dome. Tendrils of ivory light flowed away from the moon, arcing out and then narrowing, coming toward the Earth. To see this demanded substantial ionization of intervening gas, he estimated. Which required enormous energies, the fruit of the final cataclysm mercifully hidden from view. The restless glow came rushing across a quarter of a million miles, reddening as it came.

It fattened. An orange filigree laced the high air. Excited atoms fluoresced in a great green circle. *Probably*, he analyzed, *the electrodynamic effects hitting the upper atmosphere, driving a wave of ionization and charge imbalances. More lightning due, probably.*

Get back inside? No, live at the peak.

Even in death, the Eater's work was accurate, its geometry quite precise—a circle that collapsed inward in a spray of brightening yellow-green. Suddenly he realized that this was a descending cone. Energies concentrating. He did not notice his hair standing on end, or the humming air, until it was much too late.

9 Benjamin landed two full days later. A "catcher's mitt" shuttle snagged him from a looping orbit and brought him down. It was a long glide across most of the Pacific to Oahu airport, taxiing to the same spot where he had departed a thousand years before.

In yet another way, he had lost her.

Behind a gray curtain, he went through the motions of being involved. Arno and Amy met him with news of Kingsley. The Eater's final paroxysm, as its magnetic structure collapsed, had sent enormous currents through a circuit that connected moon and Earth. It had focused its energies upon Mauna Kea, and there the final vengeance had descended. Those inside the conducting Keck dome survived, since the currents remained on the outside. No others.

The black hole still remained, of course, a dead spike of gravitational gradient now. Its still-huge mass performed a slow gavotte about the moon, and vice versa, so that the Earth now had an invisible partner in its voyage around the sun. The moon lurched and gyred as the triple-mass system traced a complex curve. The moon turned its other face toward Earth for the first time since it became locked by tidal stresses, an event that had occurred well before life had advanced beyond the single-cell level. The far side had few craters and its dark skin had liquefied before the onslaught. Benjamin's first glimpse of that side momentarily startled him out of his cottony mood. Clouds trailed across the face, outgassing from the melted rock. These were the first to grace the lunar skies for probably four billion years. They lasted only days, making Luna seem a momentary twin.

Occasionally some stray mass would err into the path of the now-naked black hole. The flash was visible from Earth, if one were looking at just the right second. Astronomers immediately began using the hole as a gravitational lens to focus light from stars and galaxies passing behind it. Within weeks, papers began appearing, turning a terror into a tool.

But the billowing magnetic structure was gone. With it vanished all traces of a mind older than the solar system.

Or so they all thought, until Amy came quietly into his office in late afternoon. "Got a funny one for you."

He peered at the sheet, alarmed by her tense voice. It was a report of radio emission from the vicinity of the Eater's orbit. "High flux, picked up by the microwave network."

"One of our ships, still out there?"

"Don't think so. This looks more like emission from relativistic electrons."

He stared at her. "A . . . jet?"

"It could be."

It was. Observations over the next day showed that a fresh jet was blooming from very close to the black hole itself.

"It's alive," Amy said. "The magnetic field structure that housed the Old Ones, it must have come through okay."

"Damn. This jet—where is it pushing the hole?"

"Outward," Amy told a crowded auditorium at the base of Mauna Kea. "It's moving off in a straight line."

A voice called, "Toward what?"

"Suspiciously close to the direction in the sky of that other emission we saw, months ago. Remember?" Clearly nobody did. Amy went on, "An electromagnetic spectrum similar to Eater's. Some people wanted to bargain with the information, maybe get Eater to leave us alone."

Another voice called, "Companionship?"

Benjamin remembered Kingsley saying that the most they could hope to do was damage the thing. So Channing had died only to wound . . .

"It is notably diminished," he rose to say. "The latest radio maps of the hole vicinity show a knot of extremely intense fields anchored in the hole itself. A small accretion disk seems to be building, apparently assembled from the debris in its vicinity."

"So it can't harm us?" a voice asked anxiously.

"Not now." He felt compelled to add, "It could come back."

"Then why head out toward that source?" a woman in the back asked.

"We cannot know." His eyes swept the room and everywhere he saw naked fear. "But we can be vigilant."

The information was suppressed. The world was not able to take the shock and uncertainty of this revelation—or so higher heads than his believed.

It had been folly, he saw, to believe that a creature which had encountered myriad assaults upon itself could be killed with anything present-day physics could devise. That they had injured it was a tribute. A mere few decades earlier, humanity could have done nothing. He supposed that was some kind of distinction. Not that it helped him in the dark of night, tossing restlessly.

The hole's course held steady. It was leaving.

But humankind would eventually learn of its true fate, of that he was sure. And no one would ever truly rest easy again.

There was much to be done to make up humanity's immense losses, but Benjamin felt no urge to join in.

He knew, without being able to speak of it, that he had to complete his emotional arc. An abstract term, but he sensed a tension riding in him.

One day at sunset, he said a final goodbye to her on the beach, beneath a splendid ruddy streak of cloud. The wrecked sky above still showed orbiting debris of the battle, twinkling against the emerging stars. Vagrant energetic electrons struck auroras at the poles, where great sheets of light surged. He could see soft glows to the north. That would fade, and with it, some of the horror.

But not all of it, ever. Humanity would never again be able to gaze at the stars with anything resembling the astronomer's serenity. Or feel awe at the heavens, untinged by terror.

After the sunset, he came back into his temporary quarters and saw the hourglass she had given him. He had meant to bring it home before he left, then forgotten and left it in his car. All he had left now was a suitcase from the trunk and the hourglass. Everything in his Center office had burned.

No past. No future. Only this hovering moment.

Outside, the balmy aromas of life resurgent.

The hourglass stood on his desk and captured his gaze.

Sand at the bottom. What would she want him to do with it?

He turned it upside down, beginning his life anew.

Goodbye. Hello.

10

—pop—
—stretching pain—
—and she zoomed *out*—
—away from a brilliance at her back.

Somehow she knew that this was the twin other mouth of the Eater's black hole. She had pierced the very center of it and tunneled through an immeasurable expanse of space-time.

A white hole. Behind her erupted a tongue of plasma, licking hot at her, pursuing hard and fast—but she shot out into . . .

. . . a carnival of gaudy light.

Marvelous, airy cities hung in black space. Weird constructions rotated. In the distance hung a yellow-green star, too large, but warm.

She knew without knowing how.

She was in some other space-time, maybe not even in this universe. It *felt* different.

Here was where the doomed civilizations, swallowed by the Eater in its long journey, had ended up. Others, the Eaten, had known enough to send small missions into the fat equatorial bulge. Venturing into the realm of physics beyond calculation, they had won through.

They had colonized this space. A place hard fought for,

over more eons than flesh could know. Here swam survivors of countless alien societies, fruit of ancient desperation.

Waiting patiently in their castles. Knowing how stripped-down craft would be, after the shredding tidal forces of the hole. Ready to salvage any compressed intelligence.

Fathom it. Revive it. Her.

And now to greet. *Hello,* she thought.

Something like a hailing call came strumming redly through her sensorium.

For an astronaut, this is a heaven of sorts.

Wonders to explore.

AFTERWORD

One of the notions leading to this novel came to me while reading one of the classic texts of plasma astrophysics:

> *It appears that the radical element responsible for the continuing thread of cosmic unrest is the magnetic field. What, then, is a magnetic field . . . that, like a biological form, is able to reproduce itself and carry on an active life in the general outflow of starlight, and from there alter the behavior of stars and galaxies?*
> —*Eugene Parker,*
> Cosmical Magnetic Fields

While the ideas in this novel are offered in playful speculation, I have endeavored to show truthfully, against an extreme backdrop, how scientists do think, work, and confront the unknown. Astronomy locates its students in a perspective grander and perhaps more cold than does any other science. Though the effect is little noticed, it seems to me to have an appreciable impact, at a level often below perception, upon how astronomers see the universe and our place in it. Such lessons are among the most subtle we can learn.

The initial spur for this work came from my colleague and friend, Mark O. Martin. Jennifer Brehl's deft and insightful editing yet again contributed to improving my text.

I have also benefited from discussions with Joan Benford, Dominic Benford, John Casti, Jay Sanders, Vince Gerardis, Ralph Vicinanza, Elisabeth Malartre, Joe Miller, John Cramer, Roger Blandford, and Martin Rees.

The constant assistance of Marilyn Olsen was essential. The unattributed poem in the last Part is by Swinburne.

The black hole figure in Part V is by Nigel Sharp, and was generated from an exact computer calculation of the general relativistic conditions near a rotating black hole. It appeared first in "Demythologizing the Black Hole," by Richard Matzner, Tsvi Piran, and Tony Rothman, in *Analog Essays on Science*, edited by Stanley Schmidt, Wiley, 1990, to whom thanks go for permission to reproduce it.

July 1999

We hope you've enjoyed this Eos book. As part of our mission to give readers the best science fiction and fantasy being written today, the following pages contain a glimpse into the fascinating worlds of a select group of Eos authors.

In the following pages experience visionary science fiction from Jack McDevitt and Stephen Baxter, sweeping epic fantasy from Janny Wurts and C. J. Cherryh, and journey into the near-future with Gregory Benford and the mystic past with Stephen R. Lawhead.

Grand Conspiracy

Janny Wurts

The hard frost came to the downs of Araethura early, and the rains at their cusp laced crusts of ice through the peat stacks under the sheds. Indoors, with no fire lit to fend off autumn's breezes, the invasive cold settled at will. Crouched on her knees on the packed earthen floor beside her darkened cottage hearthstone, the Koriani enchantress Elaira cast aside her flint striker. She cupped her chilled fingers, blew on the caught spark. Well versed in the contrary nature of wet peat, she launched into strings of ridiculous endearments, coaxing damp fodder to nourish its struggling wisp of caught flame.

The fateful knock at her door, which shattered her peace, interrupted her then.

Elaira damped back her annoyance. The spill in her fingers fluttered out as she arose, resigned to the usual request for a cough remedy or a tincture to dose a sick goat. For seven years, she had lived alone, plying her herbal wisdom on the moorlands. Time had eased the innate distrust the local herders held toward practice of her craft, and families now came to her freely when trouble visited their livestock and farm-steads. While the leaves turned, and the season's late foraging sent her deep into the hills, such supplicants knew she was best found at home after sundown.

The dark in the cottage weighed like felt soaked in the sweet meadow scents of the herbs bundled to dry in the rafters. Elaira breathed in the oily must from her fleece jacket, just pulled from storage in her clothes chest. While she threaded between her sparse furnishing by touch, the pounding resumed, impatient.

"Daelion's bollocks, I hear you!" Elaira clawed under her collar, hooked out the silver chain that hung her spell crystal. The quartz as her focus, she invoked mage-sight to steer past the tumbledown stacks of herb hampers and clay jars, long since overcrowding the niche underneath the cluttered board of her work trestle. Barefoot and cold, she reached the door and fumbled with numbed hands for the latch.

Apprehension swept her, unbidden. For the crystallized span of a heartbeat, every fiber of her being clamored in primal, precognitive warning.

Then her roan gelding whinnied from the shed. His call was answered by a strange horse's wicker; a shod hoof chinked against rock, and a distinct chime of bit rings sliced the night. Innocuous sounds; yet their import snapped away the false calm she had wrested from whole years of disciplined solitude.

"Sithaer's begotten demons!" Elaira released her crystal, swept over by needling gooseflesh in the chill embrace of the dark. Those downsland herders who called needing help came on foot, or else they rode in astride scruffy moor ponies with hackamores braided from leather. Their mounts wore no tack with metal fittings. Nor did they ever fare shod.

Her left hand hovered, indecisive, while the knock resounded a third time. The rickety wood panel jounced in its frame and threatened the strapped leather hinges. Before the door gave way under punishment, Elaira tripped up the latch. Wind flung the panel against her braced shoulder and revealed what the fell night had brought her.

A Koriani enchantress stood on her threshold, ruffled into lofty disdain by the inclement Araethurian autumn.

"First Senior," Elaira greeted, the requisite formality of high office like ice chips between her locked teeth.

Lirenda unclasped her mantle, her air of reserve an acid

rebuff. "No longer First Senior." As if upbraiding a junior
initiate for an insubordinate attitude, she admitted, "The
Prime Matriarch has rescinded my privileges."

That was news; a political break of shattering magnitude,
which implied a long fall from position and favor.

The implied disgrace of an eighth-rank enchantress defied
all sane credibility. For over five decades, Lirenda had stood
second in line behind the Koriani Prime Matriarch. Morriel
was weakened by vast age, even dying, rumor said. There
seemed no imaginable intrigue or expediency that might
drive her to disown her sole groomed successor against the
hour when her faculties would finally fail her.

Despite the moiled waters of Koriani high policy.
Lirenda's arrival would not be chance, but tied like forged
chain to the name that haunted every facet of Elaira's existence.

Infinity Beach

Jack McDevitt

"Nova goes in three minutes."

Dr. Kimberly Brandywine looked out across the dozen or so faces in the briefing room. In back, lenses were pointed at her, sending the event out across the nets. Behind, her projections read HELLO TO THE UNIVERSE and KNOCK and IS ANYBODY OUT THERE?

Several flatscreens were positioned around the walls, showing technicians bent over terminals in the *Trent*. These were the teams that would ignite the nova, but the images were fourteen hours old, the time required for the hyper-comm transmissions to arrive.

Everyone present was attractive and youthful, except sometimes for their eyes. However vital and agile people were, their true age tended to reveal itself in their gaze. There was a hardness that came with advancing years, eyes that somehow lost their depth and their animation. Kim was in her midthirties, with exquisite features and hair the color of a raven's wing. In an earlier era, they would have launched ships for her. In her own age, she was just part of the crowd.

"If we haven't found anybody after all this time," the representative from Seabright Communications was saying, "it can only be because there's nobody to find. Or, if there is, they're so far away it doesn't matter."

She delivered her standard reply, discounting the great silence, pointing out that even after eight centuries humans had still inspected only a few thousand star systems. "But you may be right," she admitted. "Maybe we *are* alone. But the fact is that we really don't know. So we'll keep trying."

Kim had long since concluded that Seabright was right. They hadn't found so much as an amoeba out there. Briefly, at the beginning of the Space Age, there'd been speculation that life might exist in Europa's seas. Or in Jupiter's clouds. There'd even been a piece of meteoric rock thought to contain evidence of Martian bacteria. It was as close to extraterrestrial life as we'd ever come.

Hands were still waving.

"One more question," she said.

She gave it to Canon Woodbridge, a science advisor for the Grand Council of the Republic. He was tall, dark, bearded, almost satanic in appearance, yet a congenial fiend, one who meant no harm. "Kim," he said, "why do you think we're so afraid of being alone? Why do we want so much to find our own reflections out there?" He glanced in the direction of the screens, where the technicians continued their almost-ceremonial activities.

How on earth would she know? "I have no idea, Canon," she said.

"But you're deeply involved in the Beacon Project. And your sister devoted her life to the same goal."

"Maybe it's in the wiring." Emily, her clone actually, had vanished when Kim was seven. She paused momentarily and tried to deliver a thoughtful response, something about the human need to communicate and to explore. "I suspect," she said, "if there's really nothing out there, if the universe is *really* empty, or at least *this* part of it is, then maybe a lot of us would feel there's no point to the trip." There was more to it than that, she knew. Some primal urge not to be *alone*. But when she tried to put it into words she floundered around, gave up, and glanced at the clock.

One minute to midnight, New Year's Eve, in the two hundred eleventh year of the Republic and the six hundredth year since Marquand's landing. One minute to detonation.

"How are we doing on time?" asked one of the journalists. "Are they on schedule?"

"Yes," Kim said. "As of ten A.M. this morning." The hypercomm signal from the *Trent* required fourteen hours and some odd minutes to travel the 580 light-years from the scene of detonation. "I think we're safe to assume that the nova is imminent."

She activated an overhead screen, which picked up an image of the target star. Alpha Maxim was a bright AO-class. Hydrogen lines prominent. Surface temperature 11,000° C. Luminosity sixty times that of Helios. Five planets. All barren. Like every other known world, save the few that had been terraformed.

It would be the first of six novas. All would occur within a volume of space which measured approximately five hundred cubic light-years. And they would be triggered at sixty-day intervals. It would be a demonstration that could not help but draw the attention of anyone who might be watching. The ultimate message to the stars: *We are here.*

But she believed, as almost everyone else did, that the great silence would continue to roll back.

Fortress of Dragons

C. J. Cherryh

"Where shall we lodge?" Orien Aswydd asked him haughtily, turning and standing fast at the landing a step above him, and only a breath later did Tristen realize she was none so subtly inquiring after her former rooms. Those rooms happened to be the ducal apartment—*his* apartment.

And little as he liked his lodgings, green velvet draperies and all the heraldry of the Aswydds into the bargain, he had no intention whatsoever of allowing these women that symbolic honor of place. The ducal apartments were not merely rooms: they were an appurtenance of high office, a place from which the duke's orders flowed to all Amefel, and *no*, and twice no, Orien Aswydd should not have them.

Nor should she have any other such stately rooms, now that she made a demand of it, not a decision of spite, but rather of realization that nothing he granted her was without consequence in the view of those watching him. Her deserts were in fact the West Gate guardhouse and the headsman's block: King Cefwyn had stripped title and lands from her, but spared her life, despite the fact her crimes included attempted regicide. Cefwyn had spared her life and sent her off to the nunnery instead on the understanding she would never return to Henas'amef or set claim on the duchy.

And now, now so very soon after the new year, here she stopped at the west doors of her former hall, drew herself up straight and defiant despite the ravages of weather and a body lately failing from exhaustion, and strongly suggested she be given the honors of her birth and recent office.

One could—almost—admire her . . . but one could never, never yield to her.

"We'll find a place suitable," Tristen said curtly. "Rooms better than the guardhouse, at least." He knew the outrage he provoked by adding that last remark, but it made his point. And turning to Lusin, his chief bodyguard: "Tell Cook to come." Cook, like many of the servants, had served the Aswydd lords before he had taken the dukedom, which was to say only last year; but now he relied on her and trusted Cook as the only woman of his close acquaintance More, Cook had children, several of them, and might understand Lady Tarien's condition better than a man would.

Regarding that condition, however, Cook's was not the only advice he needed now. Master Emuin was awake, and knew, and had known about the ladies even before they reached the town gates.

—What shall I do? he asked Emuin now within the gray space wizards used. The Aswydd women might hear him, this close, but in this moment he did not care. **Where do you say should I put them?**

—I'm sure I don't know, Emuin said, and as the gray place opened wide, they stood, in their wizardous aspect, in a place of cloud and wind, equally wary of the Aswydds—who were there, unabashedly eavesdropping on them. **This is inconvenient.**

They had feared the stars, had gotten through the perilous time of change with no worse calamity than the arrival of Owl, who was somewhere about, and they had hoped that Owl was the end of the last troubled epoch and the beginning of a more auspicious age.

But, perhaps on the same night, counting the time it took to travel so far—for so it turned out—Orien and Tarien had left their exile and set out to reach Henas'amef and their former home.

—*With child, no less,* Emuin said, and turned a fierce and forbidding question toward Tarien Aswydd.—*Whose, woman?*

It was harshly, even brutally demanded, so uncharacteristically forceful that Tristen flinched. In the same instant Orien flung an arm about her sister, who shied from answering and winked out of the gray space like a candle in the wind.

Orien's was a swift, defiant retreat.

Emuin's abrupt question rid them, if only momentarily, of the Aswydds' wizardous eavesdropping, and for Tristen's part, he was no little chagrined that he had never asked so important a question in all the long walk back with the women. In his own defense, his attention in those hours had all been to the simple struggle with the snow, and with Orien's challenge to him . . . and then with the dismay his allied lords, down in the camps about the town wall, had felt very keenly, simply to see Orien back in Amefel. That Tarien was with child had seemed to him one of those things women could arrange, and one of those states women at times maintained—consequently had he, a wizard's Shaping, born of fire on a hearth, asked himself that one simple, essential question before bringing the women here?

No, he had not.

Whose child, indeed, begun in a nunnery, where, as he understood, there were only women?

Or perhaps not in the nunnery.

He felt a shadow pass in the gray space, and at the same moment, in the world, felt the wind of Owl's wings pass him and sweep on.

So Owl, who had guided him to find the sisters in the storm, was still abroad in the world. And magic was. And everything that had seemed simple now became a series of choices, each one with consequences.

Vacuum Diagrams

Stephen Baxter

The Ghost cruiser hovered between Earth and Moon.

The ship was a rough ovoid, woven from silvered rope. Instrument clusters and energy pods were knotted to the walls. Around me, Ghosts clung to the rope like grapes to a vine.

The blue of crescent Earth shimmered over their pulsating, convex surfaces.

Earth folded up and disappeared.

The first hyperspace hope was immense, thousands of light years long. Then, in a succession of bewildering leaps, we sailed out of the Galaxy.

We fell obliquely to the plane of the disc. The core was a chandelier of pink-white light, thousands of light years across, hanging over my head. Spiral arms—cloudy, streaming—moved serenely above me. There were blisters of gas sprinkled along the arms, I saw, bubbles of swollen color.

Galactic light glimmered over the silvered flesh of the Ghosts, and of my own body.

We reached the Ghosts' base—far from home, in the halo of the Galaxy.

It was a typical Ghost construct: a hollowed-out moon, a

rock ball a thousand miles wide, and it was riddled with passages and cavities. It hung beneath the great ceiling of the Galaxy, the only large object visible as other than a smudge of light.

We descended. The moon turned into a complex, machined landscape below me. Our ship shut down its drive and entered a high, looping orbit. The Ghosts drifted away from the ship and down towards the surface, bobbing like balloons, shining in Galaxy light.

I let go of the ship and floated away from its tangled hull.

Ghost ships and science platforms swept over the pocked landscape, fragments of shining net. All over the surface, vast cylindrical structures gleamed. These were intrasystem drives and hyperdrives, systems which had been used to haul this moon—at huge expense—out of the plane of the Galaxy, and to hold it here.

There was quagma down there, I saw, little packets of the primordial stuff, buried in the pits of ancient planetesimal craters. My information had been good, then.

What in Lethe were the Ghosts doing out here?

The world of the Silver Ghosts was once earthlike: blue skies, a yellow sun.

As the Ghosts climbed to awareness their sun evaporated, killed by a companion pulsar. When the atmosphere started snowing, the Ghosts rebuilt themselves.

That epochal ordeal left the Ghosts determined, secretive, often reckless. Dangerous.

They moved out into space—the Heat Sink—to fulfill their ambitions.

I had been told the Ghosts were close to completing their new quagma project. I was chief administrator of the Ghost liaison office, representing most of mankind. It was my job to stop the Ghosts endangering us all.

So that I could deal with the Ghosts, I was remade, a decade ago.

I look like a statue of a man, done in silver, or chrome. My legs are pillars. My hands and arms have been made immensely strong. I don't live behind my eyes anymore: I live in my chest cavity. I feel like a deep-sea fish, blind and almost immobile, stuck here in the dark. My mechanical eyes are like periscopes, far above "me."

I can subsist on starlight, and survive the vacuum for days at a time, enfolding my seventy-six-year-old human core—me—in warmth and darkness. I have a Ghost doctor; twice a year it opens me up and cleans me out.

I have a face, a sculpture of eyes, nose, mouth. It doesn't even look much like I used to, before. It doesn't matter; apart from the eyes, the face is non-functional, put there to reassure me.

I can run with the Ghosts. I can fly in space, if I choose to.

Eater

Gregory Benford

It began quietly.

Amy Major came into Benjamin's office and with studied care placed a sheet in front of his tired eyes. "Got a funny one for you."

Benjamin stared at the graph. In the middle of the page, a sharp peak poked up to a high level, then fell slowly to his right. He glanced at the bottom axis, showing time, and said, "So it died away in a few seconds. What's so odd?"

Amy gave him an angular grin that he knew she thought made her look tough-minded and skeptical. He had always read that expression as stubborn, but then, she so often disagreed with him. "Here's the second."

"Second?" Maybe her grin was deserved.

With a suppressed smile, she handed him another sheet. Same sort of peak, subsiding into the background noise in four seconds. "Ho hum." He raised his eyebrows in question, a look he had trained the staff to interpret as *Why are you wasting my time?*

"Could be any ordinary burster, right?"

"Yes." Amy liked to play the elephantine game out in full.

"Only it's a repeater."

"Ah. How close?"

"In space, dead on. The prelim position is right on top of the first one's." Dramatic pause. "In time, 13.45 hours."

"What?" Was this a joke? "Thirteen hours?"

"Yup."

Gamma-ray bursters were cosmological explosions, the biggest Creation had ever devised. They showed up in the highest energy spectrum of all, the fat, powerful light that emerged when atomic nuclei fell apart. The preferred model describing bursters invoked a big black hole swallowing something else quite substantial, like a massive star. Bursters were the dyspeptic belch of a spectacularly large astrophysical meal. Each one devastated a seared region of the host galaxy.

Eaten once, a star could not be ingested again, thirteen hours later.

On the off chance that this was still a joke, he said with measured deliberation, "Now, that *is* interesting." Always be positive at the beginning, or else staff would not come to you at all. He smiled wanly. "But the preliminary position is in a big box."

This was more than a judicious reservation. It was almost certainly the true explanation. The two would prove to come from different points in the sky.

They got from the discovering instrument a rough location of the burster—a box drawn on the sky map, with the source within it somewhere. Sharpening that took other instruments specially designed for the job. Same for the second burster. Once they knew accurately where this second burst was, he was sure it would turn out to be far from the earlier burst, and the excitement would be over. Best to let her down slowly, though. "Still, let's hope it's something new."

"Uh, I thought it was worth mentioning, Dr. Knowlton." Her rawboned face retreated into defensive mode, mouth pursing up as if she had drawn a string through both lips. She had been the origin of the staff's private name for him,

Dr. Know-It-All-ton. That had hurt more than he had ever let on.

"And it is, it is. You asked Space Array for a quick location?"

"Sure, and sent out an alert to everybody on Gamma Net."

"Great."

She let her skeptic-hardnose mask slip a little. "It's a real repeater. I just know it."

"I hope you're right." He had been through dozens of cases of mistaken identity and Amy had not. She was a fine operations astronomer, skilled at sampling the steady stream of data that flowed through the High Energy Astrophysics Center, though a bit too earnest for his taste.

"I know, nobody's ever seen a repeater this delayed," she said.

The Black Rood

Stephen R. Lawhead

The Feast of St. George
Anno Domini, 1132

My Dearest Caitríona,

The worst has happened. As old Pedar would say, "I am sore becalmed."

My glorious dream is ashes and dust. It died in the killing heat of a nameless Syrian desert—along with eight thousand good men whose only crime was that of fealty to a stubborn, arrogant boy. I could weep for them, but for the fact that I, no less headstrong and haughty than that misguided boy, will shortly follow them to the grave.

The Saracens insist that I am the esteemed guest of the Caliph of Cairo. In truth, this is nothing more than a polite way of saying I am a captive in his house. They treat me well; indeed, since coming to the Holy Land, I have not known such courtesy, nor such elegance. Nevertheless, I cannot leave the palace until the caliph has seen me. It is for him to decide my fate. I know too well what the outcome will be.

Be that as it may, the great caliph is pursuing enemies in

the south and is not expected to return to the city for a goodly while. Thus, I have time enough, and liberty, to set down what can be told about our great and noble purpose so you will know why your father risked all he loved best in life for a single chance to obtain that prize which surpasses all others.

Some of what I shall write is known to you. If this grows tedious, I ask you to bear with me, and remember that this, my last testament, is not for you alone, my heart, but for those who will join us in our labors in days to come. God willing, all will be told before the end.

So now, where to begin? Let us start with the day Torf-Einar came back from the dead.

I was with your grandfather Murdo at the church, helping to oversee the builders working there. The previous summer we had purchased a load of cut stone for the arches and thresholds, and were preparing the site for the arrival of the shipment which was due at any time. Your grandfather and Abbot Emlyn were standing at the table in the yard, study-ing the drawings which Brother Paulus had made for the building, when one of the monks came running from the fields to say that a boat was putting into the bay.

We quickly assembled a welcome party and went down to meet it. The ship was small—an island runner only—but it was not from Orkneyjar. Nor was it one of King Sigurd's fishing boats as some had assumed. The sailors had rowed the vessel into shallow water and were lifting down a bundle by the time we reached the cove. There were four boatmen in the water and three on deck, and they had a board between them which they were straining to lower. Obviously heavy, they were at pains to keep from dropping their cargo into the cove.

"They are traders from Eíre," suggested one of the women. "I wonder what they have brought?"

"It looks like a heap of old rags," said another.

The sailors muscled their burden over the rail, and waded

ashore. As they drew nearer, I saw that the board was really a litter with a body strapped to it. They placed this bundle of cloth and bone before us on the strand, and stepped away—as if mightily glad to have done with an onerous task. I thought it must be the body of some poor seaman, one of their own perhaps, who had died at sea.

No sooner had they put it down, however, than this corpse began to shout and thrash about. "Unbind me!" it cried, throwing its thin limbs around. "Let me up!"

Those on the strand gave a start and jumped back. Murdo, however, stepped closer and bent over the heaving mass of tatters. "Torf?" he said, stooping near. "Is that you, Torf-Einar?"

To the amazement of everyone looking on, the near-corpse replied, "And who should it be but myself? Unbind me, I say, and let me up."

"God in heaven!" cried Murdo. "Is it true?" Gesturing to some of the men, he said, "Here, my brother is back from the dead—help me loose him."

I came forward along with the abbot and several others, and we untied my long-lost uncle. He had returned from the Holy Land where he had lived since the Great Pilgrimage. The eldest of my father's two brothers, he and the next eldest, Skuli, had joined with Baldwin of Bouillon. In return for their loyal service they were given lands at Edessa where they had remained ever since.

When asked what happened to his brothers, Murdo would always say that they had died chasing their fortunes in the Holy Land. In all the years of my life till then, I had never known it to be otherwise. How not? There never came any word from them—never a letter, or even a greeting sent by way of a returning pilgrim—though opportunities must have been plentiful enough through the years. That is why Murdo said he had come back from the dead. In a way, he had; for no one had ever expected to see Torf-Einar again—either in this world *or* the next.